PRIME SUSPECT

"I think," Bolton said slowly, "that you might be in trouble. After all, you are the prime suspect."

Raoul was startled. "What do you mean?"

"The police think you killed him. After all, everyone in the university knows you couldn't stand each other."

"It's all so stupid!" Raoul paused. "I've got to find out who killed Mowatt. I can't take the chance the police will get it wrong."

Bolton nodded. If convicted, Raoul would have his magical ability and knowledge permanently blocked, in addition to the physical sentence. "I'll help any way I can, you know that. Plus," he added, with a trace of his usual humor, "it's an excuse for you to skip classes, and I can get a whopper of a story out of it. Deal?"

A shadow of a smile crossed Raoul's face. "Deal. So where do we start, Sherlock?"

Look for these Del Rey Discoveries . . .
Because something new is always worth the risk!

SHADE AND SHADOW

Francine G. Woodbury

A Del Rey® Book
BALLANTINE BOOKS • NEW YORK

For Tom
and Mom & Dad

A Del Rey® Book
Published by Ballantine Books
Copyright © 1996 by Francine G. Woodbury

All rights reserved under International and Pan-American Copyright Conventions. Published in the United States by Ballantine Books, a division of Random House, Inc., New York, and simultaneously in Canada by Random House of Canada Limited, Toronto.

http://www.randomhouse.com

Library of Congress Catalog Card Number: 95-96160

ISBN 0-345-39428-3

Manufactured in the United States of America

First Edition: June 1996

10 9 8 7 6 5 4 3 2 1

*"I love the shade and the shadow,
and would be alone with my thoughts when I may."*
—BRAM STOKER, *Dracula*

Chapter 1

"What do you mean, you can't get the blood out?" Raoul snapped into the phone. "I gave you the damned thing a full week ago, and you're calling me *now* to say it won't be ready for tonight?" He paused, listening.

"Oh, just *keep* the bloody thing, for all I care!" he shouted, and slammed the phone into its cradle. He looked down at it for a moment, then swept it and a stack of papers onto the floor, barely missing a rat that had been lunching on the crumbs from a plate of teacakes. The phone hit the floor with a discordant jangle, making the rat bolt for the safety of the curtains.

"Professor Smythe?" a concerned voice called from the hall outside the study. "I heard a noise—is everything all right?"

"Quite, Mrs. Higgins," he answered sharply. "Everything's fine. Just wonderful." He paused. "Isn't today Friday, by the way? I thought this was one of your long weekends. Why are you here?" He looked at the study door, but didn't open it.

"It's my sister, Professor. She's got a doctor's appointment in Oxford this afternoon, so it was easiest just to wait and leave today. So as she wouldn't have to drive the same bit twice in two days, you know—back and forth, back and forth. I was just doing a bit of work until she gets here. And then I heard that noise. Are you sure—"

"Fine, Mrs. Higgins, that's wonderful. And thank you for staying. Now go away. I'm working."

"Humph," Edna Higgins sniffed as she dusted the hall's

1

waist-high molding. "You'd think he'd be civil once in a while, but no, not him," she muttered. "Always was a bit short with people, from the time he was a lad." She continued down the hall toward the back staircase, dusting and grumbling as she went.

Back in the study, Professor Smythe had already spelled the papers and put the phone back on the desk. "Bloody hell," he muttered. If the robe wouldn't be ready from the cleaners until tomorrow, what would he wear tonight? Why did it take so long to remove a simple bloodstain? "Gods!" he said aloud. "Oh well, I'll muster something up, I suppose."

The problem was that the garment at the cleaners was his only dress robe, and if he merely conjured fineness onto a plain robe, anyone with half an ounce of detection would be able to tell, since the magical aura would practically scream "Look at me, I've been changed!" to anyone who bothered to check. Better to show up naked than in a hastily spelled outfit. He'd have to work a deep transformation, which was time- and energy-consuming. And even then there would be aural residue, since it was impossible to work a spell without leaving some trace. He sighed. Things would be fine if he could just wear his university robe, but the reception was to be formal. No, he needed something dressy, but he wasn't about to spend money on a new robe for Mowatt's sake.

It was bad enough that he had to attend this little gala the Whitings were putting on for old Mowatt, the department chair. And that even Assistant Professors of Magic were supposed to "look the part," as he'd so often been cautioned by Mowatt himself. On top of that, his one good robe had gotten stained at the last official outing he'd been dragged to, and now he had to find something else to wear, and all this on the first day in months he'd made real progress on his research.

The problem, as Raoul saw it, was that magic was too hidebound, too tied to outdated traditions. The whole bit of needing the proper clothing, the proper atmosphere, making the traditional movements, speaking the traditional words, sprinkling this here, that there, and so on, was ridiculous. He could appreciate that the tradition sprang from centuries-old rituals and years of academic study. But he couldn't fathom that nothing had changed for nearly a thousand years. There had to be a way, he knew, to strip off all the old bits, all the useless regalia that lingered from when magic was a religion, and not a business and an academic study, to strip it down and make it clean and almost new again.

Current magical training, Raoul proposed, was actually a form of "un-training." When a person's magical abilities developed, usually around puberty, often spontaneous acts of magic occurred, based on concentrated thought rather than words, actions, and whatnot. This, Raoul theorized, was the true potential of magic—spells worked only by the power of the mind. He was convinced it was possible—his current research concentrated on reducing complicated spells to mere words. Once he'd perfected that, he hoped to further refine the theory and one day achieve silent, thought-driven spells.

No one else seemed to think so, however. When he'd initially tried to turn his idea into a thesis, he'd almost been defrocked before he'd even been frocked. "Too radical," he'd been told, particularly by Mowatt. He'd always been told that, though. That was he, Raoul Ahmahn Giamboni Smythe, Magical Radical. Harriet Gulledge's bastard son, named for all three of the men she'd been with the week he was conceived, with that most common of names tacked on for additional confusion. Boarding-schooled since age three, shifted from one place to another until he'd bought this house, Thornhold.

No one knew where Raoul's power came from. Neither his mother, an art dealer, nor any of his three possible fathers—a banker, an antiques dealer specializing in rugs, and a cab driver, "but an exceptionally intelligent and handsome one," as his mother always added when the last was mentioned—had any magical ability whatsoever. And

Raoul's abilities had developed incredibly early and suddenly; he'd performed his first intentional spell at six. Raoul was a fluke, a changeling, as his mother had so often called him.

Raoul shook his head, forcing himself out of his reverie. He rolled his large wooden chair closer to the desk and turned on the computer. As always, it beeped frantically for a moment, then settled down to a quiet hum. Clicking on the Microsoft Spell icon, he pulled up his directory of files. He'd painstakingly entered hundreds of spells into it, listing words, actions, and ingredients for each. Some, usually the cantrips, took up only a few lines, but others went on for pages. This was the core of his research data, as well as his personal archive. The days of the handwritten spell book were long past, at least for the few magicians who would actually use computers.

Raoul's research was proving exceedingly difficult. Reducing "bring mixture to a boil, add a pinch of henbane" to a few words meant creating many separate smaller verbal-only spells to reproduce each step. The nearest comparison in the nonmagical world was writing a computer program, or more correctly, a batch file, a simple command to access much more complicated programs. However, Raoul was finding that his resulting spells took longer to cast than their standard counterparts. He'd also found that the concentration required to work them exhausted him, though he hoped his fatigue would decrease as he became used to it.

Deciding to combine obtaining an acceptable robe for the gala with his research, Raoul opened his folder of transformation spells and saw that he hadn't yet done a reduced version of fabric transformations. As his eyes moved from right to left over the Etruscan runes covering the screen, he realized that it was a more complicated spell than those he'd been working on. Luckily, as he scrolled through the description, he recognized subspells that were at least similar to ones he'd already reduced. Pausing occasionally to speak aloud, he began the reduction process, typing words in, switching from English for his notes and comments to Etruscan for the actual spell.

An hour later he left the study, closing the door behind him, and went down the hall to his bedroom. The large walk-in closet was spotless, the drawers neatly shut and clothes hanging evenly on hangers. Higgins was here, he thought, smiling. He was a slob, if left to himself. Gathering an armful of robes, spilling others onto the floor in the process, Raoul returned to the study, dropping a robe on the way and leaving it there.

He dropped the pile on the study's leather couch, then picked out a simple black silk robe. Although Oxford's other colleges had dispensed with required robes years ago for both students and professors except during examinations, Mowatt insisted that professors in the College of Magic wear robes while working spells in classes, even those that didn't require special clothing. Raoul, who was most comfortable in jeans and T-shirts, argued against this regulation at every staff meeting. In the meantime, he grudgingly wore plain black robes. For the most formal occasions, he consented to a simple embroidered pattern, usually roses. The robe at the cleaners was of black silk, with argent roses covering all but the long sleeves. The effect was that of a patterned shift over a plain robe. He detested having to wear it.

His fellow magicians generally preferred sumptuous fabrics in bright colors encrusted with embroidery and gems or stones. Raoul, in contrast, wore black. Always. Partly due to the ease of matching things, partly from liking the look, and partly from affectation. He admitted it; he knew others looked askance at him, thought him slightly sinister. Sometimes, usually at official gatherings, he felt like a raven in a flock of chattering parrots. For everyday workings, he was sufficiently radical to wear his usual jeans and T-shirt under an open robe, causing much distress to Mowatt, who considered it practically blasphemous. Tonight, however, Raoul knew he would have to look his official best. He sighed again.

He tossed the robe onto the couch, dissatisfied before he'd even begun to work the spell, and chose instead a plain moire silk. Pulling the heavy burgundy drapes closed over the window, he hung the robe from the curtain rod. Looking from the computer screen to the robe, he spoke quietly for almost half an hour, gesturing occasionally. Finally, the robe swayed slightly, as if a breeze were suddenly stirring deep within its folds, then hung still again. Raoul walked over to peer closely at the fabric, surveying the change. Nothing. He chose another spell and began again.

Four hours and five spells later, roses, black on the black robe, had appeared, formed from the moire pattern itself. He set the spell firmly and stood back. A true transformation, using nothing but words and hands. So what, that it had taken more than five times longer than if he'd just worked the spell in its original form? It was progress.

Of course, he hadn't really changed the substance of the robe, merely its appearance. Still, it wasn't a bad piece of work, he thought. Speaking a quick spell, he ran his hand over the material: no aura of magical residue. That's strange, he thought. He did a more careful reading, then another. Nothing. In no way whatsoever had this piece been subjected to magic. It was great, but as far as he knew, it was also impossible. How had he done it? The other magicians at the party would go crazy trying to find out how, if they knew. Let them figure it out, he thought smugly. But first, he himself had to figure it out. He turned back to the computer to go over every step of what he'd just done.

The phone rang. Raoul reached across the desk to pick it up.

"Rags? It's Bolton. Look, are you going to this thing tonight for dear old M? I can't believe Whiting gave the old bugger his own chair. And I've been roped into writing it up for the Daily Nuisance, can you believe it? Anyway, hello. How are you?"

Maxwell Bolton never seemed to breathe when speaking. There would be a furious rush of words, then a huge gasping pause. Raoul spoke before Bolton could prepare for another onslaught.

"Yes. I'm going, though I don't see the point. I'm the last thing the old cow probably wants to see on his night of glory. And I still don't understand why they're naming his own chair after him, anyway. He's personally set Magic back about fifty years. Classical training, he calls it. Turning out a new generation of magicians, steeped in tradition. Wallowing in it, is more like it. I'm surprised he doesn't have the lot of us running around in pointy hats cutting open chickens to see what tomorrow's weather'll be. Someone should just kill the fool and have done. *Then* they can name a chair after him and I wouldn't mind."

"Easy there, Rags. Been working today, haven't you? You wouldn't still be bitter about his telling you off, would you? You must admit he did rather a royal job of it."

Raoul didn't answer for a moment. Finally he said, "Yes, I'm still bitter. That man has no right to say what's valid research and what's not. It's not his university."

"No, but it *is* his department. And it's Whiting's university, and Mowatt's in thick. You've got to play his way or he'll boot you fast, you know."

"I know, I'm just getting fed up with hearing people tell me my ideas won't work when I know they will. If I hear one more sanctimonious ass say 'If it's not broken, don't fix it,' I'll puke on their bloody satin slippers."

"Couldn't you just turn them into frogs or something? You *are* a magician, after all. But I suppose that wouldn't be dignified, and you know the first rule of magic is that . . ." He paused, and Raoul knew what was coming, a sentence they'd both heard many times in a freshman Magic course, the first of many for Raoul, the first and last for Bolton. They spoke together.

"Dignity is the true magician's cloak." They laughed.

Chuckling, Raoul said, "Gods, that man was an ass! Mowatt must have loved him. Anyway, I've got to get some sleep; I've been up all day getting ready for this thing. I'll see you tonight."

As he was hanging up, he heard Bolton's parting shot, "You wouldn't be so tired if you weren't so vain, you damned vampire. Have a nice nap."

Raoul replaced the receiver, muttering, "And don't call me Rags!" He and Bolton had been friends since they met at the last of Raoul's many boarding schools, though Raoul still didn't know why. No, rather, he didn't want to know why, didn't want to think about the lack of something that Bolton filled for him. Still, Bolton was the only one to ever get away with calling him Rags. The first time he'd called him that—and even then Raoul had known it would stick—another boy had picked it up. At the time, Raoul had already begun carrying a small stiletto, mostly for effect, but he did know how to use it, and was suspended for weeks for slicing open the boy's cheek. He'd heard later that the man claimed it was a dueling scar.

He shook himself out of the memory. He'd been serious about needing sleep. His classes ran from ten to two, and office hours till four, though everything had been canceled today in honor of Mowatt. After paperwork and leftover errands, Raoul generally slept until midnight or so.

He worked best at night, loving the quiet misty darkness of the early hours. He'd open the drapes and balcony doors in his study and work away, the silence broken only by his muttered spells and the small clicks of the rats' claws on the wooden floor. He never felt lonely, because he always had the rats. A plate of leftovers on the floor and they were set for the night, munching and playing about quietly. Not that they didn't eat well anyway, what with Higgins putting out cream and treats all the time. She still thought he had shy cats.

He'd bought them for company, originally, two small black ratlings, and kept them in a box in his study until they were litter trained. A fun chore that had been, but he wouldn't have them caged and didn't fancy stepping in rat shit all the time. Once they'd gotten the knack of it, he'd given them the run of the house. Now they were legion, but still preferred his study to the rest of the house, with the possible exception of a Higginsless kitchen.

Smiling, Raoul closed the study door, called down to Higgins that he was going to sleep and that she should enjoy her weekend, then went to his room. Closing the heavy curtains, he stripped and got into bed. He ran through a few relaxation exercises to clear his mind, then slept.

Raoul woke in a foul mood after dreaming about old professors and current colleagues walking naked around him in a circle, chanting words he didn't understand. A fast shower and a cup of strong tea didn't help. He grumbled as he dressed, detesting the party more with each thought, until he was practically seething by the time his cab arrived. Unfortunately, bad moods weren't all that unusual for him. He knew well that he was often unable, or possibly unwilling, to calm himself and rechannel the anger he felt when forced into situations he disliked. Something nasty usually happened when he was in these moods; he seemed to lose all control over what his ears would hear his mouth saying or his eyes see his body doing. He supposed it was a power issue; he had to do something he didn't want to, and internal rebellion threatened to consume him. Unhealthy, Raoul knew, but he placated himself with the thought that was the way he was. He wasn't ashamed of it.

When the cab dropped him off at the Whitings', Raoul didn't enter the house immediately, but walked around to the garden. As chancellor of the university, Reginald Whiting and his family lived in an extremely old, relatively palatial house. Raoul had been inside only twice before, once when he'd had his third interview as a potential instructor, and the second time at Robert Marlowe's retirement reception. He'd liked the garden best then, too.

Now, standing in the shadows cast by the large trees, he looked into the bright windows, watching the people inside come together and flow apart. The full moon, hidden behind thick clouds, bathed everything in a weird half-light. It calmed him somewhat; he wished he could just stay outside

and walk off all his tension. He felt almost worse than before as he dismissed, unwillingly, the thought of just skip-
ping the party. Duty called. Duty sucked.

He walked around to the front door and knocked once.
The butler opened it and went to help Raoul with his coat,
fumbling a bit when he realized it was a cloak. Raoul
headed for the parlor, steeling himself as for an ordeal.

Sixty or so people milled about in the parlor, which
could have comfortably held twice that number. Raoul
stood in the doorway for a moment, ranging his gaze
around the room. Most of his college seemed to be present,
along with the usual social baggage types plus thirty or so
people he didn't recognize but probably knew.

His eyes were drawn to a tall blonde woman in a flowing
white-silver sequined dress. She was chatting merrily with
Mrs. Whiting in a corner of the room. He noted that her
hair, which didn't look dyed, though he knew it was, had
been cut short since the last time he'd seen her. The dress
would have looked ridiculous on most people, but she had
the height and the plank-straight figure to carry it off. She
was as coolly beautiful as ever, completely at ease. Raoul
whispered, focusing his voice so only she would hear,
"Hello, Mother."

Harriet Gulledge started, turning quickly on hearing the
voice in her ear. Catching sight of him, she tilted her head
and smiled at Raoul before turning back to her companion
with a murmured, "I'm sorry, Lesley dear, what was that
last? I didn't quite hear you."

Raoul smiled. He never could make her completely off
balance, though he didn't think he'd ever stop trying. She
did look lovely this evening. Maybe he'd get a chance to
talk to her for a bit, see how she'd been. But first he'd see
how the evening went.

An arm snaked around his waist. Starting, he turned to
look down at Catherine Moss, who had somehow sneaked
up on him. He stepped away from her arm, managing not
to grimace in distaste. "Hello, Catherine."

"Raoul, how nice to see you again! I was wondering if

you'd show up, given your obvious love for social occasions. Then again, you probably have to be here, don't you? Too bad you couldn't make our little get-together last week." Catherine's voice had a strange purring stridency which put Raoul's teeth on edge.

"Sorry, got tied up in work." Raoul was already looking for somewhere else to go. Catherine and her clique bored him to death, or annoyed him to the point of murder, depending on his mood. Tonight he could cheerfully throttle her and all her bony friends. He wondered again how Bolton could stand being with them all.

"Excuse me," he said, moving away, "I need a drink." He headed directly for the bar, skirting the various groups in the way. He raised a hand in greeting when necessary, nodded at others, but didn't stop or speak until he'd reached the bar. He asked for a Guinness. Dispensing with the glass, he stood idly sipping from the bottle, watching the crowd. His blazing anger had dulled to a vague unease, his usual feeling of being somehow different from the rest of the people milling about like so many cattle. And there in the middle of the herd, basking in the attention of various university and social luminaries, stood the new holder of the Mowatt chair of Magic, Arthur Mowatt, BMA, Ph.D., DMS. His cloth-of-gold robe gleamed under the lights, varicolored jewels glinting brightly as he moved.

Raoul sighed, compelled by duty to start toward the man. Best to get the unpleasantries over as quickly as possible, he thought. He couldn't remember exactly when the problem between he and Mowatt had begun. At first, when Raoul was only a student, Mowatt had used him as a scapegoat, an example of what not to do. Unfortunately for Mowatt, Raoul had proved to be brilliant and exceedingly powerful as well as intractable and unusual.

For his part, Raoul considered Mowatt a churlish old man, bound to his faith in tradition and with a fear of doing anything differently. He had enjoyed baiting Mowatt, egging him on by his capability and the rebellion implicit in his appearance and explicit in his actions. In return,

Mowatt viewed Raoul as the embodiment of everything he detested, of anarchy and rebellion and faithlessness and disrespect. Raoul was well aware of Mowatt's feelings. While he didn't care about the opinions others held of him and never yielded to them, he eventually stopped actively trying to annoy the man, more out of boredom than anything else.

He knew that Mowatt had fought long and hard with Sir Reginald Whiting about Raoul's acceptance into the faculty. Whiting, however, hadn't budged. Raoul had overheard them arguing more than once as he passed Mowatt's office. "The boy is eccentric, to be sure," Whiting once said, "but you can't deny the brilliance of his work in refining the art of Magic." Whiting's main argument was that at least they would control what, if not how, Raoul taught. Better for someone like him to be in a controlled environment; no telling what he'd do if left to himself. Mowatt had merely repeated his usual arguments, asking how he was to build a program of education when his own faculty was busily tearing down all it was built upon.

No, Raoul hadn't hated Mowatt at first. It wasn't until the old man had finally blown up at him in their most recent "private consultation" about Raoul's teaching habits, dress, and attitude in general that Raoul had gotten angry. He'd tried to explain what direction his research was taking, and where it could possibly lead. Startlingly, Mowatt, after telling him flatly to discontinue the research, had accused him of everything from bastardy, which Raoul couldn't deny (although he'd never been ashamed of the fact), to disregard for Magic itself. Contemptuously, Mowatt told him he would never know true Magic, because it ultimately held no meaning for him, being rather something merely to be mastered. He'd gone on from there, but Raoul had stopped listening and left without a word at the first pause. Let Mowatt think he'd shamed him into silence, Raoul thought, let him think he'd hurt him. Because in fact he had.

Magic, Raoul knew, was the only thing that had ever really mattered to him. His earliest memories were of discovering the power to change, to see beyond the ordinary, of Magic. He'd taught himself at first, learning to read Etruscan before he'd even mastered English. Nothing else, not even his few friends, his family, anything, had ever touched him so deeply. He was truly happy, he thought, only when working some complicated spell, his mind focused deeply on the power within himself, sharpening and coalescing it, reaching out to the fabric of nature itself. Then, and only then, did he feel whole. Not that anything was wrong at other times, but once he'd felt the fascination of seeing the larger view of things, he knew he'd never be able to duplicate it in any other way. It made the feeling of general dissatisfaction and unease, of being not at home in his own skin, disappear. And that was what Mowatt would take away from him if he could. Mowatt wanted Magic to be tamed and trained, dished out in drips and droplets in a certain way to certain people. He wanted to take the joy out of it. In a way, Raoul pitied him.

"Hello again, stranger." Raoul saw with a hopeless sinking feeling that Catherine had followed him across the room. He crossed his arms before she could touch him again.

Tugging at his sleeve, she prattled on obliviously. "Now, dear, you've got to come with me. I've got some people you simply must meet. You'll love them." She pulled at his arm. Resigned, he followed. At least it would put off talking to Mowatt.

She chattered along, breaking off to greet people, but never quite releasing her hold on him. "Ruthie, darling, how good to see you! Really, we must chat later! Thomas, come along with me now, I'm introducing Raoul to some new people. Raoul, you know you really need to socialize a bit more, to meet more people, make new friends. You can't live like a hermit, you know."

"Catherine, I already know quite enough people. I don't have time for any more. I can't spare time for my friends as it is. Why do you always think that a person should get to know everyone he sees? The more friends one has, the less they mean."

"Really, Raoul, you are so strange sometimes! Of course you have time for more friends! Don't be an ass, darling. Now, here we are."

She had brought him to a group of five or six people standing in a loose circle at the doorway to the garden. Pulling Raoul into the midst of the group, Catherine started in on the introductions.

"Now everyone, I've got a special present for you. This is Raoul Smythe, he's in the university's Magic faculty, kind of the *enfant terrible* there, you know. Keeps awfully to himself. Raoul, this is Patricia LeFevre, she owns a clothing store here in town, it's just adorable. She designs most of it herself, you know. And this is John Rossini, here from Italy to study at the university, and Patrick Bondler and Betty Fernwick, they're friends of mine from the Illiteracy Committee, and Mary Schoenstein, her father's the barrister, and this lovely young thing is our hosts' daughter, Anne Lesley Benson Alcroft Whiting. And that's everyone. Whew!" She paused for breath, smiling at her own witty comments.

"You'll have to excuse Catherine," Anne Whiting said dryly. "She loves to hear herself mention how many people she knows, and what she knows about them. Call me Anne, please." She held out a hand and smiled.

Raoul looked at her, wondering that she could be the daughter of Sir Reginald, a large athletic man going slowly to fat, and Lesley Alcroft Whiting, who had kept her field-hockey figure but hid her age under a thick coat of makeup and expensively tailored clothes. Anne, on the other hand, seemed a frail thing, pretty in a pale blonde inbred way, with a lovely low voice. Patricia LeFevre certainly looked like a clothing-store owner, wearing the better part of at least two unmatched outfits, to judge by sight. Rossini, an Italian by Catherine's introduction, seemed the perfect student. All his tuxedo needed was a backpack attached. Raoul thought he might have had him in a class at some point, but wasn't positive. Bondler and the Fernwick woman were nondescript in a Catherine's-friends kind of way, both gaunt and societally perfect, and probably unbearably political. Mary Schoenstein was unusual-looking, not traditionally pretty but quite arresting, with a great mass of unruly black curls overpowering her simple black dress and pale skin.

Raoul nodded in greeting at them.

"So, Raoul, what do you do at university?" Bondler asked.

"I'm an Assistant Professor of Magic."

"Oh, so you work with Professor Mowatt, then?" Anne asked.

"You could say that, I suppose. We really don't have that much contact."

"Brilliant, isn't he? It must be wonderful to work in such an innovative environment," Bondler said. "Quite an honor for someone as young as you are."

Raoul didn't answer, though he thought the comment odd, considering Bondler didn't look that much older than his own twenty-eight years. There was an odd pause as no one spoke.

Before anyone else could start chattering again, Raoul began edging away. "You'll excuse me, I hope. I need to see some of the faculty."

"Raoul, before you go," Catherine said, "we've all got a standing brunch date Saturdays, and we're trying out a new restaurant this week. Why don't you come along? You'll like it; it's supposed to be quite odd. What do you think?"

Everyone made agreeing noises, saying, "Oh, yes, do come."

"I'm very sorry, but I'll be working tomorrow."

Ignoring his protests, they insisted that he could take a few moments out to eat. Finally, exasperated, he said he'd go, just so he could get away. He'd think up an excuse later. Catherine and Mary said they would pick him up at eleven. That decided, he left quickly, before anyone volunteered him for some committee.

He started toward a group of professors who stood clustered in the middle of the room, looking a bit overdressed in their flowing robes. Before he'd gone more than a few paces, however, Whiting called him over to the corner where he and Mowatt were momentarily speaking alone.

"Well, Smythe, I'm glad you could make it," Whiting said jovially, clapping a meaty hand on his shoulder. Raoul wasn't sure if it was merely in greeting or to keep him from escaping. Still, he respected Whiting, though their contact had been extremely limited. The man seemed to really care about how the various colleges functioned, not just about how much money the university as a whole was pulling in.

Mowatt glared at Raoul. "We didn't think you'd be here, after you missed the main ceremony." He glanced down at Raoul's boots. "Couldn't find the proper footwear, I see."

Raoul looked squarely at Mowatt. "I imagined you'd prefer the occasion without my presence. Congratulations, Professor Mowatt. And now, if you'll excuse me?" Raoul started to turn away, but Whiting held him back.

"Arthur, Raoul, while I have you both alone, I'd like to mention something. I'd like you to stop this rivalry of yours, if only for the sake of the department. Your little feud is starting to take its toll, and not just on my ulcer. What do you say? Shall we give it a try?" He looked questioningly at the two men, both of whom were looking stonily at him. Whiting tried to lighten the atmosphere. "After all, you're both professors, and one a holder of an academic chair. You've got to set a good example for the troops."

"*Assistant* Professor," Mowatt snapped.

Raoul rolled his eyes.

"Actually, Arthur," Whiting said, "that's something we should probably discuss soon. I've read Raoul's research proposal, and frankly, I think it has promise."

"Reginald, what are you talking about?" Mowatt asked, his voice low but intense. "What proposal?"

"The one I sent him," Raoul said evenly. "The one you didn't really look at. I sent a copy to Sir Reginald. With a complaint." His eyes locked with Mowatt's for a second.

"Why you—" Mowatt began, then turned angrily to Whiting. "Reginald, I can't believe you would even look at such a thing! Do you see what I have to put up with? And this, this . . . and you want to promote him? You can't do that! I am Chair of the College, you know. And there is a committee that decides on issues of tenure." His face reddened. "Not to mention—"

"Arthur, stop." Whiting's voice was firm. "It wasn't my intention to upset you, especially tonight. It's an idea I had recently, pending your approval, of course, in light of the possibilities his research has. He deserves it, in my opinion. I'm sorry if you disagree. Perhaps you and I can discuss it on Monday? I'll have Robert set up a time for us to meet. But perhaps you'd both," he turned to look at Raoul for a moment, "benefit from thinking about what I've said. I want this childish jealousy settled, and soon. Why can't the two of you find a way to work together? Surely it can't be that difficult? So now, if you'll excuse me, I've got to go play gracious host. Arthur, Smythe." He nodded coolly at the two men and walked away.

"Well of all the unmitigated gall—" Mowatt began.

"He could be right, you know," Raoul mused quietly, almost to himself.

"Pardon, Smythe?" Mowatt bridled, thinking Raoul was just interrupting him for spite.

Raoul looked him in the eyes, then glanced away. "Just jealousy at the bottom of it? It could work. I've got all these new ideas, but I'm still just another assistant professor, while you're the college chair. I'm jealous? And it probably works the same for you," he said quickly, gesturing around him, thinking out loud, "to run a department, one you've built up as an altar to a tradition, and have this kid come up and tell you you're wrong, and start proving it. Jealousy . . ." He looked at Mowatt again. "He's right." He ran his fingers through his hair, making it stand more on end than usual. "I need to leave now. Good-bye."

Mowatt had the look of a man who hasn't quite followed the conversation. "What?" he asked confusedly. "Did you actually believe him? He's just playing at politics again. That's all this is you know, I've seen it before, and—"

"Excuse me, Professor, if you will. And, uh, congratulations." Raoul turned and quickly strode through the room, drinking off his beer as he walked. He tried not to look around as he passed the clumps of people chattering around him. Raoul found the butler lurking in the front hall near the door, ready to jump up and be officious at the sound of the bell. He caught the man's attention.

"My cloak?" he asked. The butler looked at him quizzically for a moment, then, realizing what was wanted, called to a young assistant to fetch the gentleman's coat, then went off to call for the cab Raoul requested. The assistant, a boy of about fifteen and obviously uncomfortable in his livery, trotted down a side hall. Raoul followed. As he passed the first door in the corridor, an arm reached out and pulled him into the room. Raoul spun around, his hand snaking down to the side of his boot and back before he saw that it was Bolton.

"Still carrying this old thing, eh?" Bolton said, gently removing the stiletto from Raoul to look at it. "Are you leaving? It's so early—what, did someone set you off already? Good thing I saw you. I'm just taking a few quick notes for tomorrow's article, who's wearing what, the usual crap, you know. So where are you going?" He handed the knife back, hilt first, placing it in Raoul's outstretched hand. Raoul wiped the spotless blade on his sleeve.

"You know," Raoul said pensively, sliding the stiletto back into its sheath, "if you insist on ambushing me like that, someday you're going to lose a finger. And I thought you never took notes."

"Never for anything I'm actually interested in. But it's not worth the mental effort to remember exactly what shade of peach Catherine Moss wore, or what new hairstyle Betty Fernwick had. So I snick off to a side room, make a few scribbles, and then dart back into the feeding frenzy. You see your mother?" Raoul nodded confirmation. "She looks great. I've got to chat her up later, get a few good quotes. So anyway, are you leaving? Have you seen Mowatt?"

"Yes, and yes. And I don't feel like talking about it. I'll see you later." Raoul left, knowing that Bolton was used to his abrupt comings and goings, and would probably call or stop by the next day. That would be fine, and it would be good to talk to him then, once he'd had a chance to think out all that had happened. Right now, though, he needed to get away from people and lights and noise and just be alone. He made it through the hall without speaking to anyone else, retrieved his cloak from the assistant, and stepped into the waiting cab.

Just past Little Barrington, Raoul asked the driver to let him out. He was almost ten miles from home, but thought a walk would clear his head. Wrapping his cloak tightly around himself and holding it closed with crossed arms to ward off the chill of the damp evening, Raoul began walking. He forced himself to move quickly, not to warm up, but to work out his tension, to hit a stride that would seem to move of itself without him. He consciously increased his pace, feeling his legs scissoring along the road, listening to his boots clocking out the passage of time, fast and regular heartbeats on stone.

He really couldn't say he hated Mowatt. He didn't think he truly hated anyone: he just couldn't bring himself to feel all that much about anyone or anything, except magic. Working spells, creating spells, thinking about the way all things worked together and affected each other, the balance. Those things interested him, held him, left no room for anyone or anything to get beyond a certain point in his life.

Except, of course, for the things and people that did. He couldn't explain away Bolton, or his mother, or even the rats. If he was so cold, why did he need them? He'd love to just be able to shut himself off from Bolton, from the often annoying interruptions of his work when his friend wanted to talk, but he couldn't. He wouldn't. He enjoyed talking to Bolton, even when they were saying nothing of import. Or having long conversations where they seemed to do nothing but complain about the stupidity of most people, excepting themselves, of course, or fall into silly reminiscences about past days that they both had hated. But if they had hated things so much, why talk about them years later? Why hold on to each other, when they were nothing but reminders of days best forgotten? But the days hadn't been forgotten or left behind, they'd been made enjoyable by the fact of companionship. Friendship. It defied definition. But he wouldn't change it if he could, even though it made his cold self-image a lie. Somewhat.

So, he didn't hate Mowatt. But that didn't mean he had to enjoy working or being with the man. He was tired of everything becoming a fight, of needing to explain and justify himself before Mowatt would even consider listening to an idea. Then again, Raoul thought, maybe he was too defensive to be objective. Mowatt did seem to seek him out to pick quarrels, but Raoul had to admit he had never made any attempt to conform.

Part of his unique charm, Raoul thought wryly, knowing it to be a lie. He was different. He'd spent many years growing his eccentricities around himself like a protective shell, and now he expected people to just deal with that, or better yet, to just leave him alone. But he was who he was—how could he change that, and why should he? To be a good sheep and do as he was told? He just couldn't see how compromise would help the situation.

Whiting appeared to want him as a full, tenured professor, and to want him enough to mention it to Mowatt in front of him. That meant he was doing something right, at least. But why so quickly, and without consulting Mowatt? Raoul wasn't even sure he wanted tenure, although it would give him more time for research. The problem was getting internal support for the results, which he didn't have and wouldn't be getting unless something changed. Unless perhaps Mowatt was on his way out, which he doubted. He needed to talk to Whiting, see what he had in mind. Perhaps tomorrow.

Chapter 2

Thornhold was dark when Raoul arrived. The walk had done him good, it seemed; he felt calmed and revitalized, ready for a quick change into real clothes, a cup of tea, and then off to the research again. He wanted to find out how he had managed to completely wipe the magical aura from the robe. Not that he could see any use for such a spell, but he needed to know how it had happened. Side spells could sometimes be dangerous; it wouldn't do to use a spell to tidy a room and accidentally make it rain in Shropshire. Nothing esoterical about it; it was pure physics. For something to become, something somewhere had to unbecome, as it were. Conservation of matter really did work, and on all scales.

Entering the house, Raoul felt the usual sense of peace steal over him. Thornhold was the only place he'd ever felt completely at home. He'd been lucky to find it, luckier to have money at the time. Before he even completed his thesis, he'd wanted to move out of his university digs, but he couldn't afford it, or rather, wouldn't take the money his mother offered. If she bought something for him, he wouldn't refuse it, but he hadn't asked her for anything since he'd first been sent off to school. It was typical of their relationship.

The money for the house had come to him through an enterprising scholarly publisher who'd seen an excerpt from his thesis and contacted him. The eventual book, *The Evil Eye: Curse Evocation and Avoidance in the Early Nineteenth Century*, came on the coattails of yet another small public scare about the unrestrained use of magic and thus sold remarkably well. Mowatt, resenting its success, still occasionally reminded Raoul that it wouldn't have happened if he hadn't vetoed Raoul's first choice of a thesis topic.

His first royalty check in his pocket, Raoul had been on his way to a weekend jaunt into Wales with Bolton when a detour forced them off the A40 west of Oxford. Driving without a map, they'd taken a tiny unpaved road somewhere near Lower Slaughter, and looking into the trees, Raoul had seen the fence. Eight feet of solid stone. It seemed so forbidding that he'd made Bolton stop so they could get a better look at it. A dirt drive snaked off toward a chained and padlocked wrought-iron gate even taller than the fence. Black wrought-iron roses twined about the gate, realistically pointed thorns poking out of the iron foliage. A tree-lined drive beyond the gate led to the house. Bolton had broken into Raoul's reverie with a snicker. "Well," he'd said, looking at the house, "if the word 'folly' isn't part of that thing's name, it damned well should be. It's ghastly!"

Raoul remained silent, staring at the house and smiling. Golden Cotswold limestone and wood rose for three stories in a bizarre mating of Cotswold cottage, Tudor mansion, and Italian villa. Windows and balconies jutted out into space, and three towers rose asymmetrically from the roof to vie with apparently innumerable chimneys. Hideous and beautiful, the house stood silently on at least an acre of half-cleared land probably intended for a formal garden, but left to grow into a riot of wildflowers and tall grass. Beyond the gardens, forest surrounded the house. There were no signs of occupancy. Raoul stood gazing silently a few moments longer, then turned to Bolton. "Let's get going. I need to go into town."

"Back to Oxford? Why?"

"No, not Oxford. The next town we come to should do."

"Oh. You should have gone before we left." Bolton laughed.

Glancing over at Bolton, Raoul rolled his eyes upward. "Idiot. No, I need to find a Realtor."

Bolton stopped, turning to face Raoul. "Oh, no. Don't tell me you're going to say what I think you're going to say . . . Rags, you can't be serious." He looked at Raoul. "Oh, gods, you are serious. I wish I were surprised. It's horrible! It's like something Bosch would live in. Or you, I suppose." He heaved a mock sigh. "Well, let's get going. A quid says the name has 'folly' in it."

Later, as Raoul signed the royalty check over to the Realtor as a down payment, he remembered to ask for a pound back. "Anyway," he said, handing the note to Bolton, "I'll be changing the name."

He smiled, remembering, as he waited for the kettle to boil. Bolton had hated the new name, as had almost everyone except his friends at the Seller. Thornhold, Slaughter. He still thought it the most wonderful address ever. So evocative. It was worth the inconvenience of being so far from Oxford, if indeed it was an inconvenience.

He carried his tea to the study, then set to work on recreating what he'd done the previous evening. He'd tried a number of spells before it worked, and needed to completely duplicate his methods before trying to isolate why the aural blanking had occurred.

Although he became sidetracked a few times, finding ways to shorten the spell files he was using, he eventually had another shirt with roses on it. But there was definitely magical residue. He'd just used a plain cotton shirt this time, so he tried raw silk instead. Still residue. The robe he'd worn to the gala had been moire, so he dug through the closet until he found another shirt of the same fabric. He worked the spell yet again, this time the spell leaving no residue whatsoever. Obviously, the materials used in the spell were important.

Moire was a fabric with a pattern actually in the cloth itself, rather than a plain or patterned weave. Whereas in the latter two the spell caused the motif to appear by either adding an image to the cloth or by rearranging the weave image, in the moire it merely shifted an image that was already an integral element, formed by nature. Maybe that was it, he thought. He needed something with a natural pattern that could be manipulated to test it. Raoul smiled. Tree bark. He printed out the spell he needed, since missing even one word would nullify the test, and went outside.

Casting the spell, he felt invigorated. The sun was near rising, lending a clean, cold cast to the last of the moonlight. This, he had always felt, was the way magic was meant to be performed; outside, not cloistered in some dank smoke-filled room.

The spell worked, leaving no aural residue on the trees, only roses and leaves formed of bark patterns twining up the trunks. They looked great, he thought. He'd already done almost an entire side of the drive when he began to tire. His eyelids were trying to close of their own accord by the time he was satisfied that no trace of magic existed on any of the trees he'd worked on. He'd been right, at least, he thought as he walked back into the house, though he still needed to isolate the reason why it was happening. Thank the gods for computers, he thought as he entered the house, otherwise he would have had to figure out each combination of words and gestures by hand.

As he passed quietly through the kitchen, trying not to wake Mrs. Higgins, Raoul remembered that she'd left the previous evening. He always seemed to lose track of the days when she was out. He checked the refrigerator to see what she'd left for him, then continued up to bed, and set the alarm to wake him at ten.

On rising, Raoul went downstairs and started the kettle for tea, telephoning for a cab while he waited. In the shower he decided to see if Whiting was at home before going to his own office to work. Raoul wanted to discuss the tenure issue with him, or at least arrange a time to meet, to see just what Whiting had in mind before Mowatt had a chance to sway him against it. He'd make it clear to Whiting that he could make much more progress on his research if he had internal support. Mowatt just wouldn't consider what it could mean to the magic community if there could be some forward motion in spell-casting. Raoul thought if he could sway Whiting, perhaps the chancellor could put pressure on Mowatt to loosen the reins a bit.

He continued looking over his printouts in the cab, writing occasional notes in the margins. He'd narrowed the cause of the aural erasure to ten lines or so, but they still had to be taken apart rune by rune, sound by sound. Unfortunately, after he spoke with Whiting, he'd have paperwork to deal with before he could play with the spell. Still, he hoped to have something by early evening at the latest. Though a completely unexpected result, discovering how to completely remove traces of magic could be the breakthrough he needed to demonstrate the possibilities of his research.

Arriving at the chancellor's house, Raoul paid off the cab and rang the bell. The butler was about to respond to his request to see Whiting when the daughter, whose name he'd forgotten, flew into the front hall, throwing a coat on and nearly colliding with the two men.

"Oh!" she said, stopping and looking confusedly at Raoul, "I thought Cat and Mary were picking you up. I'm running late, as usual. Did something happen?"

He stared at her for a moment, baffled. "Excuse me? I'm looking for—"

She broke in before she could finish. "Ah, I see. You've forgotten brunch then, haven't you?" She smiled. "No problem, you can ride with me. The girls will figure out you're not at home, I'm sure. Cat never waits for anyone, anyway."

Raoul realized it was Saturday, and that he'd completely forgotten the stupid brunch. It was pure dumb luck to have caught her on her way. He tried to beg off, but she wouldn't hear of it, and anyway, she said, her father had gone to London. "He should be back by the time we're through, though, so you can see him then. Hawkins," she said, turning to the bewildered butler, "write Raoul in Daddy's calendar for about three or four o'clock this afternoon, would you? Thanks so much." And then she pulled Raoul toward the car, before he could grasp the implication of the times she'd given.

"Three or four?" he asked as she revved the engine. "This won't take that long, will it?"

She turned to look at him, tilting her head quizzically. "You really don't get out much, do you? Of course—it's a brunch. Those usually do take a while, what with all the talking and general enjoying oneself that goes on." She smiled.

"Okay, okay," he said, throwing up his hands, "It's just that I really did have things planned for this afternoon." Actually, he was pleasantly surprised at her banter, and suspected he might actually enjoy Anne's company, though that would probably change as soon as they saw Catherine Moss. Raoul had often noted that Catherine's presence seemed to suck the intelligence out of any conversation.

They chatted on the way to the restaurant, which was in Reading. "What kind of name is 'The Wild Brunch,' anyway?" Raoul asked at one point. "It's probably some cheesy pseudobiker bar, with leather tablecloths, topless waitresses, and Brando-burgers, right?" He laughed. "Am I right?"

"That's 'The Wild One,' silly! This is the other one. You know, horses, cowboys, Peckinpah? Movie? Twentieth century?" That little quizzical tilt to the head again, and the smile. So much for baiting her, he thought. He changed the subject, asking her what she did. As it turned out, she was an assistant account executive in an Oxford advertising agency. "Run by one of Dad's friends, of course," she added. From her tone, he suspected it wasn't something she enjoyed, so he asked if that were the case.

"You don't pull your punches, do you?" she asked. "Catherine was almost right."

"What's that supposed to mean?" he replied, scowling. Although to some extent he encouraged his reputation, he hated being confronted with the fact that he might be fod-

der for people like Catherine to discuss. "What the hell
does she know about me? And anyway, what's wrong with
asking a simple question? If you don't feel like answering,
don't answer. Gods! You people spend so much time danc-
ing around each other, trying not to give offense, that I'm
surprised you can communicate at all. If people would
spend more time thinking about what to say rather than
how to say it prettily, things would be a lot simpler everywhere, I can tell you that." He stopped, realizing that he
was becoming angry. They rode in silence for a while.

"You know, you're right," Anne finally said, turning to
him. "You're rude, but you're right." Her voice held a
slight sarcastic edge.

"I prefer to think of myself as honest," he replied,
"though I'll accept rude in a pinch. I've just never bothered
too much about what other people think." He continued, almost to himself, "This wasn't such a good idea."

"No, I think it's probably good for you to come out of
your cave once in a while," she said. "Anyway, we're
here."

The restaurant turned out to have an American West
theme, with red-checked tablecloths, staff in cowboy or Na-
tive American outfits, fried foods, and people saying "y'all"
for no apparent reason. The company wasn't much better.
In addition to the people he'd met at Mowatt's party, there
were two or three new faces. Raoul faded in and out of
conversation, which as far as he could tell concerned primarily the fashions and mating habits of people who
weren't there.

". . . and then she walked out of the room, just like that.
She hasn't spoken to him since, either. Isn't it fabulous?
And then when I saw him . . ."

". . . I just finished the new Del Franco novel—it kept
me up all night . . ."

". . . Now, Raoul, is it really true that only certain fabrics
can be worn while working spells? I've been thinking of
creating a line of clothes based on magician's robes."

". . . and then Baldrick said that it was funny, because he had a thingy that looked just like a . . ."

"Well, Patricia, it all depends on the spell . . ."

Dessert was nearly finished when two men in gray suits entered the restaurant, looked around, then approached their table. Catherine looked as if she were trying to recall where she knew them from as one stopped a few feet behind Raoul while the other gently touched his arm. "Excuse me, sir, but are you Mr. Raoul Giamboni-Smythe of Lower Slaughter?" the man asked politely.

"Just Smythe," Raoul said, "and just Slaughter. Who are you?" As Raoul stood and turned, the man beside him quickly stepped back, while the other reached into his jacket.

"I'm Detective Inspector George Barnstone, sir, and my colleague is Detective Mulcahy. Would you mind stepping out with us for a bit? We'd like to talk to you."

"Out where to talk about what? What's the problem?"

"We'd like to talk to you for a moment about something, if you please. At the station." Gray suit number one put his hand back on Raoul's arm and pulled gently.

By now the table was a mass of chatter. "What's going on, then?" "Oh, dear, is there a problem?" and "What's this?" began to gain in volume and frequency, and people at the surrounding tables turned to look.

Finally, Raoul turned to the man holding his arm and said firmly, "Look, I'm going nowhere until you state what you're about, and how about some identification while you're at it?"

The man, who appeared to be in his mid- to late thirties, showed Raoul an identification card saying he was indeed Detective Inspector George Barnstone of the Oxford police. Then, addressing Raoul and the others, he said, "The problem, sir, is that you're wanted for questioning concerning the late Arthur Mowatt, and we'd like to speak to you about it. Privately. Now." On the last two words his voice became firmer, and his grip on Raoul's arm tightened.

Betty Fernwick broke the tense pause with a giggle. "Oh,

I knew there was a misunderstanding! Professor Mowatt's not dead! We just saw him last night."

Detective Inspector Barnstone turned to her. "I'm afraid he is, ma'am. Now if you'll please excuse us . . ."

He nodded at Raoul, who shrugged and said, "Lead on, then." They started toward the door, the other detective following, but after a few steps Raoul stopped and turned back to the table. "Excuse me, y'all," he drawled at the shocked group, then continued out with the detectives. He could hear the buzz of conversation start up again as they left. Mowatt dead? Raoul thought. How very strange.

The detectives ushered him into the backseat of a gray sedan. As the car pulled out into traffic, Raoul asked, "Am I under arrest, then?"

"Oh no, sir," Mulcahy responded. "You're just wanted for questioning at the moment. We'll give you all the details at the station."

"Fine," Raoul said, "but knock off with the 'sir,' will you? It's annoying." The detective didn't reply, merely turned away. Raoul sat in silence, looking out the window and thinking about the ramifications of Mowatt being dead. He noticed Barnstone glancing in the rearview mirror at him at regular intervals. He also noted there were no handles on the rear doors. It could have been worse, he thought. At least I'm out of the stupid brunch.

The ride back to Oxford passed quickly. Inside the station, he was led into a small yellow-lit office. Barnstone sat down behind a desk and motioned Raoul to take the single seat facing him. "Tea, sir—I mean Mr. Giamboni-Smythe?" Mulcahy asked. When Raoul declined, after pointing out again that his surname was simply Smythe, Mulcahy leaned against the wall beside the desk, facing Raoul.

"Now, gentlemen," Raoul said, leaning forward, "will you tell me what's going on here?"

The facts were simple. "At nine-fifteen this morning," Detective Barnstone recited, "the Oxford police received an anonymous phone call, apparently from a woman, saying that Arthur Mowatt was dead. They tried to ring him, of course, but when there was no answer, they sent men to see if anything was amiss. When the constables arrived, they found the front door open and the professor lying on the floor of his study. He appeared to have been struck on the head with a blunt instrument, and to have bled to death. Preliminary investigation has placed the time of death at sometime between two and four o'clock that morning. There are no signs of a struggle, and nothing appears to have been stolen."

Barnstone paused a moment while Raoul digested the information. "Now, if you please, Professor Smythe," Barnstone continued, "where were you during that time? We know that you left the Whitings' party between ten-thirty and eleven o'clock."

"Did I?" Raoul asked. "I hadn't remarked the time." He paused, trying to remember the exact order of events. "I took a cab back to my house, but had them leave me off just past Little Barrington."

"Why was that, if you please?" Barnstone asked, writing.

"I had a few things to think about, and I often think while walking. It clears my head."

"I see. Now approximately how far would you say you walked?"

"I can't be exact, but I expect it's roughly ten miles. You could have someone measure it."

"Just answer the questions, please. So you had the cab let you out because you had 'a few things to think about,' and then walked home? When did you arrive at your house?"

"Again, I didn't remark the time. I expect it was one or two o'clock, but I really can't be precise. Then I—"

"Excuse me again, but did you happen to see anyone while you were walking? That might help establish the time."

"No, I didn't see anyone. Perhaps someone saw me, I really can't say. It's not really a very populated area. And, as I said, I was thinking. Shall I continue?"

"Please."

"Anyway, I arrived home, made a cup of tea, and then worked in my study for a while before going outside to work on a new spell. I came back inside at around five o'clock, just after sunrise, then went to bed and woke at ten. Will that do?"

"Can anyone confirm this?"

"My housekeeper was off as of yesterday afternoon. You'll just have to take my word for it, I guess. Is there anything else?" Raoul waited while Barnstone wrote on a pad.

"Just a few more questions, sir. I'd like to be sure I have this correct: you left the party between ten-thirty and eleven, which we can verify with the cab company. You proceeded in the cab to approximately Little Barrington, again verifiable as to exact place and time, then continued on foot to your house, where you proceeded to make tea and work magic until approximately five o'clock in the morning. Is this correct?"

"Yes."

"So you were walking and thinking, making tea, and working alone in your study, and outside, during the hours of the murder."

"It appears so. Is this a problem? I realize it's fairly vague, but why would I want to kill Mowatt?" As he spoke, Raoul realized he should probably have used Mowatt's title, but it was too late.

"That's what we'd like to find out, sir. It's come to our attention that the two of you didn't really get along, and were seen arguing at the party earlier that evening. Is that true?"

"Arguing? A bit, but that's nothing unusual. It was no secret that we didn't get along."

"But wasn't he your direct superior in the college?"

"Yes, but each professor is relatively autonomous."

"But you are, of course, only an assistant professor."

"Yes, at the moment." Raoul was starting to wonder how all this was sounding to the detectives. It even sounded somewhat fishy to him, and he knew what had happened.

Then again, he supposed that interrogations were intended to make one nervous. And he was definitely beginning to feel ill at ease. "Part of the reason we were arguing at the party was that Sir Reginald Whiting appears to favor offering me tenure. Mowatt disagreed."

"And so you parted angrily?"

"I wasn't particularly angry with him, no. I think he was more angry at the idea being mentioned to both of us at once. I think he felt slighted."

"By Sir Reginald?"

"I suppose."

Raoul was determined not to break the ensuing moment of silence. Finally Barnstone said, "So was the argument with Professor Mowatt what you were thinking about on your walk back to your house on the night of the murder?"

Raoul looked evenly at Barnstone and resisted the urge to blurt out "Objection! Leading the witness!" He didn't think the detective would find it amusing.

"Do you find something amusing, Professor?" Barnstone asked him.

Raoul realized he'd smiled at his own thoughts. "No, I was just thinking. I suppose that one of the things on my mind was my *discussion* with Sir Reginald and Professor Mowatt, yes. Among other things."

"Very well, Professor. I believe that will be all for now. We'll be sure to contact you, Mr. Smythe, if anything further develops. We will also look into corroborating your times."

Raoul nodded. "Fine. Am I free to go ?" he asked, feeling relieved despite himself.

"Yes, sir. We'll draw up a statement for you to sign later. Do you need a ride anywhere?"

"I'm just going back to the university. I need to do some work in the office." He realized he must be more upset than he thought; he was starting to offer excuses for everything.

"That's no problem at all. Detective Mulcahy will take you there. Thank you again for your help." The two men escorted Raoul to the door. As Mulcahy and Raoul were leaving, Barnstone added, "Sorry to mention this, but you should plan on remaining in the country for the duration of the investigation. Standard procedure, you know."

"Certainly."

With that, Raoul left. The ride to his office was again a silent one, though he did get to sit in the front seat. When the detective stopped to let him out, Raoul thanked him, then walked across the yard to his office.

Strangely, the building was unlocked, though it was late on a weekend afternoon. As Raoul walked down the corridor, he noticed that the light inside his office clearly revealed silhouettes of at least two men. Drawing the knife from his boot and holding it lightly in his left hand, he slowly opened the door. Whiting stood talking to Bolton. They fell silent as he entered.

"Shouldn't leave your door unlocked, old man," Bolton said, rising to greet him. "You never know who might turn up. How are you?"

"Fine," Raoul answered. "Would you wait outside for a bit?" He turned to walk a step or two with Bolton, using the moment to slide the knife into the sleeve of his shirt. He held his arm stiffly, not wanting either to dislodge it or cut himself.

Bolton paused at the door, looking concerned. "I'll be next door, when you want me." Then he laughed. "Livingston doesn't lock his office, either." John Livingston, another assistant professor, occupied the office adjacent to Raoul's.

"Now, Sir Reginald," Raoul said, taking a seat behind his desk and offering a chair to the university head, "what can I do for you?"

He leaned forward against the desk, reaching down to slide the knife back into the boot sheath.

Whiting cut right to the chase. "I'm glad you finally came by. I took a chance this was where you'd come first. Horrible, isn't it, about Arthur? I hear you were called in for questioning." Before Raoul could respond, he continued, "They spoke with me in London earlier this afternoon. Very polite about it, I must say. They say it happened early this morning."

"Yes," Raoul answered, wondering where this was leading.

"It didn't appear to be a robbery, either. There was no sign of a struggle. Odd, isn't it?" Whiting appeared to be speaking out of nervousness, which was unusual for him. Raoul waited. Whiting continued. "Very bad press for the university, you know, very bad indeed. 'Newly honored department chair murdered' and such. Headlines, inquiries, trials, and the like. Very bad indeed . . . Do they think you did it?"

"Pardon?" Raoul said, surprised. "I should hope not. Not, that is," he mused, "that I have a very convincing alibi."

"No," agreed Whiting, "not really." At Raoul's inquiring look, he explained. "They called as soon as you left them, you know. They asked about you, what your relationship with Arthur had been. Told me what you'd said, asked if I believed you. I told them it sounded perfectly all right, of course. Poor old Arthur," he said, then fell silent. "He wanted me to fire you, you know," he went on after a moment. "So set in his ways." He waved Raoul to silence. "He really was. But a brilliant mind, really, simply brilliant."

Whiting looked at Raoul. "I'm sorry, bursting in here and blathering away. I'm more upset than I admit, I suppose. You know he and I have—I mean *had*—known each other for more than twenty years? I can't believe he's gone." He was silent again, but only for a moment. "So you see, Raoul, I'm in an awkward position, what with you being a suspect and all. Not that I think you did it, not at all, it's just a matter of what people will think about the university, and how disruptive it might be: police, reporters, the whole business. We don't want that, you know."

"Am I to understand," Raoul said stiffly, "that you're asking me to step down? Is that it? I'm to resign over this? Do you know what that looks like? You can't be serious."

"I don't want you to resign, Raoul, just not to teach for the duration of the investigation. You will, of course, continue to work on your research, and you'll have the full use of the university, your office, whatever you want. Just take the time off from teaching duties. Purely to avoid any negative publicity, you understand. Your classes would be covered by another professor, probably Livingston."

"Excuse me, Sir Reginald," Raoul broke in, "but you really can't be serious. Avoid negative publicity? Maybe it will for the university, but this won't reflect all that well on me, you know . . ." He trailed off, unable to express exactly what he wanted to say. "What will the police say? I am a suspect, at least for the moment . . ."

"Pish." Whiting snorted. "About as much as I am. There's really no question that it was anyone at the university. The police need to be thorough is all. And I'll let them know what has happened, of course. If you agree, that is." He paused, then continued, tempting, "Think of all the progress you can make without other responsibilities. It would be like being a research fellow."

Raoul thought for a moment. It would give him time to concentrate on the spell reductions. And if it was this important to Whiting, then it might be best to comply with his wishes. Still, it wouldn't hurt to consider all the ramifications first. "If you wouldn't mind, Sir Reginald," he asked, "I'd like to think it over for a bit."

"No problem at all. Why don't you give me your answer Monday morning. There's a meeting for your college staff at ten o'clock. Why don't you plan on either being in my office or leaving a message for me by nine. That way I can work it into the meeting." Whiting nodded to himself, thinking. "Yes, that'll be perfect," he muttered, then caught himself and turned back to Raoul. "You'll get back to me Monday morning, then? Good. I'll tell Livingston, of course, when it's necessary. Good day, Raoul." Whiting rose and shook his hand, then left, leaving the door open behind him.

Raoul turned his chair to the right to look out his office's single window. He sat for a moment, watching as Whiting exited the building and walked off in the direction of his home rather than his office. Maybe it wouldn't be so bad, he thought. After all, Whiting had made a career out of turning any possible occurrence into "good press" for the university, or at least avoiding "bad press." He'd do anything to avoid a hint of scand—A sudden noise at the door startled him. Raoul spun in his chair with a quick intake of breath.

Bolton was standing in the doorway. "Don't hiss at me, young man!" He smiled and fell into the chair Whiting had recently vacated. "So, they called you in, eh?" Despite his air of cultivated disinterest in anything not related to fashion or people of fashion, Bolton tended to know a lot about what was going on at any given moment. He'd once remarked that people were more apt to spill information to someone they considered foolish than to someone who might actually be able to add two and two. His "cultural review" column had often been the first to present information on various personages and events, all due to "dumb luck," of course. Raoul often wondered how Bolton could stand sucking up to people the way he did, but he seemed to genuinely enjoy it.

Raoul nodded. "And Whiting wants to pull me from teaching for as long as the investigation lasts. This isn't good." He paused for a moment, the thought of the morning's events bringing a wry smile to his face. "The police yanked me right out of one of Catherine's day-long lunches. Pity. Oxford detectives. What have you heard so far, by the way? I assume you've been snooping around all morning." Raoul looked at his friend, hoping he could shed some light. Right now, he had too many questions and no answers at all.

"Well, first you tell me what happened, and then maybe I can fill in some gaps. It's all that anyone's been talking about. Have you ever noticed that no matter how squeamish a person says they are, nothing brings out the talker in one quite like violent death? Not just violence, mind you, and not just death, but the particular combination of the two. Something about the randomness, I suppose. Brings out the need to rationalize things. Usually while eating, too, when you think about it. Hmmm . . ." He rolled the thought around for a moment, then looked up. "Anyway, tell."

When Raoul finished telling Bolton about all that had occurred since the previous evening, including the weird aural erasure he'd discovered, he glanced at Bolton for a reaction. Bolton was leaning back in his chair, arms crossed, watching him.

"I think," he said slowly, "that you might be in trouble, my friend." His voice was serious, a rare occurrence. "Your alibi sucks, your motive for murder doesn't, and getting pulled doesn't speak volumes for the university's faith in you, no matter what Whiting says about it being an 'opportunity.' I'd be careful, if I were you."

"What's that supposed to mean? I didn't kill the idiot, you know." *Kill,* he thought, was a strange word to be using. He still couldn't associate it with Mowatt; the man was too unpleasant to be dead. Raoul wondered if he was afraid of feeling relieved. He *had* wanted Mowatt out of his life. He wasn't even sure how he felt about it; his feelings were so mixed, a jumble of relief, guilt, and a tense uneasiness. "You know that," he said. "Don't tell me you think I could have . . ."

"No, I don't." Bolton said firmly. "But you are the prime suspect, you know."

Raoul was startled. "I'm what?" he asked, sitting upright. "They said it was just routine. What do you mean, I'm the prime suspect?"

"I mean that right now the police think you probably killed him. Think about it, Rags. Everyone in the university knows you can't stand the man, and he can't stand you. Couldn't, rather. Gossip at the party had you storming out when Mowatt opposed Whiting's hint about tenure, and Mowatt was certainly in a fine fettle after you left."

"I hadn't heard. What happened?"

"Well, after you left, Mowatt started spouting off to anyone who'd listen about how you and Whiting were conspiring to drive him out of the department. Hell, he even filled my ear for fifteen minutes or so. He'd been drinking, of course. Then he kept trying to talk to Whiting, who kept putting him off. Mrs. Whiting eventually got him calmed down. I think she put him in a cab and sent him home when the party started breaking up around midnight. You two were quite the hot item of gossip afterward," Bolton finished.

"Where?" Raoul asked.

"Oh, I ended up going clubbing with a bunch of people from the party—you know, Catherine and company, plus some of your teaching brethren. Your colleagues, in particular, seemed surprised it hadn't come sooner." He paused, waiting for Raoul to indicate if he wanted to hear more. He knew Raoul was touchy about people discussing him. Still, Bolton thought, Raoul did seem to leave an undercurrent of interest wherever he passed. He was different, and as Bolton knew only too well, difference either attracts or repels, sometimes both at once.

"What hadn't come sooner?" Raoul asked. Bolton detected a note of resignation in his voice. He had his head in his hands again, eyes closed, listening. Bolton didn't often worry about Raoul, who never seemed to be touched by events, at least outwardly, but he seemed particularly withdrawn now.

Bolton continued, watching Raoul as he spoke, "Well, the university contingent, Livingston and Barstow, you know, seemed to think you've been chafing at the bit more than usual lately, what with all the research you've been doing against Mowatt's express wishes, and with him finally telling you off last week. I think they expected last night's clash between you two at the party. They respect you, you know," he added, for no real reason. "You've quite the reputation as a wunderkind. Personally, I think Mowatt was quite right to be worried."

"Pardon?" Raoul still hadn't looked up.

"Think of all the progress Whiting has made, updating

the facilities and whatnot. Changing the university, breaking
with tradition. Mowatt was in danger of becoming an an-
achronism, and I think he knew it. Not that Whiting would
fire him or anything like that; it's just that Mowatt was losing respect. He probably viewed you as a threat, at the
least. Whiting's always looking for something to really
draw the school into the public eye. That could be you.
Magic always makes good copy, trust me."

"So people think I killed him?"

"I don't know, Rags. I just don't know. But I don't see
where you have much choice but to take Whiting up on his
offer. Use the time to think about what's happening, about
what you're going to do. At the very least, if nothing else
comes of it, you'll have him on your side. Who knows,
maybe some new evidence will turn up that's not circum-
stantial." Bolton shrugged, though Raoul's eyes were still
closed.

Raoul opened them and looked at Bolton. This was too
serious for his taste. "I know." He sighed. "It's just all so
stupid! What if nothing else turns up? What if they make
a mistake? I can't be convicted, Max. I just can't. You
know what they do. I couldn't live with that." He paused
for a moment. "I'm going to find out who did this, find out
what happened. I can't take the chance they'll be wrong."

Bolton knew what Raoul was talking about. The penal-
ties for magicians convicted of capital crimes were severe.
They had to be since, despite the careful study of the natural balance and responsibility that went into an education
in magic, there was always the possibility of someone using
magic for ill purposes. Mindful of the persecutions suffered
by magicians throughout history at the hands of frightened
mobs and cultish fanatics, the community of magicians po-
liced their own when necessary. Law enforcement agencies
had special task forces to deal with magical crime; courts
and judges had special advisory boards. If convicted,
however unlikely it might be, Raoul would have his magical ability and knowledge blocked, permanently, in addi-

tion to whatever physical sentence was pronounced. Bolton knew that the very thought would be anathema to Raoul.

Raoul was looking at him. "It'll be okay, Rags," he said nodding. "I'll help any way I can, you know that. We'll find out what happened, and it'll be fine. Plus," he added, with a trace of his usual humor, "it's an excuse for you to skip classes, and I can get a whopper of a story about it. Deal?"

A shadow of a smile crossed Raoul's face. "Deal. So where do we start, Sherlock?"

Bolton turned serious again. "We start by me getting a copy of the police transcripts, and then, my dear Watson, we visit the scene of the crime. I've got a friend in the police who owes me a favor; I'll see what he can get." He glanced at his watch. "I've got to get back to London now, though." He smiled lecherously. "Got a date. Are you going to be okay? What are you doing tonight?"

Raoul shrugged. "Tonight? I've got to meet someone at the Seller, but after that, I don't know. I need to think for a while."

"Well, don't brood, okay? I'll call you tomorrow. You'll be around?"

Raoul nodded. "Here or at home, yeah. I've got a lot to think about."

"Don't think too hard, Rags," Bolton said, crossing to the door.

Raoul snorted in response as Bolton left, then got ready to leave. He wished he hadn't made plans, but hopefully it wouldn't take long. In any case, it would probably be good for him to sit for a while, have a Guinness, and not think about Mowatt.

Raoul didn't go out much; he found most of the clubs too trendy and, more important, too full of students. There was one club, however, that he considered almost a second home. The Rat Seller was a dank pit that hadn't appreciably changed in all the years he'd known it. Bolton liked to describe it as a rest home for the incurably immature. Located on a tiny side street, with a stunningly bad view of a cemetery and the train line, its inconvenient location and bad reputation kept all but the most dedicatedly strange students away. Most of Raoul's small circle of friends frequented it.

As usual, Raoul took the longer route to the club, avoiding the crowded and noisy main streets. Even so, he was tense and irritable by the time he left the smaller college streets and entered the town proper. As usual, a group of religious fanatics stood clustered in the square where St. Giles street split into the Woodstock and Banbury roads. The spot was favored by a number of fundamentalist groups, since in addition to being convenient to traffic, across the street was a Druid-owned pub, the Hollow Man, which made a great target for their shouted comments.

As he approached the orderly mob, Raoul considered going into the Hollow Man just to spite them, but decided against it; it was usually crowded at this hour, and he was probably going to be late as it was. The group itself was a cluster of about twenty or so people, most holding either Bibles or painted signs with slogans such as MAGIC = DAMNATION, and SATAN LOVES MAGIC. The oldest member of the group, a man of about fifty or so, stood on the bottom stair leading to the church, holding his Bible aloft and shouting about how Oxford had become overrun by people using magic and those who supported them. Raoul walked straight through the group, ignoring the warding gestures and hissed comments.

Someone grabbed his sleeve, stopping him. "Have you accepted the Christ as your Savior?" the man asked.

Raoul fixed the man's hand with an angry glare. "Not yet," he snapped. "Been too busy sacrificing children. Now move your fucking hand before I move it for you." He glanced at the man's face. "Oh, it's you, Mordechai." He turned to leave.

Still holding his sleeve, the disheveled young man pulled him back. "You're damned, Raoul. Magic is evil. But it's not too late for you to—What are you doing?" he cried, stepping back a pace as Raoul began to speak quietly. The rest of the group fell silent and turned to look just as Raoul's spell took effect.

Mordechai screamed when he found he couldn't release his hold on his Bible. As he shook his right hand frantically, trying to let go of the book, Raoul grabbed the front of his shirt and pulled him close.

"Leave me the hell alone, Mordechai," he growled in the shaking man's ear. "I won't tell you again. Next time I'll just light your hand on fire." Releasing his hold, Raoul shoved Mordechai backward and made his way across the street. The spell would only last for a minute or so, but maybe this time Mordechai would get the hint. It seemed that Mordechai was always around, badgering him about his wickedness. The fact that they'd been at school together only made it worse for Raoul, since Mordechai not only knew his name, but his history. As he continued toward the club, Raoul realized that lately Mordechai had managed to find him at least once a week and seemed to be getting worse each time. Obviously, he hadn't gotten the point yet.

Raoul's friend Skank hadn't yet arrived when he reached the Rat Seller. He sat at his usual back corner table, nursing a pint of stout and watching the original *Nosferatu* projected on the wall, its soundtrack drowned by the Bauhaus compilation tape blaring from the speakers. Raoul smiled. Bryon, the bartender, always seemed to arrange interesting juxtapositions of movies and music. Leaning back, he closed his eyes, forcing himself to relax.

Hearing someone approach, Raoul opened his eyes. Skank, a drink in one hand, her guitar case in the other, flung herself into the chair beside him. "Hi," she said brightly. "I suppose I'm late, right? Sorry."

Raoul shook his head. "No problem." He nodded at the guitar case. "Is that the patient?"

"Yeah," she said, undoing the locks. She pulled out the guitar, a battered black Les Paul copy, and held it out to him. "He just won't stay in tune lately."

He took it gingerly by the neck and looked closely at it. "You know, Skank, one of these days you should get someone who knows about these things to look at this. For all I know, my spells could be damaging it."

"Yeah, I know, but that costs money," she said. "No offense intended. So can you figure out a way to keep it in tune?"

Raoul thought for a moment. "Sure," he replied. "If you tune it now, I can put a spell on the strings so that their length won't change. That'll keep it in tune, I think, plus it's a spell I think I've got with me. That sound okay?"

Skank nodded, taking the guitar and beginning to tune it while Raoul pulled a large binder out of his bag and began flipping through the pages of computer printout. When Skank was satisfied with the sound, she handed the guitar back to Raoul, who laid it on the table. He looked up from the spellbook. "Get me a glass of water, would you?"

She looked quizzically at him, but turned toward the bar without a word, returning a few minutes later with a full glass. "It's from the tap," she said, holding it out to Raoul. "Is that okay?"

He glanced up from the piece of parchment he'd begun writing on. "Fine," he said shortly. "Just set it down on the table, next to the guitar. And stand back, would you?"

Glancing at the written spell, he wrote a few more words on the rectangular piece of parchment. Recapping his fountain pen, he reached back into his bag for a small jar of what looked to Skank like dust.

"What's that?" she asked, knowing he hated to be interrupted in a spell, but wanting to know.

"Powdered earth," he snapped. "Skank, I'm trying to work here. Shhh."

"Okay," she said, taking another step back. She watched closely as Raoul shook a small amount of earth onto the rune-covered parchment and spread it carefully so that it covered all but a small space in the center. Dipping a finger into the glass of water, he let three droplets fall into the center of the parchment.

"Okay, then," he said to himself, standing up. "Here we go." Taking up the parchment, he threaded it carefully through the strings in the middle of the neck. Placing his left hand on the headstock and his right on the bridge, he began to speak. As usual, Skank thought it sounded like gibberish, but obviously he knew what he was doing, since the parchment burst suddenly into a greenish flame which didn't appear to be consuming the paper itself. Raoul spoke a few more words, then laid both hands over the flame. When he removed them, the parchment was unharmed, but completely blank. He pulled the paper nonchalantly out of the strings.

"If the runes start to show up again, the spell's wearing off," he said, handing the paper to Skank. "But you don't need to keep it if you don't want to. It should be fine now."

She picked up the guitar, looking it over carefully before strumming a chord. "Hey!" she exclaimed. "It sounds great!" She hugged the guitar to her before setting it back into its case. As she sat down again, she asked, "So, what do I owe you for this? You know I'd do *anything*, don't you?" She leered.

Raoul rolled his eyes and shook his head. "Don't be weird, Skank." He took a drink, thinking. His circle of friends operated on a loose barter system. "Cabs are always good."

Skank shook her head and laughed. "I can't believe this. I make a perfectly reasonable lewd suggestion and you're more interested in transportation. What am I going to do with you?"

"Drive me to work?" Raoul asked, feigning innocence.

"Okay, I get the point. My cousin still has his cab, and he still owes me for playing his wedding; how about five trips between Thornhold and Oxford? Is that fair?"

Raoul nodded. "Sounds great. What's his number?"

Skank opened the guitar case and consulted a list taped inside it. She rattled off the number to Raoul, who wrote it down. She pulled a wrapped package out of the case before closing it. "Oh, and I almost forgot. Bill asked me to give these to you. It's the tarot deck he promised you. He says thanks again, too."

Raoul took the package. "Bill's back in town?"

"Yeah, for a little while. He'll probably be here later tonight."

Raoul finished off his beer and stood. "I'll see him later, probably. I've got to run now. Thanks for the cabs."

Skank smiled up at him. "My pleasure, really."

Later that evening at Thornhold, Raoul felt restless. On returning, he'd done a little work on the aural erasure, trying to find out what had caused it, but found himself unable to concentrate. He turned off the computer in the study, picked up a book on early Etruscan inscriptions, and put it down a moment later, realizing he'd been reading the same sentence over and over. He walked through the empty house to the parlor, turned on the television, switched rapidly between channels, then turned it off again. Upstairs again, he decided to go to bed, but was unable to sleep, even after meditation exercises.

Sighing, Raoul turned on the bedside lamp and picked up the deck of cards he'd placed there earlier. He had loved playing solitaire since he was a child and kept the habit as he'd grown older, knowing that part of his enjoyment was the memory of the quiet, happy hours when the game had provided refuge from a bothersome world. Idly, he shuffled the cards. He hadn't really looked at the deck since unwrapping it when he'd gotten home. It was a tarot deck; he didn't own any standard card decks.

Although all magicians were trained in most forms of cartomancy, Raoul didn't have a lot of use for it. Though he knew his view was prejudicial, he considered cartomancy, and the tarot in particular, as more of a trick for the untrained than a useful magical tool. After all, magical ability had nothing to do with reading the cards, which probably had a lot to do with their popularity.

He cut the deck into three piles with his left hand, then recombined the piles and began to lay out a hand. Although there were twenty-two more cards in a tarot deck than in a standard deck, he'd never let that stop him. He just picked out the Major Arcana as they turned up.

He turned over the first card and scowled down at his own face looking up at him; Bill had done a pen and ink sketch of him as The Magician. Laying the card aside, Raoul snorted quietly, thinking of the card's meaning: the need to take chances. He continued laying out the cards in a standard seven-pile game. Another trump appeared: The High Priestess, symbol of creative effort, academic excellence, marriage, and sometimes children. Hopefully, it referred to the former two, he thought. Rolling his eyes at his own silliness, Raoul nevertheless laid the card sideways across The Magician, as the crossing influence in a Celtic cross pattern. So, the Magician needed to take chances academically or creatively. Big surprise. He finished laying out the solitaire pattern without finding any more trumps, and began to play.

The next trump card, Justice, appeared when Raoul set the Ace of Wands on the scoring pile. He placed it directly below the two trumps already in place, in the spot representing the aim of the tarot reading. Okay, he thought, so this was a little weird, what with Mowatt's murder and all. He smiled grimly as he continued playing, remembering how reading for oneself was supposedly bad luck. Not that my luck could be much worse at the moment, he thought.

The Devil, symbol of cruelty, lack of concern, the inevitable, or the ascendancy of earthly matters, turned up next. Raoul placed it to the left of the two crossed trumps, where it represented recent developments. The reading seemed strangely accurate, he thought, mentally adding the phrase "if you believed in that sort of thing." His resolve not to pay any more attention to the trumps was broken when he tossed the next trump in the general direction of the spread and it landed in the proper place for the fifth card.

The fifth card showed possible developments. The Hermit had landed in the reversed position, meaning self-deceit, concealment, or immaturity. My own immaturity? Raoul wondered. He decided to continue the game, laying the trumps in reading position as they came up, and do a full read once the spread was complete. Not that he believed what the cards would tell him, but he did admit that sometimes what you read into them could show what you were really thinking or feeling about an issue.

As he laid down the last trump of the spread, The Tower, Raoul realized that the solitaire game was unwinnable. Gathering up the rest of the cards and setting them aside, he looked at the spread. First came the central issue, The Magician, crossed by The High Priestess and based on, or aimed toward, Justice. Fairly accurate, he thought. The Devil showed recent developments. The Hermit possible ones. The Moon was the approaching influence, meaning danger or bad luck for someone close to him, and the possibility of secret enemies. Raoul wondered if it referred to Mowatt's antagonism or his death.

He himself, he noted, was represented by The Hanged Man, which usually signified rebellion, decisions involving sacrifice, and occult investigation. Rebellion was right on the mark, he thought, but perhaps the "occult investigation" referred to his research. The eighth card, representing others, was The Emperor, reversed—Raoul wondered how the issue of dependence on parents or ill luck with an inheritance fit the reading. His own hopes and fears were represented by the ninth card, The Lovers. He snorted aloud again: while wish fulfillment fit the pattern, the card's additional meanings of attraction and beauty were neither hopeful nor fearful for him. Romance wasn't a part of his life, he thought, mostly because he didn't want it to be.

He picked up the last card, representing the outcome. If he was looking for a reading assuring him that the murder investigation was going to turn out fine, he'd gotten the wrong card. He tried to shake off the sudden feeling of worry, but the whole thing suddenly seemed more than just a joke. And The Tower's only positive meaning as an outcome was in the sense that the unexpected bad luck, deception, natural calamity, or unsettled home life it referred to would be momentary, a passing condition. All in all, Raoul thought, a lousy read. And he still wasn't tired, just the opposite. He gathered the cards back into a single pile, then replaced them on the table.

Rising, he threw on a robe and padded barefoot down to the kitchen to make tea. If he couldn't sleep, he decided, he might as well stay awake and think some more about the aural erasure and how it might fit into his research. After all, he could always sleep tomorrow, since he didn't need to be anywhere until Monday.

Chapter 3

"You're quiet today," Bolton remarked a few minutes after picking Raoul up at his office on Monday. "What's up? How'd the big meeting go?" As he drove he turned to look at Raoul, moping in the passenger seat.

Raoul grunted a response.

"C'mon, Rags, talk. Something's pissed you off, I can tell. So what happened? Did you see Whiting? What'd you tell him?"

Realizing Bolton wasn't going to relent, Raoul replied, "Yeah, I saw him. I went to his office before nine and told him that I'd step down from teaching for the time being, but *only* if he made it perfectly clear to everyone that I was doing it to work on special research. Not that it'll fool anyone, but at least it will make me feel slightly better about it."

Bolton nodded understandingly. "So what'd he say?"

Raoul shrugged. "He agreed. It's not as if he wants to fire me or anything, or that I'm not doing a good job. He's just trying to protect the university. Not that I like the idea, mind you, but if it's going to happen anyway, I may as well get something out of it. Afterward, he announced it to the entire department at the staff meeting. By the way, you're not planning on printing this, are you?" He looked pointedly at Bolton, who turned away and concentrated on the road ahead, but smiled.

"Of course I am! Don't worry, I'll barely mention you."

"Why do you have to mention me at all?"

Bolton sighed. They went over this every time he wrote

anything about Oxford. "Because, dear boy, if I mention *you*, then I can talk about your mother, who makes amazingly good copy. Any idea who she's seeing these days, by the way?" Bolton adored Raoul's mother and never missed a chance to mention her in his column, much to Raoul's annoyance and her delight.

Raoul snorted. "Two sheiks, a banker, and a bishop, who knows? You talk to her more than I do, anyway. Look, do you want to hear about the meeting or not?"

"Please. Who was there?"

"All the College of Magic faculty, even the teaching assistants. Turns out he had another meeting directly afterward, for the chairs of the other departments, to tell them what was going on so they could pass it along to the underlings. Our chair, of course, is dead, so we got the royal treatment."

"So what's going on?"

"Well, the gist is that Whiting isn't going to appoint just anyone to the position; he's going to wait until he finds the perfect person, 'Of course we're all very sorry about Professor Mowatt, but we've got to look at this as an opportunity,' that kind of thing. In the meantime, of course, all the administrative stuff will go through him." Raoul shook his head, wondering. "As if he doesn't have enough to do as is. Politics . . . No Magic classes for a week, funeral on Friday . . ." He trailed off, thinking about the meeting he'd had with Whiting, and the staff meeting that followed.

He had entered Whiting's secretary's office just before nine o'clock, and was surprised to see Whiting himself behind the desk, working at the computer "Oh, hello, Raoul," Whiting had said, standing up. "Robert's on vacation today; there's a temp on the way, but I need a file and I can't seem to get it. You're pretty handy with computers, aren't you?"

Raoul nodded and crossed the room. Whiting waved him into the chair and explained what he was trying to do. It turned out to be fairly simple; Whiting just hadn't known the right command to access the word-processing program. In less than a minute Raoul had the file printing out. Whiting clapped a heavy hand on Raoul's shoulder. "Great, just great!" he said, taking the pages from the printer. "Wonderful things, computers. I don't know how we ever got along without them. You're here to see me, I assume, so why don't we just step into my office."

Raoul followed him into the corner office. Whiting motioned him to sit in the well-padded leather chair in front of his desk. Raoul found himself looking up at Whiting from the low-set chair, across the top of the large mahogany desk, though when standing up they'd been nearly the same height. Attempting not to smile at the obvious power ploy, Raoul glanced around the room while Whiting shuffled through some papers.

The office was large, nearly three times the size of Raoul's. A large oval table of the same burnished mahogany as the desk occupied almost half the floor space. One wall held a built-in floor-to-ceiling bookshelf, while the other three walls were covered with prints. Raoul noted the framed charters dating the founding of the various colleges, the colorful prints of the college seals and flags, and an enlarged copy of the University Charter Revision of 1955, which had changed the names of all the individual colleges to their present titles, referring to specific disciplines.

"So, Raoul," Whiting said, suddenly all business, "have you reached a decision? Will you take the time off?"

"I'll do it, but I'd like there to be some mention of how I'm taking the time to do research. To avoid idle gossip." He waited for Whiting's reaction.

"Hmmm . . ." Whiting made a steeple of his fingers, resting his chin on his thumb. He thought a moment, then nodded. "Yes, I see . . ." He paused again, then slapped one hand on the table, pointing the forefinger of his other hand at Raoul. "You know, that's a good idea. It wouldn't do to have the rest of the staff wondering why all this is happening. There's going to be enough loose talk about Arthur's death as it is. A very good idea, Raoul. I'll mention it at the meeting." He glanced at his watch.

"Sir?" Raoul broke in.

Whiting glanced at him. "Yes? Is there something else you wanted?"

Raoul paused. This could be awkward, and he needed to be tactful, something he didn't usually bother with. "I was wondering . . . at the party for Professor Mowatt, you mentioned a promotion. This is probably a bad time, I realize, but I'd like to know more about what you were considering."

Whiting nodded slowly. "Right, we did mention that, didn't we? Well, Raoul, this really isn't the best time to discuss it, as you noted, what with Arthur's death and—" He glanced at his watch again. "—a staff meeting in a few minutes. I do want you to know, however, that once everything has calmed down, I'd like to sit down and discuss this with you. I think you have a very bright future, Raoul. But things being what they are at the moment . . ."

Raoul knew better than to press the point, though he wasn't satisfied with Whiting's answer. "Fine, then. We'll talk later." He rose. "I'll leave you to prepare for the meeting."

Whiting also stood. "No rush, Raoul. As a matter of fact, I'm ready to walk over myself. Care to join me?"

The staff meeting was being held in one of the smaller lecture halls of the College of Magic, a short walk from the administrative offices. Raoul broke away from Whiting as they entered the hall, since he wanted a seat behind the rest of the attendees. The magic faculty was of average size: excluding Mowatt, there were only ten people on the teaching staff: two senior professors, two full professors, three assistant professors, and three graduate students serving as teaching assistants. Four administrative assistants filled out the number.

"I can't believe you're actually on time, Professor. What's the occasion?" Raoul turned to look at Miriam Materides, his teaching assistant and most promising graduate student, and moved over one seat to make room for her. "Can you believe it about Professor Mowatt?" she asked.

"Good morning, Miriam," he said as she sat down. "Yeah, I heard."

Miriam's presence had been another thorn in Mowatt's side, Raoul thought. Assistant professors were not supposed to rate teaching assistants, but Miriam had specifically requested him because of his work with magic and computers. Mowatt denied the request, but was forced to back down when Miriam went directly to Whiting about it. Raoul knew that she hadn't had anything against Mowatt, but she was direct about what she wanted—and usually got it. It was one of the reasons they got along so well.

"What do you think—" Miriam broke off as Whiting stood up.

Sitting in Bolton's car, Raoul felt himself grow angry again at the memory of Whiting's speech. Most of it had been fairly routine, considering the circumstances. In honor of Mowatt, all classes were to be suspended for the week. A service would be held in University Temple on Friday. Staff attendance, Whiting hinted, was mandatory. Regular classes would begin again the following Monday, and so on. He'd mentioned that the search for Mowatt's replacement would begin immediately, and that he himself would assume responsibility for the college until the position was filled. Then he spoke briefly about Mowatt's career, breaking off only once, when his voice caught.

For Raoul, the surprise came at the end of the meeting, after Whiting had answered the few questions asked. Before adjourning, he'd added, almost as an afterthought, one last piece of business: Raoul Smythe was taking a temporary leave of absence from teaching in order to complete a particular piece of research at his, Whiting's, request. Leave was effective immediately, and John Livingston would be taking over Raoul's teaching duties in the interim. Raoul noted that none of the professors, especially Livingston, seemed surprised at the news. As the meeting broke up, Raoul sought Livingston out.

"I must say you don't seem very surprised, John," Raoul told him.

Livingston looked quizzically back at him. "Well, I'm not, really," he replied. "Sir Reginald told me about it right away."

Right away? Raoul thought. He'd only told Whiting he accepted the offer this morning, and he'd been with Whiting until the meeting began. "When did he tell you?" he asked.

"He called me at home Saturday afternoon," Livingston said, still looking confused. "Around five o'clock. Is everything okay, Raoul?"

Five o'clock? Raoul realized that Whiting must have called Livingston immediately after they'd spoken on Saturday. Obviously, the decision hadn't been his after all. Hiding his anger, he waved Livingston's concern off. "No, no, everything's fine. I was just curious. I've got to run, John. I'll stop by later and drop off the syllabi for the classes."

Avoiding looking at anyone else, he slipped out of the hall and strode purposefully in the direction of his office. He couldn't talk to Whiting then; he was too angry, and in any case, what was there to say?

"Professor Smythe?" Miriam called from behind him when he'd nearly reached the Magic offices. Raoul turned. She was hurrying along the path, trying to catch up to him. She began speaking again before she'd reached him.

"I don't understand what's going on, Professor. Why won't you be teaching?" She looked worried.

Raoul resumed walking, slower this time. He smiled thinly. "Miriam, everything's fine. You heard Whiting; I think I've hit on something in my research, that's all, and he's supporting it. The timing, however, sucks." Which was true, Raoul thought, up to a point.

"Your reduced spells?" Miriam said. "That's great, especially after Professor Mowatt ... I mean ..." She trailed off. They'd never spoken about Mowatt's refusal to support Raoul's work, though Miriam had worked with Raoul on the spell reductions for months. "That's great," she repeated. "But what about classes?"

Raoul shrugged. "You'll be doing the same work you

have been, only with Livingston instead of me. For your teaching responsibilities, I mean. I'll still be around for your thesis, of course." He smiled at her reassuringly. "It's not as if I'm disappearing, you know."

Miriam looked relieved. "Well, good," she said, then looked down at her watch. "Blast! I'm going to be late for class! I've got to run, Professor. I'll see you later." Miriam's graduate studies were in two specializations, Computer Science and Magic, the course work for which, in addition to her teaching responsibilities and work on her thesis, kept her exceedingly busy. He watched her jog toward the College of Science buildings, then continued walking.

When he reached his office, Raoul realized he wasn't in the mood for work, and since the week's classes had been canceled, he didn't need to see Livingston right away. He spoke a quick spell to shut the door and picked up the phone.

"Any luck with the police files?" he asked when Bolton answered.

"What? Oh, hi, Rags. The files? Of course I got them—what do you take me for, O Faithless One? I was going to drop them by tonight."

"How about now?"

Bolton chuckled. "Taking the day off, are we?"

"Classes are canceled all week. Death in the family, you know. How about it? Can you leave work?"

Bolton laughed again. "Right, it's so strict here. I'll have to get permission to unchain the leg irons, but I think I should be able to manage it. I'll be there in forty-five or so. Where are you?"

The trip from the paper's London office, Raoul knew, should take well over an hour, but Bolton was a notoriously fast driver. Unbeknownst to Bolton, Raoul kept a spell against accidents on his car, updating it every few weeks. So far, it had worked. "In my office. See you."

Less than an hour later Bolton appeared, smiling broadly and waving a folder from the doorway of Raoul's office as

Raoul explained his class schedule to John Livingston, who'd popped in after the meeting. Raoul found an excuse to get rid of Livingston, then he and Bolton set off to break into Mowatt's house.

"What?" Raoul asked, turning toward Bolton in the car. "Sorry, did you say something?"

Bolton looked at him. "You mean, what have I been saying for the last five minutes? Oh, nothing much, just telling you about the cure for cancer I've discovered, my new proof for the Theory of Relativity and how I've found the secret of eternal life. You know, everyday stuff. If you're finished daydreaming, you might actually take a look at that file you're holding." Raoul looked down at the file in his hand, then flipped it open. Sure enough, Bolton had managed to get photocopies of everything in the police files.

"You really are amazing, aren't you?" Raoul said admiringly.

"*Moi?*" Bolton replied, smiling. "Oh, it was nothing, really. My friend's a police clerk. Simple, really." He smirked.

Raoul shook his head. "What'd you do? Threaten to print something about his mother?"

Bolton laughed. "Nothing so crass, my dear," he replied smugly. "I merely helped Rodger out of a somewhat nasty affair once, and he owed me a favor."

"Hmmm," Raoul said, "must have been some problem, if he makes copies of case files for you."

"Let's just say I convinced someone that it might be wise to take his wife on vacation for a while. Rodger, by the way, isn't married."

"Oh," Raoul said, "I get the picture. And you say the Seller attracts all the reprobates! Nice friends you've got!" He laughed.

"Look who's talking!"

Their good mood, however, began to sober as they neared Mowatt's house. Raoul had suggested it might be useful to try magically reconstructing as much of the scene as he could at the murder site. The police report stated that an attempt made by a police magician had revealed nothing, but it couldn't hurt to try again. The police were already saying the crime probably had nothing to do with magic, an idea enhanced by their discovery of an opened basement window, though they couldn't say if it had been opened by the murderer. Raoul idly flipped through the report as they drove, unconsciously grimacing when he saw his own name.

"Hey," he exclaimed, "did you read this yet?"

"Yeah," Bolton replied. "I take it you just found the witness?"

Raoul nodded. "The cab driver who drove him home after the party saw someone standing at the side of the house, huh? A 'tallish, darkish man'—good description. They should have no problem finding him at all." He read on. "None of the neighbors saw or heard anything, of course. How handy. What the hell would someone be doing hanging around waiting for Mowatt at twelve-thirty in the morning, I wonder? It can't just be coincidence, though, since he was killed sometime between two and four. Hmmm . . .

"What we need to do, really," Raoul mused, unaware he was speaking aloud, "is to find out why he was killed. That's almost more important than how, when you get down to it. Someone had to have a motive. Then again, it's not as if he was all that popular to begin with . . . Wait, I think that's the house."

Mowatt's house was located in Headington, a short drive from the university. The street was empty as they pulled up and parked well away from the driveway, hoping the police weren't still watching the site.

The house was a modest two story Tudor surrounded by a tall holly hedge. Luckily, there appeared to be no one near to see the two young men who were obviously not policemen pass through the front gate and pause at the door. A single strip of bright yellow POLICE SCENE DO NOT CROSS tape blocked the front door. Before moving it aside, Raoul took a few moments to work a simple spell on himself and Bolton to ensure they would leave neither foot- nor fingerprints.

Raoul paused, looking at the lock.

"Hurry up, Rags," Bolton said, looking around. "Spell it open before someone sees us."

Raoul turned to Bolton. "And just how am I supposed to spell open a lock I've never seen, smartass? It could be any kind of lock."

"Oh, damn, Rags . . ." Bolton said in frustration. "Hey, what are you—"

Raoul was probing at the lock with his stiletto blade. A moment later tumblers clicked into place and he pushed the door open. "No problem," he said, smiling as he held the door for Bolton to enter.

Bolton's retort was cut short as they entered the house. No lights were on, and drapes were drawn over each window. Neither man spoke as the door swung quietly shut behind them.

Standing in the still, dim hall, Raoul said quietly, "You know, I wonder if it felt different here when he was alive." His voice sounded strange in the dead air.

"Do you, well . . . *sense* anything?" Bolton asked hesitantly.

Raoul scowled wryly at him. "You mean with my great mystical sensing abilities, my unseen third eye?" He snorted. "I thought you knew better than to ask stupid questions like that." He shook his head. "No, all I *sense* is nothing. There's no dust, everything appears neat." He gestured vaguely around the hall. "But it just feels like no one lives here. It's empty."

"That's what I meant in the first place," Bolton retorted. "Want to look around a bit, or do you just want to see the library?" His unspoken "that's where the body was" hung in the air.

"Let's look around first. I want to see how he lived, get a feel for the place."

They stood in a wide front hall running the length of the house. Raoul turned to his left, entering the dining room.

He walked around the table, looking at the antique botanical prints ranging along the walls. While he was positive it was a decorator's dream, the room seemed to him overly formal and utterly devoid of personality. He resumed his trek through the hall, Bolton following quietly. On their right stood a double doorway, blocked by another strip of police tape. The library.

"Let's wait on this one, shall we?" Raoul said, continuing past the door. They wandered through the rest of the first floor, past a small den furnished only with a television set, couch, and chair, peered into a bathroom and two closets, looked into the large kitchen, then made their way upstairs.

The upper level contained two bedrooms, a study, and, surprisingly, a small darkroom. "That's funny," Raoul said as he and Bolton looked at the photography equipment neatly arranged on the darkroom shelves. "He was a photographer? The man didn't have a single picture in his office! Weird."

"Well," Bolton replied, "I don't see any in here, either. Let's check the other rooms."

The left-hand front room, facing the driveway, appeared to have been used as a study. Again Raoul noted the spartan furnishings. A large wooden desk and matching leather chair, two large bookcases packed with cheap paperback editions of various reference works, and a single wooden filing cabinet, were all the room contained. More antique prints covered the walls, this time of what appeared to be prize-winning farm animals.

"Hey, Rags, look at this," Bolton said, flipping the pages of a binder he'd pulled off a bookshelf. "I think we've found the photos."

Raoul walked over and peered over Bolton's shoulder at the carefully laid-out photos. "Hey," he said, "that's the College of Magic in most of these. Nice pictures." He reached down and pulled out another binder. More photographs of buildings and scenery, this time of a place he didn't recognize. Strangely, there were no people to be seen in any of the photographs. "You know," Raoul said, "these aren't bad at all. He had a good eye for composition."

"Well, he certainly didn't have one for decorating, that's for sure," Bolton remarked sarcastically, fingering the dark floral draperies. "This had to have been done by a decorator, you know? No one can be this dull without special training."

Raoul agreed. "And the parlor downstairs, too. Pretty much the whole house. Sterile. Doesn't seem like anyone lived here, you know? I wonder . . . did he have a house-keeper?"

"The police report didn't say. I suppose it would be easy enough to find out, though. I'll look into it this afternoon." Bolton pulled a pad out of his jacket pocket and jotted a note. Catching Raoul's skeptical look, he said, "Yes, I know, I know, I never take notes, right? Well, I have a feeling I'll be taking a lot of them for a while. So there, Mister I-can't-work-a-spell-without-a-printout-in-front-of-me!"

"C'mon," Raoul said, "let's look around some more."

A connecting door in the study led directly into a bedroom, as soulless and traditional as the other rooms. "This has to be a guest room," Raoul said, looking into the empty drawers of the single bureau. The walk-in closet held only a single hanging sachet exuding a faint scent of lavender.

"This bath is glorious, Rags!" Bolton called from across the hall. "You've got to see it!" Raoul left the empty bedroom behind and crossed the hall to the bath. Bolton was right. The room belonged in a different house; it had nothing at all of the ambience of the other rooms. The painted walls were a rich, pale sea-green which complemented the dark green floor tiles. An antique free-standing tub, easily large enough for two, rested to one side of the room. A tall cabinet beside the basin held shaving accoutrements, soaps, shampoo, and the like, and a great number of bottles and jars of varying skin creams.

"I don't get it," Raoul said, looking around. "I just don't see any connection. There's comfort here, but still no personality."

"Well," Bolton said, holding up a large, unopened bottle of rose oil, "he may have been a bastard, but at least he had soft skin." He laughed.

Raoul rolled his eyes and shook his head. "Wait a minute," he said, scanning the shelves of the cabinets. "This is odd. These are all unopened, did you notice? Why the hell would he have bought all this and then not used it?"

"Maybe the decorator stocked it." Bolton laughed. "You know, window dressing?"

Raoul shook his head. Ignoring Bolton's comment, he asked, "So what's in there?" and pointed to the room's other door.

"The master bedroom, I'd guess. Let's have a look."

While decidedly not as sumptuous as the room they'd just been in, the master bedroom nevertheless displayed a less minimalist style than the other rooms. And, though immaculately clean, there was at least evidence of occupation. A bureau held clothing and a few toiletries, and the walk-in closet was filled with dark suits and robes of various color, cloth, and design, many of which Raoul recognized. A number of pairs of shoes were neatly arranged to one side of the closet, and a high shelf held hatboxes of varying sizes and shapes. The bed itself was queen-sized, with pristine white bed linen. A number of walking sticks and staffs filled a brass urn in one corner.

"I'm going back downstairs," Raoul said. "Let's see the library." They passed back into the upstairs hallway and retraced their route down to the front hall and the double wooden doors. Raoul spelled the barrier aside and opened the doors. The room was massive, running nearly the entire length of the house. The high ceilings were much more noticeable here than in the other rooms, due to floor-to-ceiling bookshelves lining all but the outside wall. That wall, which they faced, was broken in the center by a wide stone fireplace. The ornately carved mantel held a number of candlesticks supporting candles of various colors. On the wide marble hearth, and partially on the polished wooden floor, lay the outline of a body.

"Sad sight, isn't it?" Bolton said from behind Raoul, who solemnly nodded assent, not interrupting his appraisal of the room.

"This is where he lived," he said. "Just this room." Indeed, the library held all the personality that the rest of the house lacked. This was different from the sensuous atmosphere of the bath upstairs, and somehow less contrived and more alive than the other rooms. The bookshelves were completely filled, a quick perusal of the spines revealing a mix of classic and recent titles on topics ranging from magic to criticism to literature. The highest shelf was fitted with a brass railing, and each of the three walls had a rolling ladder attached for easy access to the higher shelves.

Crossing to the left of the fireplace, carefully avoiding stepping on the outline, Raoul looked down at the leather top of the wide wooden desk. Except for the massive leatherbound book on a reading stand, it looked exactly like Mowatt's desk at the university. A full leather in-box, an empty out-box, a reference book with slips of paper sticking out, and a number of file folders were all neatly arranged on the desktop. Carefully, Raoul opened the book on the reading stand. Meticulously hand-lettered runes covered the page; he recognized the purification spell immediately. He flipped a few pages forward in the book—another carefully handwritten spell.

"What's that?" Bolton asked, peering over his shoulder.

"Mowatt's spellbook," Raoul replied. "Will you look at this? Handwritten, hand-indexed . . . This must have taken him years." He shook his head in wonder. "It's beautiful, but what a waste of time! No wonder he wouldn't even look at my printouts." He could appreciate the care that had gone into creating it, sadly aware that in a few years it would probably be a museum piece. Gently closing the cover, he turned to survey the rest of the room.

The desk faced a wide picture window, which, when Raoul pulled aside the heavy drapes, revealed a pleasant if small garden. "We should check if there was a gardener, too," he told Bolton. Reclosing the drapes, he moved to the

large wooden cabinet on the other side of the fireplace.
Finding it unlocked, he opened it, finding inside a variety
of magical implements, a clean robe, and a number of carefully labeled jars, bottles, and packets. Nothing unusual, he
thought as he closed the door. He glanced around the room,
trying to garner an impression of it as a whole. In addition
to the desk, cabinet, and two armchairs with matching end
tables, a medium-size table stood at one end of the room,
and another tall wooden file cabinet stood near the desk.

"Hey, Rags," Bolton called from the opposite end of the
room, where he stood looking at the wall, "I think these
might be some of his photos."

Raoul walked over to look. Among the old maps of Oxford and the inevitable framed degrees, were a number of
enlargements of color photographs. The carefully matted
and framed photos were of various historical magical sites,
mostly related to druidry. He turned one around, and saw
that Mowatt had handwritten the location and the date of
the picture on the backing paper. The photos were quite
good, Raoul thought, and there was one of the Sacred Oak
of Donar in Germany which was truly spectacular.
"Hmmm," he muttered. He was still having trouble with
Mowatt's being creative in any way.

He turned his attention to the place where the body had
lain. "So," he said to Bolton, who was now looking through
the files on the desk, "what do the police say happened
again?"

Bolton looked in his notebook. "They think the murderer
entered in one of two ways, either by the front door, which
was left open, or by prying open the basement window
under the kitchen. There was no sign of forced entry or a
struggle, and nothing in here was broken or taken. He was
struck on the back of the head, once, with what we don't
know. You know, the standard 'blunt instrument.' Maybe
the murderer brought it in with him, or took it out, though
nothing seems to be missing. The coroner says that he
probably fell here immediately, unconscious, and died
within fifteen minutes from internal hemorrhaging of the

brain. There was some external bleeding, but nothing in-
consistent with the coroner's statement. There were no foot-
prints or fingerprints found."

"Not even Mowatt's?" Raoul asked

"It doesn't say. If his prints weren't, it would mean
someone had wiped everything down, though, and I think
they'd have mentioned it. I'll check it through Rodger if
you want, though."

"That would be great. While you're at it, ask him about
a housekeeper or a gardener." He glanced around the room.
"I need to read the room's aura . . . Have you seen my bag
anywhere?"

"It's in the car," Bolton replied, laughing. "Do you ever
remember anything, Rags?" He held his hands out in mock
terror at Raoul's glare. "Ooh, I'm *so* frightened! I'll just get
your bag, shall I? Since I remember where we parked, that
is." Without waiting for a response, he left the room.

Raoul glanced around the room as he cleared his mind in
preparation for reading the room's aura, the first step in the
scrying spell. Reading the past was more difficult than most
people expected. Non-magicians, and even some magicians,
somehow seemed to think that any event left some kind of
marker or afterimage in time, which was definitely not the
case. No one could just conjure up pictures of what had
gone before or what was to come.

Scrying was indeed used to find out what had, or would,
transpire at a certain moment in time, but the images invoked, though generally accurate, were vague and symbolic
at best. Information was gleaned by a combination of the
scryer's ability to read magical signs and symbols, and
plain old guesswork. It was generally more reliable than a
tarot reading, but not by much.

When scrying into the present, seeing what was happening somewhere else, all that was necessary was to magically create a sort of eye in space that would present a
symbolic manifestation of the event being "seen" in the
glass. The trick was to get the physical location exactly
right, and to read the signs correctly. While not foolproof,

it was subject to far fewer variables than scrying into the past or future. Scrying events from different times required the scryer to take into account not only physical conditions such as light and weather, but also to prognosticate a complicated series of probable events leading to a certain moment. It was difficult to be completely accurate, since the future was never certain and the past was rarely clear. Still, it was worth a try, Raoul thought.

First, however, he needed to read the aura of the room itself, for magical residue always affected the scry. Time-scrying was somewhat easier when one was searching for magical events, or events connected to the use of magic: the residue of magical auras generally appeared fairly clearly, and a strong magician could sometimes tell exactly what spell had been used, merely from the aura. The flip side, of course, was that occasionally magical auras appearing in the scrying glass were so strong they overpowered all other images.

Raoul seated himself on the floor, facing the outlined body and the fireplace, and closed his eyes. He meditated, regulating his breathing and heartbeat to reflect an inner calm. When he opened his eyes, he saw that Bolton had placed the scrying glass, a bottle of spring water, a sheaf of parchment, a quill pen, and a small glass jar containing ram's blood in front of him, not touching the outlined body. To his side lay the ring binder holding his printed spells. He could feel, rather than see, Bolton sitting in the leather chair.

Deciding to forego using the printouts, since Bolton's throwaway comment about his memory had struck home, Raoul spoke the words that would read the magical aura of the room. As he spoke, he rose, walking around the room and using his hands to delineate the space to be read, the entire room in this case. As he said the last words of the spell, he concentrated, willing the aura to appear.

A faint bluish tinge, striped with purple, appeared throughout the room, which Raoul recognized as the residue of an aural read. He noted that the residue was slightly different from what his version of the spell usually left. Beyond that, the room had no aura whatsoever. None. "Damn," Raoul muttered to himself. He reached down for the binder, chagrined. Maybe he'd forgotten something, hadn't read deeply enough. He read through the spell again, this time reciting straight from the book.

Now the aura was tinged with more purple, the result of his first read through the spell, but still nothing else. This was very strange, Raoul thought. "Bolton," he called, "c'mere for a minute." He spoke a quick cantrip, changing the color of Bolton's tie. Looking down, Bolton watched as the color seemed to slide from light blue to black, and felt the usual fleeting moment of jealousy at his friend's abilities. He himself could barely do the most simple cantrips, and not without full regalia and a pronunciation guide. Magic was so much a part of Raoul that it never occurred to him to bother with the display and mystery necessary for others to focus themselves, he made it look easy. That in itself explained why so many people resented him.

Raoul read the aural spell again. The tie clearly reflected magical residue, and there was an echo of the other aural reads that had been done. Other than that, the room was still magically pure, untampered with. A magician's study. "Not bloody likely," Raoul murmured. He stepped outside the room and read the hallway. Faint residue showed in a few spots. "Hmmm."

"What?" Bolton asked.

"The spell works, definitely. It looks like only a few spells have been worked down here, though; the auras are really faint. But they're *there*. So why nothing in the study, I wonder?"

"It's like when you erased the aura on that robe," Bolton said. "But isn't that nearly impossible? I thought you'd only done it by accident."

"It is, and I did. But it looks like someone else knows how as well, or else stumbled upon whatever it is that does it. Maybe Mowatt himself. I can't even tell when it happened! Blast!"

Raoul began pacing, speaking aloud to himself as much as to Bolton. "I can't go to the police with this, you know. Not until I find out how it's done. Even then, I can't just go up to them and say, 'Look, I've found this weird magical thing at the scene of the crime, which might have bearing on the case. You see, all the residue of magic has been completely obliterated, which means that Mowatt could have been killed using magic, and then had it covered up. So possibly the murderer is a magician. Oh, and by the way, I happen to be the only person who's ever done it.' They'd hang me, you know?" He stopped pacing for a moment and looked at Bolton. "Right?"

"This is weird, Rags," Bolton said. He frowned. "This is truly weird. We have to find out who did this. I mean us, you and me. We have to. Then we can go to the police, and let them come to the same conclusion. But you and I have to come up with a murderer, a motive, Mrs. Brown in the cupboard with a can of mace, whatever."

Now Bolton was pacing. "Okay," he said, stopping, "here's what we do. When you get back to the university, start asking people about Mowatt. Whiting said he'd been acting oddly lately: find out how, and to whom. Find out anything, everything. And work on that spell, the one that blanks everything. I'll get started with the housekeeper-gardener thing, and see what I can find out about his private life. Someone's got to know what he did! He can't have just taken baths and worked in here, you know, no matter what it looks like . . . Phil."

"What?" Raoul said. "I caught all but the last bit."

"Phil," Bolton repeated, obviously still thinking. "Phil Lynchfield. Reporter. Knows absolutely *everyone*." Catching Raoul's look, he added, "Yes, it *is* possible to know more people than I do." He smiled. "Okay that's a good plan. What now?"

"Well, I want to try a few more reads in here. You can leave if you'd like; it's a short enough walk back to my office."

"That's great, if you're sure you don't need me. I'll call

Phil right away and see what he can tell me." Bolton turned
to go. At the door he paused. "Oh, and Rags . . .?"

Raoul looked up from his magical equipment.

"When you do leave, just be careful that no one sees
you. And remember to shut the door, okay?"

Raoul rolled his eyes at him. "Yes, Mother. I'll talk to
you later."

When the door had closed behind Bolton, Raoul turned
back to his spellbook. The lack of aura bothered him. As
far as he knew, aural erasure just didn't happen. Ever. Not
completely, anyway. Auras degenerated over time, to be
sure, but it usually took quite a while. And suddenly here
it was, twice in one week. He'd stumbled onto something
very, very powerful, either completely new or extremely
old. In either case, all that was required to isolate it was
time and some hard thinking.

Suddenly, it struck him: What if—and it was a very large
if—the problem lay in the word combinations he'd used in
his batch spell? Perhaps there were hidden words, hidden
sounds, that he hadn't taken into account? He smiled to
himself, his eyes lighting as an idea began to form: What
if he'd discovered the pronunciation of one of the unknown
Etruscan runes? The pronunciation of the seven runes, their
use dating back at least to the beginnings of Etruscan writing in 700 BCE, had never been deciphered, existing only in
fragmentary spells without pronunciation glosses. Tomes of
information existed on the various hypotheses concerning
their meaning and use, but no one had ever found out just
how to say them to make them work. It was worth a try,
Raoul thought, even if nothing came of it.

Sitting on the floor of Mowatt's library, he decided to ask
Miriam to load all known fragments containing the lost
runes into a computer program for him, as a special project.
She was working toward her doctorate in both magic theory
and computer programming, so writing the program would
be good practice for her, and when he had a moment, he
could use the spell he'd created to compare rune sequences
with the fragments. With someone else loading the info, not

to mention writing the program, it would free his time to think of other possibilities about the spell and to talk to people about Mowatt. He felt uncomfortable about prying into other people's opinions about the man. A loner himself, Raoul respected the desire to keep one's life private. Still, there was something odd about the way people seemed to be saying how strangely the man had been acting recently. And then there was the matter of this house and its atmosphere.

Raoul looked around the library again, the only room in the house where any trace of Mowatt's personality showed. The other rooms seemed to be just window dressing. It would be interesting to know if someone had done the decorating, or if Mowatt had done it himself. Maybe he'd spoken about it, or perhaps Bolton could ferret the information out of someone. Thinking of Bolton reminded him that there were more things to be done. He'd been up all day, and was starting to feel it.

There was nothing more he could do in the library without knowing the aura of the room. Scowling, he walked into the hall and rapidly ran through the aural read again, taking in the entire house. He walked through the rooms again, checking for aural residue as he went. Most of the rooms were blank, with the occasional residue that he knew from experience went with being a magician—the auras looked to him mostly like cantrips, probably spells to pick up spills and the like. Though magical training placed great theoretical value on not using magic for trivial purposes, Raoul knew from experience that it was easy to get lazy and use spells for the most common tasks. After all, why reach down to get something that had fallen when you could magically pick it up? Somehow, the aural residue of the small spells gave Mowatt's house at least a slight air of humanity.

Nothing unusual turned up in the rest of the house. Frustrated, Raoul gathered together his scrying utensils from the study and left, remembering to check for passersby and to spell the barriers back across the doors.

As he walked back toward the university, he scanned the ground for small stones. Seeing one, he stooped and picked it up, continuing on his way. Matching his words to his stride, he cleansed the stone of all residue and charge until it read a perfect blank. He primed it with a receptive charge, then infused it with the thought of inquiring into who had decorated Mowatt's house. The reminder set, he dropped the stone into a pocket and went back to looking for more stones as he walked.

By the time Raoul reached his office, he had a pocketful of memory stones, reminding him of all the things that needed to be done. Holding a stone in his hand and speaking a single keyword would be all that was required to release the reminder. It was easier than taking notes, he thought, though he stood a chance of carrying around quite a load if things got too complicated.

In his office, he settled behind his desk, removing the memory stones from his pocket and clearing a small spot for them on the desktop. He flipped through the piles of papers in front of him for blank paper, found none, and finally pulled a clean sheet out of the printer. He wrote a detailed note to Miriam explaining what he needed for the runic program, folded it, addressed it to her, then slid it into his pocket. He'd drop it in the university post on his way out of the building. Gathering up his papers, he closed his office door behind him and went off to wait for the cab he'd called for.

When he arrived home, Mrs. Higgins was lurking in the parlor, obviously waiting for him. "Good evening, Mr. Smythe," she began, "is there something wrong? The police rang today while you were out and were asking all sorts of questions about you." She sounded upset. "Is this something to do with poor Mr. Mowatt dying?"

He asked her to make a pot of tea for both of them while he settled in, and then to join him in the parlor for a chat. Ten minutes later he was giving her a condensed version of the events of the weekend, including his decision to look into the murder for himself. Higgins sat silently, hands

crossed on her lap, not moving except to shake her head
now and again and then smooth back a wayward lock of
hair loosened by the movement.

"Ah," she said softly when Raoul was finished, "this is
terrible, isn't it? Just terrible. You poor thing." She looked
at him with concern. "Isn't there some way you can just
find out who did it, using your magic, I mean? Look into
a crystal ball or something?" Higgins didn't really know
much about magic, it being to her as music was to the tone
deaf.

Raoul shook his head, smiling sadly. "Unfortunately, it
doesn't quite work that way. I'm going to do all I can,
though. Mostly, I think, I'll need to talk to people and think
things out for myself. Plus, Bolton's helping."

"Ah." She nodded, as if Bolton's involvement made
everything all right. Shaking her head, she reverted to her
usual imperturbable self. "Well, then, will you be needing
more tea while you work?" He nodded. "Shall I bring it up
to the study? Are you hungry?"

"If you could manage a sandwich or something, that
would be great. I'm not all that famished."

She smiled at him as she rose. "Don't worry," she said,
"I'm sure everything will turn out just fine."

He successfully avoided laughing at her good-natured
naiveté. "You're an optimist, Mrs. Higgins," he said as he
followed her as far as the front stairs, then continued up to
his study.

"Well, *someone* has to be," she called after him seriously.

Perhaps he was being too negative, Raoul thought as he
sat down at his desk and turned on the computer. Maybe he
hadn't yet exhausted all he could do to find out what had
occurred at Mowatt's house the night he died. Perhaps the
aural blanking might only affect a localized reading; if that
were the case, he could try scrying from here and see what
happened. He shook his head, irritated. This aural erasure
problem had thrown a wrench into everything he'd tried to
do recently. He wanted to figure it out, and quickly. But
first he'd try the scry again.

He glanced at the candles held in wall sconces around the room; there was nothing flammable near them, so he spoke one of his batch spells, a five-word string of gibberish pronounced in the Etruscan mode. Immediately, the wicks sprang into flame, lending a golden glow to the room. Raoul walked over to the light switch and turned off the electric lights in the room. He was still working on a batch spell to magically shut off the lights, but so far the best he'd been able to do was blow all the fuses in the house at once. Satisfied with the room's light, he picked up his bag and returned to the desk.

He took the scrying implements out of his bag and cleared a space on the desk. On it he placed his scrying glass, which wasn't a glass at all but a flat copper bowl, the inside of which had been painted black. He gently set a small piece of parchment in the bottom of the bowl, then opened the bottle of water and slowly filled the bowl, careful to avoid splashing or dislodging the paper. When the bowl was full, he unstoppered the small jar of ram's blood and dipped the tip of the quill pen into it.

The quill was a personal touch; almost everyone else he knew who used this particular scrying method simply poured out a single drop of blood into the center of the bowl. Raoul, however, had never had much luck with that method, since he usually spilled out too much, and had once dropped the entire jar in by mistake, while teaching the spell in class. Easier by far to use the quill, he thought as he watched a single droplet fall slowly into the water, directly above the parchment. Immediately a pinkish cloud began to form, reflections of candlelight glinting on its surface. Turning his thoughts to Mowatt and envisioning the fireplace and hearth of the dead man's study, Raoul set his hands on the desk, on either side of the bowl, leaned forward, and concentrated on the cloud, waiting. When the color was correct, he spoke the short spell, then mentally fixed the exact moment he wanted, remembering the weather, the time, the probable position of the moon . . .

As always, the vision was a long time coming. The

candlelight began to flicker brightly on the edges of Raoul's vision, and he felt the strain of staring into the water begin to tell on his eyes. Finally, the center of the pink cloud began to darken, a sure sign that something was soon to appear. Raoul deepened his concentration on Mowatt and watched as the darkness spread to cover the entire surface of the water.

When the now-darkened cloud covered it completely, Raoul further focused his thoughts into a single question: Who had killed Mowatt? He inhaled deeply, feeling the strange mental pressure he associated with scrying, as if the air he drew in were expanding within his skull.

The change in the cloud was immediate; instantly its color lightened and its size contracted until it seemed to be only a faint shadow deep underwater. An image appeared, unclear and covered by the shadow, which was unusual; images in the glass were usually relatively clear. The image reminded Raoul of the ripples and rings that appeared when a stone was thrown into still water. The image then changed to something like a wave cresting. Raoul scowled, still deep in concentration: What did images of water have to do with Mowatt's death? He refocused on his original question.

The image flickered into nothingness, but the shadow remained, almost obscuring the sight of a pale square swaying gently from side to side, like a piece of paper floating down through the air. Raoul had barely registered the image when it changed again, the pale paper, if it was paper, stopping its movement and gradually enlarging and changing color until it was almost pinkish, with spots of darker red and an almost blinding white. He had no clue as to what it was, or its relation to his question. And the shadow in the water still partially obscured the vision. Inhaling still more deeply, he decided to try another question: What would happen as a result of his investigation with Bolton?

Again the image shifted. The dark red spots on the pinkish image seemed to flare as points of red for a moment, but were almost instantly obscured by the shadow, which changed to a lighter shade of gray and then slowly broke up in the water, drifting into nothingness. Raoul was left staring into a bowl of clear water with a sodden piece of parchment floating in it.

He shook his head violently and leaned back in the chair, exhaling hugely. Water and paper, then whatever the last two had been, all obscured by shades and shadows. "What was *that*?" he muttered angrily to himself. Feeling drained, he slowly stood and crossed to the light switch, leaning on the wall for a moment's support before turning the lights back on. He walked slowly around the room, one hand on the wall, and blew out the candles. A single quiet knock sounded at the door. "Come in," he called out, appalled at how tired he suddenly sounded and felt.

Mrs. Higgins came into the room with a covered tray. "I waited until the candles were out," she said by way of explanation.

Raoul nodded, the hint of a smile flickering over his face. "Thanks," he said simply, sitting heavily back down in his chair. "No," he added quickly, seeing Higgins about to move the scrying glass, "I'll take care of it. Just set the tray on the couch or something." He passed a hand over his eyes. "Thanks," he repeated as Higgins left with a backward glance at him. As she closed the door, he leaned his head back for a moment, closing his eyes. He couldn't believe how exhausted he was, and from such a bad reading. He'd never seen anything like that shadow before, nor had such an unclear reading. He wondered if it had something to do with the aural erasure or if it was just a bad scry. Scrying, after all, was an uncertain proposal at best, but this one had certainly been the worst ever.

Moving the tray to a side table, he stretched himself out on the couch and picked up half of the sandwich Higgins had left. As he ate he thought more about the images he'd seen. They'd been vague enough even without taking the shadow into account. Water, paper, the pinkish thing, and a brief flash of points of red. Not much to go on, he thought wryly. He wondered if the shadow itself might have meaning, and not be merely an obstruction. That was also a possibility, but what it could mean, beyond the obvious interpretation of obscurement, he didn't know. He leaned back and closed his eyes again, trying to picture the different images and understand their significance.

Waking suddenly, Raoul opened his eyes and squinted against the lights. He must have fallen asleep. Not that he felt particularly awake at the moment. He stood and walked to the computer, where he checked the time: it was after midnight. Well, at least I'm right on schedule, he thought. He looked down at the scrying glass on the desk, swirled the bloody quill tip in the water to clean it, removed the parchment, then opened one of the glass doors, and carried the bowl to the balcony.

A light rain was falling. Raoul stood a moment, enjoying the chill air, then emptied the bowl over the railing, hearing the water splash onto the rosebushes below. He turned back into the study, where he carefully set the bowl back on its shelf in the large open cabinet he used to hold his magical instruments. He picked up the quill and jar of blood from the desk and placed them next to the bowl. Crossing back to the couch, he felt the teapot to see if there was any chance it was still warm. It wasn't. He left the plate with the remaining half sandwich in a corner for the rats, then carried the tray quietly down through the darkened house to the kitchen.

Waiting for the kettle to boil for tea, Raoul walked to the front of the house, looking about him as if for the first time. Reminded by the quiet of Mowatt's house, he wondered if a stranger doing the same would have any idea of the man who lived here. He stood with his back to the carved front door. No feeling of closed-off rooms here. The parlor, to his left, was an open space, hedged only by the outside walls and by the wall of the lavatory toward the back of the house. A fireplace stood near the back wall. He looked around the room, originally intended as a modern version of a medieval great hall.

He'd left the stone walls uncovered, with only the

occasional period weapon hanging as decoration. Heavy
tapestry-patterned drapes obscured the tall bay windows on
either side of the fireplace, and the dark wood couches and
chairs were upholstered in a deep, rich red that complemented the drapes. A large carved armoire in the corner
housed the television and stereo. Raoul nodded to himself.
A good room. Opposite the parlor was the dining room,
with massive double glass doors opening onto a small
stone-paved terrace. The circular staircase of open ironwork
separated the parlor from the dining room.

Hearing the kettle hiss, he passed through the dining
room on his way to the kitchen, running his hand gently
over the intentionally scarred wooden surface of the long
rectangular table, a re-creation of a medieval hall piece. A
cast-iron chandelier hung over it, each candle-shaped light
held by a grinning gargoyle. Pewter dishes and stone and
glass goblets in heavy, open wood cabinets rimmed the
room. He stepped through the narrow doorway to the
kitchen. As he made his tea, Raoul remembered the first
time he'd seen the inside of the house, walking in with Bolton and the Realtor.

Sheila something, her name had been. She'd gestured
around the medieval furnishings, explaining that the previous owner had been a history buff and that the distant rela-
tives who were selling the house didn't care for any of the
house's furnishings. "Of course, you'll probably want to re-
decorate," she had continued. "It's all so dark and gloomy-
looking!" She'd laughed, too, the ignorant sap, probably
envisioning the place all done over in pastels or something
equally foul. Raoul had merely asked to see the upper
floors, leaving the architectural questions to Bolton.

Raoul carried his cup up the back staircase, which cut
between the kitchen and the room he'd done over for Mrs.
Higgins, meanwhile thinking how odd it was that Mowatt
had most likely paid someone to decorate a house in a style
reflecting nothing of himself, while he had lucked into buying a house that had been utterly perfect from the start.
Well, he amended, the ground floor had been utterly per-

fect. He'd had to almost completely renovate the top two floors, which had been left unfinished. Luckily, many of his friends from the Seller were artisans or knew workmen who would work for barter. A spell here, a dresser there. He'd gotten his computer setup that way, from a dealer who had already had two DUI convictions. A somewhat complicated geas that made him unable to drive when he'd had more than two drinks had gotten Raoul his PC. He'd had to pay cash for the printer, though.

The second floor of the house had been a mass of raw wall space and structural supports when he'd moved in, allowing Raoul to decide just what he wanted before having anything built. The final result was a wide corridor running the length of the house, from the round staircase in front to the small stair he'd just ascended at the back. Four large rooms had been created; the master bedroom at the back of the house, a small library next to it, another library, specifically for magic texts, across from it, and his study on the diagonal, connected to the magic library by two large carved wooden doors. He'd had the rooms done mostly in dark wood and leather furnishings, lending them a comforting feel, like being deep in the bowels of one of the university libraries, but without the annoyance of students.

Entering his study, he settled himself at his desk and looked around. He'd had the walls in here paneled as well, not that anyone could tell, with all the papers tacked and taped to them. Newspaper clippings, printouts, notes to himself, pictures he liked, and more all vied for space with the few framed prints. A large print of a page from the Emperor Claudius' Etruscan dictionary hung beside a small framed copy of Richard Dadd's *The Fairy-Feller's Master Stroke* on the wall to his right. They were both slightly askew. Idly, Raoul thought about straightening them, but didn't. Spinning his chair, he popped his feet on the desk and leaned back, continuing to think about the house.

He wouldn't bother going up to the third floor, which held the stairs to the towers and four guest rooms, one of which was permanently reserved for, and had been completely decorated by, Bolton. The others he'd left as he'd found them, just stuck some furniture in. The three stone towers on the roof were also completely untouched; unheated and undecorated except for cold stone benches built into the walls, and lit only by small rectangular window slits and wall sconces. Raoul didn't go up there much, except when in the mood to do some sky-watching or quiet thinking.

All in all, he thought, Thornhold could indeed tell who and what he was, if you knew what to look for. He stopped, sitting up quickly. That might be it. He hadn't been looking for anything at Mowatt's, he'd just been expecting something to jump out at him. But what did he need to look for? Maybe once he found out more about Mowatt, about his personal life and beliefs, he could go back and see if the house had anything more to say. He wrote a note to himself to that effect and taped it to the side of the monitor. Pouring himself a cup of tea, he began to enter an account of the scry he'd done into his files.

Chapter 4

Mowatt was on fire. His skin crackled and changed color, turning as red as the flames that engulfed him but did not burn. "Hurry up, Smythe," he snapped. "Can't you do anything right, you little bastard? What are you waiting for?" Strangely, the flames didn't seem to bother him at all. Raoul suddenly realized he was holding a bucket, and without thinking threw the contents at Mowatt. Papers flew out, completely obscuring Mowatt's body for a moment, then all seemed to catch fire at once. Mowatt began to scream.

"Oh, come *on*, Raoul," Anne Whiting said, tugging at his arm. "We're late for brunch! It's a barbecue, don't you know? Catherine hates it when we're late! Stop worrying about *him*!" He followed her into a room where a number of people stood clustered around a massive fireplace. Anne shoved her way to the front, pulling Raoul behind her. Her father was turning slowly on a spit, chatting idly with Catherine Moss and Bolton. "Oh, *there* you are, finally," Sir Reginald said to Raoul. "I've been waiting for you. You're next." He reached out for Raoul with blackened hands, a metallic shriek issuing from his lips.

Raoul jerked upright in bed, Whiting's cry resolving into the shrilling of the alarm clock. Raoul reached over to shut it off, feeling the sweat covering his body turn suddenly cold as he threw off the covers. He shook his head violently, trying to clear away the last image of the burned and bloody hands reaching out for him. He couldn't remember the last time he'd even had a nightmare, least of all one so vivid. He rose and went into the shower, forcing himself to think of all he had to do the rest of his day.

He'd spent the remainder of the previous night comparing the words of his batch spell against an Etruscan dictionary. Many of the words were gibberish as far as meanings went, but Raoul thought it worth checking for word combinations that might have the same pronunciation as real words, much the way the words "rose says," aloud, could be mistaken for "roses." By six o'clock in the morning he'd gone through the entire spell, finding only five Etruscan words embedded in the spell: trunk, cart, beehive, prayer, and, strangely enough, flower. None of the words, however, had any special magical efficacy as far as he could tell. At that point he'd given up and decided to catch a few hours of sleep.

"Mr. Smythe?"

Raoul heard Higgins' voice over the sound of the water and poked his head around the curtain.

"What?"

"I've brought you a tray. I'll leave it on the table."

"Thanks." He drew his head back.

Raoul dressed and ate quickly, then went into his study to work before the cab arrived. If he was going to spend the day questioning people about Mowatt, there was a spell he wanted to use as an aid. He knew his own limitations, and didn't want to forget any of the conversations he might be having, but he also didn't want to take notes. He doubted that people would speak freely if he were busily scribbling down everything they said. He already had a memory-enhancing spell that ensured total recall at a later time, but he wanted to doctor it so he could turn it on and off at will so he could retain the conversations themselves in subconscious memory, not everything that he said or heard during the entire day. What he needed was a key word to activate and deactivate the spell without breaking it completely. He set to work on the spell.

Two hours later Raoul was in Livingston's office, explaining where he was in his four undergraduate and two graduate courses. Miriam already handled most of the teaching for two undergraduate classes, and could probably take on the second-year class in Etruscan runic incantations as well. Livingston himself would probably be best for the last of the undergraduate classes—a fourth-year seminar in different magical systems of weather forecasting—as well as the two graduate courses, both of which dealt with practical applications of various types of magic. Livingston was silently flipping through the syllabi, nodding to himself and jotting notes in the margins.

Privately, Raoul thought Livingston had been the best choice to take on his classes. Whereas his own specialty, if it could be called such, was Practical Magic—teaching students how to actually use magical systems, and particularly the uses of magic in the "real" world—Livingston specialized in Comparative Magic. Of course, Whiting's choice of Livingston probably had nothing to do with the magical considerations, Raoul realized. He, Livingston, and Michelle Fein were the department's three assistant professors, lowest on the academic totem pole. Michelle's class schedule was always full, since at the moment she was the only specialist in Northern European magic, her specific area being history and her pet subject druidic magic. She couldn't have taken on another class, which left Livingston. Biting back a sigh at yet another instance of office politics, Raoul glanced around while Livingston finished taking down notes.

As in almost every other office, the bookshelves were crammed to overflowing. Increasing the crowding of the shelves were the numerous models Livingston had placed in front of, and sometimes on top of, the books. One shelf held, in addition to its load of books, plastic models of the Egyptian, Babylonian, and Etruscan calves' livers used for divination. A set of children's blocks carved with the Hebrew, English, Etruscan, and Norse alphabets ranged across another shelf. Raoul looked up, suddenly aware that Livingston had finished writing and was watching him. "Sorry," he said. "I was admiring your blocks."

Livingston smiled. "Thanks. I've had them since I was a kid. I think I've pretty much got a handle on the classes, then. Can you think of anything else?"

Raoul shook his head. "Not really, no. Thanks again. I realize it's an imposition . . ."

Livingston shook his head, still smiling. "No problem. I just hope everything will be okay." He paused, obviously thinking he'd let something slip, then added, "With your research, I mean."

Raoul smiled slightly. This was the opportunity he'd hoped for. "John, can I ask you something?" he asked, glancing pointedly at the open door.

Livingston looked nervous for a second, then said, "Sure, Raoul. What about?" He rose and gently pushed the door shut, then sat again. He was intrigued; while perfectly friendly, he and Raoul had never been what he'd call "chummy." He waited for Raoul to continue.

"This is a little . . . awkward for me," Raoul said. "I'm wondering if you've heard anything about why I'm taking time off."

"Well, your research, for one," Livingston began.

Without speaking, Raoul lowered his head slightly, looking at Livingston from under his eyebrows.

Livingston laughed nervously, looking away. He sighed. "Okay, Raoul, so people have mentioned that it might have something to do with the investigation into Mowatt's death. You were called in for questioning, weren't you? But," he added quickly, "it's not as if anyone here thinks you had anything to do with it. Really. I figure it's probably just Whiting being overcautious. Right?" He looked at Raoul as if seeking confirmation.

Raoul smiled. "Thanks for being honest with me. I'd wondered how much everyone knew. And I think you're probably right about Whiting. I just wish this whole thing were done with, frankly. It's pretty weird." As if changing the subject, he continued, "Had *you* noticed anything different about Mowatt, lately? They certainly grilled me about what I thought about him. They talked to you, too, didn't they?" Raoul found that the pronoun "they" was easier to say than "the police." He felt odd leading Livingston on, but needed to know what he'd thought of Mowatt. He waited as Livingston paused to think.

Finally Livingston nodded, biting his lips. "Yeah, they talked to me. Here, of course. I didn't need to actually go anywhere with them. You know," he mused, almost to himself, "it's strange. I really couldn't tell them all that much; it kind of hit me while I was talking to them. I've been here for five years, worked for Mowatt the entire time, and probably never said fifty words to him at once. I mean, it's not like he ignored me, but it kind of is, if you know what I mean. I guess I've been lucky, in a way. We never argued, he supported the papers I've published, he never complained about me, but I'm still an assistant professor after five years. And I'm a good professor, you know that. It's as if I weren't here, as if he forgot about me if I wasn't talking directly to him. Look at it this way, Raoul—sure, he singled you out a lot of the time, but at least he noticed you."

Strangely, Raoul thought he detected a note of jealousy in Livingston's voice.

Livingston continued with a dry chuckle, "So in a way, Raoul, this whole thing has been pretty good for me. At least Whiting knows I'm alive. That sounds horrible, doesn't it?"

Raoul shook his head. "No, not at all. I think this whole business has shaken everyone up, made us think about what we're doing and where we are. And it's not always pleasant." He rose. "Anyway, I should run. Thanks again for taking over the classes, and for the talk."

Livingston also rose. There was an awkward moment; the conversation almost seemed to call for a handshake, but they knew each other too well for such a businesslike gesture. Livingston placed both hands on his desk. "It's no problem, really. And I understand why you wanted to know; we're in a gossipy business, after all." He smiled and opened the door. "You'll be around, right?" Raoul nodded as he walked to the door. "Good luck with your research, then, Raoul."

"Thanks, John. I'll see you later."

Raoul walked down the hall to his own office. He needed to write notes on what Livingston had said; he'd realized halfway through their conversation that he'd forgotten to use the mnemonic spell he'd placed on himself before leaving Thornhold. "Damn," he muttered, settling himself at his computer. "Bloody lot of good the spell does if I forget to use it." He noticed a folded note on the desktop, his name scrawled on the front in Miriam's handwriting.

"Got your note," it read. "I'll start writing a program immediately and drop by tomorrow or Wednesday to go over it with you. Miriam." Good, Raoul thought, jotting a list of faculty members he wanted to talk to on the back of the note. He placed a check next to Livingston's name, then opened a new file in the computer and began to key in the gist of their conversation. Funny how he'd never noticed that Mowatt had apparently ignored Livingston. Lucky guy, Raoul thought.

By the time the cab dropped him off at Thornhold just after six that evening, Raoul felt exhausted. Talking, he realized, was hard work. And *this* is what Bolton does all day? he wondered. He'd never think Bolton had it easy again. And he'd only talked to four people—others hadn't been in their offices, and he hadn't wanted to call attention to his poking around, asking about Mowatt. He'd see the rest tomorrow. He hoped he'd gotten something out of the three conversations he'd had after talking to Livingston, though. He'd remembered to set the mnemonic spell before he began each interview, and to reset it afterward, so his short-term memory of each conversation was extremely limited; if he hadn't checked their names off the list, he doubted he'd remember exactly who he'd spoken with, much less anything that had been said.

The mnemonic spell would hold the information in his memory until he recalled it in a trance state, which was best performed as a two-person job. Before leaving his office, he'd left a message for Bolton, asking him to come by Thornhold for dinner and to help him retrieve the memories. First, however, he needed to relax. There wasn't enough time to take a nap, so he thought he'd do some reading. On his way upstairs Raoul asked Higgins if she would bring him a pot of extra strong tea.

"Certainly," she replied. "What time would you like dinner, by the way? And will Mr. Bolton be joining you? Would you like me to make anything in particular?"

Raoul didn't care much about food—he'd eat it if it was in front of him and like as not forget if it wasn't—and left all matters pertaining to meals to Higgins. She shopped and cooked, and had over the years from nanny to housekeeper developed an idea of his likes and dislikes. If Bolton was coming, however, she would cater to his tastes, since he always told her how wonderful a cook she was, and was forever jokingly trying to woo her services away from Raoul. Mrs. Higgins adored Bolton and was secretly much flattered by his attentions. He reminded her of her own son at that age, twenty years ago, though she was hardly consciously aware of it and would never think to mention it if she had been. Raoul told her to go ahead and make whatever she felt like, and that yes, Bolton would probably show up. She nodded and went off to the kitchen.

As Raoul dropped off his bag in the study, there was a slight movement in the corner, reminding him that he should change the rats' litter and ask Higgins for a plate of leftovers. Idly, he wondered what her reaction would be when she finally realized he didn't have cats. He wandered across the hall to the library and found a large volume on the history of Etruscan runes and a slim book on unexplained phenomena, which he vaguely recalled mentioning true transformations. Looking at the packed shelves, his eye was caught by Mowatt's name. He picked up the book, a survey of religious customs relating to spell preparation in differing magical systems. He tucked that under his arm with the other two and returned to the study. Higgins was just coming out of the room and gave a low cry as she saw him, her hand flying up to her throat in surprise.

"Sorry," he said, "I didn't mean to startle you."

"Oh, no," she clucked. "It's my fault. Your tea is on the desk, by the way. Will you need anything else?"

Raoul shook his head. "No, thanks. But when Bolton gets here, just send him up, would you? Thanks."

Sitting at his desk, idly thumbing through the books while the tea steeped, he realized he wasn't thinking clearly. A shower and a change would probably clear his head, he thought.

He took a long, hot shower, which helped soothe his aching neck muscles. Refreshed, Raoul threw on a black T-shirt and jeans. Leaving his feet bare, he returned to the study, still drying his hair.

Bolton was sitting on the floor, hand-feeding bits of chicken from a plate to an entranced crowd of four or five rats. He looked up as Raoul entered. "Well, aren't we clean! I've been entertaining the kids with some of Higgins' scraps." Stretching out a finger, he lightly stroked the top of a rat's head. It writhed in pleasure, nosing his hand for more food. "They've really grown, haven't they?" He rose, leaving the plate in the corner. "So how did your day go? Any luck?"

Raoul explained that he didn't know, and wouldn't until he retrieved the memories. "Which you can help me with, now that you're here. Later, though. What about you? Any results with the housekeeper or gardener?" Tossing the damp towel onto the couch, Raoul walked to his desk and sat down, moving the books aside so he could put his feet up and still see Bolton.

Bolton gingerly picked up the towel and laid it carefully over a chair back, then stretched himself out on the couch. He put his hands behind his head and looked at the ceiling. "Yes and no. There was a housekeeper, somebody Howard or something like that."

At Raoul's look, he tapped his jacket's breast pocket. "Don't worry, exact names and such are all in my notes.

Anyway, she came in usually once or twice a week. Mowatt always called the day before to specifically request her. She did basic tidying, a little cooking—which I suppose went into the freezer for him to reheat—laundry, and generally looked after the place. He left a key for her, and she put it back when she was done. She came in when he was gone, left before he returned. She only met him two or three times. Says he was very fussy about how the place was kept, wouldn't let her do more than dust in the library, and the guest bed wasn't used more than twice a year. But," he continued, sitting up, "and she didn't really want to mention this, but being a cad, I forced it out of her—" He chuckled. "—it did appear that each week there were more plates than just one person could account for, unless Mowatt ate an awful lot."

"What?" Raoul asked. "He had someone living with him?"

"I don't think so. I checked with the closest neighbors, and they say that every few days when he'd come home, there'd be another car right behind. They don't think it stayed overnight, by the way. Sometimes the other car would show up on weekends or late at night. A light blue something, no one was really sure of the make. So he had a regular guest, did our Mowatt."

"What about a gardener? He might know something about it."

"No gardener, it appears. Mowatt bought the house ten or eleven years ago—"

"About when we were graduating," Raoul mused.

"Right. He bought it from a Realtor, who I tracked down by asking the neighbors if they knew who owned the house before. The previous owner was a little old lady who owned it for years with her husband and sold it on his death. Sweet little thing; she makes the most marvelous little cakes, you wouldn't believe them ... Anyway, she, the little old lady, still had a card from the Realtor. Some people just save *everything*, you know? The Realtor put me on the track of a decorator she'd—the Realtor, that is—

suggested to Mowatt. Turns out the decorator is her cousin's brother-in-law, so she still uses him.

"So anyhow, I found the decorator, who says that he did do the house, but not really, since Mowatt wanted the most dull surroundings he'd ever seen. Really traditional and all."

"Yes, it is, isn't it? Did he do the whole house?" Raoul asked. Bolton could never seem to avoid putting in all the unimportant details of a story, making it excruciatingly long.

"I'm getting there. Stop interrupting or I'll never finish." Catching Raoul's muttered "Right, in about five years," he pulled a face then continued.

"So, he did what Mowatt asked and did up the kitchen, the front room, the bedrooms, the hall, and the bath. Very straight, very traditional." He held up his hand, stopping Raoul from interrupting again. "Then, about six months ago, he got a call from the very same Professor Mowatt, asking him to *redo* the upstairs bath. He said Mowatt gave him a picture out of some magazine, he didn't remember which, for the bath, and asked for something similar. Something very lavish, and said he could go all out. Which he did, as we've seen. Oh, and going back to when he originally did the rest of the house, he said Mowatt also asked for him to lay out a garden design, but not to arrange for a landscape contractor. Said he'd do it himself. Which he did, apparently. No gardener."

"So maybe he liked gardening. That's odd about the bath being done so recently. What about the library?"

"Well, Bernard said—he's the decorator—that Mowatt asked him to only do the floor, the fireplace, and to have shelves made. Nothing else. When the rest of the house was finished, Bernard said the library was still empty except for what little he'd done. So Mowatt must have put the room together himself, after. The funny thing is, the library had the only furnishings he brought with him, since he had Bernard buy everything else. Beds, tables, pictures, whatever. Everything was new. Bernard remembered because it was so odd that he—I mean Mowatt—didn't seem to care about any of it at all, just said to make it 'traditional' and that was it."

"Where did he live before he bought the house?"

"I don't know. Maybe at the university? I could look into it," Bolton said, reaching into his pocket for the notebook.

"No, don't bother. I can check tomorrow. It probably doesn't matter, anyway." He wrote a note to himself on a clean sheet of paper. "So, was that it for today?"

"That's all I got. How about you?"

Starting with his work on the aural erasure, Raoul concisely explained his idea about the unknown runes and the program Miriam would be developing. "As far as asking around about Mowatt," he continued, "I only managed to catch two or three people today, though. Shall we see what I found out?"

"Sure. What do I need to do?"

Raoul explained the procedure. To retrieve the conversations, he'd need to put himself in a state of deep meditation and relive the events. He'd set the recall spell so he would be speaking out loud. They could record the memories on a tape, or Bolton could try and take it down.

"Dictation, huh?" Bolton asked. "Good idea, you don't want a tape laying around, even if nothing turns up. But what if I fall behind?"

"Oh, you can stop and start the recall at will, once I get started. All you have to do is say 'stop' or 'begin,' " Raoul replied. "It's just that I'll be in trance until it's completely finished. You need to tell me when and where to start up again. But don't get too far behind, since once everything's fully recalled, I'll remember them the same way I would normally."

"Which is to say, not at all." Bolton smiled. "Handy little spell, that."

"Yes and no. It only works once for each memory recalled, and retelling them is in 'real' time. The conversations will take as long to relate as when they were taking place. This could take a few hours. Is that all right with your schedule?"

Bolton checked his watch. "Well, it's seven-thirty now, and I've nowhere to be this evening. How about a bite of dinner before we begin, though?"

Raoul agreed. He hadn't eaten since that morning. They went down to the kitchen, where Mrs. Higgins was just pulling a pie from the oven. Over her protestations that she would take care of everything, the two men fixed their own plates and carried them into the small dining room. Bolton opened a bottle of wine, and during dinner they spoke of nothing but the murder, the police investigation, and the erasure spell. Raoul told Bolton what Livingston had said, and also mentioned the strange scry he'd done the previous evening.

When finished, they cleared the table, again over Higgins' complaints, then returned to the study. Bolton brought the wine with him, and poured out a fresh glass while Raoul prepared himself. Bolton sat on the couch again, a pad balanced on his lap, and Raoul sat at his desk. Bolton watched Raoul's eyes slowly glaze over as he retreated into his own subconscious. When Raoul had been still and unmoving for a few minutes, Bolton said clearly, "Begin," and Raoul began to speak.

"Excuse me, Professor Llewellyn-Jones," Raoul said in an oddly flat, uninflected voice, "may I speak with you for a moment?

"Certainly," he continued. "Please, come in." Bolton couldn't quite put his finger on why, but he could definitely tell the difference between Raoul's voice and the voice of whomever he was speaking with. Odd, he thought, as he struggled to keep up his transcription of the conversation.

Transcribing, with a number of stops and starts for Bolton to catch up or rest his hand, took just over three hours. It had been quite odd, watching it end. Raoul had said, in the flat voice, "Thank you again, Cara. You've been really helpful," and then, seemingly out of nowhere, "Did you get everything, Bolton?" in his usual voice. The difference startled him and he'd dropped the pad. Raoul, the cad, had actually laughed, Bolton's shocked face being his first sight as he came out of trance.

The wine was long gone, so Bolton went downstairs to get a fresh bottle while Raoul stretched his cramped muscles. Returning to the study, he found Raoul poring over the pages of scrawled script.

"I will never understand," Raoul said, "why you refuse to use computers. Now I'll have to enter all this in myself, you know."

"Computers?" Bolton answered. "They're beastly, sly little machines, and someday people will realize that. I used one once, and it ate an entire article. I had to rewrite the whole thing, and I've never touched one since, and I never will. What about you? You're the one who refuses to have his picture taken, you know!"

"That's different. And I don't refuse, I just prefer not to. Unlike some people, I don't need photographs to remind me of what I've done or where I've been. Anyway, I'll key this in later on, if that's all right with you. I'll print out a copy for you when I do. So what do you think?"

"Well," Bolton said, "the three professors you talked to don't seem to have had a very high opinion of Mowatt, that's for sure. What do you remember of it now?"

"Most everything. It seems I'm not the only one who thought he was a mean-spirited old crank. I really didn't know anyone else had had problems with him."

"From what we heard, it doesn't sound as if there were too many who hadn't had problems with him of one kind or another. And now we've got a few more people to check out. What say we split the list? I'll take the people outside Oxford and you can add the others to your list, if they're not already on it."

"Sounds like you're trying to keep me within the bounds of the university, Bolton." Raoul was serious.

So was Bolton. "It's better if you don't do too much public snooping, I think. It'll be hard to explain away if anyone gets wind of it." Bolton didn't say exactly who might find out and cause problems, but Raoul knew who he meant.

"Don't worry. After all, no one saw us at Mowatt's yesterday."

"I know that, but you've got to be careful, you know. It's no problem for me to go nosing around people's houses and histories, it's what I do, and anyway, I'm not a suspect. You are. You need to be careful. It's bad enough you're asking around at the university. So let me deal with the outside people, will you?"

Raoul reluctantly agreed, and they spoke for a while about how best to approach the various people. Eventually Bolton decided to go home, since he wanted to get an early start in the morning. He planned on trying to find Mowatt's mystery visitor, and promised to call the next afternoon with any new developments. When he was gone, Raoul decided to take a walk before transcribing Bolton's scribbles.

He walked among the trees, pausing now and then to look up at the full moon. Although he subscribed to no particular religion, another point on which Mowatt had thought him delinquent—believing, as he did, that magic and religion should be indistinguishable—Raoul had always felt a special fondness for the moon, and never failed to greet her appearance with a kind of quiet joy. Idly, he wondered which cult, or cults, Mowatt had followed. There were a lot of photographs in the study of sites sacred to Teutonic druidry, he recalled. That might prove to be another area for investigation. He'd ask around at the university tomorrow. Probably Whiting would know, if they had been such good friends. He sighed and turned back toward the house, beckoned by the single light shining from his study window.

Since it was still early, at least by his schedule, he set about transcribing Bolton's notes. The information he'd gotten from the three professors intrigued him. He'd always assumed he was the only person with whom Mowatt didn't see eye-to-eye, but that didn't appear to be the case.

Lloyd Llewellyn-Jones, a senior professor, specialized in the history and development of Western magic. He'd been

with the department only two years, having been hired
when Robert Marlowe retired. Keying in their conversation, Raoul was reminded of his own experience with
Mowatt. After professing his shock and regret over
Mowatt's death, Llewellyn-Jones had described an idea
he'd had over a year ago for a new class, an idea that
Mowatt had quickly killed. Lloyd thought there might be
benefits in exploring the correlation between magic and
violence, but not in the usual negative sense. Instead he believed that the violence and virtual blood lust of the early
users of magic, the priests of the various religions, had had
positive effects in the eventual development of magic as a
science. Mowatt had disagreed, refusing to even consider
the idea. Llewellyn-Jones went ahead on his own, finally
producing a book on the subject which he had self-
published, lacking university support. He'd never quite forgiven Mowatt for the slight.

And rightly so, Raoul thought as he typed. Teaching a
class while preparing a thesis for publication was invaluable
for seeing how people reacted to the ideas presented. He'd
read Lloyd's book, and while it was a bit vague, he found
it interesting and the subject itself fascinating. He continued
transcribing.

Llewellyn-Jones and Mowatt had had other disagree-
ments, as well. Lloyd had run through a list of six or seven
instances where he'd disagreed with Mowatt to the point of
going over his head to Whiting. Strangely enough, Raoul
noted, the points in question seemed to be fairly minor,
things that should have been left to Llewellyn-Jones' dis-
cretion as a senior professor. Lloyd had mentioned such di-
verse and trivial examples as where particular classes were
held, the number and type of examinations, and his personal grading methods.

One case in point concerned Lloyd's wanting to use a
particular textbook that dealt with the relatively recent phe-
nomenon of using magic as a business tool. Mowatt canceled the order for the texts, on the precept that he'd met
the author, a professor at London University, and thought

his methodology presented a poor view of magicians. Llewellyn-Jones lost that particular argument and had to choose a different book.

Raoul switched to a new document for a moment to record the London University professor's name. Bolton might want to talk to him later. He returned to the transcription file.

"It's as if he didn't trust *anyone*," Lloyd had said. "He wanted to be completely in control of everything that went on in every class. I know Edgar had the same problems as I did, too."

Edgar Waller, Raoul knew, was a full professor who dealt primarily with magic as used in religion. Drawing his list of staff members out of the pile of papers near him, Raoul circled Waller's name.

Llewellyn-Jones had continued, "I mean, I don't want to speak ill of the dead, but the man just wasn't a good manager. At a certain point you have to let things go and not niggle over every detail. I was fortunate in that Sir Reginald would usually back me up, or at least force some kind of compromise, but I'm sure that Mowatt resented it to no end. At least he wasn't openly hostile, the way he was with you, Raoul. To tell the truth, I don't see how you put up with it." The conversation had then turned to a discussion of Raoul's work on the batch spells, which Llewellyn-Jones had heard about and admired.

That transcript completed, Raoul finished the next quickly, since he'd only spoken briefly with Rani Kasir. Rani, another senior professor, had been with the department for more than eight years, and felt that Mowatt had held his career back, but he wouldn't detail the reasons why. He stressed, however, that he felt no bitterness toward Mowatt, that if the situation had truly been intolerable, he would have left long ago. Raoul didn't know the man well enough to say if it were true or not, but suspected that Kasir had become accustomed to his position and the situation. Raoul knew well the complacency that comes with giving in just once.

Kasir did mention, however, that he thought Mowatt didn't get along with other college chairs. When Raoul had pressed him for an example, he'd mentioned Lydia Stillman, Chair of the College of English Studies. Apparently, Kasir had once heard her complaining after a meeting that Mowatt spoke of things he didn't know about, and then expected people to listen to him merely because of who he was. Raoul added Stillman's name to his list of staff members. Unfortunately, he only knew her by sight. Still, he'd figure out some pretext to talk to her.

As he typed, Raoul wondered whether the conversations would have taken the same negative turn had Mowatt only been injured. He doubted it. There appeared to be something cathartic in speaking of the dead, especially speaking negatively, no matter what people said to the contrary. Cordially disliked while living, now that Mowatt was dead he presented a focus for everyone's undefined angers and fears. Well, mostly everyone, Raoul mentally amended, keying in his final interview.

Cara Barstow, a full professor of Modern Eastern Magic, had no opinion of Mowatt, or so it seemed. Keying in her vague answers, Raoul would have said she hadn't even known the man. Nothing positive, nothing negative. He had been a good administrator, a good role model. Nice. No, he'd never complained about anything she'd done, he'd always been supportive. Not that they'd really spoken all that often, she'd just had the impression that he would have been supportive if she'd needed it.

Raoul rolled his eyes. Cara Barstow exemplified much of what he couldn't stand about most people. She had no opinions save those of whomever she was speaking with—which was usually, unfortunately, Catherine Moss and company. Catherine's friendship with Cara surprised Raoul, now that he thought about it. Catherine's friends, though annoying, did have a certain "beautiful people" quality to them, whereas Cara seemed almost a nonentity to Raoul. It wasn't that Cara was unpleasant or unattractive, he thought, but that she wasn't *noticeable*. She wore her straight nondescript brown hair in a nondescript pageboy, wore clothes of classic styling rather than current fashion, and generally did all the things a young lady of good breeding should.

Raoul had always found her almost cloyingly sweet; he couldn't recall her ever saying anything negative about anyone. Her office decor reflected this, the walls covered by pastel flowery prints bearing pictures of small woodland creatures and saccharine platitudes about how good everything was, and how much better it would be in the next life. Cara was a Celtic school druid, though of a particularly naive type that Raoul had never been able to reconcile with his knowledge of the sect's beliefs. Cara's thoughts on reincarnation, Raoul thought, were perfectly expressed by a small framed print in her office that showed a kitten playing with a butterfly, obviously with no harmful intent. The text assured the reader that the writer would be sure to "take the time to chase more butterflies, play with more kittens, follow more rainbows," and other such drivel in the next pass through life. It struck Raoul as sad, for it seemed to him that somewhere deep inside her, Cara recognized that she'd wasted her current lifetime in meaningless politeness, and he wondered if she'd written it herself. In short, he thought, she was perfectly politically correct, perfectly middle-of-the-road in her teaching, and perfectly dull. No wonder Mowatt hadn't had any problems with her, or vice versa.

Finishing the transcriptions, he saved the file and exited the program. Looking at the blank screen, he debated doing some work on the aural erasure, but decided instead in favor of a cup of tea and reading. Maybe he'd skim through Mowatt's book first, see if that gave him any more insight into the man.

Chapter 5

Raoul woke to the sound of thunder and of rain hitting the window. He opened his eyes, wincing at the bright light of the monitor in front of him, groaning as he lifted his legs off the desk. Squinting, he read the time from the screen display. Nine o'clock in the morning; he must have slept most of the night. He rubbed his eyes, unsure whether to go back to bed—a real bed—or to just consider himself awake. He didn't feel so much tired as stiff. "I hate mornings," he growled aloud, getting to his feet and sitting rapidly back down as pins and needles coursed through his legs. "Blast!" He rose again, more carefully this time, and moved slowly toward the stairs.

"Mrs. Higgins?" he called.

"Sir?" came the response from the kitchen. "Are you up?" She ascended the first few stairs to catch a glimpse of Raoul clutching the banister. "Oh, dear!" Mrs. Higgins cried as she saw him. "Did you fall asleep at your desk again?" Without waiting for an answer, she continued, "Well, off to the bath with you, and I'll have a hot cup of tea ready when you're out."

He nodded thanks and entered his room, still moving slowly and carefully. Part of him wanted to hate the way Higgins sometimes mothered him, but he also found it oddly comforting. Come to think of it, he supposed it was only natural, since she'd taken care of him nearly all his life. His real mother wasn't the comforting or caring type. Not that he needed any of it, he told himself as he headed for the shower, shedding clothes while crossing the room.

Thinking of his mother reminded him that he should call her. He paused, resting his head against the cool tile and letting the shower's hot water sluice over him. She'd probably heard about Mowatt by now, and he should let her know what was happening. She might want him to go down to London and see her, though, and he always felt out of place around her when he visited, as if her life had neither relation to nor space for him in it.

Sighing, Raoul turned off the tap and dried himself, shaking out his wet hair. It was getting a big shaggy. He'd have to decide soon whether to chop it all off again or to just start pulling it back. Mowatt'll probably take me to task for a ponytail again, he thought; he bitches if it sticks out too much, he bitches if it's too long. He stood still for a moment, suddenly recalling that Mowatt wouldn't be doing any more complaining about his hair, or anything else for that matter, and that it didn't matter anyway, since he himself wouldn't be teaching for a while.

He took his time dressing, sipping the promised tea. First he needed to get back to the office, talk to a few more people. Lloyd Llewellyn-Jones had mentioned that Edgar Waller, another senior professor, might be good to talk to, since he'd been with the department almost as long as Mowatt. Raoul also wanted to talk to Jean Morris, Mowatt's assistant. He'd nose around a bit, talk to Miriam about the runic program and then see if he could get some time with Whiting. Whiting, if he was in the proper mood, should be able to shed some light on Mowatt's character, at least.

Raoul went into the study to gather his things for the office. He had just put the phone down, having called for a cab into Oxford, when it rang again. He picked it up midring and continued putting his papers into his bag as Catherine spewed inanities into his ear.

"No, Catherine," he sighed, "I was not arrested . . . I don't know who did it, Catherine . . . I'm afraid I'm not free for lunch . . . Yes, I know that. I'm taking a break from classes . . . Catherine, if you know all about this, then why are you asking me? . . . Yes, I saw Cara yesterday . . . No,

I did not notice her hair . . . Catherine, I really have to go . . . No, Catherine, I hate parties, you know that . . . Funeral? . . . Yes, I'll probably go . . . Catherine, why would I have any idea what people will be wearing? It's a funeral! People will wear what they usually wear to funerals! Why are you worrying about this? . . . Anne who? . . . Oh, right. No, I haven't seen her lately, why would I have seen her? Look, I really do have to go now, I've got a ride waiting . . . No, I don't want to see that, I've no time . . . No thanks. Anyway, good-bye . . . Good-bye . . . Hang up, Catherine . . .

"Argh!" he cried, slamming the phone down. "I hate that idiot!"

"Is everything all right, Mr. Smythe?" Mrs. Higgins asked, coming up from the kitchen and drying her hands on a towel. "Is something wrong?"

"Fine, Mrs. Higgins, really." Raoul looked at her, annoyed. "Please don't hover," he snapped, "everything is fine." She was standing still, staring at him. "Go," he said. She returned to the kitchen, muttering something about ingratitude. No way was he going to start explaining everything that happened to him to her. A little comfort was fine, if that's what she wanted to give, but it was also all he would take, and that not always. He ran his hands through his hair, trying to remember what he'd been doing when Beast Catherine had called. Cab, that was it. He'd been getting ready to leave.

Satisfied that he hadn't forgotten anything, he went down to the kitchen and told Higgins that he expected to be out late and that she could take the afternoon off if she wished. He'd find his own dinner, in any case. She replied curtly. Well, he thought, he'd try to be nice to her for a few days. He really hated it when people expected things of him. It was hard enough living up to one's own view of oneself, he thought, as he heard a car pull up to the gate, without having to meet others' expectations as well.

Miriam was waiting outside his office when he arrived,

a stack of books on the floor beside her. "Hi!" she chirped when she saw him.

"How in the world can you manage to be quite so perky every morning?" Raoul asked her, by way of greeting. "And you know the office is never locked, you could just go in."

She smiled at him, used to his manner after two years as his teaching assistant. As they entered the office, she began explaining about a program she'd found that would allow them to sort through the runic components of the spell in different ways.

"Now if I can cross-reference this back to the spell you're trying to break down, this baby should be able to spit out a listing of what each element of the spell does. I'd like to initially break it down phonetically, running all the different combinations of sounds, of course, as well as cryptographically, and I think we should do the same to at least two similar spells so we'll have some kind of baseline. That'll give both the runes and their English letter equivalents, because a couple of the runes have multiple pronunciation possibilities. I'll need to write a quick and dirty analysis program to sort the results, but that shouldn't be a problem. What do you think?"

"I think I'm very, very glad that you decided to split your studies between magic and computers. It sounds great, but how long will something like this take? Do you even have this runic program?"

"You've still got a modem, right?" she asked, walking to the desk to peer at the wiring behind the computer.

"Of course." That had been another battle with Mowatt, who didn't think magic and computers were compatible to begin with. Luckily, Mowatt had been overruled by Whiting, who understood that networks could refer to something other than one's sociopolitical circle.

"Then I've got the program," she continued, as Raoul laughed, "and if the spells aren't too long, I could have the first couple of passes done a few hours after I get the spells in and the program written. Which," she plowed on, expecting his next question, "should take about three to five hours, depending on the length of the spells and their linguistic complexity. I've started on the programming already, I just wanted to be sure we were thinking along the same lines. So give me at least a day, since I've got other things to do, including teaching some of your classes." She smiled. "When do you need it?"

"I don't have a hard deadline, but the sooner I have it, the better."

"Should I be asking why you need this?"

Raoul grimaced. "Actually, Miriam, I'd prefer you didn't. And, to be frank, at the moment this is completely personal business for me, so there's no credit attached. Will that be a problem?" He was fairly sure it wouldn't, otherwise he wouldn't have asked this of her in the first place, but he needed to be sure.

She snorted in reply. "Don't be silly, Professor. Of course it's fine."

"Good, then." Raoul smiled. "You can use my computer as much as you'd like, since I've got some other things to take care of in the next day or so. And now I'll get out of your way. If you need me, leave a note here, or leave a message at Thornhold. As I said, I'm going to be running around for the next few days, but I'll try to keep popping in. And I'd actually like to keep the office locked for a while. You know where the extra key is, if you need to leave?"

She shook her head.

"See the paperweight, there?" Raoul asked, pointing to a two-inch ball of clear crystal, a key embedded deep within it. "Now, pick it up."

Miriam did so, looking at him strangely. "Yeah, so?" she asked.

"Concentrate on the paperweight," Raoul said. "Now what's the Etruscan word for 'ghost'? Don't look at me, look at the weight."

Miriam thought a moment, her eyes never leaving the key in the crystal. *"Hinthial,"* she said. Immediately, her face lit in pleased surprise as she exclaimed, "It's just a key!" The crystal had completely disappeared.

"Uh-huh," Raoul agreed, pleased at her reaction. "Last place you'd look, right?"

Miriam was still marveling over the key. "That is *so* cool. What is it, just a glamour? But how did you give it weight? Is this one of the reduced spells you've been working on?"

"That's it. And, yes, it's a glamour, but I added a substance-enhancing spell. Good thinking, you figured it out. Are you all set, then?"

"Wait. How do I . . . oh!" Miriam had replaced the key on the top of the pile of papers she had taken it from. The moment it left her hand, the paperweight was back. She looked up at him, distracted, her attention still on the paperweight. "What? Oh, yeah, I'm all set."

Turning back at the door, Raoul said, "Oh, and Miriam . . . ?"

"Yes?" She looked up.

"Thank you. Really." He closed the door behind him and walked down the hall to see if Edgar Waller was in.

By two-thirty he was exhausted, frustrated, and hungry. He'd only managed to find three of the people he'd been looking for, and would have to wait until Bolton next popped over to Thornhold to review what they'd said. From the length of time he'd spent with two of them, he didn't expect much. He'd had a little more luck with Bob Parker, Whiting's assistant, who'd been in Mowatt's office when Raoul had arrived. Mowatt's assistant, Jean, was apparently out sick. Parker had been very helpful, giving Raoul a copy of Mowatt's curriculum vitae and just talking about the man.

Raoul hadn't bothered with the mnemonic spell before talking to Parker, so he needed a quiet place to write notes and hopefully get some food. He decided on the Hollow Man. The usual crowd of religious fanatics were chanting in the square in front of it, but this time no one accosted him.

Since it was too late for the real lunch crowd, the pub was subdued. Raoul hung his coat on the rack of hooks to the right of the door and waited a moment for his eyes to adjust. Day or night, the interior of the pub always held a kind of twilight atmosphere, a sense of separateness from the passage of time outside. He chose a table in a corner of the back room, as far from the two other occupied tables as possible. In a few moments the barkeep, Edward, came over with a pint of Guinness.

"Afternoon, Raoul," Edward said, "your pie'll be out in a few moments."

"Hi, Edward," Raoul said, smiling. "How's business?"

"Fine, as usual. Had quite a crowd over the weekend, but it's quieted a bit now. Hear you've had some excitement yourself. Sad thing, that happening to Professor Mowatt. Didn't know him myself. You holding up?"

Raoul nodded, taking a sip from the glass. "Yeah," he said, "I'm doing okay."

Edward laid a hand on his shoulder. "Good," he said, then turning back to the bar. "Evie'll bring your pie out."

Raoul sat drinking for a few moments, thinking about the first time Edward had appeared with his food before he'd actually ordered it. He'd been in his third year of undergraduate work at the time and had been coming to the pub occasionally for a year or more. He'd stared at Edward with such surprise that the barkeep had laughed and sat down for a moment. "Easy, son," he'd said, still chuckling. "I've a bit of the second sight I show off now and again to those I like. I'm Edward."

They'd spoken briefly, Raoul explaining who he was, and Edward doing the same. Raoul had been surprised at how easy it was to talk to him. "You're a quiet one, I know," Edward said, "which is why I came over. You've a good aura." His response to Raoul's question about how long he'd been barkeep had also been a surprise. "Oh, I guess it's about three hundred and forty, maybe three hundred and sixty years now." Again, seeing the look on Raoul's face, he'd laughed and explained.

Early in the seventeenth century, Edward said, a group of Celtic druids decided to buy a pub. Since then they'd been running the place, and as they died they were reborn, eventually making their way back to it. "So, Rory—that's another one of us—he'll be about—" He paused a moment to think. "—sixteen, I think, wherever he is. Anyway, he and I have been tending the till here since 1632." He continued, "Now, not everyone believes what we believe, and that's fine, and I'm not asking you to agree, I'm just telling you what I believe the answer to your question is." He'd waited for a response.

Raoul had replied that since all he knew about druidry was from a survey course in modern religions he'd taken the previous year, he was not one to judge what anyone believed. This had apparently been acceptable to Edward, for since then he'd nearly always taken the trouble to bring Raoul's order over himself and to say hello. It was odd, Raoul thought, how he'd always felt comfortable around the man. Edward once said it was because they'd been friends in a previous life. Raoul wasn't sure if that was the case, but he couldn't deny that he considered the man a friend, though he knew almost nothing about him and they'd never had more than a few words of conversation at a time. However, certain things did give Raoul pause for thought, such as the day two years ago when a young bartender named Rory had appeared and slid into the bar's routine as if he'd known it all his life.

Evie's arrival with a steaming hot shepherd's pie interrupted his thoughts, and he hungrily dug in. When he had finished, and started on a second pint of stout, he turned to taking down his notes for the morning. Increasingly, he felt he was merely flailing around aimlessly, and that was no good at all. Taking up a pen, he began to write.

"Mowatt?" Parker had replied to Raoul's question. "I still can't believe he's dead, you know. I keep expecting him to walk in any moment with some utterly urgent request. Everything always had to be done right away for him; the man had no sense of timing or priorities. Anyway," he'd said, looking shrewdly at Raoul, "why're you so interested?"

Raoul had explained, honestly, what he needed to know, and why. Parker understood, and said he'd give him all he could. "I've already spoken to the police, too," he'd said, then paused. "I gave them your name as someone to talk to. Sorry." He looked awkward.

"That's fine," Raoul said, and surprisingly, it was. "You were doing what you needed to. Anyway, it's not as if it was a secret that we didn't get along. So what was it like, working with him?"

"You probably know already. He was pretty much the same with everyone. It's hard to describe, as I told the police. I told them it was as if he didn't trust *anyone*, not even me. I was his assistant for almost three years before Sir Reginald hired me, and during all that time he never even trusted me to draft a memo for him. Had to do everything himself, you see. And then he'd check it after I'd typed it, too. He was like that with everything, and everyone. It all had to be done his way."

Raoul knew that well from his own experience. "What about his friends?" he asked.

"You really should talk to Jean, you know? I think they got on well, so she might know. Mowatt's friends? Here? He didn't seem to have any. Everything was business. He'd have lunch with Sir Reginald every now and again, but it was always for university business. He—Mowatt, I mean—was always trying make things more formal, it seemed. You know, fill out forms instead of just asking for things, that kind of thing. Sometimes I think that's all he did, we did so many memos and letters asking to change this or that. And he always sent copies to the Trustees' Board as well."

"What kind of things was he trying to change?"

"Silly things, I always thought." Parker paused a moment, remembering. "Things like redoing the tenure review procedure for professors . . ."

"That doesn't seem too odd."

Parker grimaced. "No?" he asked. "That's because you haven't gone through a tenure review yet, no offense. Try having every student in every class filling out evaluation forms, then cross referencing each evaluation against grades, weeding out the highest and lowest, then averaging those. And that's only the student part. Then you have to go through the board evaluations, checking each member for personal bias, for or against. Average those. And so on, and the final decision rests with the chair anyway. Mowatt always seemed to want more authority. What do you think of that, now?"

Raoul didn't reply. Instead, he asked, "Was everything like that? So complicated?"

Parker nodded. "Oh, yes, at least from what I've seen, both working for and with him. Forms in triplicate. He was always creating charts, graphs, and whatever, of the information he'd get. Jean still calls me for help on them sometimes. I don't think he really looked at any of it, he just wanted to have it done. Jean's got files and files of memos to the board about everything. I've got them, too."

"What about Whiting? Why didn't Mowatt just ask him in person for what he wanted? Aren't they—I mean, weren't they friends?"

"I really don't know; neither ever really talked about the other. I got the feeling, though, that lately Sir Reginald felt there were better ways to spend his time than by listening to Mowatt." He added, somewhat shyly, "I didn't tell that to the police."

"Why not? What do you mean?"

"I've no proof, it's just a feeling. Sir Reginald hadn't had lunch with him for over a month, hadn't made any appointments to talk to him about anything. He used to schedule a visit at least once or twice a week. Mowatt had Jean calling and calling for an appointment lately, but nothing was scheduled."

Raoul couldn't think of anything more to ask. Just as the situation began to feel awkward, the telephone rang. Raoul stood. "Thanks," he said, "you've really been helpful."

Parker held up a finger for him to wait, and picked up the phone. As he spoke he rummaged in the files, finally drawing out a few pages.

Hanging up the phone, he handed them to Raoul. "This may come in handy, I don't know," Parker said. "It's Mowatt's curriculum vitae. He always liked to keep it updated, I don't know why. It's not as if he'd ever have left here." He smiled. "Jean keeps it in the same place I always did. He never liked anything to change."

Sitting in the pub, Raoul put his pen down and took the pages Parker had given him out of his bag, skimming the information. Mowatt had graduated Oxford with an initial degree in Magic, without any honors or special accolades, Raoul noted somewhat smugly. There was no college name because all the Oxford colleges had been unified into the single university name in 1955, with the colleges merely providing specialization of study. Mowatt finished his doctorate in 1967, taught at a boys' school for a year, then returned to Oxford as a tutor, moving up to senior professor over the next eight years. He'd become the college chair in 1979. On the whole, Raoul thought, a fairly dull career, never really leaving the scholastic nest. Then again, he realized with some discomfort, he'd done the same thing himself. "Only," he muttered aloud, "I appear to have gotten into a bit more trouble on the way."

Catching Edward's eye, he signaled for another stout, then ran his hands through his hair in frustration. To find out who had killed Mowatt, he needed to know why anyone would have wanted to kill him. He knew how he'd been killed: a blow to the head. But that's where the aural erasure might come into play. Raoul could think of three possibilities: that magic had been used to kill him and then erase the aura, that magic had not been used and the aura erased anyway, or that the aural erasure was just a fluke and had nothing to do with Mowatt's death at all. He could imagine why someone would want to cover up a magical crime, making it look like a simple break-in, but not why someone, having coshed a man on the head, would need to erase magic traces. It was too complicated to think about without more information.

Raoul mentally reviewed what he knew. Prior to his death, Mowatt had been acting somewhat differently than usual, that much was clear. His relations with Whiting, and with him, too, had been more strained, more volatile. Why? And who was the mystery visitor to his house? A lover? Raoul couldn't bring himself to imagine Mowatt in a romantic relationship—it was too alien to his conception of the man.

Thinking about it, Raoul realized he had absolutely no suspects. He sighed, and started adding to the list of people he needed to talk to. First of all, he needed to see Whiting, to find out just how close he and Mowatt had been. He would stop by Whiting's office on the way back to his own. Irritably, he realized he could have just asked Parker if Whiting would be in this afternoon. And he still needed to see Edgar Waller. Leaving money on the table, he gathered his papers and headed back to the university, hoping that Bolton's day had been more fruitful than his own.

Raoul tried Waller's office first, and was told he'd already left for the day, so he walked back to his own office to see how Miriam was doing. His door was locked, the office dark. He spelled open the door and upon entering, he saw a note taped to the darkened monitor screen. The CPU console light was on, however, and flashing; the computer was running something. He glanced at the note.

In black marker, the note stated: PROGRAM RUNNING. DO NOT TURN OFF MACHINE. The back of the note was more edifying. In Miriam's cramped handwriting, Raoul read: "Prof. Smythe: The program works fine. I loaded in the three spells, and I'm running it now to break them down into all possible pronunciation configurations. When that's done it'll automatically run the program I wrote to collate the results. It might take a while—I'll check in first thing in the morning—I have the key. M." The note continued lower on the page, "Oh—two calls while you were out, Mr. Bolton and Mr. Barnstone both want you to call them. M."

It took a moment for Raoul to recall just who Mr. Barnstone was. The detective inspector. He wondered what the man wanted. He'd call him later. He left, spelling the door locked behind him.

Raoul stood before the locked door of the main administration building, which housed Whiting's office, cursing quietly. "Doesn't anyone in the blasted place believe in working late anymore?" he wondered, unaware he'd spoken aloud until someone behind him chuckled. He spun, a rapid breath hissing through his teeth.

Anne Whiting stood before him, arms crossed, laughing quietly. "Hi," she said, smiling. "Did I scare you?"

Raoul took a deep breath, willing himself to relax despite the adrenaline flooding his system. He was more tense than he'd realized. "Uh, no," he responded, running his fingers through his hair and feeling silly. He chuckled lightly. "Okay, well, maybe you startled me." He breathed deeply again. "So, what are you doing here?" he asked.

Anne shrugged. "Looking for my father. We were *supposed* to have dinner tonight. How about you?"

For some reason, Raoul felt awkward. "Me? I was looking for your father, too. I ran into his assistant in Mowatt's office."

"Jean?" Anne asked, puzzled.

"No, Bob Parker. Jean's not in. Why do you ask?"

"I didn't think she'd be in. She's been out sick all week, some kind of flu or something, I think. Hadn't you heard?"

"No," Raoul replied, somewhat stiffly, "I haven't been around that much this week." Come to think of it, though, he did remember that he hadn't seen her at the meeting on Monday.

Anne's hand flew to her mouth, her face contorting in an embarrassed grimace. "Oh!" she exclaimed, shaking her head. "I'm so sorry. I'd forgotten. Sorry." Obviously, she knew about the suspension, that it wasn't just for research.

Raoul found the look of pity in her eyes unbearable, and looked away. "Don't worry about it," he said. He looked back at her, saw the hesitation still in her eyes and said the first thing that occurred to him, surprising himself: "Look, do you want to go for a drink or something?"

At least it made her face lose its look of confusion and hurt. "What?" she asked.

This time he had to think about it, making it that much harder to ask. He repeated the question, enunciating carefully: "Do you want to go out for a drink with me?"

Anne's eyes were downcast as she considered. Looking up, she nodded. "Okay," she said, and smiled. "Where to?"

"How about my club?" Raoul asked, and in response to her doubtful look, added, "It's not a private club or anything, just a nightclub that serves food. I just call it mine because I practically live there. You probably know it—the Rat Seller." He waited for the look of horror to cross her face. It wasn't long in coming.

"That place!" she exclaimed. "You mean people really go there? Normal people, I mean." Embarrassment colored her cheeks as she realized what she'd said. "Not that you're not normal, of course," she began, then noticed his expression. Raoul leaned back against the iron stair railing, arms crossed, smirking. Indignant, she shook a finger in his face. "You did that on purpose, didn't you? And I fell for it like a prize fish." At this last, one of Raoul's eyebrows rose and his smirk widened to a grin. She turned, took a few steps away, then turned back. "Well?" she asked. "Are we going or not? Do you want to take my car?"

Raoul shook his head. "No," he answered, "it's too hard to find by car, and nearly impossible to park. Squirrely old medieval streets, you know. It's faster to walk." Shouldering his bag, he gestured for her to walk with him.

The Seller was located in the basement of an old grain storehouse which now functioned as a seedy hotel. Club rumor had it that the club and hotel were owned by the same person, but since none of the regulars had ever found out who owned either one, the story remained myth. Raoul had once asked Bryon, the manager and bartender, if he knew who owned the place, since Bryon was known to live in the hotel itself. Bryon, never talkative in any case, had merely shrugged, and Raoul hadn't pressed the issue.

Now, approaching the building, he glanced at Anne, walking beside him, and wondered what she thought of it. Her gaze moved across the row of dirty storefronts occasionally topped by apartments, then said to him, "I don't want to offend you, Raoul, but you *like* coming here?"

He laughed. "You think it's bad now, wait till we get inside." He gestured widely at the doorway in front of them. A large wooden sign hung above, depicting a man in medieval garb displaying a large cage filled with rodents, under the words THE RAT SELLER. Raoul indicated that she should precede him.

"Downstairs" he said, after she entered and faced the two darkened staircases, one leading up into shadow, the other only a few steps down to a dark corner As they rounded the corner, the dimly lit stair straightened, leading them farther down, to an old oaken door. Raoul pushed it open, and was struck by an almost palpable wave of loudly throbbing drums and bass, smoke, and the relatively indescribable odor of the club itself, which had something to do with the music, the smoke, the alcohol, the clientele, and the basement location. He breathed deeply, feeling completely at home. Standing on the landing next to Anne, he suddenly felt he was seeing the club again for the first time.

Most of the twenty or so people in the front room turned briefly to see who had entered. Anne noted their stares, and turned to Raoul. "It's fine," he told her, smiling. "Not many new people come here. Or stay if they do. Come on." He led her in a straight path from the door, past the tables against the front wall, stopping to greet or be greeted by a few people. They ended up at a small table in the front corner, close to the small bar standing against the wall opposite the door, and with a view of the entire club.

Before Anne had even removed her coat, Bryon appeared with a pint of stout, which he set in front of Raoul. "Hey," Raoul said by way of greeting. Bryon's cigarette nodded a response. Anne asked for a glass of white wine. The barkeep looked at Raoul, shrugged, then walked back to the bar. A few moments later a glass of yellow liquid appeared on the edge of the bar. Raoul walked over and retrieved it, setting it in front of Anne.

"Why didn't the bartender bring it over?" she asked, gingerly taking a sip.

"Bryon? He generally doesn't come out to do anything but gather up the empties. He'll sometimes bring me over the first pint of the night because we're friends." He paused, then continued with a nervous chuckle, "Plus, he probably wanted to check you out. I usually come alone."

She looked around in silence for a moment, taking in the painted abstract mural on the opposite wall, the small stage on the other side of the bar. "What's back there?" she asked, gesturing at the rough doorway to the right of the stage.

"The back room, a few more tables, another bar, then the kitchen. Plus, you can get to a bathroom from there, but you probably don't want to try." She looked questioningly at him, so he continued, "It's upstairs, in the hotel. You never know what'll be up there."

She didn't respond, and they sat silently for a while, looking around. Just as Raoul began to regret his rash invitation, she asked, "Why'd you invite me here?"

The question threw him. "Why?" he repeated. "I don't know." He paused, feeling like an idiot. "I guess because I enjoyed talking to you in the car the other day, and . . ." He trailed off. "I don't know why, really."

"I didn't ask why you asked me out, Raoul," she said, and smiled. "I think I figured that part out myself." Before he could respond, she continued, "I asked why you brought me here, to this place."

"Oh." Suddenly, he wanted nothing more than to be safely ensconced in his study at Thornhold, rather than here having to think about how to answer that question.

"I mean, are you trying to make me feel uncomfortable or out of place? Because I do. But that's not exactly what I mean," she continued, before he could respond. "This isn't a place I'd come to on my own, that's clear. I don't know anyone here, and it's not really my style. But what I think I'm trying to ask is whether or not you brought me here to . . . I don't know, get back at my father or Catherine or something. I don't like feeling like I'm being used. Or tested." She stopped, looking at him.

He lowered his head, ran his fingers back and forth through his hair a few times, then looked back at her. "I don't know," he replied, holding up a hand to stop her answer. "I'm not using you to get back at either your father or Catherine, that I'm sure about. Nothing to get back at them for." He paused, thinking. "I know this isn't your type of place, that these aren't your type of people, that you probably don't listen to music like this when you're on your own. But I do. This isn't just my type of place, it *is* my place. I feel at home here, these are my friends. I didn't think about bringing you here. Well, I mean I did, but . . ."

He couldn't seem to say what he meant. He tried again: "If I'm testing you, I don't mean to. I don't know what else to say. We can leave if you'd like." He felt supremely awkward, half hoping she'd take him up on the offer. Why had he asked her out anyway? he wondered.

"No," she said, "it's okay." She laughed nervously. "I really put you on the spot, didn't I? Sorry. I needed to know, I guess." Rising, she picked up her glass. "Do you want another?" At his nod, she took both glasses and waited at the bar for a refill.

Returning, she asked, "Okay, so tell me about this place. How long have you been coming here? How'd you find out about it?"

Raoul smiled, starting to relax again. Maybe this wouldn't be that bad after all, he thought. He looked around the room, remembering. "I heard about it a few months after I'd come up to Oxford. I was feeling a bit, uh, 'uncomfortable and out of place,' as it were." He waved away her grimace, smiling. "You know, everyone else seemed to think the university meant nice suits, short hair, and making contacts for a wonderful career in business. Even the people in Magic."

She feigned shock. "And you didn't? How odd!" She laughed. "Go on."

"Well, I heard a few suits speaking in quiet, horrified tones about this place they'd been to, where everyone sat around on cushions listening to odd, loud music and smoking all kinds of strange things in hookahs."

"So you went that night?"

"Actually, it took me about a week to find it. Once I got here, I was hooked. Of course it was nothing like they'd described, but I'd expected that. It was pretty much as it is now." He looked around fondly. "Just a bunch of people being exactly what they are, with no pretense and no attitude. And no suits." Looking over her shoulder, he said in a louder voice, "Of course, if I'd known about some of the weirdos that come in here, I'd have avoided the place like the plague."

She turned to look behind her. A man with bright white hair and baggy multicolored clothing was approaching. He carried a glass and a sketch pad. She couldn't tell if his hair was bleached or naturally white; he could have been anywhere between thirty and fifty. He pulled a chair from the next table and sat down beside her.

"Excuse me, miss, but is this—" He looked at Raoul and snorted. "—*person* bothering you?" He lifted her hand from the table and kissed it. "Bill Hat, at your service, my lady. How goes it, Raoul?" Anne looked silently from the man to Raoul, her eyes wide.

"It goes, Bill. I was just telling Anne about how I started coming here. Anne, this is Bill. Don't believe a word he says."

Bill addressed Anne directly: "Now, I don't know what he's told you about the Seller yet, but you have to understand, it was a much, much better place until he started showing up. A perfectly respectable jazz club. And now look at it!" He gestured around with open arms and smiled broadly at her.

"Was it really a jazz club, Mr. Hat?"

"No 'misters' in here, my dear; 'Bill' will do just fine. And yes, it was. Almost twenty years ago. That only lasted a few years, though. Now the mural is all that's left from those days. Besides me, that is."

"Better compliment him on the mural, Anne. He painted it," Raoul said.

"Really? Then you're an artist?"

"A painter. Houses, signs, whatnot, just to get me enough to travel on. Architectural portraits are my first love, you see. Ever seen the Parthenon? The pyramids? The Temple of Sethlans in old Volterra? Glorious, all of them. I could spend my life looking at them, drawing them."

"Bill's been around the world more times than the moon, I think," Raoul said to Anne. He turned back to Bill. "By the way, thanks for the cards—they're gorgeous. How long are you back for this time?"

"Only a week or two, I think. I've got a couple of jobs lined up, should get me enough to head back out. Anyway, I've got to run. It's been a true pleasure meeting you, my dear," he said, again raising Anne's hand to his lips, "although your taste in men appears to be deplorable. I'll see you later, Raoul; I need to get another set of your famous luggage wards. Ta."

Anne waited until Bill was safely out of earshot before asking, "Luggage wards? Do tell . . ."

Raoul chuckled, raising his eyes to the ceiling. "It's a spell of mine. It keeps one's bags from being moved unless a keyword is spoken. He uses it when he's traveling to make sure no one makes off with his paintings." He shrugged. "It's kind of simple."

"No, it's not. That's super!" Anne said. "Can anyone use it?"

"It takes a certain amount of ability. Not a lot, though."

"Oh . . . Could you explain something for me?" she asked. "I should probably know all this, but I never really studied magic. How do you tell if you've got magical ability, or how much? Can't you just learn the spells and then use them?"

Raoul sighed. "You know, I'm always shocked at how little people know about it. No offense, of course." He thought a moment. "The easiest way to tell if you've got magic is to try it. If it works, or if you feel that it should be working, you've probably got some ability. There're tests you can do, too. It's kind of like music." Anne looked confused, so he continued.

"Look at it this way—some people, like Mozart or any other musical prodigy, just seem to know how to play from birth. The ability is innate, and training just—well, seems to fine-tune it. Other people need years of training and hard work to reach a similar level. On the other end of the scale are the tone deaf, who may appreciate good music when they hear it, but have no ability to play at all. That's what magical ability is like.

"Some of the professors I work with, for example," he continued, "have no ability at all, but they can teach about the ethics or the history of magic far better than most people with the ability to perform spells. Take Robert Marlowe, for example." Anne shook her head, not recognizing the name. "He retired a couple of years ago, so you may not have known him. A great professor, one of the best. Anyway, he's a man who knows the history of magic backward and forward, has amazing insights into its workings, but he can't work even the simplest spell himself. And then there's someone like Bill, who's got no interest whatsoever in magic as a science, but has enough talent to use certain spells that make his life easier. It all depends on the person, really. Does that make sense?"

Anne thought a moment before replying. "Yes," she said slowly, "so then people with only a little ability will only be able to work simple spells? And the really talented people can do whatever they'd like?"

Raoul shook his head. "Nope. Magical ability, and what one does with that ability, are really two very separate things. Physicists have been studying it for years, trying to figure out what makes it work. So have most religions. What it comes down to is that if a person with magical ability is handed a spell, it won't work unless that person has some understanding of what it is they're trying to accomplish. It's why so many magicians specialize. Where the ability comes in is how strong the spell will be, how long it will last, that kind of thing."

"You've lost me."

"That's okay, it's confusing to everyone. Here's an example: Suppose a magician gets locked out of his house one day, but doesn't know any spells to open locks. He can do two things. One, he can go to someone who does know spells to open locks, and they can come over and open the door for him. Or he can choose the other option, which is to have someone teach him how a lock works, and then he can either borrow a spell from his lock-opening friend, or he can even create one himself, if he's into it. Once he understands how the lock works, and what the spell needs to do, he can use just about any lock-opening spell that exists, for that type of lock. Unless, of course, the locks have been magically altered. Is that better?"

"I think so. So if our friend's lock was a dead bolt, and he learned how to open it with a spell, he still wouldn't be able to open a combination lock, right?"

"Right. Not unless he learned how combination locks work."

"Okay, so then a magician who knows how something is done can do it magically. So why don't more magicians rob banks?" She smiled.

Raoul laughed. He was enjoying this. "Ah, you've now entered the field of magical ethics! You see, ethics is part of the formal training for anyone who's going to practice magic. Entire courses are devoted to why magicians shouldn't use magic to harm anyone . . ."

"Black magic?"

"Right, though we don't call it that. Also, the history of magic is full of these great little moral tales where bad magicians get burned at the stake, or cause persecutions against magic-users in general, etcetera . . ."

"You know, you're really good at explaining this stuff."

Raoul looked up quickly. "Oh, gods, I'm not boring you, am I? I'll shut up. It's a disease all teachers have, running off at the mouth like this."

"No!" She patted his arm. "No, I didn't mean it like that at all. Anyway, it's interesting when you tell it, and I did ask. And it's neat watching you be so interested in something. You kind of light up."

Raoul looked uncomfortable. He'd never been able to deal with compliments, even vague ones. "You're sure I'm not boring you?"

"Raoul, I'd tell you if you were, don't worry. It's fascinating. I wish I cared that much about something. Hang on, I'll get another round." She rose and headed for the bar.

When she returned, a young woman with multicolored dreadlocks was sitting in the seat Bill had vacated, laughing with Raoul. "Hi," said the strange girl. "I was just trying to convince Raoul to come up and do a number with the band later, but he's not budging." She smiled.

Anne looked at Raoul curiously. "Oh?" she said in a tight voice. "I didn't know you played an instrument."

The woman laughed. "He doesn't, really, but he does an amazing light show! I guess you're still a little too sober, hey?"

Raoul looked uncomfortable. "Anne," he said, "this is Skank. She's an old friend—" He looked at Skank. "—with a long memory. Skank, this is Anne Whiting."

Anne, who had sat down again, was looking intently at Skank. "Have we met before?" she asked. "I'd swear I knew you." She thought a moment. "Did you by any chance go to the Leighton School?"

The smile left Skank's face and her manner became cool. "My sister did. I was only there for a year."

"I knew it! What's your sister's name?"

"Lillian." Skank forced the word out.

"Not Lillian Darrow?" Anne cried. "Then you must be

Margaret! You know, I saw your parents the other day. They were at the party for Arthur Mowatt. Raoul, you were there, you probably saw them." She turned back to Skank, who hadn't said a word. "How is Lillian? I haven't seen her since school."

"Neither have I, really. I haven't seen her, or my parents, in about three years. We don't have a lot in common, it seems. And I don't really like talking about it. Anyway, Raoul," she said, turning pointedly to him, "you're staying for the show, right? Squid'll be glad to see you. And I think I heard Pocker was going to show up, too."

"Pox?" Raoul said. "You know, I haven't seen him since he left the band. I hope he shows. Friends," he explained to Anne.

She was obviously feeling hurt from the exchange with Skank. "Squid and Pocker?" she asked. "Doesn't anyone who comes here use their real name?"

Skank answered before Raoul: "No offense, Anne, but most of us aren't the people our parents named us to be, if you know what I mean."

Anne remained silent, and after a while said quietly, "I know, Skank. Believe me, I know what you mean." Even more quietly, she added, "Lucky."

The conversation had become awkward. Skank rose and picked up her guitar case, her cockiness returning, "Well, kiddies," she said heartily, "I've got to go warm up. That invite to join us is still open, Raoul," she added, laughing. She turned to Anne, touching her lightly and quickly on the shoulder. "Look, I'm sorry if I upset you. Just forget about it, okay?" She winked at Raoul and left.

As she walked away toward the stage, they heard her say, loudly, "Piss off, Mordechai! Asshole . . ." Raoul's head jerked up and around at the name. Anne followed his gaze to a burly young man coming their way.

Later, as they walked back to the university, still somewhat deafened by the loudness of the band, Anne said, "I still cannot believe you lit that poor man's hand on fire!"

Raoul sighed. They'd already been through this. "First, I

did not light his hand, I lit the card he was about to shove in my face. It's not my fault he didn't let go of it. And second, I've warned that idiot a thousand times what I was going to do to him if he didn't start leaving me and, I should add, my friends, alone. He's always after me."

"But who is he?"

"Mordechai? He was at school with Bolton and me, but I never knew him all that well. Spotty little git. His family belongs to a very strict christian sect; any contact with magic, except what their priests use in ceremony, is strictly forbidden. So he and I never had a lot to say to each other."

"But then why was he coming to see you? Wouldn't he want to stay as far away as he could?" She grinned. "Especially since you apparently like lighting him on fire . . ."

"I don't know. Like I said, he's been bothering me all the time lately. He's got a thing for fire, it seems. He tries to convince me of the wickedness of what I do, threatening me with hellfire and brimstone and the like. He's always done it to some extent, but he's gotten really bad in the last few months or so. Seems to spend his spare time handing out tracts and the like. He's really nothing to worry about."

It seemed impossible to Raoul that he'd spent so many hours with Anne, but when they finally reached her house, it was almost two. Over his protests, she drove him back to Thornhold.

He got out at the gate. "Thanks for coming out with me tonight," he said. "I'm sorry about the Mordechai business."

As he turned to go into the house, Anne said, "Will I . . ." and paused.

He turned back to her. "Pardon?"

"Nothing," she said. "Have a nice night. I'll see you," and drove off.

Inside, Raoul set the kettle on for tea. He debated whether to stay up and work or just get a few hours sleep, in a bed this time. Deciding on sleep, he sipped his tea as he unpacked his bag. "Crap," he muttered, fingering the note to call Bolton and Barnstone. "Well, they can wait till morning, I'm sure."

Later, as he lay in the dark planning what to do in the morning, he found himself thinking about Anne. She was certainly a strange one. Perfectly enjoyable one minute, and then turning on the finishing-school attitude with Skank like that. She'd been fine again after that, though. Strange girl. Kind of cute, though, and easy to talk to. He drifted into sleep, smiling.

Chapter 6

"Where the hell were you last night? Didn't you get my message?" Bolton asked as he slammed the bedroom door open. Raoul jerked awake, then fell back as he realized who it was. Bolton stood expectantly in the doorway, cradling a steaming cup of tea. "So?" he asked again.

"Out," Raoul mumbled, "I was out."

"Well, you're not going to believe what's happened, my friend. I got this package in yesterday's mail, and . . . Don't you want to hear this?" Raoul had walked into the bathroom, shutting the door between them.

From the bathroom came a muffled reply. "Not until I'm awake. Give me a second, will you? And how about getting me a cup of tea, unless you've drunk it all?"

Bolton grumbled his way to the kitchen and back, returning with a tray prepared by Mrs. Higgins, who'd anticipated the need. Raoul was toweling his hair in the study.

"Now, what's happened that emboldened you to get me up at—" Raoul glanced at the clock "—seven-thirty in the thrice-damned morning? It better be worth it . . ."

Smugly, Bolton handed him a typewritten sheet, obviously a photocopy. "This, as I was saying, came in the mail yesterday, at the office. Addressed to me personally. No return address, of course." He fell silent, watching Raoul's face as he read.

Raoul read the short note through twice before looking at Bolton. "Do you know what this is?" he asked.

"Am I stupid?" Bolton replied tartly. "It appears to be a blackmail note, or rather, a copy of one. Addressed to our

friend Sir Reginald Whiting, and signed by our dead friend
Mowatt. Or," he added, innocently, "were you thinking it
was something else?"

Raoul ignored the last comment. " 'If you don't want the
world to know how Montgomery-Lewis died . . .' " he read.
"Who's Montgomery-Lewis? This makes it sound like
Whiting killed him or something." He paused, and musing
aloud, said, "You know, that name is familiar . . ."

"I looked him up yesterday, while I was waiting for you
to get back to me." Bolton glanced at Raoul, then continued. "George Montgomery-Lewis happened to be the
seventy-second or so chancellor of one Oxford University.
As it happens, he drowned while boating in Scotland in
1968. He was on holiday at the time, with his wife and two
young friends from the university, one a lowly assistant
professor, the other an even lowlier graduate student. They
were his protégés." He paused dramatically.

Raoul looked up from the letter with a sinking feeling.
"Whiting and Mowatt?" he asked. "They knew each other
that long ago?"

"It appears so. So, what do you think? Is it real?"

"What do you mean, 'real'? I think it's a photocopy of
a note. It could just be some fool sending out crank letters,
you know that. Mowatt's death has certainly been in the
news enough. Still, we should probably check it out, find
out about Lewis' death—"

"Montgomery-Lewis," Bolton corrected.

"Whoever," Raoul continued. "He drowned, you say? In
water?"

Bolton eyed him curiously. "That's where drowning usually happens, Rags," he said. "Why?"

Raoul shook his head, trying to pinpoint what was bothering him. "Wait . . ." he said. After a moment it hit him.
"Water!" he cried, sitting up. "My scry! Paper and water
and the rest . . . I told you about that, didn't I?"

"Yeah, you did," Bolton said. "Paper . . ." He pointed to
the note Raoul was holding. "And water. Hmmm. What
were the other things you saw again?"

Raoul looked uneasily down at the paper in his hand. The problem with unclear scrys was that the symbols didn't become clear until after something happened. He paused, remembering the images from the scry. "The paper changed color," he said slowly. "It got bigger and kind of pinkish, almost spotted. Then there was a flash of red and then the whole thing went gray and disappeared. Not too much to go on, huh?"

Bolton thought. "What do you mean, 'went gray'? Like smoke or something?"

Raoul shook his head. "Not really, no. I don't think so, at least. More like a shadow falling across something, or a shade, a cloud . . . I don't know." He shook his head, more violently this time. "Anyway, where was I? We should find out about this guy's death, look into how long Whiting and Mowatt have known each other, what their relationship was like, that kind of thing. You know, it's funny, I talked to Whiting's secretary yesterday, and he said it seemed the two of them hadn't been getting along lately. I wonder . . ." He trailed off, unsure of just what it was that he wondered about. "And incidentally, you should probably let the police know about this. It'll endear you to them even more. The police . . . damn, I'm supposed to remember something about them . . . Miriam, it had something to do with . . . Oh, right—Barnstone called me." A movement caught his eye.

Bolton was shaking his head, chuckling.

"What?" Raoul snapped.

"Sorry. I just love watching you talk to yourself. Barnstone the detective, I assume? What did he want?"

"I don't know. I haven't called him back yet. I'll call him later. Now, while I've got you here, I need you to write down the two conversations I had yesterday. You up for some scribbling?"

Bolton checked the teapot and warmed up both their cups. "Sure," he said. "I'll get my things while you prepare."

Raoul's first conversation, with Lydia Stillman, Chair of

the College of English, didn't contain much of interest. She hadn't wanted to talk about Mowatt, claiming she didn't really know him all that well. Raoul had gotten her to talk about his behavior at staff meetings, revealing the unsurprising news that he was usually impatient with anything not directly involving him, but full of suggestions for how other people should run things.

The one interesting bit about the whole conversation, Bolton thought as he was writing, was that apparently Mowatt attended every meeting of the college chairs, whether the College of Magic was directly involved or not. "It was as if he couldn't bear to be left out of anything," Stillman had mused. "He apparently needed to know everything about what was happening at the university." She also mentioned that she thought he wanted to succeed Whiting as chancellor, but said that was just her opinion and shouldn't count for anything.

Bolton stopped Raoul's recall at the end of the conversation to make some additional notes, including a reminder to himself to ask Raoul about the succession idea. As he prepared a clean page for the next set of notes, he heard Mrs. Higgins' voice downstairs. He could hear her quite well, which was odd. Usually one had to shout to be heard from one floor to the next. He stopped, listening.

". . . now, just you wait! I don't care who you're with or what you're from . . . just wait a minute while I let the gentlemen know you're here! Will you please stop?" She continued on in this vein, her voice becoming increasingly loud. Bolton rose and headed for the door, glancing once back at Raoul, who sat in deep meditation.

A knock sounded at the door just as he reached for the handle.

"Mr. Smythe?" Mrs. Higgins said, "There's a gentleman here to see you . . ."

The door opened. Bolton found himself facing a man in his mid-thirties in a slightly baggy gray suit, a sheaf of papers in one hand, his hat in the other. He looked appraisingly at Bolton. "I'm looking for Professor Smythe," he said, peering guardedly around Bolton. "Is he here?"

Bolton checked a sigh and affected his most officious because-I'm-a-journalist pose. "Yes, the professor is in, but I'm afraid he's rather indisposed at the moment. And you would be . . . ?" He waited.

"My name is Barnstone. Detective Inspector George Barnstone, Oxford police. I'm here on official business. Would you mind, Mister . . . I'm afraid I didn't catch your name."

"Bolton."

Barnstone nodded. "Ah, right. Maxwell Bolton, I should have realized. I'd heard that you and the professor are good friends. My wife reads your column in the *News*. Quite interesting, she says. In any case, Mr. Bolton, I'm afraid I'm going to have to disturb Professor Smythe. It's somewhat urgent."

Bolton mentally willed himself to ignore the flattery, difficult as that might be. He decided to bluff. Pushing the door wide, he pointed to Raoul's still form. "As I said, I'm afraid Raoul's indisposed." He added, in a confidential stage whisper, "He's meditating."

Infuriatingly, Barnstone was unfazed. "Fine," he said, leaning on the arm of a side chair, "I'll just wait until he comes 'round, then." He took a long look around the room before returning his gaze to Bolton. He didn't quite smirk. Turning to the obviously distressed housekeeper, he said, "Thank you. I think that'll be all for now." Higgins scowled silently at him, but at Bolton's nod left the room with a huff.

Bolton tried to think through what was happening. The problem was that Raoul wasn't going to "come 'round" until the recall was finished. And he didn't relish the idea of explaining to Barnstone either why Raoul would be meditating quite so long or why he'd need the detective to leave the room for who knew how long before Raoul would be ready to see him. What was so important anyway for him to come barging in? Bolton wondered. He realized Barnstone was watching him. He needed a diversion.

"So, Detective, would you care for a cup of tea or something? This could take some time. Raoul often meditates for hours, you know. Shall we go downstairs where it's more comfortable?" Even as he spoke, Bolton realized how lame he sounded. He smiled at Barnstone, waiting for a response.

Barnstone took his time replying. Finally he said, with a sigh, "You know, Mr. Bolton, this case has really gotten under my skin. Nothing at all seems simple; nothing is clear-cut." He met Bolton's eyes. "It's all rather frustrating. Your friend here," he nodded at Raoul, "fits in somewhere, but I'm not sure how. He just seems to come up anytime the case is being discuss. Odd, wouldn't you say?" He didn't wait for an answer. "I think so. And now you're here. Kind of early in the day, I'd think. I wonder . . . just over for a chat, were you?"

Bolton managed to look surprised. "Are you interrogating me, Detective Inspector? How funny! Raoul is my best friend, as I'm sure you know. I come here often, and I don't need a particular reason to do so. Satisfied?"

Barnstone stood, stretching. "As a matter of fact, no. Take a seat, Mr. Bolton. I've a short story to tell you. You see, I'm here to find out if your friend knows anything that might relate to a certain document received by the Yard yesterday morning." He paused, looked directly at Bolton, then turned and plucked a sheet of paper off Raoul's desk. With a sinking feeling Bolton noted that it was the note he'd brought with him. Barnstone looked at it for a moment, then waved it in his direction. "So, imagine my surprise when I see that he's already got a copy. Now, why don't you begin—"

"Hi, Michelle. Have you got a moment . . . ?" Barnstone and Bolton both started as Raoul began to speak in the flat voice Bolton now associated with magical recall.

"Stop!" Bolton cried. Barnstone had triggered the recall by saying "begin." Bolton looked at the detective and shrugged guiltily. "I guess you want to know what's going on," he said. Barnstone nodded, crossing his arms. Bolton sighed. "Well, it's a long story, and I do want Raoul awake for it, so . . ." He paused, then came out with it in a rush: "Raoul and I have been doing our own investigating of the murder. My idea, really. He can't take notes to save his life, so he's put himself under a mnemonic spell to recall conversations he's had with faculty. I need to take notes while he relives it, so he can come out of meditation. And, by the way, I should mention that the note in Raoul's hand is mine; it came to me at the office yesterday and I brought it here to show Raoul. Anyway, the recall will take exactly as long as the original conversation, which may be quite some time. I suppose you want to wait?"

"Oh, yes. I wouldn't miss this for the world."

"I was afraid of that. Okay, let me get my notes. You can sit, if you'd like . . ." Bolton settled himself on the couch, facing Raoul. He muttered, "Okay, let's see, he started with 'Hi, Michelle, got a moment,' right?"

"Right," agreed Barnstone. "Who's Michelle?"

Bolton finished taking the statement down, then said, "He'll tell us after. Begin." Immediately, Raoul began to speak.

Raoul had spoken with Michelle, obviously a professor, for only about fifteen minutes. Bolton, writing, thought to himself that she wasn't contributing anything new to their store of information about Mowatt. Apparently, she and Mowatt had gotten on well enough; she said he'd sometimes stop by just to talk about the history of the northern religions, which was her specialty. She did make one interesting comment, that she thought the reason they got on was that it wasn't as if she was trying anything new, or making any changes, the implication being that Raoul was. Interesting, though not really surprising.

Bolton was still writing when Raoul came out of meditation. Stretching, he shook his head, "Whew! I'm stiff— feels like I've been sitting for hours . . . What the . . . ! Oh. Hello, Detective Inspector." Raoul looked at Bolton, who shrugged.

"Social call?" Raoul asked sarcastically. Still stiff and slightly groggy, he gingerly poured himself a cup of tea, waiting for Barnstone to speak.

Surprisingly, the detective's first question was directed at Bolton. "So, perhaps you'd like to tell me about this?" He shook the photocopied note, which he'd been holding all through Raoul's recall.

Looking guiltily at Raoul, Bolton explained to Barnstone why he'd brought the note to Raoul rather than straight to the police. Barnstone listened attentively, occasionally writing in a small notebook. Throughout the conversation, Raoul remained seated at his desk, toying with a pen. When Barnstone finally turned his attention to him, Raoul cut him off before he could begin.

"Excuse me, but just what's going on here?" he asked coldly, scowling equally at Barnstone and Bolton. "Why are you in my house, and how did you get up here?"

"He wouldn't stay downstairs, sir." All three men turned to the doorway, where Mrs. Higgins stood holding a covered tray.

Raoul crossed to her from behind the desk. "I'll bet he wouldn't," he said, taking the plate. "Thanks, Mrs. Higgins. It's okay." Smiling gently at her worried look, he closed the door behind her.

He walked back to the desk, setting the plate down precariously on a stack of papers. He removed the cover and took one of the scones Mrs. Higgins had made, gesturing for the others to do the same. Only after he had slowly chewed and swallowed a bite did he speak.

"Detective Inspector Barnstone"—Raoul stressed the man's title—"I hope you have a better reason for disturbing us than just going over Bolton's junk mail. Shall I assume that's why you came by? And that finding me in meditation was just a pleasant excuse to listen in on the private conversations of a suspect? I am still a suspect, I assume."

"Yes." Barnstone paused, letting that sink in as the answer to both questions, then continued. "That is, yes, I did come by to talk to you about the letter which I received anonymously, and yes, we're still considering you. It was merely fortuitous that I came by while you were in the process of magically retrieving conversations you'd had concerning the deceased Professor Mowatt. Mr. Bolton tells me you've been having quite a few of those lately. Mind if I ask why?"

Raoul shot an angry glare at Bolton, not caring how it looked, before turning back to the detective. "Just bored, I guess," he replied snidely. "The teaching business is kind of slow these days, as I'm sure you're aware. And if your next question is whether I've discovered anything, the answer is no. I've spoken with six or seven people at the university, and no one has revealed any grave information. No secret plots, no hidden identities, no clandestine affairs, no anything. Does that cover it? Frankly, most people just didn't like the man, and I can't say I blame them. Any other questions, Detective Inspector? I really should be getting to my research. It's not often I get so much free time to work on it." The corners of his mouth turned up in a small smile that didn't reach his eyes.

Barnstone waited a moment, his gaze holding Raoul's, before replying. "No," he said slowly, "I don't have any more questions at the moment." He turned toward the door, paused and turned back, addressing Bolton. "And Mr. Bolton, if you receive any more interesting tidbits—" He again waved the letter in his hand. "—I'd appreciate it if you'd share them with the police. Good day to you both. I'll show myself out."

"Oh, it's no problem," Raoul said, rising and crossing the room. Bolton followed behind them. No one spoke as they walked through the house to the door.

As he left, Barnstone said, rather insincerely, "Thank you. This has been quite informative."

Raoul nodded and stood watching silently from the outer doorway as the detective drove down the drive, stopped to open the gate, drove through, and stopped again to close the gate. Only when the sound of the car had disappeared down the road did Raoul shut the door, after first speaking the spell that locked the gate. He stood, leaning his head against the inside of the door for a few moments, surprised by the virulence of his anger that someone had entered Thornhold without his permission. He breathed deeply until he felt some of the tightness leave his body, then turned back into the parlor.

Bolton sat draped across a leather armchair, legs dangling, watching Raoul with concerned eyes. Silently, he twisted in the chair to watch as Raoul crossed the room and stood in front of the fireplace with his back to him. "Rags," he said softly, "are you okay?" He knew only too well how Raoul could work himself into a fury when something was out of his control, and Raoul's continued silence worried him. Raoul quietly and tightly spoke a single Etruscan word, and the logs on the dragon-shaped firedogs suddenly exploded in flame. Within moments Bolton could feel the heat of the fire from across the room, but still Raoul didn't move. Finally, Raoul picked up a log from the stack of wood beside the hearth and added it to the fire, then practically flung himself onto the couch with an explosive sigh. Watching him, Bolton recognized the signs that the tantrum had probably been averted.

"So," Raoul said after a few minutes of silence, "what do we do now?" He sat up.

"Well," Bolton said, relieved, "his timing was certainly unfortunate, that's for sure. I think we look into the letter, don't you? He certainly seemed to believe it was important." He paused for a moment, troubled by something. Raoul waited. "Something's bothering me about that letter, you know? I just can't put my finger on it . . ."

"Well," Raoul said slowly, "it's odd that he had it. Why send it to the police and to your paper as well?"

"Publicity?" Bolton suggested.

"Maybe. But then why send it to the police, too? Investigations usually don't make that kind of information available to the papers, do they? And I'll bet it's not as if it's the only piece of mail they've received. Maybe whoever sent it wanted it to be singled out." Bolton hummed to himself, thinking. Raoul continued. "Can you find out if any of the other papers got one? That should tell us if whoever sent it was just looking for publicity—"

"Why me?" Bolton broke in. Raoul looked up, confused. Bolton explained, "I mean, why send it to me at the paper, and not to one of the crime reporters? My column is weekly, not daily, and I've only mentioned Mowatt's death in passing. So why send it to me?"

Raoul spoke quietly. "Maybe because you're my friend?" He stopped. "Gods, that's not too paranoid, is it? Maybe I'm losing my mind," he said.

"Maybe not," Bolton replied. Catching Raoul's look, he amended, "Paranoid, I mean." He chuckled briefly, then continued. "But we won't know anything until we know who sent it. And we can't even start to think about who sent it until we know if it's real or not, if it's true. So that's where I say we start."

"When did what's-his-name die again? The old chancellor."

"Twenty-eight years ago this September."

"Who in the world is going to remember something that happened almost thirty years ago?" He shook his head. "It'll have to be a paper trail, then. Can you get copies of articles about it? Obituaries, things like that?"

"No problem. I'll just have Brenda pull them." Brenda was Bolton's assistant, a pert twenty-two-year-old trying to break into journalism. Bolton had been trying to get her to go out with him for months, but his reputation had preceded him. "I'll even send her off to the library, have her look up everything, not just the Nuisance's stuff. It'll give us a chance to work more closely together." He leered. "Are you dropping the university completely, then?"

"I think I've just about exhausted people there, and I'm not too keen on Barnstone knowing all about what I'm doing. I'd like to spend some time on the magic aspect, if you don't mind. I really want to know if the aural erasure has anything to do with any of this. Can you also keep digging on Mowatt's mystery friend? That may go somewhere as well."

Bolton agreed, and collected his bag from the study before going off to his office.

After he'd gone, Raoul decided he needed a walk to clear his head. On his way out he asked Mrs. Higgins to have a light lunch ready in an hour or so, managing to avoid her unspoken questions by being abrupt. He didn't mean to hurt her, he just didn't feel all that reassuring himself.

During his walk it began to rain lightly, by the time he returned to the house he was drenched and feeling chilled. He decided not to go into Oxford that afternoon to work, and stood dripping in the hall while he called Miriam at his office number.

"I've already been in for about two hours," she told him. "The reports are just printing out now."

"That's great, Miriam," Raoul replied. "How do the results look? Did it work okay?"

"I think so, but I haven't had a chance to go over them yet. And I've got to work on another project this afternoon. Will it be okay if I do it this evening? Or do you want to go over them yourself?"

They decided that it was easiest for Raoul to do the analysis himself, since he had the time at the moment. She said she'd send the printouts over to Thornhold right away. He thanked her and said he'd see her the next afternoon, after Mowatt's funeral.

He stopped in the kitchen to let Mrs. Higgins know he was back and that he'd be staying in all day. He was expecting a delivery soon, he said, and asked her to bring the package up as soon as it arrived. She'd have to unlock the gate when they buzzed to let her know they'd arrived, he mentioned in passing.

"The gate's locked?" she asked, surprised. "Is there something wrong?"

Raoul smiled at her. "No, not really. I just need some privacy today, is all." Noting her concerned look he added,

"Really. It has nothing to do with this morning. You did all you could, short of tackling the man on the stairs." She laughed, blushing, obviously relieved. He thanked her again and went up to change, taking the lunch tray with him.

Although he hadn't yet seen the reports, Raoul was almost positive that he was going to come up against the usual problems with Etruscan, the base language for written and spoken incantations. In addition to the seven runes whose pronunciation was unknown, there were literally hundreds of words whose meanings had been lost. The problem, which he had often pondered, went back to the four centuries after the birth of the first christian cult, centuries marked by conflicts between christian and pagan. Although the final result had been a melding of cultures and the eventual development of magic as a science, getting to that point had resulted in the loss of much of the Etruscan culture and language. A good deal of the information on early Etruscan magic actually came from the early Renaissance, and was therefore suspect. So Raoul knew that to work with early spells, he'd have to be certain they were actually from the Etruscan era, and not medieval recreations based on false information and suppositions. Which meant everything would need to be cross-checked. More time lost.

When the reports arrived forty-five minutes later, he was curled on the study couch, skimming through the English side of the Harvard edition of the Emperor Julian's treatises on magic, looking for references to auras. The translation, he thought, was horrible, but although he could read Greek—given a good dictionary and a large amount of time—he just wasn't in the mood to fight with the original.

He called out for Mrs. Higgins to enter when she knocked, since he'd heard a car pull into the drive moments earlier. She laughed, seeing his jaw drop as she walked in with an armful of papers. She carefully cleared a place for them on the desk, then left him to it. Raoul idly picked up the first page, which was an explanatory note from Miriam.

Prof. Smythe, hope you don't mind I ran this on contin-
uous paper—it's pretty big. Although the spells were fairly
short, they ran about twenty pages because of the runic analysis. The program generated all the possible runic elements in each spell. I ran two copies of each spell—one in
your original runes, and one phonetically in English, to see
if there's anything different there. The phonetic versions ran
almost double the originals. I also included the results on
disk, in case you want to work on-line. I'll be home tonight
if you have any questions. M.

Raoul looked from the stack of pages to his already
crowded desktop and sighed. He moved the reports to the
relative safety of the couch, put Holst's *The Planets* on the
stereo, then got to work.

It took almost an hour, but eventually the desk was clear
but for the computer, the reports—separated into three
piles—a pad for notes, and his battered copies of Liddell
and Scott's *Etruscan-English Lexicon* and the *Oxford Book
of Common Spells* for reference.

Printing out clean copies of the three original spells he'd
used, Raoul glanced through to refamiliarize himself with
them. The first was his "batch" spell, the one he was really
interested in. The other two were the "normal" spells he'd
referenced when creating the newer one. He'd chosen them
originally for their ease of casting, since neither involved
anything more complicated than a pinch or two of incense
and some minor arm-waving. All three spells used standard spell language, which he privately referred to as
"spell-speak"—a combination of meaningless words with
Etruscan pronunciation and actual Etruscan words. It was
accepted by all but the most fanatically religious magicians
that magic wasn't based on actual word meanings, but on
the combination of sounds used to make them. Another private theory of Raoul's was that the sounds had come first
and the meanings after, but there was no way to prove such
an idea. The spoken Etruscan used for spells had almost a
tonal quality to it, which he thought was yet another reason

the language had died out of common use, since a missed
intonation could change an entire spell.

Taking up the first analysis of his batch spell, he looked
at what Miriam had done. The Etruscan rune words of the
spell ran, in order, vertically down the right side. Next to
each were variants of the words, using different combinations of all possible runes.

Every word used had at least two or more variant spellings, and he'd have to look up each one. Raoul noted that
Miriam had also printed out a basic English transliteration
using common spellings and deleting spaces between
words, and then run the program again to see if any new
runic words were created. That had created more printouts—for each of the spelling variants—but luckily for him,
she'd also cross-referenced the programs so that duplicate
combinations for each word were deleted. Still, most of the
words came up with at least one new variant. More things
to look up.

"Whee," Raoul murmured quietly to himself, and began
to combine the files on his hard disk to make working with
them easier.

A touch on his shoulder made him practically leap from
his chair. He spun around to face Mrs. Higgins, who
gasped, startled herself. "What!" Raoul cried, then turned
down the stereo, shook his head and ruffled his hair. "Ever
hear of knocking?"

Mrs. Higgins drew herself up and scowled at him. "Excuse me, Mr. Smythe, but I did knock. About twelve times,
in fact." She looked at the file cabinet, where the telephone
sat, its cord dangling unplugged. Looking back at Raoul,
she continued, "Sir Reginald Whiting's on the line for you.
Shall I tell him you're busy?"

Raoul thought a moment. "No," he said, "I'll talk to
him." He stopped her as she reached for the cord. "No, I
can get it, thanks. I was cleaning in here and—" She turned
and walked for the door, barely turning back when he
called apologetically, "I'm sorry I yelled at you. I guess I
was pretty involved with this program."

After plugging the jack in, he picked up the phone. "Smythe here."

Whiting wasted no time getting to the point. "Good afternoon, Raoul. I just wanted to make sure you're planning to attend the funeral tomorrow. I want the department fully represented, and it might look strange if you in particular weren't there."

Raoul paused a moment before answering. He'd been planning on going, but it was a different thing to be told that he had to. His first instinct was to flatly refuse, but he knew that wasn't a good idea. Not appearing would probably lead to another visit from the charming Detective Inspector Barnstone, a person he hoped to never see at Thornhold again. Or anywhere else, for that matter.

"Smythe?" Whiting's voice broke in. "Are you there?"

"Yes." Raoul realized he probably sounded sullen, but he just wasn't ready to answer yet. Whiting was coming on unusually strong. Probably worried about the blackmail note, Raoul thought, since it only made sense that the police would have already questioned him about it. Idly, Raoul wondered again if the note was real, and if the police had told Whiting that he had seen it. Best not to mention it at all, he thought. Aloud, he repeated, "Yes, I'm here."

"Look, Raoul, I realize I'm telling you what to do, and I apologize. Things are very . . . well, I don't know if you realize how serious this all is. I'm trying to keep things on an even keel, but frankly, it's a scandal, and the university does not need this kind of exposure."

The police have seen him, Raoul thought as Whiting continued.

"So I'd appreciate it if you would attend tomorrow. Will you?"

"Yes. I was planning on it anyway." He paused, then asked, "Is there anything I can . . ." He paused again, unsure of what he was asking.

"No, but thank you," Whiting said, his usual confidence creeping back into his voice. "I'm afraid I may have painted rather too dire a picture. I really believe everything will be resolved soon. Still, it's best for the university that we all come together at a time like this, present a unified front, to use a military metaphor. Especially the Magic faculty; you know there are still people who believe the teaching of magic should have never been separated from religious teaching, and this unfortunate situation could be used as fuel for their fires. And in any case, Arthur headed the college for almost twenty years. No matter what anyone thought of him personally," he said pointedly, "we need to respect that, at least." He continued, again quietly serious, "So I'll see you tomorrow morning. The service, as you know, is at University Temple. The open service begins at ten o'clock sharp. It's a Teutonic druid ceremony, so remember, no cold iron."

"Good-bye, Sir Reginald."

"Until tomorrow, then."

Hanging up the phone, Raoul muttered mockingly, "So, remember, no cold iron . . ." As if he didn't know. It never ceased to amaze him that people constantly assumed that since he wasn't himself religious, he knew nothing about any of them. Whiting, of all people, should know what went into the university training, any university's training, of a practicing magician. Theory, practice, history, and a plethora of religious historical background. Especially for magicians like him, whose specialty was Practical Magic.

But then again, Raoul thought, maybe Whiting wouldn't know that. Offhand, he couldn't recall what Whiting's own area of study had been, but he was fairly certain it hadn't been Magic. The man was an administrator, for crying out loud. And a good one, at that, Raoul mused wryly, recalling how well Whiting worked an audience, even an audience of one. Still, he did obviously care about what happened to the university itself. He jotted down a note about the service's time. He'd call Bolton later to make sure he knew as well, since it was a cinch Bolton would be covering it for the Nuisance. Unplugging the phone again, he turned back to his reports.

Hours later he'd narrowed the spell-word possibilities

down to only six possible variations. It felt as if he'd spent days testing the variants of individual words, sounds, and combinations, but it was well worth it. Looking at the six printouts spread before the keyboard, he smiled. He still needed to narrow the possibilities down to one version, but that would probably be fairly simple at this point, since he figured he'd already found what he was looking for. Miriam's phonetic program had provided the answer when the runes were transliterated into the English alphabet, analyzed, and then translated back into Etruscan runes.

In each of the six variant versions of the batch spell, a letter combination appeared that couldn't be pronounced using the known Etruscan alphabet. Idly, he circled the hole in the runic translations next to the combination on each page. His stomach growled with hunger. Glancing at the on-screen clock, he realized he'd been working all day. Funny that Higgins hadn't checked on him, he thought, then remembered his brusque reception of her earlier interruption. Oh well, he'd make it up to her somehow.

When he entered the kitchen, Higgins glanced at him from the refrigerator, where she stood looking into the icebox. "Good evening," she said, and turned back to her work. "I'm just finishing up. There's a leg of lamb in the oven, and a pie in the freezer for reheating. That should see you through the weekend."

He'd forgotten it was Thursday. Her arrangement, made through his mother, was that she alternated working three and four days each week. It suited both Higgins and Raoul well. Mrs. Higgins usually put up enough food on Wednesdays and Thursdays to carry him through the weekend, and she got to spend quite a bit of time with her sister and her friends.

"That'll be fine, I'm sure. Thanks," he said. When she didn't reply, he went on: "Look, I'm sorry about this afternoon. I didn't mean to upset you. I can't help the way I am." Facing her, he crossed his arms on his chest. "Face it," he said seriously, "I'm just never going to be a nice person."

Relenting, Higgins smiled.

Raoul relaxed, relieved. "So, are you leaving now, or do you want to have dinner here?"

"I promised Marie I'd take her out to dinner tonight. Sorry. But I'm not leaving yet."

Raoul smiled. "Then keep me company while I eat? No, I can do it," he said when she reached for the oven.

He fixed a plate for himself while she sat, listening to him describe the program's results. Talking about it, Raoul felt strangely buoyant, considering he was no farther along than before. He occasionally got into this talkative mood, usually when his work was going well, where he just chattered away. He supposed it was because he spent so much time alone; every once in a while he'd start bouncing off the walls. It balanced his fits of anger, he supposed.

Mrs. Higgins asked a question now and then, but mostly just listened. She'd heard him talk about his work enough to follow him, although she had neither magical ability nor any real interest in it. She knew Raoul well enough, however, to enjoy his good moods when they were upon him.

The buzzer sounded as Raoul finished washing up. "That'll be Marie," Higgins said. When not working, she shared a small cottage in Chipping Norton with her sister. Raoul spelled the gate open while she went to gather her things. As usual, Marie waited in the car. Higgins had once confided to him that Marie, who'd become a christian after the death of her husband, felt uncomfortable with the "dark magician" her sister worked for. Edna, who was more open-minded, was constantly assuring Marie that magic wasn't evil, that her soul wasn't in danger by the association. Over the years, Marie had begun to accept Raoul more, at least conceptually, but she had never actually set foot in Thornhold while he was present.

Once he'd seen Higgins off and relocked the gate, Raoul returned to his research. He needed to isolate the exact wording from the remaining versions of his batch spell, and then see if he could isolate the same occurrence in either of the two "normal" spells. He didn't know what he'd do

if the runic hole didn't appear in the two spells, since anyone who might have magically changed something in
Mowatt's library certainly wouldn't have used a spell Raoul
had created the day of the murder. So he needed to find the
same pronunciation combination in another spell to make
his theory work. If it did, he thought, it was likely he'd discovered a lost rune. The notion that he might have isolated
the sound of one of the lost runes was just incredible. This
could be the break he'd needed to make people realize the
importance of what he was doing.

That thought was immediately followed by the realization that all his work could be lost, or worse, finished by
someone else, if he was arrested. He'd know it had been
his, but be unable to do anything. That was the worst of it.
Raoul sat immobile, his heart pounding as he tried to calm
himself. Rationally, part of him realized he must be having
some kind of a panic attack, but he couldn't think of anything but what it could possibly feel like to live without
magic. He felt frozen, chilled. All his work on the spell,
what would it really prove? Nothing, he thought; not even
whether or not the crime was magical, since Mowatt could
have done it himself and then been killed. Nothing, all for
nothing. What the police needed was a murderer, and all
they had was him and a possible blackmail note. The note,
Raoul realized, could be the answer. Raising clenched fists
to his forehead, he closed his eyes and breathed deeply, trying to quell the tension that set his entire body quivering,
as if he'd had too much caffeine.

"Stop it," he said aloud through clenched teeth, "stop it
now." He sat back, laying his hands flat on the desk, and
exhaled fully. Freaking out was not an option. The police
and Bolton would look into whether or not the note was
real, which would take care of that. He couldn't do anything there. What he could do was work on the magic aspect. If the note was real, then . . . "Whiting?" he said
aloud to himself. "But that makes no sense . . . No. I'm not
going to worry about this now. I'm going to work on this
program, see what turns up. I'm going to isolate what made

the auras disappear. And," he continued aloud, feeling a semblance of self-control return, "I am going to stop talking to myself. Now. Okay."

Raoul decided to make a pot of tea, *de*caffeinated, and work through the night. Part of the problem, he realized, was that his schedule had been upset. He'd lost his routine, gotten either not enough or too much sleep in the past few days. He'd start changing that now, get back to his usual pattern. He'd work through the night, go to the funeral, check in with Miriam and Bolton, and then sleep. He'd be exhausted by then, so he'd need to. And then he'd be back on track.

The next morning at eight, the computer alarm's bleeping startled him. He'd been engrossed in reading a text about the influence of Etruscan and Latin magic on Gallic and Celtic druidry. Turning off the alarm, he spelled the book to open to the same page the next time he picked it up. After phoning for a cab to pick him up at nine-thirty, he began to gather everything he'd need to give Miriam in the afternoon.

With the sheaf of printouts and the updated disk safely stowed in his bag and carefully laid in front of the front door where he couldn't possibly forget it, Raoul began to prepare for the funeral. Freshly showered and shaved, he thought about wearing the moire robe, but decided it would be in bad taste to wear to Mowatt's funeral what he'd had on the night he'd died. Instead, he pulled out the dress robe used for university functions. Basic black, with the red, silver, and blue striped baldric of the College of Magic.

Fully dressed, he checked himself in the mirror, pleased with the results. He changed the gold hoop in his ear for a small silver one which better matched the baldric, and slid a thin solid silver knife into his boot sheath.

A horn sounded from the lane. Throwing a cloak over his shoulder, he carried his bag out to where the car waited. "University Temple, Oxford," he told the driver. On the way there, he remembered that he'd meant to call Bolton.

Oh well, he thought, if he's covering it, he knows where it is and what to wear. I hope.

He arrived early, but was pleased to see he wasn't the first of the nonparticipants. A small knot of people stood to one side of the temple entrance, politely looking away, in deference to the secret ritual within, and speaking in hushed tones. Standing to the side, Raoul looked up at the sky and decided it was a perfect day for a funeral; the sky was gray and overcast, but looked as if it would stay that way and not rain. A slight breeze ruffled the leaves on the trees surrounding the other three sides of the temple. The sacred oak grove of the druids was on the left.

Someone approached him. He recognized the man, but couldn't remember his name or where he'd seen him before. "Hello," Raoul said, hoping the man would introduce himself.

"Hi," he replied. "I'm not sure if you remember me, but Max Bolton introduced us once a few years ago. I'm Phil Lynchfield, from the *News*. Max asked me to give you this. He can't make it today." He handed Raoul a large, thick envelope. Before Raoul could reply, a chime sounded from within the temple, signaling the end of the closed ceremony. Raoul turned and followed the reporter into the temple.

Mowatt had drawn quite a crowd, Raoul thought, looking around from his vantage point on the third lowest row on the left side of the altar. Well over a hundred people had come to the temple, nearly filling it.

He recognized most of the people. Across the temple he spotted Whiting and his wife in the first row, both looking serious. He couldn't find Anne, though he did see a number of university staff, including all of the Magic faculty. Mowatt's secretary, Jean, stood at the back, crying, next to Robert Parker. Raoul thought she looked wretched, then remembered that she'd been ill. He suppressed a sneer when he caught sight of Barnstone lurking at the back of the crowd, then turned his attention to the ceremony, which was about to begin.

Slowly, the druids in their undyed white wool robes filed in from the grove, until they stood in a semi-circle behind the altar. Raoul recognized members of various colleges among the celebrants. The high druid, distinguished by her tall headdress, entered last, and moved to the front of the altar. She stood for a moment facing the grove in silence. Another chime sounded, beginning the ceremony.

Raoul had ample time to reflect during the hour-long ritual. Although not a believer, he appreciated the concepts behind the ceremony. The high druid spoke movingly, though obviously for the crowd's benefit, on the meanings of the various ritual elements. The mistletoe, she explained, holding it aloft on a thin round of polished oak, cut with a silver sickle knife at dawn that morning from one of the vines growing on the sacred oaks, represented their brother, the thread of whose life had been cut. The sheaf of wheat symbolized the breadth of the knowledge he had possessed, and the oak seed the wealth of possibilities open to him in his new life as he was reborn.

The ceremony went smoothly, being as much a welcoming of a "new" member, the reborn Mowatt who was not present at this time, as a farewell to the man everyone had known, whose cremated body was present though his soul had flown to a new housing. At the end of the temple ceremony the druids led the crowd out into the grove. The final ritual, where the ashes of the mistletoe and wheat were mixed with the ashen remains of the man and then planted in the grove, together with the oak seed, was truly beautiful, Raoul thought.

The ceremony over, the funeral-goers moved silently back through the temple. Although he nodded in greeting to Sir Reginald, Raoul avoided speaking to anyone as he left. He felt sobered, but not saddened, by the ceremony. Occasionally when something like a religious ceremony moved him, he keenly felt his own lack of faith in anything. He supposed he was too analytical to really believe in anything he couldn't define.

Miriam wasn't in his office and didn't answer her home

phone, so he left a message that he'd be back in the office in an hour or so, and went to the Hollow Man for a pint and to look through Bolton's envelope.

Raoul settled himself in a corner booth and dug the envelope out of his bag. It was packed with loose papers, mostly photocopies of newspaper articles. Bolton had left a note dated the previous evening.

> Rags, I figure you'll read this in the Hollow Man, since funerals always make you morbid and feeling morbid makes you want to sit in a pub. Have one for me. I've enclosed everything Brenda found about the Montgomery-Lewis case. The papers ate it up, which isn't surprising. The distinguished university man and his lovely young wife, who was a real dish if the photos don't lie. Throw in two young graduate students and a semimysterious death and you've got a newspaper field day. I also included some notes and miscellaneous things from the files. I've sent a copy of all this to our friend Barnstone, since I'm *such* a dutiful citizen. Should win him over, ha ha. The point of all this, by the way, is that I'm off to Scotland to do a little field work at the scene of the crime, as it were. I'll be back in a few days, but I'll call if anything interesting turns up.

An addition at the bottom of the note read, "P.S. Saw your little girlfriend and family at dinner. I told her I was off on a highland fling and asked her to get in touch with you, in case you were lonely. *Hope* you don't mind ..."

"Asshole," Raoul muttered, then laughed quietly. Bolton had never understood that he just wasn't interested in the whole dating concept. Bolton was always pointing out anyone relatively attractive, and had once gone as far as setting up a surprise blind date for him. The woman had been nice enough, but Raoul had spent the entire evening trying to look as if he wouldn't rather be working alone in his study. He'd failed, as had the date. Bolton's attempts to interest him in relationship-hunting had been reduced to gentle ribbing, however, since the night Bolton had dragged him to one of Catherine's parties. They'd been standing in a group of six or seven people, and Bolton had brought up Raoul's reticence to dating.

Suddenly Raoul and his love life had become the subject of the conversation. Questions, stories, and advice followed, until finally someone asked the magic question, "But what about sex?" With everyone's eyes on him, Raoul nonchalantly replied, "Well, I masturbate quite a bit, and do you know, that seems to take care of it." The dead silence had been broken only by Bolton's laughter. Since then the topic had become more of a private joke.

Raoul chuckled quietly to himself, remembering. He really did enjoy Anne's company. Bolton would be thrilled. Someone behind him cleared their throat, and he turned, expecting Edward or Evie. Looking up, he saw Mordechai standing beside the table. Raoul leapt to his feet, upsetting his beer.

"What the fuck are you doing here?" he asked, glaring, quickly stuffing the papers under the envelope. Guinness dripped onto the floor.

Mordechai looked trapped, glancing from Raoul to the spill and back. "Look, I'm sorry ... I ..." Helplessly, he held out his empty hands.

With an undisguised sneer of distaste, Raoul noted that Mordechai's nails were bitten to the quick and the skin of his hands dry to the point of flaking. "Leave," Raoul said firmly, moving out of the booth as Evie approached with a towel.

Mordechai stepped back as Raoul moved toward him. "What?" he asked.

"Leave," Raoul repeated. "Go away. Now." He took another step toward him.

Mordechai stood his ground, though he threw a wild look around the room as if looking for help. "I ... I can't," he stuttered. As Raoul took another step forward, Mordechai threw his hands up as if to ward him off. "I need to talk to you!"

Raoul stopped. He turned to Evie, who'd finished mopping up the spill. "I'll take another, thanks." Evie looked questioningly between him and Mordechai. "Nothing for him. He won't be staying," Raoul said. As Evie walked back toward the bar, he continued, "You need to talk to me? What could you possibly have to talk to me about? Not your little god and his dislike of magic, I hope?" He smiled at Mordechai's warding gesture.

Mordechai looked around the room again and sighed. "I . . ." he began. "Look, can I sit down? It's not what you think. It's important." His eyes looked desperate.

Knowing he'd probably regret it, Raoul relented, sitting back down and gesturing for Mordechai to do the same as Evie arrived with a fresh pint. She looked at Raoul, who nodded. She turned to Mordechai. "Water," he said, "just water, please."

Raoul sipped his drink. "You wanted to talk," he said, "so talk." He waited.

The younger man looked down at the table, idly scratching at the back of one hand. He sighed, then began speaking in a low voice. "This is hard for me. I know we've never gotten along—" Raoul snorted. Mordechai continued, "You've got to understand, it was never you personally, it was just that I was raised to think people like you were, well, wrong." He looked up at Raoul. "I'm sorry." He turned his eyes back down to the table.

Raoul waited a moment, then asked, confused, "That's it? 'I'm sorry?' That's what all this is about? Excuse me, but—"

"No," Mordechai interrupted, "that's not it. There's more." He took a deep breath. "My father died last year, you see. My mother died when I was at school. When we were at school." He paused, waiting for a response.

Raoul was uncomfortable. "Sorry," he said, "I didn't know that." He wondered where this was leading.

"It's okay. I kept it quiet at the time. So, anyway, my father really raised me. He was pretty strict. Our sect doesn't believe in a lot of socializing outside. Anyway, that's not important. I'm sorry, I'm probably not making a lot of sense. So he died last year. It was really sudden. Heart attack. I was at work, the hospital called me." He stopped and sipped at the water Evie had brought, then scratched at the back of his neck. "After the funeral, I had to go through his things, sort stuff out. There was a letter for me, sealed, with the will. It—" He paused, then brought it out in a rush, "—it said I was adopted."

Oh gods, we're related, Raoul thought, but managed to remain silent.

"It said my real parents hadn't wanted me. I guess my parents, I mean my parents who adopted me, had tried and prayed to have a child, but God hadn't given them one. So they petitioned the Elders to let them adopt a child. That was me. I was adopted."

"And?" Raoul prompted, still not seeing where this was leading. He'd never really wondered about his own unknown father—he had enough problems with the parent he had—but he didn't want to be related to Mordechai.

"And that was it, then. I threw myself into the sect, as you probably know. That was when I started going after . . . well, after people like you."

"Magicians?" Raoul prompted again. Gods, the man couldn't even say the word! "Go on."

"So anyway, everything was fine then, until—" He drank again, swallowing noisily. "—until about six months ago. I was serving as acolyte one Sunday, and I lowered my head to pray before lighting one of the altar candles. I guess I was thinking about lighting it. When I raised my head, it was lit. I didn't know what to do, I didn't know if anyone else had seen, so I just went on. After the service, though, the priest-celebrant called me aside. He asked if I'd noticed anything odd when the candles were lit. I had to tell him what had happened."

Raoul nodded. Sometimes spontaneous acts of magic occurred as the ability developed, usually around puberty. Apparently Mordechai was a late bloomer as far as magic went. He really, really didn't want to be related to Mordechai. Raoul sighed.

"I'm sorry, I'm really taking a long time to tell this, aren't I?" Mordechai looked embarrassed, then pushed on. "So he talked to the Elders about it, and they sent me out for tests. I can do magic." He stopped, looking directly at Raoul.

"So, what does this have to do with me?" Raoul asked, dreading the answer.

"I went back and looked up my adoption records. I went to the hospital and talked to people. I found out who my birth parents were. The magic comes from my birth father."

Raoul repeated his last question. "Mordechai, get to the point. What does this have to do with me?" Here it comes, he thought. Damn fathers, anyway!

"I need you to help me get rid of it."

"What?" Thank the gods, they weren't related! "Get rid of what?" Raoul tried not to sound relieved.

"The magic. I've already tried. I've been exorcised. I've taken holy waters at six different shrines around the world. I've fasted, I've purged, I've abased my flesh, I've prayed. Oh God, how I've prayed! And nothing has worked. It's been six months, and I've tried everything, but nothing has worked. You've got to help me. You've just got to."

"Let me get this straight. You want me to help you get rid of your magical ability. Why?"

"Because you're magic yourself. You know how, or you must know someone who does. I've got to get rid of it. It's bad, it's evil. If you only knew . . ."

Raoul sighed again, boggled by this young idiot's problem. He knew scads of people who would kill to have any ability at all. "Frankly, Mordechai, why don't you just keep it? It can come in handy sometimes."

"The Church," Mordechai whispered. "They won't let me stay if I don't."

"What?"

"The Elders. They told me I'd have to leave if I can't rid myself of the taint. You don't understand! The Church is my life! It's all I have left now." His voice was ragged. "Can't you help me? Can you? Please? You're the only one left . . . I mean, the only . . . magician . . . I know."

Suddenly, Raoul felt for him. He imagined what it would feel like if he himself had to walk into, say, Hagia Sophia and ask the pope for help. He must be at the end of his rope to even talk to me, he thought. He took a deep breath. "Okay," he said. Mordechai's face lit up. Raoul held up a hand. "Okay, I'll try to help. I'll get you some information. And that's it. Do you understand?" He felt tired, drained.

Mordechai was ebullient in his thanks. Raoul took down a phone number where he could reach him, and told Mordechai he'd call when he found something out. Mordechai was to ask the Elders exactly what they needed to allow him to return to the fold, and to let him know when he called. Wanting to cut the encounter short, Raoul stood. "Look, I've got to go. I'll call when I've found something out." He left money for the beer, refusing Mordechai's offer to pay, and left.

Walking back to his office, he was troubled by the problem. He thought he knew exactly what Mordechai was looking for; it was what happened to magicians who were convicted of capital offenses, such as, oh, say murder. To have one's ability blocked, completely and irretrievably. Raoul wasn't even sure he remembered how it was done, though, or who actually performed the "operation." It was something one learned about briefly in ethics classes, but something most magicians didn't like to talk, or even think, about. He'd need to do some reading on it, distasteful as it might be. And who knew, he thought bitterly, it might even come in handy for himself, if things didn't work out.

The conversation with Mordechai had taken more time than he'd wanted to spare. Miriam was still out when he returned to his office, so he left a message asking if her new phonetic program could handle scanning for a particular set of letters or sounds in a variety of spells. He wanted to check all the spells in his computer spellbook, as well as a number of older, classic spells. He told her he'd leave a

copy of his notes in the office for her, and that she could
call him at Thornhold if she had questions. Otherwise, he'd
talk to her sometime tomorrow.

Raoul debated reviewing the articles Bolton had given
him, but decided that his concentration was far from what
it could be at the moment. Maybe he'd do better at
Thornhold.

Chapter 7

FATAL HEART ATTACK CLAIMS VACATIONING SCHOLAR, the first article proclaimed. He checked the paper's date: August 12, 1968. He glanced quickly through the rest of the articles, the tone of which appeared to be split evenly between straightforward and sensational, then sorted the articles chronologically. He'd save the notes and miscellaneous pieces for later.

Turning on the computer, he created a file and took notes as he read the first of the articles, dated the day after the accident. The story seemed fairly simple: On the morning of Saturday, August 10, 1968, fifty-five-year-old George Montgomery-Lewis died of a heart attack while boating on Loch Tay in Scotland. He'd been vacationing in the nearby town of Killin with his wife and two friends, both of whom were also employed by Oxford. The inquest was to be held the following Wednesday, before the body was returned to Oxford for burial.

The other article from the same date added only the names of Montgomery-Lewis' wife, Jeanine, and his two companions, Arthur Mowatt and Reginald Whiting, and also mentioned that the party was staying at a guest house on the loch owned by Mrs. Duncan O'Connor of Killin.

As Raoul worked through the stack, more details emerged. Montgomery-Lewis had apparently been married for three years at the time of his death. Prior to that, his wife, the former Jeanine Arbuthnot, had been his personal secretary. At the time of his death, the couple had no children. According to a statement made by Mrs. O'Connor,

Montgomery-Lewis had been coming to the same place for a two-week holiday every year for more than ten years. Though his two young friends, Mowatt and Whiting, had been joining him for perhaps four years, this had been the first time Mrs. Montgomery-Lewis accompanied her husband. Montgomery-Lewis had apparently been quite an avid fisherman, spending much of each day fishing on the loch, often accompanied by one or both of his friends. Mrs. Montgomery-Lewis did not fish.

Despite the sometimes lurid headlines, Raoul found no indication that anyone considered Montgomery-Lewis' death anything more than an unfortunate accident. The brief mentions of the inquest indicated that there had been no sign of foul play. One of the papers, however, managed to subtly hint at some undefined impropriety in the fact that Montgomery-Lewis' two friends and his wife were all much younger than Montgomery-Lewis himself. Raoul paused in his reading to dig out his notes about Mowatt. He'd been fifty-seven at the time of his death, which meant that he'd have been about thirty in 1968. Raoul wasn't sure if Mowatt and Whiting were the same age, but he imagined Whiting to be in his early fifties. He jotted down a note to remind himself to find out exactly how old Whiting and Montgomery-Lewis' wife were, and if the wife was still alive.

Returning to the articles, Raoul couldn't help smiling at the stereotype of the middle-aged academic falling for the young secretary. His smirk grew into a snort of amusement when the next article provided him with an answer to the age question. Mrs. Montgomery-Lewis was only twenty-six at the time of her husband's death, his friends Mowatt and Whiting thirty and twenty-eight, respectively. The piece went on to explain that both men had been students of Montgomery-Lewis during his tenure as headmaster of Whitethorne Academy, a prestigious school for boys. Mowatt, in fact, had recently been hired by Oxford as a Magic tutor from a teaching position at Whitethorne. Whiting, who apparently was not employed by Oxford, despite what some of the articles reported, was pursuing graduate studies in both history and business. Both young men were deeply upset by the death of their friend and mentor, the reports stated. An obituary from the Oxford University paper mentioned that Whiting had delivered one of the more moving addresses at the graveside ceremony.

The articles gradually died out over a period of two weeks or so. Next in the pile was a large envelope filled with photographs of those involved. The first was a picture taken at the time of Montgomery-Lewis' withdrawal from Whitethorne Academy. The caption pointed out Montgomery-Lewis to one side, and someone had circled two faces in the crowd of students, apparently Whiting and Mowatt. Squinting, Raoul couldn't see more than a passing resemblance to the men he knew, partly due to the grainy texture of the photo itself and partly to their extreme youth. A series of newspaper photos of Montgomery-Lewis at various university functions followed, spanning a number of years. Mowatt and Whiting appeared in some of the later photos. Sandwiched in among the newspaper photos was a color snapshot from Montgomery-Lewis' wedding. Jeanine Arbuthnot Montgomery-Lewis was indeed lovely, Raoul thought, though her white suit and high bouffant hairdo looked dated. She had one of those faces that always seem familiar. Idly, Raoul wondered where Bolton had found the photograph.

Under the envelope of photos, Raoul found a stack of what he assumed to be notes from the *News'* files. For the most part they merely confirmed the information from the various articles, but one piece in particular piqued his interest. It was a photocopy of Montgomery-Lewis' death certificate, which stated that the cause of death had been drowning as a result of falling out of the boat during a heart attack. None of the papers had mentioned anything but the heart attack itself. Raoul wondered why not, then turned to the last item in Bolton's pile of information.

The large envelope was sealed, and had a penciled note from Bolton on the front. "R: I (obviously) didn't give

Barnstone a copy of *this* bit. B." Intrigued, Raoul carefully opened the envelope, which contained a manila folder. Inside were photocopies of Scottish police reports concerning Montgomery-Lewis' death. Raoul shook his head, not even wanting to wonder how Bolton had managed to get them.

A single page summarized the facts of the case, followed by five transcribed statements, from Mrs. Montgomery-Lewis, Whiting, Mowatt, Mrs. O'Connor, and Mr. Dhugal Armstrong. Raoul didn't recognize the last name, but he curbed his interest and began with the summary.

The vacationing party, that is, the Montgomery-Lewises and their two guests, had all breakfasted together at eleven o'clock at Mrs. O'Connor's. Though the guest cottage in which they were all staying was equipped with both kitchen and dining room, traditionally Montgomery-Lewis asked that meals be cooked and served by Mrs. O'Connor in the main lodge. At around noon the party split up, Arthur Mowatt hiking off to look for a rumored standing stone, and the other three returning to the guest cottage. At approximately one o'clock Montgomery-Lewis left to go fishing, stating that he would return in time for tea, which was generally served at four-thirty. Whiting declined his offer to accompany him, preferring instead to do some reading. Mrs. Montgomery-Lewis also stayed behind to read and catch up on her correspondence.

At approximately four o'clock Dhugal Armstrong of Killin was returning across the loch, having spent an hour or so fishing, when he heard someone shouting. A man was running along the shore, pointing to Montgomery-Lewis' boat in the middle of the loch. Armstrong turned and saw that Montgomery-Lewis' boat was empty. He'd seen him earlier on his way across the loch, and they'd exchanged shouted pleasantries. Armstrong rowed his boat closer, and at that time saw the deceased floating, facedown, about five feet from the boat. Armstrong pulled him into his own boat and rowed toward the landing nearest Mrs. O'Connor's, while the man on shore, later identified as Mowatt, waded out to help beach the boat.

After landing the boat, Armstrong, on Mowatt's suggestion, went to the main cottage to telephone for help. After approximately ten minutes he returned to the landing, with Mrs. O'Connor, to find Mowatt trying to resuscitate Montgomery-Lewis, and also to find Mrs. Montgomery-Lewis, who had arrived and fainted and was being revived by Whiting.

The ambulance, accompanied by the police, arrived at 4:36 and pronounced the victim dead at the scene. The body was taken to the local doctor's for examination. Statements were taken from Mrs. Montgomery-Lewis, Whiting, Mowatt, Armstrong, and Mrs. O'Connor.

The notes ended there. Raoul had just settled himself with his feet on the desk to read through the statements when the phone rang. He almost fell out of the chair reaching for the phone, and was trying not to laugh as he answered. "Smythe," he snorted, thinking it was probably Bolton.

"Uh, hi. This is Anne Whiting. Raoul?"

"Oh. Hi." He paused, pleased to hear from her, but with absolutely no idea of what to say. "So, hi," he repeated. Snappy, he thought, really snappy dialogue.

"Is this a bad time to call? You sound kind of strange."

"No, it's fine. It's just that I almost flipped my chair over getting to the phone and—"

"Oh. Well, I was just calling to say hello and see how you were doing. I saw Max last night."

Max? Raoul thought. Who the hell was ... oh, right. Bolton. "Right, he mentioned that."

"Really? I thought he was leaving for vacation."

"Well, he is, I mean he did. He dropped me a note."

"Oh," she said, "that was nice of him." This time she paused. "So, what are you up to?"

"Me? Oh, I was just doing some reading. Nothing much." He didn't want to mention that he was researching her father's past. Best to just change the subject. "How about you?"

"Oh, not too much. Just doing some research for work,

plus a few meetings. Pretty boring, really." Another silence. "So, anyway, would you like to get together sometime again? I enjoyed talking to you last time. Even if," she laughed nervously, "no police officers showed up."

Raoul smiled. "Well, nothing's perfect, you know. And anyway, they were detectives. Sure, I'd like that." He plunged ahead, "How about tonight?"

She was quiet for a moment, and sounded confused when she answered. "I can't. I'm in Manchester. Didn't Max tell you I was going off on a business trip?"

"No, he didn't. When did you leave?" She was calling from Manchester, just to chat? Idiotically, he realized he was smiling.

"Last night, after dinner."

"Ah. Well, I guess tonight really isn't good, then, is it?"

"No. But I'll be back in town tomorrow afternoon, so we could get together then. That is, if you'd like."

He thought a moment. He'd have to be in his office anyway, despite the fact that it would be Saturday, to see Miriam and do a few things. "No, that's fine. Do you want to meet me at my office?"

"Sure. What time's good for you?"

"Whenever you'd like. After five?"

"Perfect. Five-thirty?"

"Sure." More silence. Sometimes he hated phones, Raoul thought.

"Okay, so I'll see you then."

"Okay."

"Well, 'bye."

" 'Bye. Thanks for calling, Anne. I'll see you later." Feeling foolish, Raoul hung up the phone. She'd called him. He pulled a wry face, thinking she'd probably only done it because of Bolton's prompting, but part of him was deeply pleased. He wanted to reflect on what a good listener she was, how easy it seemed for them to talk to each other, but his mind kept returning to how soft her hair looked, and the quizzical tilt of her head that made his palms itch to cup her face in his hands. "Oh, shit." He spoke aloud, drawing the words out. "I don't need this, not now, not her."

Although he'd never mentioned it to Bolton, or anyone else for that matter, he wasn't as asexual as he pretended. Not always, at least. It was true that most of the time he was simply too involved with, and intrigued by, his magic, to want anything else. Nor did he lack for friendship or companionship, what with Bolton always around, and his friends at the Hollow Man and the Seller. He'd never felt lonely, rather the opposite; no matter how much he enjoyed his friends, there were always times when he would have preferred to be by himself.

But still, every once in a while someone—never anyone he was close to—would writhe their way into his subconscious. He'd be working on something, or reading, or just ruminating, and suddenly he'd be thinking about someone. Mostly they'd been students or people he'd seen at a club. Never anyone he knew, never anyone close. He shuddered, remembering the feeling of helplessness, of being held in the grip of his own thoughts, that the waking fantasies brought. At least it was usually only momentary, leaving only a sour taste in his mind and a lingering erection that he refused to do anything about.

He'd lied to Bolton at the party a few years ago when he said he masturbated as release. By then he'd given up on it, preferring the discomfort to the realization that he was only treating a symptom. Not that there was anything wrong with it; it just didn't seem to resolve anything. He remembered only too well the empty, frustrated feeling that remained even after physical desire had been satisfied. "Shit," he repeated, shaking off his thoughts. He'd just have to deal with this. Anne wasn't crush material, she was a friend. Or rather, she could be, once they'd gotten to know each other better. He wasn't looking for anything more. Sighing, he picked up the statements again.

Reading through Armstrong's and O'Connor's versions of their involvement, Raoul found nothing that hadn't been previously covered by either the articles or the police notes.

The other three statements, however, contained details that were completely new to him.

He'd known that the four companions had split up just after noon, and that Mowatt had gone off alone while the other three returned to the cottage. Mowatt stated that he'd heard in town of a standing stone in an old grove, only three or four miles away, and had gotten directions to the site. He'd set off immediately after lunch, stopping once to ask directions of a farmer working near the road. A penciled note on the side of the statement indicated that a Robert Aulay had confirmed that he'd been questioned by Mowatt at about one o'clock. Mowatt had reached the site, taken a few photographs, then returned to the guest house just before four o'clock. No one else was in the cottage at that time, so he went down to the lake to see if they were perhaps boating.

He'd reached the shore in time to see Montgomery-Lewis fall from the boat. He'd watched for a moment, confused, before realizing something was wrong, that Montgomery-Lewis wasn't getting back in the boat or swimming. Looking around for help, he spotted Armstrong's boat farther up the lake and ran along the shore toward it, shouting and trying to get his attention. Whiting and Mrs. Montgomery-Lewis appeared within five minutes of the body being brought to shore. The rest of the statement was the same as in the notes.

Whiting and Mrs. Montgomery-Lewis' statements mirrored each other. Having stayed behind when Montgomery-Lewis went off to fish, Mrs. Montgomery-Lewis decided at approximately three o'clock to go for a walk on the shore, and Whiting said he'd accompany her. They had turned around and were nearing the guest house when they heard shouting. They ran toward the landing, reaching the boat while Mowatt was trying to revive the deceased. When she realized what was happening, Mrs. Montgomery-Lewis fainted.

Raoul finished putting the information from the statements into his notes, then reread what he'd written. He didn't see anything suspicious. The timing of Mowatt's return seemed somewhat fortuitous, but that had been corroborated by the farmer's statement, and the distances worked with the times given. It seemed fairly straightforward, although Bolton obviously thought it warranted further checking. Oh, well, Raoul thought as he stood and stretched, Bolton would call soon enough.

He checked the time on the computer; it was nearly three o'clock. Since he couldn't call Miriam until morning, he decided to do more reading on the lost runes. Checking the library, he found he had at least four books on the subject, with topics ranging from pure magic to history to linguistics. He picked out the two that looked most interesting and brought them downstairs. He built up a fire in the living room while waiting for the kettle to boil.

Hours later, as the taxi sped toward Oxford, Raoul was still musing on what he'd read that morning: Gervase Martin's *Etruscan Language and Magic*, a study of the linguistic development of magic. The subject was fascinating; the Etruscan pronunciation system was unlike any other, because the spoken language itself was so intimately tied to magic.

Martin's theory was that Etruscan was the first known runic language, and that it had gradually spread to other magic-using cultures, evolving as it traveled. According to this theory, Gallic, Teutonic, and Norse runes, as well as the Celtic ogam system, all descended from Etruscan writing, having been assimilated into those cultures as they came into contact with the sea-faring Etruscans. It made sense; in each of the rune-using cultures mentioned, magic had nothing to do with the spoken language, but rather with a runic alphabet that had no relation to the spoken language alphabet. Raoul agreed with much of what Martin thought, but was particularly interested in what the book proposed about the so-called "lost runes."

The seven "lost runes," Martin theorized, were not just runic symbols whose pronunciation had been lost. They stopped appearing in public inscriptions after the second century BCE, and from private spellbooks by the first century CE. Martin was certain they were still known at that time, however, since at least five of the runes appeared in spellbooks written during the reign of the Roman mage-emperor Julian in the third century.

Martin posited that the last known use of the runes was in the early ninth century, during the first Great Alliance against Charles the Great. However, no documentation existed for such a theory; contemporary references stated only that "hidden knowledge" and "secret power" of the Etruscans were employed by the magicians of the Lombard court. Martin theorized that the seven runes were somehow more powerful than the others, and that knowledge of their use had been limited only to a select few. Unfortunately, during the dark ages with its plagues and resulting witch hunts, much had been lost, including the pronunciation of the runes.

"Excuse me, sir, but we've arrived." The cabbie's voice jolted Raoul out of his thoughts. Distracted, he handed the cabbie a handful of bills and left the car. He walked toward Whiting's office, his eyes unfocused as he continued ruminating on the connections between the lost runes and the aural erasure spell. The final test would be to try out entire spells containing the runes, using the new pronunciation.

The door of Whiting's office was open. Raoul walked in, surprising Robert Parker, who spun around at the sound of the door opening. The two men stared at each other silently for a moment, Raoul with his hand still on the doorknob and Parker with a file clutched in one hand.

Parker broke the silence. "Raoul! You surprised me! Come on in. Sir Reginald's not here, I'm afraid, if you're looking for him. Can I help you with anything?"

In fact, Raoul was relieved that Whiting wasn't in, since he didn't want to explain why he needed a list of the still-living professors who'd been at Oxford during Montgomery-Lewis' tenure. He didn't want to explain it to Parker, either. "Thanks, Bob," he replied, closing the door behind him and perching on the arm of Parker's guest chair. "Looks like you're keeping pretty busy."

Parker leaned back over the open file drawer and replaced the file he'd been holding. "What, this?" he asked. "It's been absolutely insane around here, so I needed to catch up on the paperwork. We've gotten a temp in to cover for Jean while she's out sick, but frankly," he lowered his voice, "He's just not working out all that well. So I've really been doing two jobs." He shook his head. "So anyway, what are *you* doing here on a Saturday?"

"Me?" Raoul wasn't about to tell Parker that he and Bolton were investigating on their own, but he couldn't lie, either. Not outright, anyway. Damn ethics, he thought. "Well," he began, "I've come up against something weird in my research." That much at least was true. He rushed on, hoping Parker wouldn't think about it too much. "And I need to consult with some old staff members. I was wondering if I could get addresses or phone numbers, and I figured you might be able to help."

Parker appeared unsure. "I don't know . . ."

"Look," Raoul said, "I don't want you to go to any trouble. If you can give me a cross-college list, I'll even narrow it down myself." He paused. "This is possible, right?"

"Well . . ."

Raoul moved around the desk to look at Parker's computer. "You know," he mused aloud, "I bet you could do it, if you can do a search by multiple variables. You've got access to the personnel database, right?"

"Of course," Parker bridled. "I can access almost every system from here. What do you mean 'search by multiple variables'?"

"Let me show you."

Five minutes later Raoul walked out of the office with the list in hand. "Hey," Parker called after him, "thanks for showing me how to do that. It'll come in handy."

Raoul smiled. "No problem at all. My pleasure."

As he walked, glancing at the list, a name caught his eye:

Robert Marlowe. Marlowe had retired as Senior Professor of Magical History just a year after Raoul was hired, and had been replaced by Lloyd Llewellyn-Jones. When Raoul was a student, he'd always gotten along with Marlowe, and had enjoyed knowing him as a colleague as well. Himself a bit of a radical, Marlowe had always been a supporter of Raoul's ideas. According to the address on the list, Marlowe lived in Headington, the same suburb as Mowatt, though Raoul didn't recognize the street name. He tried the number from his office and was pleasantly surprised when Marlowe not only was home, but recognized his name immediately. He said he'd love for Raoul to stop by and chat, and gave directions. Marlowe lived only about a mile and a half from the College of Magic buildings; he was sure of the distance, he said, because the doctors had advised him to walk for exercise and he'd gotten one of those walking meters that recorded how far he went and how many calories he burned. He would have continued chatting away, but Raoul gently broke off the conversation, saying he'd walk right over.

On the way to Marlowe's, he ruefully realized he'd only seen the man a few times in the years since his retirement, mostly at official functions. Marlowe had been at least in his late sixties when he'd retired, which would make him seventy or so now. The personnel listing had stated that Marlowe was hired as a full professor in 1963. Both Mowatt and Whiting would have been working on their graduate degrees then, although Whiting had been in a different college. It was odd, Raoul thought, how Marlowe had possibly taught Mowatt, had had seniority over him, but hadn't been chosen to run the department when the previous chair retired. He'd have made a great chair, Raoul thought.

Marlowe lived in one of the faux Edwardian blocks of flat complexes that had sprung up in recent years, blocks that somehow managed to look attractive and artificial at the same time. A sign in front announced it as HIGHBRIDGE CLOSE. The building was surrounded by a well-kept lawn,

bordered with late flowers. Two or three people were working in the flower beds as Raoul walked up the pathway to
the door. Noting their age, Raoul idly wondered if this was
some kind of retirement community. It seemed very quiet.

Entering the front door, he pressed the button marked
R. MARLOWE and waited. The door unlocked with a buzz,
and he entered. Marlowe had directed him to turn left outside the elevator on the third floor; his flat was number 313. Raoul found the correct door and knocked rather
than pressing the buzzer. After a few moments the door
opened and he was shown in by a smiling Marlowe.

The first thing Raoul noticed was the almost overpowering odor of incense. It was strong enough that he couldn't
identify the exact scent. He swallowed and blinked, slowly
adjusting to it as Marlowe greeted him and gave him a
quick tour of his rooms. The four-room apartment was a
jumble of mismatched furniture and bookcases filled to
overflowing. One small room held a candlelit shrine to
Vanth, the Etruscan goddess of Death, incense burners, a
number of spirit masks hanging on the walls, and a single
tatami mat on the floor before the altar. A screen door off
the main room led to a balcony overlooking a small courtyard. Raoul noted with a smile that nearly every flat surface
held at least one book, slips of paper sticking out as page
markers. Settling into a comfortably overstuffed chair, he
listened to the play of water in the courtyard fountain while
Marlowe made tea.

"Quite an uproar these days at the university, I imagine,"
Marlowe said as he returned with cups and a pot. "I saw
you at the funeral yesterday. Pity poor Mowatt dying so
young. I hear there's an investigation going on. Have you
heard what the police think yet?"

"There's nothing definite, but they're leaning toward
murder, rather than it just having been a break-in. I know
they've got a few suspects in mind." Raoul grimaced.

Marlowe chuckled. "You, I presume? Who else?"

"Sir Reginald, I think. And possibly someone else who

has yet to be identified. Excuse me, Professor, but you don't seem all that surprised."

Marlowe leaned forward. "Frankly, Raoul, I'm not. Arthur Mowatt was a man who made enemies easily, held grudges, and could be a real bastard when he chose to. So I'm not surprised if someone killed him. But—" he held up a hand, stopping Raoul. "—he was also a brilliant researcher, and a friend. I don't like to blind myself by having a one-sided view of people. All in all, I'd say, he was a good man. Not very outgoing, you understand, and, well, stern. But you knew him as well. You said Whiting was also a suspect? As well as you . . ." He paused for a moment to pour out two cups of tea. "Now, I don't mean any offense by this, but indulge an old man for a moment. Did you kill him?"

Raoul was startled. "No," he said. Marlowe held up his hand again, cutting off the rest of Raoul's explanation.

"Good," he said, leaning back with his tea. "You've always been honest. So then why come to see me? Or is this merely a social call?" He waited, the corners of his eyes crinkling into a multitude of lines as a small smile played on his lips.

Raoul smiled, recalling how much he'd always liked this man, more familiar to him as a teacher than as a colleague. He'd taken several semesters with Marlowe over the years, and had always respected the man's crusty bluntness, as well as his encyclopedic knowledge of magical history. "Well, Professor," he began, "I don't know if you've heard, but I've been suspended from teaching until this is over, since I'm a suspect." Try as he might, he couldn't help the bitter note in his voice. "So I'm looking into it myself for a number of reasons, now that I have all this free time."

Marlowe nodded, waiting for him to continue.

"As I said, I believe Whiting is now a suspect. I'm not free to say exactly for what reason, but I think it has something to do with the death of George Montgomery-Lewis. I thought I'd talk to you first, because you were here at the time of his death, along with Mowatt and Sir Reginald. You knew them all."

"George Montgomery-Lewis? Hmmm," Marlowe mused. "That's thirty years ago, son, a long time to remember. Nineteen . . . sixty-eight he died, if I'm not mistaken, wasn't it?"

Raoul smiled. "Yes. Late summer, August." Marlowe's memory for dates was as sharp as ever, he thought.

"Right. He'd gone on vacation with Jeanine and Arthur and Reg." Catching Raoul's look, Marlowe explained, "Reg. Reginald Whiting. Now, Jeanine, there was a lovely, lovely girl. Shocked the whole school when he married her, George did. People started calling him 'Mr. Chips' behind his back, that kind of thing." He chuckled, then glanced at Raoul, who looked puzzled. "Mr. Chips," he said. "You know, *Goodbye, Mr. Chips*, the novel? James Hilton. Huge bestseller when I was a boy. Also a movie with Ronald Colman. Lovely, sweet story."

"*Goodbye, Mr. Chips?* I thought Peter O'Toole was in that."

Marlowe rolled his eyes to the ceiling and sighed, laughing. "In any case," he continued, "George hated knowing that people were joking about the May-December aspect of it all. He was dreadfully sensitive about decorum. Used to always chide me about this," he mused, rubbing his long beard. He fell silent for a moment. "Arthur had just been hired as a tutor back then, you know," he continued. "He'd been a student of mine, and then taught for a year at his old school before coming back. Probably trying to follow in George's footsteps.

"He and Reg were what I suppose you'd call pets of George's. He'd taught them, and brought them to Oxford, and took a great interest in them. And they, of course, were the best of friends. Reg pretty much did everything Arthur did. I remember being somewhat surprised that Reg was reading history for his doctorate and not magic, but then again, he never did have a lot of use for magic."

Raoul had to interrupt. "You mean, Whiting followed Mowatt's lead? That's a bit odd, wouldn't you think? Whiting has always seemed so much more—" He paused, searching for the right word. "—dynamic."

"It's not really that odd. When I first met them, Arthur was the 'dynamic' one. Reginald seemed a bit of a tag-along. After all, Arthur was the elder, more 'experienced' one, if you will. Reg didn't quite come into his own until after George died. I don't think Reg knew what he wanted to do until then; he always seemed to do whatever George or Arthur thought was right. George's death seemed to shock him into thinking for himself. Before that he always struck me as rather aimlessly ambitious."

"What about the wife?"

"Whiting's wife? He didn't marry her until after he'd begun teaching at the university. Well-connected girl, Lesley." Noting the shake of Raoul's head, he corrected himself. "Oh, you meant Jeanine. What about her?"

"Well, how did she fit into Montgomery-Lewis' friendship with Whiting and Mowatt? Do you remember how they felt about her?"

"Now, you've got to remember that I wasn't a part of their group. I knew them all, of course, but I probably knew Arthur the best, since he'd been a student and was actually tutoring for some of my classes. A teaching assistant, you'd call him now, only back then they couldn't really teach until after they'd gotten their degrees. A much better system, now, when you think about it. But I digress. Jeanine . . . Jeanine I knew from the year she'd spent as George's secretary. So you really shouldn't place too much emphasis on my personal opinion, especially after thirty years."

"I understand. What are you leading up to?"

Marlowe smiled. "Good boy. Well, the long and the short of it is that I always rather thought Arthur was in love with Jeanine."

"In love with? They were having an affair?" That would certainly change the color of things, Raoul thought. He still couldn't picture a young Mowatt, much less one young and in love.

"Heavens, no! As I said, it's only my perception at work here. No, I think he worshiped her from afar, as it were. He spent much of his free time with her, when George was away, talking and taking her places. George encouraged it, since he didn't really enjoy doing what he called 'young things,' but wanted her to do whatever she wanted. Of course, Reginald was there, as well, so it wasn't as if the two of them were alone."

"I wonder how she felt about Mowatt?"

"Well, she never seemed to favor one more than the other, except George, of course. I think that because he loved Arthur and Reg, she loved them, too. I think he thought of them as his sons, and they were more than willing to see him as a father figure. So she probably functioned, unknowingly, as a kind of mother-playmate for them. And I think Arthur was desperately besotted with her, for those same reasons, with never a thought of actually doing anything about it. It seems a bit strange now, but at the time it seemed perfectly natural. Then again, I was much older than the three of them, so I may just be patronizing in retrospect." He smiled.

"What about Whiting?" Raoul asked, wishing he'd either been taking notes or had thought to put himself into the mnemonic recall spell. "Was he in love with her as well?"

Marlowe thought a moment before replying. "No . . ." he said slowly, then repeated himself more firmly, "No. I wish I could recall something specific about why I think that, but I can't. There was a difference in how they treated each other, but I can't even say what it was. Perhaps it was just a feeling I had." He shrugged.

"What happened after Montgomery-Lewis died? Do you remember what people thought about it? What was said?"

Marlowe refreshed their tea. "After George died? Everyone was shocked, of course. So unexpected, and it happened right before the term began, so it really was the major topic of conversation. Absolutely everyone was talking about it.

But, rumors? It all seemed so straightforward, it wasn't gossip in the usual sense. It was just something that was spoken about often. Of course, some of the more prurient types were waiting with bated breath for Arthur or Reg to take up with Jeanine, but they were sorely disappointed."

"I don't understand. What happened?"

"Why, she left England altogether, I believe. From what I recall, she was just crushed by George's death, and as soon as his affairs were settled, she left for the Continent. I never heard where. Arthur never mentioned her afterward, to my knowledge. I think it was hard on both of them."

"Mowatt and Jeanine?"

"Arthur and Reginald. As I said, Reg threw himself into his work as a result, finally settled down with a goal. Arthur did the same, but not with such spectacular results." Again he caught Raoul's look and explained. "Reg got his final degrees early, about a year after George died. He then took a position in the history department—assistant professor, I think. Skipped right over tutoring. And then within ten years he was chancellor of the entire university. Fastest rise through the ranks in Oxford history."

"I hadn't realized that," Raoul said, surprised. It was quite a feat.

"I always thought Arthur was a bit jealous, you know. After all, he'd only been hired as a tutor, and though he eventually did chair the department, it took until, oh, let me think . . . 1979." He nodded, "Yes, that was it. It was after Reg became chancellor, I remember. I think that had something to do with it as well, which had to have rankled Arthur even more."

"But they're still—I mean, they were still friends, even then?" Raoul asked. He found himself unwilling to ask why Marlowe himself had been passed over as department chair. From the sound of it, it had probably just been politics.

"Oh, yes," Marlowe answered, nodding. "but I think they cooled toward each other over the years. They certainly didn't see as much of each other as before George died, that's certain. For one thing, Reg had married by then, and then little Anne came along, so I imagine he didn't have nearly as much time for his friends as he'd like. And as I've said, I think Arthur was a bit resentful. You'll understand when I say that Arthur plodded toward his successes, whereas Reg made his happen."

Raoul nodded, agreeing. Marlowe, noting the teapot was empty and cold, asked Raoul if he'd like a bite to eat. "I seem to eat earlier every day," he said, smiling. "It comes with age."

Raoul, noting that it was nearly one o'clock, politely declined the offer. At the door Marlowe said, "I hope I haven't bored you with an old man's reminiscing." Raoul said that he hadn't, not at all, and asked if he could come back some other time, to discuss less unpleasant matters. He really did enjoy Marlowe's company. Walking back to his office, he realized he'd never gotten to know him all that well, and he regretted it.

As he'd expected, his office was empty when he arrived. He entered Marlowe's comments into the computer, idly munching on the sandwich he'd bought on the way and wishing he had time to stop in at the Hollow Man for a pint. Unfortunately, he needed to snatch a few hours sleep before Anne arrived at five-thirty, so there wasn't time.

Staring blankly at his notes, Raoul tried to fit the pieces together into some kind of coherent theory. The problem was that nowhere at all could he find a shred of proof that Montgomery-Lewis' death was anything but an unfortunate accident, which negated the blackmail note as a motive to murder. But if the note wasn't real, why would someone have sent it, or even written it in the first place? Nothing seemed to tie together. He chuckled quietly at the thought of how easily mysteries were solved on television or in books.

What the whole thing came down to, he thought, shutting down the computer and propping his feet on the desk, was nothing. Hints and hints and hints, all of which could be coincidental, accidental, or purely imaginary. Leaning back and closing his eyes, he wondered if Mowatt's death hadn't been an accident after all. Maybe someone had been in the house, a burglar perhaps, and Mowatt had surprised him. Mowatt could have been killed in a struggle, and whoever had done it could have panicked and left. The problem with that theory was the same as with all the others: no proof whatsoever. No sign of forced entry, no sign of a struggle, no fingerprints, nothing stolen. In short, nothing at all. Taking a deep breath and exhaling loudly, Raoul forced himself to stop thinking about it and to clear his mind for meditation and a quick nap . . .

"Ow!" he snapped aloud as he jerked painfully awake. He must have been more tired than he'd realized to have slept so deeply. Rubbing his neck, he checked the time. It was past six. "Damn it," he muttered. The door to the building was locked; he'd probably missed Anne, unless she was waiting outside or running late as well. Cramming his printouts and notes into his bag, he left in a rush. Outside, he looked around but didn't see Anne. He started walking quickly toward her house, hoping she'd just gone home.

The Whitings' house was completely lit up, and a number of cars were parked in front. Two dark-suited men stood near one of the cars, talking quietly. Something was going on, Raoul thought, and it certainly didn't look like a party. Scowling and confused, Raoul looked closely at the men as he walked to the front door. They fell silent as he passed. Raoul pressed the bell and waited for someone to open the door.

A long moment later another dark suit opened the door, but stood blocking the entrance. "Yes?" the man asked.

"Who is it?" Anne's voice came from farther inside the house. Raoul heard light footsteps approaching the entryway. Peering around the man in the doorway, Raoul saw Anne walking toward him, a smile lighting her face as she caught sight of him. She looked up at the man in the doorway, saying, "Excuse us," and staring at him with narrowed eyes until he moved out of the way.

Raoul stepped inside. "Anne, is everything all right?

What's going on?" The sound of people milling around came from the other rooms.

Anne shook her head at him, smiling grimly and glancing around. "I was hoping you'd come by. I'm sorry I'm late. It's a madhouse. That's what's going on. Wait a moment while I get my coat." She went back down the hall, after throwing another glare at the silent and motionless man who had remained near the door. She returned a few minutes later with the butler, who listened to her directions as he helped her with her coat. "Now," she said, speaking to the butler but occasionally looking at the dark-suited man, "I'm going out. I'm of no use here, and the doctor's up giving Mother a sedative, so she won't need me, either. If anything happens I'll be at the Hollow Man; it's a pub in town." She paused, as if waiting for the man to stop her, then turned to Raoul. "Let's go." She led the way out of the house, back down the path to the street.

Neither spoke until they'd put the house out of sight behind them. Actually, Raoul was waiting for her to speak first. He walked along with his hands in the pockets of his trench coat, matching his pace to hers and glancing at her every few steps. Anne walked quickly, her hands fiddling with the buttons of her coat, her eyes straight ahead. Finally, she slowed her pace and said flatly, without turning her head. "I'm sorry about that little scene back there. Something terrible has happened."

Raoul couldn't stand it. He stopped, putting a hand on her arm to bring her to a halt while turning her to face him. "Look," he said, "are you okay? Just what the hell was going on back there?" As he waited for her answer, he became aware that his hand was still holding her arm. As he awkwardly released her, his hand brushed against hers. She took his hand and smiled wanly. The pressure of her hand on his pressed his large silver ring uncomfortably into his fingers, but he didn't move.

"Come on," she said, pulling him forward again, "I'll explain when we're sitting down. Is the Seller open now?"

He was confused. "But you told them you'd be at the—"

"I know," she interrupted, "but I don't want to go there right now. Is it open?" She squeezed his hand, again pressing the ring into his fingers.

"Uh, yes," he answered, desperately wanting to move his hand, but worried that it might make her either drop his hand or hold it more tightly. He wasn't sure which was worse, so he left his hand dangling loosely in hers. As they walked on in silence, Raoul found himself remembering how he'd found the ring in an antique store when he was thirteen.

During the yule holidays he'd stayed at the latest school, since his mother was off somewhere in Italy. He'd enjoyed the solitude, using the time to read and practice spells, but couldn't bear the pitying looks from the remaining staff. Even worse were the comments of the other students when they'd returned; by the beginning of the term he'd already gotten into three fights, all over comments involving the word "bastard." Feeling angry and trapped, he'd even shut Bolton out. Needing to get away one day, he'd just started walking to escape the noise and the crowded feeling of the school grounds, and ended up in town.

He'd been struck by the window of the store, and stood idly gazing at the jumble of artifacts within before realizing he could just as easily go in and get warm. He and the thirtyish proprietor were the only ones in the store. The man had tried to open a conversation with some inanity like, "Smile, you'll feel better," and Raoul immediately launched into a tirade about how people who smiled all the time were probably idiots and little worse than people who went about checking to see if other people were smiling. Recalling that, Raoul winced at what a defensive little paranoid git he'd been, always spoiling for an argument or a fight.

Fortunately, the proprietor had withdrawn, allowing Raoul to lose himself in browsing. Eventually Raoul's eye was caught by an ornate silver sealing ring bearing the initial S.

"Ah, that," the proprietor said, noting Raoul's interest. "Now there's a sad piece."

"What do you mean?" Raoul asked.

"Well," the proprietor said, leaning forward on the glass case to look more closely at it, "I purchased that particular ring a few years ago. I remember it pretty clearly; it was a cold wet winter day much like today, and the young man who walked into the store looked frozen. His clothes had seen better days, and it looked like maybe he had, too. He nosed around the shop for a bit, waiting until the other customers had gone, then came up to me. He pulled out this ring and told me he needed to sell it. 'Needed,' I remember he said, not 'wanted.'

"I hate to admit it, but my first thought was that the ring was stolen, so I asked him where it had come from. He had a crafty look about him, you see. I remember he laughed when I'd asked him, a hard, grating laugh, and then he told me his story. He'd been a foundling, he said, left at an orphanage door with nothing to identify him but the ring around his neck on a string. His life at the orphanage had been brutal; his only escape was his dream of finding his real family. He'd run away when he was twelve, taking any work he could over the years while he searched for clues to who he was. I won't tell you some of the things he said he did; let's just say that his life had been an ugly one, but he'd never given up hope."

"But what about the ring?" Raoul had asked.

The proprietor laughed. "You know, that's exactly what I asked then. When I did, he laughed again, and said he didn't need it anymore, since he'd found his family all right. He was still laughing when he pulled another ring, the duplicate of the first, out of his pocket. 'Now buy the ring or send me on my way,' was all he would say after that. Well, he'd gotten me interested, so I bought it."

"And?" Raoul asked. "Did you ever find out who he was?"

"I think so," the proprietor said. "Not that I expected to. But the next day I read in the paper about a wealthy businessman who'd been murdered in London a few days earlier. No one knew why he'd been killed, since nothing had been taken except an heirloom silver ring. His name, of course, began with the letter S."

Raoul, of course, bought the ring on the spot. Families, after all, were hell.

Lost in recollection, Raoul tried to spin the ring on his finger, inadvertently squeezing Anne's hand. Turning to look up at him, she pressed his hand in return and sighed. "I'm afraid I'm not being very good company," she said quietly. Without thinking, Raoul shifted his hand, twining his fingers with hers, instantly aware of the increased contact. Her hand seemed very small in his. He held it lightly, as he would a small animal he didn't want to crush.

"It's okay," he said. As they walked the last few blocks to the club, he kept glancing around, self-conscious about walking while holding Anne's hand.

As they approached the front door, Anne said, "I thought you said it was open."

"It opens late on weekends. Hang on a bit." Releasing her hand as they entered the main door, Raoul asked her to wait while he went upstairs. "It's okay," he said, smiling, when he returned a few minutes later, "it's open for us." Turning his attention to the lock, he spoke a few words, unintelligible to Anne. The lock clicked, and he pushed the door open, then relocked it behind them after they'd entered. Anne was looking at him with a strange half smile.

"What?" he laughed nervously. "What?" He crossed to the front bar and, stepping behind it, began pouring out a pint of stout. Anne sat at the bar, still looking at him.

"Nothing," she said, "I've just never seen you work before. I like it. No," she interrupted herself, seeing him reach for a wineglass. "Just a pint of something. Not stout." Raoul raised an eyebrow at her and poured out a glass of lager. He walked around the bar to sit beside her.

He took a long drink. "So," he said finally, turning to her, "what's the matter? Who were all those men?"

She took a long drink, holding the glass in both hands like a child, then sighed, still holding the glass aloft. "Detectives," she answered bitterly. "They took my father away."

"What? Wait, start at the beginning."

"When I got to the house, at about four o'clock, there were all these cars outside, more than when you got there. There were men all over the place. Police." She took another long drink. "They were looking everywhere in the house, everywhere. Mother was hysterical. She said that they'd come to see Daddy because they found out about that note. The blackmail note."

Raoul nodded, not wanting to cut her off, and also not sure just how to tell her he already knew about it.

"They'd talked to him before about it, Mother said. It was signed by Arthur Mowatt, and said that Dad knew something about when Mr. Montgomery-Lewis died. That was before I was born, but I've heard Daddy talk about him. He and Professor Mowatt were really close to him. Anyway, the note was supposedly signed by Professor Mowatt, but no one thought it was real. Today they found out it was done on the typewriter outside my father's office. So the detectives came to ask about it, and Mother said they had some kind of warrant. When I came home, they were searching the house and Dad was in his study with four or five of them. After about half an hour Dad came out with one of them and talked to Mother." She finished her beer and held out the glass to Raoul, who walked behind the bar and refilled both their glasses. She waited until he was seated again to continue.

"And then he left with them. Not all of them, you saw the ones who stayed. Mother said that they'd found two more notes in his office. They took him just to question him, he said, not to arrest him. There's no proof, you see, just notes that make it look like he was being blackmailed. Even if he was, there's no law against being blackmailed, is there? They can't think he killed Professor

Mowatt!" Her voice grew louder. "They just can't! He didn't even leave the house after the party! He was talking to me until three-thirty in the damn morning! So he can't have had anything to do with it! Why won't they just leave him alone? This wasn't supposed to happen—" She broke off, breathing heavily, lowered her face into her hands and began to cry.

Raoul didn't know what to do. Tentatively, he put a hand on her shoulder. Anne was quivering, her entire body shaking with hiccuping sobs. He stroked her shoulder, muttering, "It's okay, it's okay, it's going to be okay . . ." It didn't help. She began to say something, but couldn't. Instead she spun on the stool and put her face to his shoulder, clutching his arms to support herself. He looked around the empty room, then slowly put his arms around her. Gradually she quieted, until finally she pushed him away.

She rubbed at her eyes, which were red and smeared with makeup. "Oh, gods," she said, sniffling, "I'm so sorry. I must look a wreck. I'm sorry . . ."

A key turning in the door lock made Raoul jump and Anne look wildly around the room. As the door opened she said quickly, "I can't see anyone now, I can't! Where's the rest room?" She seemed on the edge of hysteria again.

Raoul pointed to the back room. "Back there. Up the stairs, first door at the top. Are you all right?"

She nodded as she slipped off the chair, then walked rapidly away.

"Ahem." Bryon stood inside the door, holding it open. "Sorry about that, but I need to get ready to open the—"

Raoul interrupted, walking toward him. "No problem. Rather, I'm sorry. I know it was an imposition asking to come in early."

Bryon waved him off. "You don't ask for what you don't need, Raoul. Is she okay?" He looked in the direction Anne had gone.

"Yes. She's just upset. Family stuff," Raoul said, intentionally vague. Bryon nodded, understanding that Raoul didn't want to talk about it. He patted Raoul on the shoulder as he passed him. Raoul glanced at the clock, surprised that only an hour had passed since he'd gone to the Whitings'.

A crowd had trickled in by the time Anne returned, her reapplied makeup failing to conceal that she'd been crying. She walked to the bar, looking around confusedly until she spotted Raoul beckoning to her from his usual table. She sat, gratefully sipping at the fresh pint he'd gotten her. After a moment she said quietly, "Thank you. I'm okay now. I'm really sorry I threw such a hissy fit, but—"

He cut her off. "Don't be silly, Anne. It's fine, I understand. Do you want to leave?"

"No," she said, "I think I'd just like to sit for a while and try not to think about it, if that's okay." She looked up at him. He nodded. They sat silently for a few moments, then both tried to speak at the same time. Their laughter cleared even more tension from the air.

Smiling, Raoul said, "No, you first."

"I was just thinking how weird it was that this," she gestured around the club, "was the first place I thought of going. Why is that, do you think?"

Raoul looked around the room, which had grown much noisier with the addition of the twenty or so people now in it. "It's comfortable," he replied carefully. "No one cares what you do here or who you are. Hell," he chuckled, "at least you didn't break any bottles."

She looked questioningly at him. He had just started to explain when Bryon walked over to whisper something in his ear. Raoul stood. "Excuse me for a second, will you, Anne? There's a call for me." As he followed Bryon he added, almost to himself, "Who's calling me here? Probably Bolton . . ." A phone was laid on the back bar. Picking up the receiver, he said shortly, "Smythe here. What?"

Moments later he returned to the table, his face even more pale than usual. Gathering his coat, he said quietly but urgently to Anne, "I've got to take you home. Something's come up."

She asked what had happened as she put on her coat. "That was Phil Lynchfield from the *News*," he replied. "I've got to get to London. Bolton's been in an accident. He's being flown down from Scotland."

Chapter 8

". . . And do you know, this one," Bolton said, gesturing at Raoul, "rushed over here as soon as Phil," here he nodded at Phil Lynchfield, who was leaning against a wall of the crowded hospital room, "told him the news. Isn't that amazing? I didn't even get here for three hours, and I was still unconscious when I got in. *And* he's been here the whole time." He turned to Raoul and batted his eyelashes. "And I thought you didn't care." The other six people in the room laughed as Raoul rolled his eyes. Bolton's voice was still groggy from the medication, but at least his sense of humor had returned in full.

"Don't flatter yourself," Raoul responded tartly. "I was just trying to convince them to remove your vocal cords while they had the chance, right, Dr. Sandler?"

The physician chuckled, throwing a nervous glance around the room. He'd never seen a sickroom crowd quite like this, but was enjoying the banter. Now, however, he needed to get to work. "Unfortunately, ladies and gentlemen, I'm afraid I have to break up the party," he said. "If you'll excuse us?"

Catherine Moss was the first of the group to rise. "Oh, Max," she said, kissing Bolton on the cheek, "I'm just so happy that you're going to be fine. I was so worried about you, wasn't I, Mary?" She looked to her companion for confirmation.

"She was," Mary Schoenstein said, shaking her head at Bolton and smiling. She patted his shoulder, since his hands were both encased in bandages. "Be well, will you? And don't bother the doctor too much." As they left, Catherine glanced in Anne's direction, who in turn looked quickly at Raoul.

"I'll be along directly," she said to Catherine and Mary. "Wait for me, would you?"

Bolton, noting the look she'd shot Raoul, raised an eyebrow at him. Raoul raised one back without changing expression at all. Bolton laughed.

"What's so funny?" asked Brenda, Bolton's assistant, crossing to the bed.

"Ah, Brenda, dear." Bolton tried to sit, failed, and lay back again. "There's just a couple of things I need to fill you in on before you go . . ."

Phil Lynchfield took Brenda's arm, pulling her toward the door. "No, you don't," he called over his shoulder to Bolton. "We've got everything under control, and you're not to worry, since you're not to work. We'll call if we have any questions. So, rest! I'll be back tomorrow." Brenda called out a good-bye as Phil hustled her out the door.

"Why, of all the . . ." Bolton sputtered. "I should . . . You know," he said, turning to Raoul, "I think that man's enjoying this. He's sick! And frankly," he said in a stage whisper, "I don't think he's a good influence on Brenda."

Raoul laughed. The departure of Brenda and Phil left only himself, the doctor, Anne, and Rodger Collings in the room. Raoul turned first to Dr. Sandler. "Doctor, would you mind horribly if Rodger and I stay while you work on him? We've got some things to discuss, and I don't think you changing a dressing will bother us. Is that okay?"

Sandler looked at Bolton, who nodded. "Well, all right," he responded, "but it's a bit irregular."

Raoul nodded, then turned to Anne. Before he could speak, she stood. "Well, I suppose I'll be going as well. I'm glad you're going to be fine, Max." She kissed Bolton on the cheek. "I'll see you later?" she asked Raoul from the door. Bolton, Collings, and even the doctor turned to him.

Flustered, he answered her shortly. "I don't know yet. I'll call you."

She smiled and left.

"Well?" Bolton asked.

"Well what?"

"So what's going on with you two?" Bolton laughed, enjoying putting Raoul on the spot.

Raoul didn't take the bait. "Nothing. She drove me here, remember? We're friends, that's all. Of course," he added, addressing the other two men and gesturing at Bolton, "he probably wouldn't know much about that, since he doesn't have any." The others laughed.

Bolton gave up, throwing his bandaged hands up and grimacing as they fell back on the covers. The doctor was instantly at his side, gently lifting first one, then the other. Raoul and Collings moved their chairs farther to each side of the bed, getting out of his way.

"You really should try to be careful," Sandler said as he gently unwrapped Bolton's right hand. "This is serous, Max. I'm not positive we won't have to do grafts as it is, and you bouncing around isn't helping matters. You're lucky you've still got all your fingers." He crossed the room to a covered rolling tray holding bottles, tubes of ointment, and fresh bandages.

"Ah, Doc," Bolton whined after him, "it's not that bad, really. I got burned on my hands and knocked about the head a bit. Seriously, it doesn't even hurt that badly!"

The doctor returned to Bolton's side and gently began unwrapping the other hand. "Max," he replied, "there's no pain because I've got you drugged out of your mind. Now hold still, will you, and let me work." He concentrated on changing the dressings.

The other men, Bolton included, tried hard not to look at the reddened mass of burns covering the back of Bolton's hands and arms almost to the elbow. Maybe they weren't life-threatening or even permanently disfiguring, but they certainly weren't pretty.

Bolton drew a deep breath and turned pointedly to Raoul. "So," he said, "what's happened? What have I missed? It's pretty big, or else you," he glanced at Collings, "wouldn't be here. So tell, someone."

"I'll give you the quick rundown," Raoul said, "and then I'll let Collings here fill in the details. Then you can tell us what you found out in Scotland." Bolton and Collings nodded, agreeing. The doctor glanced at the three men and shrugged, then continued working on Bolton's hands.

Raoul shifted in his chair, getting comfortable. "Well, first there's the matter of Montgomery-Lewis' death. I read through your packet, then decided to see if anyone at the university remembered anything. I spoke with Robert Marlowe, who was not only teaching in the College of Magic at the time, but had also taught both Mowatt and Whiting as undergraduates . . ."

Bolton interrupted occasionally with questions while Raoul recounted his conversation with Marlowe. At one point all conversation stopped as Bolton grimaced in pain. Sandler asked a few questions and fussed with Bolton's right arm for a few moments. "Okay, that's better," Bolton finally said. "Go on, Rags."

Raoul finished describing his meeting with Marlowe, then moved on to what he knew of recent happenings at the Whitings'. ". . . So that's all I know; more letters were found, but I've nothing definite about what they said."

"I think I can be of help there," Rodger Collings said. Both Raoul and Bolton looked at him. "I've been making notes of the information that's come in," he continued as he thumbed through his briefcase. "Don't worry, we lowly clerks are *supposed* to take an interest in ongoing cases." He smiled conspiratorially. Pulling out a page covered in close handwriting, he referred to it as he spoke. "Let's see, you both know about the first note, right? The one you have a copy of." They nodded. "Okay, that note was a copy, not the original; copies were sent to you," he looked at Bolton, "and also to the police. The original hasn't been found. Tests show that the note was typed, not printed from a computer, and that the machine used was in the office of Sir Reginald's own assistant, Robert Parker. He was questioned about it, denying ever having seen the note, of course, but it also appears he often leaves the office completely open. Really, almost anyone could have done it."

"What about Whiting himself?" Raoul asked. "What did he have to say about it?" He felt both relieved that he was no longer the main focus of the investigation and uncomfortable that the new suspect was Anne's father.

"He also denied having seen it before, much less receiving it," Collings said. "And he also offered to take a lie detector test. It's strange," he added, referring to his notes, "but it looks like Barnstone called him and tried to set up a meeting at his house, but Whiting offered to come in, and did. Apparently, Barnstone still had doubts, though," Collings looked up, "because he's the one who requested the warrant to search Whiting's residence." He added, "Whiting's alibi for the night of the murder isn't that great. It's his daughter. She says the two of them were up talking from after the party ended until about four. The wife turned in soon after people left, about one-thirty." He turned the page over and quickly skimmed it.

"What about the search yesterday afternoon?" Raoul asked impatiently. "They found two more notes, right? What about them?"

"Right. The two notes were found in a locked drawer in Whiting's desk, and he's the only one with a key. He doesn't deny that. He pretty much refused to say anything else, however. He won't say if he actually paid what the notes ask or not, but we'll know that soon. His bank records are being pulled. Frankly, unless it's obvious from the bank records that those exact amounts were taken out, we don't have much to go on. Even if we did, it would still be difficult. The two notes aren't addressed to anyone or signed, the way the first one was."

"What exactly did the notes say?" Bolton asked. "Were they the same as the first one?"

"That's the interesting part. They're different from the one you received. Though the text of all three notes refers to the Montgomery-Lewis death, the two found in Whiting's house don't hint at murder. They're much less threatening, implying that something happened *when* Montgomery-Lewis died, something both the writer and Whiting are aware of. The two notes share almost the same wording, and both ask for twenty-five thousand pounds, as does the third."

"Hmmm," Bolton mused, "that's really not too much, is it?" Noting Raoul looking at him, he added, "I mean, if you're going to blackmail the Chancellor of Oxford, why not ask for fifty thousand? Or even more? Whiting is obviously well-off. It just seems strange. But do go on, Rodger. What about the typewriter?"

Collings smiled at Bolton. "It's a different machine," he said. "And what's more, it's just been identified as the one in the office of Mowatt's own secretary, Jean Morris."

At this, both Raoul and Bolton exclaimed, "What!" Collings stopped, waiting for one of them to continue.

"What do you mean, it was done on Jean's typewriter?" Raoul asked. "Did anyone question her?"

At this point Sandler, who'd been working quietly but steadily, stood and stretched. "Well, gentlemen, it looks like I'm through here." He addressed Raoul and Collings. "Try not to tire him out too much, will you? And you," he poked Bolton in the chest with a finger, "don't let them tire you out. I'd really like to get rid of you as soon as possible—" he smiled. "—and you're not going to heal without sleep. So take the pills the nurse gives you, when she brings them. Good luck with whatever it is you're working on. I'll shut the door, but remember, a nurse will be by in—" He checked his watch. "—an hour to check on the patient."

Collings paused a moment, collecting his thoughts. "So where were we? Oh, right. Jean Morris, Mowatt's secretary. The answer to your question is yes," he said finally. "She was brought in for questioning earlier this morning. She said she hadn't written the notes and pointed out that any-time the office was open almost anyone would have access to the machine. Practically the same thing Parker said. She offered to take a lie detector test, but that didn't seem necessary. By the way, she also has a strong alibi for the night of Mowatt's murder—she was staying at a friend's house, helping with the friend's mother, who was just back from the hospital. Back operation. She left for home just before eight, changed, then went straight to work. Says she got there at about nine-thirty."

"On a Saturday?" Raoul asked. "What was she doing there so early?"

Collins nodded. "Good catch, Raoul. Apparently she's been rather ill lately and needed to catch up. We've got confirmation of her being there from the janitorial staff, in any case."

"So what does Barnstone think?" Raoul asked. "It sounds like there's still no concrete evidence except a dead man and some possible blackmail which may or may not be related to his death. And anyway, you can't arrest Whiting for being blackmailed, can you? And am I finally out of this?"

Collings nodded slowly. "As far as your last question, technically you'll probably still be a suspect for a while, but yes, I think you're pretty well out of it now. Truthfully, at the moment most of the attention is being focused on Reginald Whiting." He looked up at the ceiling, making a steeple of his hands. "Let's see. There are a couple of theories being thrown around. So far I've heard that Whiting committed murder to avoid being blackmailed, but that was before the new notes were found. Maybe he did it to avoid *more* blackmail. There's also the theory that Whiting himself sent the first note out, to get publicity, but that seems idiotic, although it would explain why the typewriter used was outside his office. I've also started hearing that Mowatt wasn't really blackmailing Whiting at all, but sent the letter out himself to spite Whiting, and then killed himself.

Frankly, no one knows what to think about all this. It's all guesswork.

"And then," he went on, looking pointedly at Bolton, "then we've got the matter of a certain meddling reporter who took it upon himself to go to Scotland, where the inn he's staying at promptly and mysteriously burns down. The same inn, I should add, where the death referred to in all three notes took place thirty years ago. That's a pretty hot topic as well, no pun intended. You know," he added, sitting back, "I'm really glad I'm not officially involved with this at all. It's too messy. So unofficially, Max, what exactly were you looking for up there? And what did you find?"

"My turn, eh?" Bolton said, shifting his position slightly. "Hand me that glass of water, Rags, would you?" He waved a bandaged hand at a side table.

"How about I hold it for you? And stop calling me that." Raoul picked up the glass and held it to Bolton's lips, disturbed to be so clearly reminded of Bolton's helplessness at the moment. When Bolton had finished, Raoul wiped his mouth with a tissue. Bolton smiled wryly. "Thanks, Rags. You'll make someone a great little nurse someday." Raoul returned to his seat without responding. He knew Bolton must be as uncomfortable as he was, if not more so.

Bolton shifted position again. "Why did I go?" he said, returning to Collings' question. "I'm really not sure. I don't know if you've read through everything I sent," Collings shook his head, "but it just seemed awfully pat." He glanced at Raoul, who was nodding agreement. "I had a hunch there might be more, so I went up to see if the people involved were still around and talk to them."

"And . . . ?" Raoul prompted.

"And nothing. Most of the principals are dead. I spoke to the woman who runs the place, the daughter of the woman who ran it thirty years ago, and she didn't know a thing except what she'd heard from her mother and others. The man who rowed the body in is dead as well. I even took a boat out and rowed around the lake, but nothing struck me. Until, of course," he grimaced, "that flaming timber did."

"Exactly what did happen to you?" Collings asked. "It looks pretty serious, and I know there's an investigation going on about it. I've heard they suspect arson. Unfortunately, there's damned little evidence left to prove if it was or wasn't. Nice dry timbers . . . I'm sorry, Max, go on."

"What happened? It's embarrassingly simple. I'd rented the same guest house that the Montgomery-Lewises had. I went to sleep, and woke up in the middle of the night smelling smoke. Instead of thinking intelligently and jumping safely out my second-story bedroom window, I decided to use the door. The hallway was filled with smoke, so I put my coat over my head and held my breath. I checked the two other rooms on the floor, since I wasn't sure if anyone else was staying there or not. Anyway, I kicked the doors open, didn't see anyone, then decided to leave, since the smoke was getting worse. The first floor was hellish." He paused, remembering. "Completely aflame. I made a mad dash for the door, and almost made it out when a piece of the ceiling hit me. Luckily, I still had the coat over my head, so my hair didn't go up, but I have a very nasty bump which they tell me is a concussion, and these—" He held up his bandaged hands. "—from where I pushed it off me. First degree, some second. People from the other guest house pulled me out, I hear. So much for hunches, eh?"

"You said there's an investigation, though?" Raoul asked Collings. "So they don't think it was just an accident?"

"No. I'm not sure exactly what, if any, hard evidence they've found, but I've heard the word 'arson' tossed around, as I said. It's just too much of a coincidence. So you might have been on to something, after all, Max."

"Oh, gosh, Rog, that makes me feel so much better," Bolton said sarcastically.

"Well, it should." Collings glanced at his watch. "Anyway, I've got to be going. Two-hour lunches are frowned on at my level. I hope you're better soon, Max. I'll leave you my notes. Nice meeting you, Raoul."

After Collings had gone, Bolton yawned. "So, what's next for you?"

"Well, I'm still suspended until the investigation is over, so I'm going to keep working on the aural erasure. It looks like it's runic, at this point. You know," he mused, "this could be really big. I mean, I don't want to say too much before I know for sure what causes it, but . . . What about you?"

"Me?" Bolton raised his eyebrows. "Oh, I thought I'd just hang around here for a while. *Such* a nice place, you know. Real ambience."

"You know what I mean. What are they doing for you?"

"I've got healings almost every day for the next week or so. If magically inducing new skin growth doesn't take, they'll do grafts, but it's ninety percent sure the healing will work. Drugs and magic, you know. They've got to wait for my concussion to leave, though, before they can do anything."

Raoul nodded. "That makes sense." They fell silent again.

"So I guess you're pretty much giving up on the murder?" Bolton asked. "Now that you're out of the running, that is."

Raoul looked around the room. "Uh, well actually, no, not really," he muttered. "I mean," he continued, "it's still kind of personal, what with Scotland and all." He paused before adding, "And Whiting."

"Oh, really?" Bolton nodded. "Scotland, eh? Well, thanks for worrying about me, Rags. And Whiting, you say? Now, I wonder why you might be interested in him? This wouldn't have anything to do with a certain blonde, would it?"

Raoul shrugged. "Anne asked me to keep looking into it, for her father's sake. As well as my own." He avoided meeting Bolton's eyes. "I said I would. Since I'm still looking into it anyway." It was true, he thought to himself. Even if she hadn't asked, he'd still want to find out the truth now that Bolton had been injured. But he couldn't tell Bolton how frightened he'd been by his injury. Easier by far to take the teasing.

Bolton didn't answer for a long moment. Finally, Raoul looked up at him. Bolton was silently chortling and shaking his head. "What?" Raoul snapped.

"Oh, nothing, nothing." Bolton got himself under control, forcing an innocent expression onto his face. "That makes perfect sense, really, when you think about it. And just think, Rags, it's *such* a great excuse to call her!" He laughed again briefly, making a warding gesture against Raoul's glare. "Seriously, my friend, I'm glad you're keeping a hand in our little mystery. It's gotten personal for me, as well. I'm having Brenda send me anything else she can dig up on the Montgomery-Lewises. There's got to be something there, I'm sure of it. Something big enough to warrant arson, maybe . . ." He yawned again.

"You're tired," Raoul said, rising. "I'm heading out. I'll keep you posted on what I find." Taking up his coat and bag, he walked to the door, pausing before he opened it. "Be well," he said quietly.

Bolton smiled, settling deep into the covers, "Yes, Doctor." As Raoul turned to leave, Bolton called out, "Rags?"

"Yes?"

"What are you going to do if it *was* Whiting? He's the logical choice, at this point. For the murder, I mean."

Raoul stood with his hand on the doorknob, looking at Bolton. He shook his head slowly. "I don't know. I really don't know. Sleep now, okay? I'll call you later."

"It's funny, isn't it?" Bolton said softly as Raoul opened the door.

Raoul turned again, pausing. "What's funny?"

"I was right after all."

"About what?"

"Your scry." Raoul looked at Bolton strangely, wondering what he was talking about. Bolton continued, his voice sounding even more dreamy. "It *was* smoke you saw, I bet. Funny, isn't it?"

"Hilarious. Sleep now, will you?" Bolton's eyes closed.

Raoul left, shutting the door quietly behind him. The thought that Bolton might have been right about the smoke imagery troubled him. It meant that he might have been able to prevent all this from happening.

Anne was waiting in the lobby. He didn't see her at first, but turned when she called out his name. "Hi," he said, surprised. "I thought you'd left."

She smiled at him. "Well, I was going to leave with Catherine and Mary, but I wasn't really in the mood to talk to anyone, so I begged off. I was just going to drive home anyway, so I figured I'd wait and see if you wanted a ride." She paused. "So, do you want a ride?"

"Uh, sure," Raoul said, ruffling his hair. Once again he felt uncomfortable. "That is, if you're sure it's no trouble." Bolton's teasing had made him excruciatingly aware of just how much time he'd spent with Anne lately, though he could find logical excuses for most of it.

"None at all," she said brightly. "Are you ready?"

Walking to the car, they spoke about Bolton. Settling into the passenger seat, Raoul found himself explaining the procedures for magically speeding the natural healing process and inducing new skin growth. Eventually he fell silent, staring out the window while Anne kept a running commentary of small talk.

He glanced over at her. She really was lovely. A line from Coleridge's *The Rime of the Ancient Mariner* popped into his head: "Her lips were red, her looks were free, Her locks were yellow as gold: Her skin was as white as leprosy . . ." Pretty apt, he thought. Of course, he didn't think Coleridge had meant to describe someone who was actually attractive, since the lines applied to "the Nightmare Life-in-Death," but they fit, for the most part. Okay, he thought, so maybe her skin wasn't "as white as leprosy," but she certainly was pale. He glanced at her hands. A fine tracery of blue veins on the backs led to long white fingers, capped by that weird nail polish that was pink with white tips. She wore a number of rings, small gold bands capped with various precious stones. Nice-girl-from-a-good-school hands, he thought. He shifted in his seat, staring out the window again.

So she was attractive. No, that wasn't it. He was sure he knew a lot of attractive women, though it wasn't usually something he noticed. No, the problem with Anne was that he was attracted to her. And, to complicate matters, she seemed to enjoy his company as well. He had no idea of where he wanted this to go, if it was going anywhere. They were so very different from each other, and anyway, he'd always hated the idea of having "a relationship," of being expected to call, expected to be with someone. But then again, he'd never quite enjoyed being with anyone quite the way he enjoyed being with Anne. It was strange; at times he felt almost as comfortable with her as with Bolton, but there was always something more lurking behind every word, every action. That something more was what worried him.

It was probably good that Anne had refused to let him continue from her house by cab the night of Bolton's injury and had driven him herself. Truly, it had been a relief to just have her there, not that he'd spoken a word until they arrived at the hospital. And what about Bolton? He'd never admit it to him, but when he'd heard the news, he'd been terrified, and then furious.

Arson. Raoul felt helpless and angry that he couldn't do anything to find out about the fire, since he couldn't leave the area without informing the police. Not that it would do any good, he thought, since he hadn't even been able to figure anything out where he was. All he'd done so far was almost get Bolton killed. He wanted this solved, and quickly, before he could get anyone else hurt, or worse. If only I'd read the scry right, he thought. He smacked his forehead on the window.

"Raoul!" Anne said. "What's the matter?" He hadn't noticed that she'd fallen silent.

He looked over at her. "I've been thinking," he said simply.

She looked at him as if she couldn't quite decide whether to worry or not. "Well," she said, "try not to hurt yourself, all right?"

He gave her a weak smile, then turned back to the window. He closed his eyes and ran through a simple exercise to clear his mind.

"Raoul?" Anne said quietly. She gently touched his arm. He sprang awake, turning in the seat.

"What?" he snapped.

Taken aback, she leaned quickly away. "Nothing. We're here. You were asleep."

"Oh. Thanks." Stretching, he looked out the window. They were parked in front of her house. He reached into the backseat for his bag and coat. Getting out, he crossed to the front of the car. "Well, thanks for the ride. I probably wasn't much company . . ."

"No problem. Do you need a ride back to Thornhold?" She got out of the car and stood next to it, crossed arms hugging her coat to her.

"No, thanks. I've got some things to do here. Thanks, though." He was doing it again, he thought, having another absolutely inane conversation where he couldn't think of anything to say. "So," he continued, "I'm off. I'll see you." He walked off in the direction of the Magic buildings, consciously not looking back. He'd gone only a few steps when she called out his name. Turning, he saw that she had her datebook laid on the top of the car and was writing something. She tore out the page and walked over to hand it to him.

"It's my work number," she said shyly, "in case you want to call me there."

"Uh, thanks," he said, putting the slip of paper into his coat pocket. "Maybe I will. See you later, Anne." He turned and walked away again.

Outside his building he stopped, undecided. He could either go in and try calling Miriam about the program, or he could see if Jean was back in yet. And he still needed to spend some time at the library, researching how to remove magical ability for Mordechai. Raoul smiled to himself at that thought, realizing the idea didn't horrify him quite as much now that he knew it probably wouldn't be happening to him. He'd look for Jean first, he decided.

This seems to be my day for parties, he thought as he walked into Jean's office. There were at least ten people ranged around the room, including Whiting, Parker, and Jean herself. Two or three open packing boxes were set against a wall, and most of Jean's desktop was occupied by a large cake, which someone was cutting, partially obscured by a brace of multicolored balloons. He stood awkwardly in the doorway while deciding whether he should come back later. Parker caught his eye.

"Come in, Professor Smythe," Parker called from across the room. Everyone turned to face Raoul, who forced a smile.

"Am I interrupting anything?" He asked. "I could come back . . ."

"Oh, no," Jean said, crossing to him and patting his arm. The first thing that struck him was that she was wearing white cotton gloves. As she led him over to the desk, where pieces of cake were now being handed out, he saw that most of the skin on her face and neck was reddened and rough-looking, flaking to an almost silvery sheen in spots. He tried to remember if it had been that way when he'd seen her before, but decided he would have noticed if it had. He wondered if it had something to do with her recent illness.

"What's the occasion?" Raoul asked, trying not to stare at her face. He looked at the cake instead. By the time he'd puzzled out the remaining letters that had spelled "Happy Retirement" in blue icing, Jean was explaining that she'd decided to take an early retirement due to her health, and that the staff had thrown a small party for her.

"Nothing too serious, I hope?" Raoul asked, referring to her health. "I'd heard you'd been out."

She glanced at her hands for a moment. "It's just a skin problem. It's gotten worse lately." She laughed nervously and spoke louder. "Plus, it's not as if I'm retiring all that early, you know."

Raoul smiled slightly in response. He politely refused a piece of cake, but did accept a small plastic glass of champagne. He walked over to where Parker was standing.

Parker glanced around as he approached. Raoul wondered if it had something to do with his having been questioned by the police. "How are you doing, Bob?" he asked.

Parker smiled. Raoul thought it looked forced. "Fine, Professor. You know, I wouldn't have figured you for the going-away party type. How's your investigation going, by the way?"

If he'd been questioned about the notes, Raoul thought, then he knew they concerned Montgomery-Lewis—who'd been here thirty years ago, the precise period Raoul had wanted a staff list for. He looked stonily at Parker, wishing the man would be quiet. He wasn't sure what to think about him; he'd been helpful enough when they'd spoken about Mowatt, but something about Parker irritated him. It wasn't that he was ingratiating, but there seemed to be a certain edge to everything he said or did. Perhaps it was just his obvious liking for being in the know about things. Parker met Raoul's eyes for a moment, then glanced away.

"It was never really an investigation, to tell the truth," Raoul said quietly. "I suppose I'm just fascinated by the morbid side of things. Lots of excitement around here, then?" He quirked an eyebrow and nodded his head at the rest of the room.

Parker was off like a shot. "I'll say there is. Frankly, it's been a madhouse lately, what with Jean out and now retiring. And the police around all the time."

"Ah," Raoul said, nodding agreement. "They certainly have a way of upsetting things. What about Jean? Do you think they'll replace her right away?"

"Well, not until they announce the new chair. Which, between you and me, probably won't be for some time. Sir Reginald will run things, on top of all he already does, until he's found the perfect person. It'll mean lots more work for me, of course, but at least it won't be boring, if you know what I mean."

Raoul nodded, though office politics always confused him. "So, anyway, what exactly is the matter with her?"

"Well, you know she's been out since . . . well, since Mowatt died? And even before, she wasn't too well. So," he continued, "it turns out she's always had this skin problem, psoriasis, that's really gotten out of control lately. It's hereditary, I guess, and she was born with it. I mean, I'd heard of it before, but I always thought it was just dry skin. Hers never seemed all that bad before, but now . . . Her doctor told her that stress was probably making it worse. I mean, she can hardly use her hands anymore, and she said that it can actually be fatal if it gets too far along, and even if it's not, there can be all kinds of complications. So she figured she'd retire now and see if she can get it back under control. Poor thing." He glanced in Jean's direction then turned back to Raoul.

"Hmmm," Raoul responded, for lack of anything else to say. It really was too bad. Idly, he wondered how you would treat something like that. Medication, diet . . . Maybe he'd ask Dr. Sandler about it when he next saw Bolton. He looked around, noting that one or two more people had appeared since he'd been speaking to Parker. He probably wouldn't get a chance to talk to Jean alone, he thought, and anyway, this wasn't the best time for the kind of conversation he wanted to have. He excused himself to Parker and made his way over to Jean to say good-bye. She stood near her desk, chatting while she told the people who were helping her pack which box things should go into. Standing beside her, Raoul waited for a break in the conversation.

"Jean, where've you been putting your pictures?" someone asked from beside Raoul, behind the desk.

"In that box over by the wall," Jean replied. "Just be careful that the glass doesn't break."

"No glass," the woman said, holding up a photograph. "See? It looks kind of old, though. Who are they?"

As he turned his head to see the photo, Raoul heard Jean's quick intake of breath. "Where'd you find that?" she asked. "That's not mine."

"It was in the bottom drawer," the woman replied. "In the back. I wonder how long it's been in there, then. Who do you think they are?"

Raoul looked at the picture of the three smiling men. Two days ago he wouldn't have recognized Mowatt and Whiting in their younger incarnations, or known who Montgomery-Lewis was. Now, however, he said nothing, wondering what it could mean.

A hand fell heavily on his shoulder. It was Whiting, who gestured for Raoul to follow him. Raoul excused himself to Jean and followed Whiting to the door of Mowatt's old office.

"So, how's the research coming along, Raoul?" Whiting asked, leaning casually against the door frame.

Raoul started, wondering what Whiting knew, or if he'd seen the photo, then realized Whiting was referring to his magical research. "Quite well, actually," Raoul replied, trying not to look or sound relieved. Briefly, he considered asking if he would be reinstated soon, but decided it was a bad time for that particular question and all its ramifications. "I think I may be on to something."

"That's wonderful. You'll have to tell me all about it sometime." For all his professed interest, Raoul thought Whiting seemed distracted. Then Whiting continued, speaking softly, so only Raoul could hear.

"So, I hear you've been spending a bit of time with my daughter, eh?" he asked.

Oh gods, Raoul thought, I don't need this. "I guess I have," he replied carefully. "She's quite, er—" He paused, trying to find something uncompromising. "—uh, personable." He nodded, smiling weakly and feeling like an idiot.

"I've always thought so myself." Whiting said jovially. "She thinks very highly of you, you know."

"Really? Well, um, great, I guess. Great." He was still nodding, he realized, and forced himself to stop.

Whiting chuckled. "Sorry, Raoul. I don't mean to play the prying parent. It's good to see her involved with someone I like myself, though." He clapped Raoul heartily on the shoulder. "Well, I've got a university to run. You'll keep me posted on that research, won't you?"

"Of course." Raoul managed to walk, not run, to the door, nodding again to Parker on his way out. He walked dazedly in the direction of the library. Involved, he thought. Involved. Every fucking person in the world seemed to think he was "involved" with Anne. They'd seen each other two or three times, but none of the occasions was what he'd call a "date." He hated feeling that he was being forced into something; it always made him immediately reject whatever was being thrust upon him, whether it was something he truly wanted or not. And he wasn't even sure how he felt about her. He hadn't had the chance to think about it yet without someone or something interrupting. Sometimes he wished he could just stay inside Thornhold, lock himself away where no one, including Bolton and all his other so-called friends, could ever come.

He stalked into the library, past the guard, glaring about and mentally daring anyone to speak to him. Technically, he needed to show his university identification card to the guard on entering, but he'd been coming here for years. Additionally, he supposed they remembered the incident when a guard had stopped him and he hadn't had his card with him, since he never carried it. He'd refused to argue with the man beyond the point of stating that he was a professor. One of the librarians had even vouched for him, but the guard had been adamant. No ID, no entry. Raoul had given him an immediate and rather severe case of intestinal gas which lasted the rest of the man's shift. Nothing harmful, merely embarrassing. Since then, he'd had no problems with any of the guards in any of the buildings. Another plus for a bad reputation, he supposed. Stalking up to the main desk, he asked to borrow the phone. He dialed Bolton's hospital number and spoke quietly and quickly when Bolton answered.

"It's Raoul. I really can't talk now, but I've got a fun project for you. Any idea why Mowatt's secretary would have an old photo of Mowatt, Whiting, and Montgomery-

Lewis lying around? I just saw it in her office—someone found it in the desk."

"Hmmm, that's weird, Rags. Let me look into it, and I'll call you if anything turns up. Will you be around tonight?"

"I should be, later on. Anyway, I've got to go. 'Bye." He handed the handset back to the librarian. "Thanks," he said, then crossed to the computer terminal which had replaced the old card cataloging system. He hated using it. Raoul considered himself as receptive to progress as most people, if not more so, but he still missed the calm that came from flipping through hundreds of cards. Pulling up a file or doing a search just didn't have the same effect.

Letting his breath hiss out in an angry sigh, he entered the key words "magic removal" and "magic blocking" as the initial search criteria. A few moment's wait retrieved a two-screen list of books and articles. Limiting the list to books only and adding the words "intentional" and "permanent" cut the list to a tolerable twelve titles.

Eight of the books looked to be primarily related to ethics. Three of the remaining four were located in the history section, and the other was in the reference section. Raoul printed out the entire list, then did another search, this time for books on the lost runes. Armed with his two printouts, he headed for the history section. It took him a while to gather the books, since he was an inveterate browser, but eventually he settled himself into a corner carrel with the books on magic blockage and two titles dealing with the lost runes.

He laid a notepad from his bag in front of him and took off his coat. A slip of paper fell out of the pocket; Anne's work number. He picked it up and took his address book out of his bag. As he added her number, he noted that she had the kind of handwriting that revealed nothing except that she'd probably won penmanship awards in school.

Three hours later he was comfortably ensconced back in his office. He finished entering his new notes into the computer, then rummaged in his bag for the napkin with Mordechai's telephone number scribbled on it. Mordechai answered on the first ring. Grimacing, because feeling sorry for the man didn't mean he enjoyed either his conversation or his company, Raoul identified himself.

Mordechai probably felt the same way about him, judging from the slight hesitation before he said, "Ah. Hello. Can you hold on? I need to close the door." There was a pause on his end of the line. "Thank you for getting back to me. Were you able to find anything?"

"Yes. I think I may have found what you were looking for. It's not what I thought it was going to be, though. I'll give you the long version, since it will be good background for you if you decide to go through with this. All right?"

"Yes," Mordechai answered, "go ahead. Should I take notes or anything?"

"You'll need to write down a name later. Other than that, it's up to you."

"Hang on again, then, would you? I need paper and a pen." The line went silent again. A moment later Mordechai said, "Go on, please."

"Fine. The first thing I looked into is a procedure that's done when any trained magician is convicted of a capital crime. It's only invoked when dealing with crimes actually involving magic in their commission, and only people who have been trained, in one way or another, in the use of their magical abilities. Do you follow that?"

"I think so. Any witch or warlock who uses their power for evil and is caught has their powers removed. Is that right?"

Raoul rolled his eyes. "Mordechai, I don't know what you know about magic, but I think it's not very much. Let me explain something: I am a magician. I have a number of diplomas which prove that I studied for years and passed all kinds of nasty examinations. That makes me a magician, just as it makes every other person who passes those same examinations magicians. It's like being a doctor or a physicist, or anything else like that. Witches and warlocks are people who choose to practice magic without the benefit of that training and those diplomas. Some have some schooling, others are self-taught. Think of them as midwives as opposed to doctors. Evil has nothing whatsoever to do with magic. In many cases, religion has nothing whatsoever to do with magic. It's a personal decision, and I for one don't give a rat's ass what religion people choose, as long as it doesn't interfere with my life. We're talking magic and crime here, not religion and evil. Do you understand?"

There was a pause on the other end. Raoul imagined Mordechai was crossing himself or something. He smiled. Finally, a meek "Yes" sounded in his ear.

"Good," he continued. "Where was I? Right, capital crimes. So when a magician is convicted of a capital crime involving magic, a certain ritual is performed after sentencing. It's very complicated, and I won't go into detail, since you wouldn't understand it anyway. The important thing you should know is that it's a very serious undertaking. The power needed to perform the ritual—and it is a ritual, not just a spell—requires a convocation, which is a gathering of at least thirteen magicians. In this case, it's the Magician's Judicial Board, which has fifteen members, all of whom are judges in their own right. Each country has such a board, which presides over the final decision of all cases involving magic or magicians. The members of the board, as far as I know, are the only people who know the full ritual."

Mordechai broke in excitedly, "So how do I contact them?"

Raoul sighed. "You don't. As I said, it's a judicial thing. It'd be like asking to be put in prison for no reason, just because you wanted to. But," he said, cutting off any objection Mordechai might make, "there is something that might help you. When I was reading up on the ritual, there was a brief mention of a clinic in Switzerland, a kind of combination psychiatric clinic, nursing home, and religious retreat. It's run by a magician named Franklin Eiseler, who is also a psychiatrist, and, I should add, a religious fanatic. The place is called God's Eye."

"I've heard of that, I think."

"Probably," Raoul answered wryly. "It's been in the news quite a few times. The good doctor evidently didn't believe in paying taxes when he lived here. In any case, part of what the clinic does is block magical ability for those who don't want it. Eiseler has started his own cult, which believes that magic is an aberration that needs to be removed before the faithful can become 'pure.' With the exception of the doctor himself, of course. I think he's probably what you're looking for, though I can't say I recommend it. If you need more information, you can write or call the clinic itself. I've got an address but no phone number. You'll have to find that yourself."

Mordechai sighed in relief. "I don't think I can ever thank you enough for what you've done."

"Don't thank me too fast," Raoul said. "It's pretty expensive. The good doctor needs to be kept in style, you know. You may not be able to afford it."

"I'm not worried about that. Thank you so much."

"Don't worry about it. Just stop trying to save my soul or whatever is you're always on about."

"Okay, but I will pray for you. I wish you could understand how evil magic is and what it can—"

Raoul hung up.

He sat for a moment, staring at the telephone, wondering why Mordechai bothered him so. He'd come up against prejudice before, but no one had ever gotten to him as personally as Mordechai did. Even just talking to him got under his skin. He supposed it was because he'd known Mordechai since his teens. At least it was done now. He picked the phone up again and dialed Miriam's number.

"C'mon, Miriam, pick up the phone," Raoul said to the ringing on the other end. He tried to still his irritation, remembering that she actually did have other things to do. Still, he wanted to talk to her, since the library books had provided spell fragments containing each of the lost runes. He thought that by trying the pronunciation he'd found on each spell and seeing which, if any, worked, he could isolate the specific rune he'd rediscovered. He left a message on her machine, saying he was returning to Thornhold, then called for a taxi.

Mrs. Higgins flew at him the moment he came through the door, full of questions about Bolton. He allayed her fears as best he could, giving her a short version of what had happened, leaving out that Bolton had been researching ties to Mowatt's death, and telling her what the doctor and Bolton himself had said about his injuries and treatment. "A week or so more, you said?" she asked. "Oh, the poor boy! You'll be going back to see him, I hope?" Raoul nodded. "Good, then I'll cook up a pie for him—that is, if you wouldn't mind taking one with you? They can't be feeding him well."

Raoul laughed, nodding again. "I'm sure he'd love that, Mrs. Higgins. Any calls while I was out?"

She picked up a sheet of paper from beside the phone. "Oh, yes. A young woman named Miriam called last night, asking you to call her back. Professor Livingston called this morning, just to let you know all was going well in your classes. That was nice of him, wasn't it? And," she continued with an air of saving the best for last, "Mrs. Gulledge called. You're to call her back directly."

"Mother called?" Raoul asked. Mrs. Higgins nodded, smiling. She adored Harriet Gulledge, and Raoul believed she secretly harbored the belief that he ignored his mother too much. "I wonder what she wants?" he muttered.

"I'm sure I don't know," Mrs. Higgins replied. "I wrote down the number, in case you needed it." She handed him the paper and waited.

"Thank you, Mrs. Higgins." He made no move to pick up the phone. "I wonder if you could rummage up some tea and a bite to eat? I'm famished."

"Certainly. Where will you take it?"

"Upstairs in the study, if it's no trouble. Thanks."

Throwing his coat over the couch, he carried his bag and the list of calls up to the study. He brought the phone across the room to the window and dialed his mother's number. The maid answered on the third ring.

"Hi, Laura. It's Raoul. Is she about?"

"Raoul! Hi! We haven't heard from you in ages! Things are fine, I hope? And yes, she's just down the hall. I'll run and get her. Hang on, okay?"

Raoul stood, phone in hand, looking out the window. The leaves were just beginning to fall from the trees, giving the forest a somewhat stark look offset by the profusion of color blanketing the ground. After a few minutes his mother came on the line.

"Darling! I'm so glad you finally called! Have you seen Max yet? How is the poor dear? I've heard his burns are mostly superficial, but that he'll be in for another week or so. How's he bearing up? I hope you gave him my love."

He never ceased to be amazed by the amount of information his mother always just seemed to pick up. No wonder she and Bolton get on so well, he thought. He repeated what he'd told Mrs. Higgins and assured his mother that he'd given Bolton her regards. "So," he finally asked, "was that why you called?"

She laughed musically. Involuntarily, Raoul smiled. He loved the sound of her voice, no matter that what she said usually annoyed him. "Well, partially, of course! But really, it's been so long since we've spoken; I just wanted to know how you're doing. It's been months since you've been here, and we never got a chance to talk that night at the Whitings. And I imagine it's been hectic for you since then . . . So you'll have to come by soon and tell me what's been happening. Maybe the next time you visit dear Maxwell." She paused. "But I did call to let you know something." She waited.

"Yes?" He hated it when she made him prompt her.

"Well," she said, sounding pleased, "I had lunch with Madelyn Harrison today, Chief Inspector Harrison's wife, and she told me, in the strictest confidence, of course, that you're fine."

Raoul rolled his eyes. He decided to bait her. "Why, of course I'm fine, Mother. My health's never been better. How nice of her to pass it along to you, though."

She sighed. "Don't be childish, Raoul. You know what I'm talking about." A slight edge crept into her voice. "I'll spell it out for you, if you insist. The Chief Inspector of Scotland Yard mentioned to his wife, a personal friend of mine, that my son was no longer the prime suspect in the possible murder of the chair of his college. The college from which, I should add, he's been suspended because of his possible involvement in said murder inquiry. Is that clear enough for you, darling?"

"Well, I'm sorry if you were embarrassed by what's happened, if that's what you want me to say."

"I don't *want* you to say anything, Raoul. I merely thought you might *possibly* be interested. Obviously I was wrong. Why are you being so difficult? Is it because you're worried about Maxwell?"

"I'm not being difficult, Mother. You were hedging the issue. And no, I'm not worried about Bolton. He's going to be fine. Why do you always have to make up excuses for how I am, anyway?" As usual, he thought, not five minutes go by and we're arguing.

"Raoul, has it ever crossed your mind that perhaps the reason this is all happening is perhaps because of how you are? Your reputation isn't exactly the best, you know."

"Mother, I do not want to go into this—"

"And why do you always refuse to listen to what I have to say?"

"I don't refuse to listen. It's just that I know what you're going to say and it has nothing to do with me. I've heard it before, anyway."

"Oh really? So just what was I going to say?"

"You were going to start in on how my life would be so much easier if I'd 'just *try* to fit in more.' You know, the speech you've been giving me since I was six. Anyway, Mother, I don't want to argue."

She sniffed, but said nothing. He'd gotten to her, he thought. Yes, but he'd also upset her, which he disliked doing. It was hard enough for them to get along as it was. He waited for her to break the silence. It wasn't as if what he'd said wasn't true; he'd worked his first spell at six, and still hadn't heard the end of it from her.

Finally, he gave in, the way he always seemed to. "I'm sorry. I've upset you. Thank you for letting me know what Mrs. Harrison said. Actually, I knew that already. There've been some new developments."

Her voice warmed a bit from its earlier glacial tone. "So I've heard. Poor Reginald! Let's hope it all comes to nothing. This whole business is quite upsetting. I don't know how you can stand it."

Raoul made a noncommittal noise.

"Raoul?" Her voice became hesitant.

"Yes?"

"Now, please don't get upset at this, and I don't want to pry, but is it *really* such a good idea for you to be seeing Anne Whiting, now that all this is happening? Not, mind you," she cut him off, "that I'm not pleased. She's a wonderful, sweet girl. So nice. And it's about time, I might add. It's just that the timing might be . . . well, inauspicious."

Christ on a stick! Raoul thought. Does everyone know what I do? "Mother, I don't want to discuss this. We're friends. Period. End of sentence. Don't worry your pretty head about it. And now," it was his turn to cut her off, "I've got to go. Thank you for calling. I'll try to stop by next time I'm in London."

She sighed again. "That would be nice, dear. Perhaps Mrs. Stephens could entice you to stay for dinner?"

Raoul smiled. Her cook was forever trying to get him to eat more. "Who knows? I'll call you later. 'Bye."

"Ciao, darling. *Do* be careful, won't you?"

"Good-bye, Mother." Raoul gently laid the receiver down, successfully resisting the urge to throw it across the room in frustration. He loved her dearly, but he just couldn't seem to talk to or even be around her for ten minutes without an argument ensuing. "Ah, well," he sighed, then chuckled quietly. She really did know everything that was going on. To a fault.

His stomach growling reminded him that he hadn't eaten all day. He'd call Miriam later, he decided.

Chapter 9

When the phone rang at five past ten the next morning, Raoul shouted "I've got it" loud enough for Mrs. Higgins to hear. He picked it up, expecting to hear Miriam's voice. He'd finally managed to get her on the phone the previous evening, but she hadn't had time to talk. Surprisingly, it was Bolton on the line.

"Rags, it's me. Can you come over?"

"Good morning," Raoul said sarcastically. "Why? What's up?"

"Sorry. I've got the answer to your question, but I think you need to see it. When can you get here?"

"What is it?"

"You need to see it. Trust me. Are you coming or what?"

"Okay, okay! I'll be there as soon as I can. And Bolton, this better be good." Why the secrecy? he wondered.

"Oh, don't worry about that. See you." Bolton rang off.

As he hung up, Raoul wondered how Bolton had held the phone. Probably someone had held it for him; perhaps that was why he'd been so cryptic. He walked to the top of the stairs and called for Mrs. Higgins.

"Yes?" She came to the bottom of the staircase.

"I'm going to need a cab to London as fast as it can get here. Would you ring for one?"

"Certainly. Are you going to see Mr. Bolton?"

Raoul nodded.

"Oh, good. I'll get a little package ready."

Raoul returned to the study and rang Miriam. As usual, there was no answer. He told the answering machine he was leaving for London and probably wouldn't be back until late in the afternoon.

After hanging up, he spent a few minutes keying in more of the archaic spell fragments he'd found. He wanted at least two spell examples to test for each of the missing runes. The problem had been finding fragments that had clear definitions of what the spell was supposed to do, since otherwise they were worthless. He made a disk for Miriam, jammed more books and papers into his already crowded bag, then went downstairs to wait for the car.

Mrs. Higgins waylaid him as he passed the kitchen door. Indicating a bag on the table, she said, "I've made up a little something for Mr. Bolton, if you don't mind taking it with you."

"Not at all," Raoul replied, lifting the bag. Its weight surprised him. "What's in here, anyway? Lead cake?"

Chagrined, she smiled. "Well, you know how bad hospital food is, so I made up a stack of sandwiches for him. And some soup. And one of the German chocolate cakes he likes so much."

Raoul feigned shock. "That's all?"

"Well, there's also some cookies and tarts, and scones for breakfast, but that's all I've had time to make." She paused, concerned. "Do you think he needs more?"

Raoul laughed. "I'm sure he'll be more pleased than he can say. In addition to becoming the most popular man in the building. That is, at least while the food lasts . . ." The gate buzzer sounded. "Well, there's my ride. I'll be back later, I'm not sure when."

To avoid passing the time in idle speculation about what Bolton had found out about Jean and the photo, Raoul looked through the books he'd brought, marking more spells he wanted to try out. He'd gotten partly through the second book when the driver said they'd arrived.

The woman working behind the desk didn't even give him time to speak. "You're here for Mr. Bolton, aren't you?" she asked. Surprised, he nodded. Noting his puzzled look, she continued with a smile, "You probably don't remember, but I was here at the desk when he came in. I have a good memory for faces. You can go right on up."

Bolton was alone, sitting in bed reading a folder that lay on his lap. He looked up as Raoul entered and smiled. "Look at what Brenda rigged up for me last night!" he crowed. "I can read again!" He laid the palm of his bandaged right hand on the loose page in front of him. The page stuck to the bandage as he moved it aside. He put the page back, using his left elbow to hold the sheet down as he loosened the page from the bandage. He held up his right hand again for Raoul to see the double-sided tape affixed to the palm. "Ingenious, isn't she? Between this and the speaker phone, I'm actually not doing too badly."

Raoul laid his coat across the bottom of the bed and pulled up a chair. "So, where's this amazing piece of top secret news? No, wait. Higgins sent something for you." He picked up the bag, and with dramatic flourishes produced each item. When the bag was finally empty, Bolton looked at the side table, overflowing with food, and laughed. "That's all? She must not love me anymore."

Raoul chuckled. "You know, that's just what I said to her this morning. Should I put these back?"

"Hell, no! Maybe later I can get lovely nurse Liza to feed me some cake."

"Ah. She would be the matronly one I saw earlier, then? Hair in a bun, about two hundred fifty pounds, all muscle, of course, and *such* a lovely smile. I think I saw her carrying an enema bag this way." He smiled wickedly.

Bolton scowled at him. "Not quite. No, Liza's one of the candy stripers. One of the young ones." He leered, then grimaced. "Actually, the one you just described does exist." He shuddered. "I don't want to think about it. Now Liza, on the other hand . . ."

Raoul rolled his eyes. "Oh, great, I can hear it now. 'Want a cookie, little girl?' I thought you'd stopped using that line years ago. Two years, isn't it?"

Bolton smiled again, then became serious. "Anyway, my friend, enough playful repartee. Pull over here so you can see this." He waited while Raoul complied. "Now," he said, once Raoul was settled, "after you called, I asked Brenda to bring me over any articles about the Oxford staff from the past few years. I'll let you turn the pages, since you're faster at it than I am. Flip to the second picture."

The photograph was a black and white newspaper reproduction of a standing group, identified by the caption as the administrative staff of the entire university. Raoul looked up at Bolton. "That's Montgomery-Lewis, isn't it?"

"Circa 1965 or 'sixty-six." Bolton replied, nodding. "Note young Jeanine, there on the left. I don't think they were married yet." He paused while Raoul picked up the picture to get a better look. "Now flip forward a few pictures. It's another group shot."

He waited while Raoul turned the pages. "Stop. That's the one. Administrative staff from four months ago. Note Jeanine there in the middle."

Raoul looked closely at the color photo. "You mean Jean," he corrected.

"No, I mean Jeanine Lydia Arbuthnot Montgomery-Lewis, also known as Jean Morris." Bolton said. "Same woman thirty years later. Look at her."

Raoul did. From what he could tell, the two women were about the same height, but the resemblance ended there. One was a young attractive brunette, the other a middle-aged blonde. He scowled. "You're pulling my leg. I just saw her yesterday. No way."

"Use your eyes, Rags. Just compare the two pictures. Plus, I called a friend of mine at the tax office, who confirmed it. Same woman. Changed her name in 'sixty-nine."

Raoul shook his head. He couldn't believe it, much less try and think of the implications. "How . . ." He trailed off.

"How did I figure it out?" Bolton asked for him. "Oh, it was rather simple, really. Rodger left me copies of the statements made by Parker and Jean when they were questioned about the blackmail notes. I've been going over these things for days now."

"And?" Raoul asked, unsure where Bolton was leading.

"And I've been staring at these, as well as the Montgomery-Lewis case statements. They're all signed. Jean Morris' signature looked familiar, and I've never met the woman or heard from her. And then when you called it all just clicked together. I checked through the other papers I've got here, and voilà! Her signature matched Jeanine Montgomery-Lewis'. I *do* have an eye for detail, you know."

Raoul shook his head. "You're too much, do you know that? I can't believe it. She—"

"Looks so different? Thirty years is a long time, my friend. Plus, no one at the college knew her when her husband was alive. No one, that is—"

"Except Whiting and Mowatt." Raoul finished the sentence for him. "So, do they—I mean, did they know? Does Whiting know? How could they not know?"

Bolton shrugged. "Whiting might not. How much physical contact does he actually have with her? Assuming he hadn't seen her for almost thirty years, he might not have recognized her. She really does look different, you know. And then again, maybe he did recognize her. Mowatt, on the other hand, worked with her every day. Maybe he did, maybe he didn't, only we can't ask *him*. Or rather, *you* can't ask him. Whiting's a different story."

Raoul leaned back in the chair, crossing an ankle over his knee. He drummed his hands on his boot, thinking. "Ask Whiting?" he finally asked. "What if he says he didn't know? What if he says he did? What does it prove either way?"

Bolton thought a moment. "Essentially, nothing. You're right. Anyway, he could lie through his teeth and you wouldn't know. What about her? Can you talk to her?"

Raoul was still having difficulty adjusting to the idea. "I'm not sure. She retired. And what good would that do, anyway?"

"What? I thought you just saw her yesterday?"

"Right. She retired yesterday. I can get her address, though. But what do I say? 'Hi, Jean. I just dropped by wondering why you changed your name and came back to work around a man who may have killed your husband. Who's being blackmailed. Oh, and by the way, what did you have to do with Mowatt's death, and where were you the night the Scottish inn burned down?' Sure, that'll be great. She'll open right up."

"Scare her," Bolton said.

"What?"

"Scare her," he repeated firmly. "How much does she know about magic?"

"Who knows? Why?"

"So go see her, and if she doesn't fall for the old 'my powers reveal all' trick, tell her you're going to the police. You've got a brain, use it. Think up something."

Raoul sighed. "Great. Thanks. Is that it?"

"Is what what?"

"Is that the only revelation for now? If it isn't, I've got to get going, if I'm supposed to find Jean—I mean, Jeanine—today. I can't believe this," Raoul said, standing.

"Believe it. And yes, that's it. I've got another healing session later today, but I'll have Brenda try to dig up more info on Jeanine Montgomery-Lewis. Call me tonight?"

"Sure. How's the healing going, by the way?" Raoul felt a pang of guilt; Bolton seemed so much his usual self, he'd forgotten where they were and why. "Is it working?"

"Pretty well. I've only had one session so far, but my hands feel better already. It's probably only psychological at this point, though. The concussion, at least, is gone."

"Thanks to that hard head of yours. Anyway, I'm glad you're better. I'll call you tonight." Raoul left.

He called Bob Parker from a pay phone in the reception area and asked for Jean's address, which turned out to be in Summertown, a suburb to the north of Oxford. He avoided Parker's nosy questions by muttering something about wanting to send flowers. As Raoul walked toward the cab stand he was reminded that he was spending much too much money on transportation lately. Perhaps when Bolton was out he'd ask him about teaching him to drive, and then about purchasing a car. Bolton would just love that, Raoul was sure. Something else to pick on him about.

He gave the driver the address, then pulled out a pad and started jotting down things he wanted to ask Jean. He still wasn't sold on the idea of purposely frightening her. Usually, he'd found that most people with something to hide will eventually let it slip, as long as they're convinced they're just chatting. Of course, he usually used it on students who hadn't prepared for classes, but the concept was sound.

A little more than an hour later the cabbie sang out that they were nearing the address. "Damn!" Raoul cried, realizing what he'd forgotten. "Take me back to town, would you? I need to find a florist."

"Got a date, eh?" the driver asked.

Raoul, unamused, declined to respond. When they found a flower shop, he bought a large mixed arrangement. At Jean's address, a small cottage, he quickly paid the fare and walked up to the door, passing a light blue Morris parked in the short drive. Something told him that was significant, but he couldn't quite put his finger on why, and there was no time to check his notes. He pressed the bell.

Raoul suppressed the urge to wince when Jean opened the door. Direct sunlight wasn't kind to the silvery-red lesions on her exposed skin. He forced a smile and held out the flowers. "Hi, Jean. These are for you."

She held the door open, but didn't invite him in. Looking puzzled, she took the flowers. "Why, thank you, Professor Smythe. That's very kind of you. But, why?"

He shrugged. "I just stumbled into the party yesterday. I wanted to get you something."

She smiled, shaking her head. "You know, you didn't have to do that. Thank you, though. Would you care to come in for a moment?"

"Certainly." He followed her into the house. It seemed even smaller than it had from the outside. Sunlight streaming through the pinkish curtains gave the room a twilight atmosphere, which was heightened by the clutter. It seemed that every imaginable space held photographs or small porcelain figurines. The floral pattern of the curtains was repeated in the upholstery of the couch and two side chairs, and a faint scent of potpourri filled the air. Feeling slightly claustrophobic, Raoul took a seat on the couch, which softly enveloped him. Jean sat in one of the side chairs, then stood back up, as if she'd forgotten something.

"Could I offer you some tea?" she asked.

"Only if it's no trouble." Raoul felt strange, knowing who she really was. He wondered if she thought of herself as Jean or Jeanine, if she'd truly become a different person in the past thirty years.

"None at all. Make yourself at home. I'll only be a minute."

Relieved, he rose from the couch to look around as she went into the kitchen. A small side table held a number of photographs. Not wanting to pick them up, he leaned down for a better look.

They were mostly pictures of children of varying ages. One photo in particular caught his eye; a color photo of Jean herself, holding a very young baby. He picked it up for a better look. It was a striking photograph, for though Jean's skin appeared relatively clear, the child's face and hands were covered with the same reddened scales that Jean now bore.

"That's my little nephew, Colin," Jean said from behind him. Raoul spun guiltily around. She placed a large tray of tea things on the small center table, then crossed to where he stood and gently took the photo from him. "Isn't he sweet?"

"For a moment, I thought it was your child," Raoul said. "You look so happy, holding him."

She put the photo back down. "No," she said sadly, "he's not mine." She returned to her chair, and said, "But I can see why you thought that." She gestured at her face. "It's hereditary, though the doctors are unclear on just how it's passed along. It often skips, even within the same family. Poor little Colin."

"How old is he?" Raoul had no idea where the conversation might lead.

"Colin? He's—" She thought a moment. "—he's fifteen months now. I haven't seen him since the picture was taken, though. My sister and her family moved to America soon after Colin was born." She leaned forward to pour out the tea.

Raoul saw his opening. Careful to keep his voice conversational, he asked, "So, then, you and Mr. Montgomery-Lewis didn't have any children?"

Her head was down as she concentrated on pouring. She didn't respond or look up, but the thin stream of tea began to shake and missed the cup, puddling in the saucer. The tray rattled as she quickly set the pot down. She remained silent for a moment, putting one hand up to rub her forehead. She sighed, then leaned back and met Raoul's gaze. Her eyes were bright with moisture. "How did you find out?"

"The photograph in your office," he answered simply, "and then signatures."

"What do you want? The police already spoke to me about the notes. I offered to take a lie detector test. They didn't think it was necessary."

"Yes, but you only offered to take the test *after* Robert Parker had offered, and been let go, without the test. You also used practically the same wording as Parker when you talked about people having open access to the typewriter. Would you have really taken the test? I don't think so, since I think you wrote the three blackmail notes."

"And I think you should leave now," she said stiffly.

"I can't do that, Jean. I need some information."

"I don't want to talk to you. You'd better leave."

"And go straight to the police? I hear they're in the market for a blackmailer these days. Not to mention a murderer. Or murderess." He held her gaze. Her eyes dropped first.

"Why are you doing this?" she asked. "What does it matter to you?" When Raoul didn't respond, she sagged back in her chair, her defiance gone. "I didn't kill Arthur. I couldn't have."

"But you were blackmailing Whiting, weren't you? And making it look as if Mowatt were sending the notes, so suspicion would fall on him. Is that it? And why couldn't you have killed him? You look strong enough to me."

"No. You're wrong. Arthur wasn't involved at all."

"But you were blackmailing Whiting, right? Why? Is it because you think he killed your husband?"

"I can't tell you that, but you're wrong, that's not what it was about. It has nothing to do with George's death. That was an accident, believe me. Reg had nothing to do with it."

"Then why hint at it in the first note? The one the police received."

"I told you I didn't write that. The police showed it to me. It's not mine."

"What?" Raoul was confused. "What about the other two notes? Did you write them? The ones done on your typewriter?"

Jean nodded.

"Then who wrote the other? Maybe Whiting was blackmailing himself? That makes a lot of sense, doesn't it? Or maybe you just wanted to use another typewriter for a change? Or maybe," he said, thinking aloud, "maybe you're in it with Parker? And where does Mowatt fit in?"

Jean sighed. "You don't understand," she repeated. "Robert Parker, and especially Arthur, had nothing whatsoever to do with this. It was between Reg and me, and Reg knew that. No one else even knew about it. Will you please believe that?"

Raoul thought a moment. "So Whiting knows who was sending the notes." He looked at Jean, who nodded. "Does he know who sent the other note?"

She shook her head. "I don't know."

"You haven't talked to him about that note, then?"

She stared at him, puzzled. "I haven't talked to him about anything. Reginald Whiting doesn't know who I am.

He thinks I'm just—or rather, I was just—Arthur's secretary. He doesn't know I'm me. Just what is it you do know, if you don't know that?" Her eyes narrowed.

"He doesn't know," Raoul said quietly to himself. That changed things. Instead of answering her question, he posed another of his own. An idea was beginning to take shape. "But Mowatt knew, didn't he? He knew that you're really Jeanine Montgomery-Lewis."

Jean didn't respond. She looked stonily past him.

Suddenly he had it. Her car, the blue Morris. The unidentified light blue car Mowatt's neighbors had seen. "You were lovers, weren't you? Did you fight? Is that how he died?"

"No! I didn't kill him!" she cried. "I don't know who did!" She began to sob, tears slowly rolling down her face as she gripped the chair arms as if holding on for life. "Why won't you listen to me? I didn't kill him! I loved him! Oh, God, if only I'd known that before . . ." She trailed off, raising a fist to her mouth and biting at her knuckles. "I didn't kill him. I couldn't have done that to him. It was horrible."

Something in her voice made another piece click into place for Raoul. "You found him, didn't you? It was you who called the police. Before you went to work on a Saturday. And I'll bet you hadn't planned to go to work. It was an alibi, wasn't it? After you found him dead."

Still trying to get herself under control, she could only nod. Raoul poured a cup of tea and handed it to her. She held it in both hands and sipped. After a few moments she carefully replaced the cup on the tray and rubbed a hand across her eyes.

When she finally spoke, she sounded relieved, as if some barrier had been crossed. "We weren't lovers. He wanted to but I . . . I didn't think I loved him. We were friends, that was all. We spent a lot of time with each other, but I didn't want anyone to see us together. And then we argued about . . . that, and I left. That's when I began to miss work—I just didn't want to see him, and the stress it brought on . . .

But I went back that morning, to see if we could talk, and he was . . . I couldn't tell anyone, so I called the police. Oh, poor Arthur . . . dear Arthur . . .

"He knew, you see," she continued, "from the first day I walked into the office. *He* recognized me, even after all those years." She paused, a slight smile passing over her face. "I told him I didn't want anything to do with my previous life, I just needed a job. That's why I'd moved, why I'd changed my name. I came back only because . . . I took the job because it was a job. Simply that. I'm a different person now. And do you know what?" she asked Raoul.

"What?"

"Arthur respected that. That's the kind of man he was. He understood, and agreed not to say anything to anyone, especially not to Reginald. And he never asked questions, he accepted that I didn't want to talk about it. I thought we were fine, but then a few weeks ago he . . . he told me he loved me, that he'd always loved me. That I was the reason he'd never married. He showed me what he'd done for me—"

Raoul broke in, gently. "The bathroom. He redecorated it for you, didn't he? For your skin, to make it more comfortable for you to take long baths. Buying up skin creams that might help you."

Jean nodded. "Yes. Anything to keep moisture in the skin helps it. Since George's death all those years ago, it's gotten worse. Arthur wanted to help me. That's the kind of man he was, so sweet . . . and I couldn't face it, I didn't know how I felt. Not until . . ." She looked up at Raoul.

"So you and Mowatt argued about your relationship. Not about your blackmailing Whiting?"

She shook her head violently. "No! I told you he didn't even know about it."

"So what about Whiting?"

"What do you mean?"

"How did your relationship affect Mowatt's attitude toward Whiting?"

Jean thought a moment. "I've told you, we didn't have

a 'relationship.' Arthur was angry at Reg, though; he refused to believe that Reg couldn't recognize me, especially since . . ." She paused. "I think he gradually grew colder toward Reg, but it wasn't just because of me. Arthur cared very deeply about his work, and he didn't agree with Reg's ideas about how the college should be run. *You* should know that." She spoke the last sentence accusingly.

Raoul changed the subject, not wanting either to explain his own attitude toward Mowatt or to hear what Mowatt had thought of him.

"So you don't know who killed him?"

She sighed. "No."

"How did you find him?" Raoul asked.

"I was just stopping by to talk, and I . . . I let myself in, and then I saw him, but he was . . ." She breathed deeply. "He was already dead. It was horrible. I let myself out and wiped off the door, then called the police. And that's all I know."

"You don't know of anyone who might have had a reason to kill him? Anyone who was angry with him?"

Jean lowered her eyes. "No," she replied shortly.

Raoul thought she was lying. "No ideas at all?" he asked. "Surely there must be someone you could think of—"

"I said I didn't know," she snapped, still staring at her hands.

He thought briefly about trying Bolton's idea of frightening her, but decided it probably wouldn't work. As the secretary and friend of a magician, Jean probably had at least some clue about what magic could and couldn't do. Rather than risk her calling his bluff, he changed the subject. "Why were you blackmailing Whiting?"

She looked up, scowling. "I said I can't tell you that. And I won't. Why do you want to know all this, anyway? Are you going to tell the police about me? Is this just to stop them asking questions about you?"

Raoul had already thought about this. "No, it's not. And, no, I don't think I'm going to tell the police. I don't know why, but I think you're telling the truth when you say you didn't kill him. But I also think you haven't told me everything you know."

"Are you going to tell the police?" she repeated.

"No," he said, deciding. "Let them find out for themselves. And they probably will, you know."

"I don't care." She seemed tired, and idly scratched at the backs of her hands. "Are you done? I need to put on more medication." She looked at him coldly.

Raoul rose. "I'm sorry if I upset you. I can find my own way out."

Jean didn't reply, but sat silently watching until he'd closed the door behind him. Standing on the stoop, he heard her cross to the door and turn the locks. He decided to walk back into town; he needed the time to think about all he'd heard.

The walk took almost an hour. Back in his office, he immediately phoned Bolton. The nurse who answered said that Bolton was unavailable, which meant he was probably in another healing session. Raoul left a message for him to call back as soon as possible. Then he tried Miriam's number, to no avail, and left another message for her.

He added a summary of his conversation with Jean to his notes. He still couldn't put his finger on just why he believed her, but he did. And if she was telling the truth, then she hadn't killed Mowatt or written the note that had been sent to Bolton and the police. But she admitted she *had* been blackmailing Whiting, and Raoul thought she had an idea of who had killed Mowatt. It had to have something to do with the first note, he thought, but who'd written it? That one had been done on Parker's machine, outside Whiting's office. Had he written it? But he'd already been questioned, and had been the first to offer to take a lie detector test. And just why did Jean need money from Whiting? Raoul needed to find out if Whiting had actually paid or not. He wrote himself a reminder to have Bolton ask Collings what the police had discovered in Whiting's bank records. It seemed that the more information had, the more confusing the whole issue became. When the two notes had been found at Whiting's house, Raoul had started to believe that perhaps Anne's father had killed Mowatt. But if Jeanine had been the one blackmailing Whiting, and Whiting had known that, and Jean hadn't written the note that was sent to Bolton and the police—

Abruptly, Raoul realized there was no proof that Whiting had ever gotten a copy of that particular note. Everyone had just assumed he had. If suspicion had fallen on him because of that note alone, then there was no longer any concrete reason to believe that his being blackmailed had anything to do with Mowatt's death. It did imply, however, that someone, the person who actually wrote and sent the note, wanted Whiting blamed for the death and also knew about the blackmail. But who wrote the note?

He was thinking in circles, Raoul thought. He needed a break. Pulling the file on the aural erasure out of his bag, he copied the new spells from the disk onto his hard drive and set about adding the new spells he'd found on the way to London that morning. A few lines into the first spell, he canceled the new file. He just wasn't in the mood. As he gazed around his office, his eyes lit on the phone.

"Screw it," he said aloud. Taking out his address book, he dialed Anne Whiting's work number. After three rings someone picked up the line. "Uh, hello. Is Anne available? It's Raoul Smythe."

Anne came on the line a moment later. "Raoul? Hi," she said. She sounded as if she were smiling. "You're lucky. I was just on my way out the door."

"I'm glad I caught you," he replied, smiling himself. "Long time no see." She laughed. "I was wondering," he continued, "If you wanted to have dinner or a drink or something."

"Tonight?"

"Yeah."

"I'd love to. Where are you?"

"I'm at the office. Do you want me to come by your house later?"

"Actually, why don't I pick you up? We'll get dinner and then have a drink at the Seller, if you'd like. Our last time there wasn't very fun." She sounded rueful. "This way, we can make up for it."

"Sounds good. When do you want to come by?"

"Well, I'll need to change, so why don't we say half an hour or so? Is that okay?"

"Sure. I'll see you later, then."

Raoul put down the receiver, then picked it up again. Mrs. Higgins picked up on the second ring. "Good even—" she began.

Raoul cut her off. "Hi, it's me. How long does it take to make dinner for two?"

"That depends on what's being cooked," she replied, puzzled.

"Well, what do we have in the house? I'm thinking of having someone over."

She thought a moment. "Well," she said, "there's a chicken I could roast. That's always good. It could be ready in, say, an hour and a half or so."

Raoul paused, considering his options. "An hour and a half," he repeated, thinking. Half an hour till she arrived, then an hour to get to Thornhold, if they stopped for a drink on the way. "That sounds great. Go ahead with that."

"Certainly. What else would you like with dinner?"

He rolled his eyes. "I don't know. Food. Something simple. I'll serve it myself, by the way. You can have the night off." He surprised even himself with that last statement.

"Pardon?"

"I said you can have the night off. If you can whip something up for dinner and just leave it in the oven or something, I'll deal with it myself. Will that work?"

"Yes," she said slowly. He could tell she was dying to know what was going on. "When should I come back?"

"I don't know," he replied, "sometime tomorrow afternoon should be fine. Is this all right with you? I know it's kind of sudden. Oh, wait, this is a short week for you anyway, right?"

"Yes . . ."

"You know, why don't you just take the rest of the week off? It'll be a good break for you. That is, if you'd like."

"Really? Well, I guess that would be fine . . . I'll just pop over to my sister's. No problem at all. Thank you."

"Fine, then. Leave me a note, and I'll see you next week."

"Good night, then."

"Good night. And thanks, Mrs. Higgins." Raoul hung up the phone, then sat thinking about what he'd done. Well, Anne had said she'd like to see Thornhold. And he certainly didn't want Higgins poking around. No, he decided, this was definitely for the best. A nice quiet evening, with no one around to ask questions or make snide comments later. This way, he thought, maybe he could actually get to talk to her, without distractions. Without anyone around to wonder just what their "relationship" was. "Except me," he said aloud, then laughed at himself, and began gathering his things together. He thought he'd wait for her outside the building.

Anne arrived a few minutes early. "Hi!" she called from several feet away.

Raoul sat up from the wide stone banister where he'd been stretched out, staring at the sky.

"Napping?" she asked, and laughed.

"No," he replied, smiling, "just thinking. So, hi." He stood up.

"Are you all set?" she asked.

He nodded. "I was thinking . . ." he began.

She smiled. "So you said."

He raised an eyebrow. "I was thinking," he repeated, "that maybe you'd like to have dinner at Thornhold."

She looked at him. "Really?" she asked. "Afraid to be seen with me in public?"

"No, that's not what I meant. I mean . . ." he stuttered. She'd come too close to his own thoughts.

She laughed and patted his arm. "It's a great idea, and I'd love to."

Walking back to her car, they chatted vaguely about her day at work. As Raoul listened, part of him was also thinking about how friendship was, in many ways, based on storytelling. The trick was to find someone whose stories interested you, and hope that they were interested in yours. Conversations were only shared anecdotes, either from one's own past or present, or about other people whose stories somehow touched one's own. But what was really being shared wasn't the actual information; rather, the storytelling provided clues to who someone really was, their opinions, likes, and dislikes. The trick was to read beyond the words to the person behind them.

"So, anyway," Anne continued, "that was my day. What did you do? Have you talked to Max? How's he doing?"

"Bolton? I went down again this morning, as a matter of fact." He filled her in on Bolton, leaving out any mention of their research into Mowatt's death. Although he'd told her he'd let her know if he found out anything about her father, he didn't plan on involving her at all. It would make for needless complications, and he was especially hesitant after what had happened to Bolton. It was one thing that Bolton was still actively involved—Raoul didn't think it was humanly possible to stop Bolton from getting information, and the hospital was probably the safest place for him—it was another thing to possibly subject Anne to danger.

The ride to Thornhold passed swiftly and pleasantly. Raoul found himself telling her about how he'd come to own Thornhold. As usual, talking about it put him in a good mood. As they approached, Anne slowed the car, expecting he'd get out and open the gates. Instead, glancing quickly at her, he spoke the spell to unlock and open them. He knew he was showing off, but didn't particularly care.

She was suitably impressed. "Did you just do that?"

He nodded, trying not to smile.

"That's wonderful! It really is. You must get sick of people saying that, though."

He laughed. "Actually, I don't. It's funny; I use magic so much that sometimes I stop noticing it. Other people's reactions make me see it through their eyes. It brings back the—if you'll excuse the pun—magic of it. Makes it seem fresh again. Does that make sense? Drive right up to the house, by the way."

As they pulled into the drive, she had her first good look at Thornhold itself. She glanced at Raoul, who was again waiting for her reaction. He was smiling. "I know, I know," he said, laughing, "I'm the only person I know who likes it. It's okay. Believe me, you should ask Bolton what he thinks of it."

Anne opened her mouth to speak, decided against it, then forged ahead. "It is ... interesting," she said hesitantly. "It's kind of, well ... It's ..." She grimaced and fell silent, looking at Raoul, who was shaking with suppressed laughter at her discomfort. Finally she burst out giggling as well. "I'm sorry, Raoul, but it's really ugly! I'm sorry," she repeated as they got out of the car.

Raoul had to stop laughing to speak the spell that opened the door. He couldn't do it; they'd glance at each other and start laughing again.

"Maybe you should try using the key," Anne sputtered.

"I don't have one!" he responded. His stomach was starting to hurt. "I mean, I do, but I don't carry it around. Why would I need to?" That set him off again. Finally, with a muttered, "Oh, damn it!" he gave in and rang the doorbell. This, of course, got them both laughing again. They were still chuckling when Mrs. Higgins opened the door. She held the door open for them to enter, looking confusedly from Raoul to Anne.

"Welcome home," she said. "You're earlier than I expected. Everything's not quite done yet. Good evening, miss."

Raoul had managed to get himself back under some semblance of control. He smiled at Mrs. Higgins. "No problem at all," he replied, taking off his coat, then helping Anne with hers. "Just show me what to do and I'll take care of it." Higgins looked at him, surprised. As far as she knew, Raoul's culinary talents were limited to boiling water and ordering take-out food. "No, really," he repeated, nodding at her and smiling. "How hard can it be?"

Anne broke in, "No harder than opening a door, I imagine." She laughed, turning to Mrs. Higgins. "I'm Anne Whiting, by the way. You must be Mrs. Higgins. I'm pleased to meet you."

Mrs. Higgins beamed at her. "Well, hello. Would you happen to be related to Sir Reginald Whiting at the university?"

Anne nodded. "He's my father."

Raoul addressed Mrs. Higgins again, speaking as he moved toward the kitchen. "So, why don't you show me what I need to do? Have you called for a cab yet, or is your sister coming by? Anne, make yourself at home. Would you like something to drink? Wine or anything?"

"Wine would be fine. White, if it's no trouble. Would you like me to help?"

"No, thanks. I'll be back in a moment. Sorry, Mrs. Higgins. You were saying?"

As Higgins showed Raoul exactly what needed to be done, she explained that her sister was coming to pick her up. Raoul opened the wine, asking questions about the timing of the vegetables as compared to that of the chicken. As Mrs. Higgins set out the serving dishes she said, "Now, the table's all set, but I didn't have time to make anything for dessert. Are you sure you don't want me to stay? It's really no trouble if you do."

Raoul shook his head, "No, thanks. I'll be fine. Really. Please stop worrying." He spoke more firmly; her concern was starting to feel cloying.

Luckily, she'd been with him long enough to pick up on his moods. She nodded. "Well, I'll just finish up in here until Marie arrives." She made a shooing motion at him. "Go on in, you shouldn't neglect your guest."

He grinned in response, picked up two glasses and the wine, and headed back to the living room.

Anne was standing to the right of the fireplace, looking up at the sword, a claymore, hanging there. "Gorgeous, isn't it?" Raoul asked as he crossed to her. "That one's an original, not a reproduction. Supposedly it was used at the Battle of Bannockburn in 1314, but of course there's no proof. Still . . ." He held out one of the glasses to her. She took it, and both stood silently for a moment. Finally Raoul raised his glass toward her. *"Alpnu,"* he said, then gently touched her glass with his own. The crystal chimed quietly.

"It's the closest thing Etruscan has to a toast," he explained in response to her look. "Literally it means 'gladly' or 'willingly,' but there's a secondary meaning of something being given willingly or 'as a gift.' Apparently the Etruscans didn't care about health as much as we do. I guess you can take it to mean that I'm glad you've come over."

Anne nodded. "Well, then, *alpnu*," she said, raising her glass to him in turn. She smiled, gesturing around the room. "Did you do all this yourself?"

Raoul shook his head. "Not this floor," he said. "Almost all of this came with the house. Some of the swords are mine, but that's about it. I wouldn't change a thing, though. I'm sorry, would you like the full tour?"

"Of course."

They wound their way slowly through the house, finishing on the rooftop walkway between the towers. "What a lovely view," Anne murmured, looking out over the patchwork hills.

"It is, isn't it?" Raoul replied. He wasn't sure he'd ever noticed before.

Higgins' sister's car pulled up to the gate, which swung open a moment after she buzzed. She parked in front of the house, and a few moments later Mrs. Higgins came out. Raoul called down to Higgins to have a nice time, and he and Anne both waved as the car drove off.

They returned downstairs. While showing her the kitchen

and pointing out the outside herb garden, Raoul checked on the chicken, which according to Higgins' note was ready to serve. Over his protestations that he could handle it, Anne helped. Finally, they sat down to eat. Anne raised her glass in a toast. *"Alpnu,"* she said, smiling.

The meal was quite good, Raoul thought, feeling somewhat proprietary even though he'd had nothing to do with the cooking itself. He and Anne spent most of dinner discussing how important it was that where one lived reflect one's own personality. He was pleased to hear that she thought, as he did, that Thornhold was perfect for him. Without mentioning Mowatt's name, he spoke about how he had felt in a house almost completely without personality. "It's horrible to even think about it, really," he said. "I just can't imagine how anyone could live like that, surrounded by things they didn't care about. How can you spend so much time somewhere without leaving any sort of mark?"

"I wish I knew," Anne said. "I think I live that way now. I mean, my parents' house is lovely, but it's not mine. I'd love to have the chance to have a place that was completely mine, that I could decorate however I'd like to, to make it what I wanted it to be."

Raoul nodded. "I know the feeling. It's the nesting urge, I think." He smiled before continuing. "Why don't you just move out?"

Anne snorted. "If only it were that easy," she said. "No, it's another one of those things where Dad insists on having his own way but makes it look like my decision. Which it is, really. I guess I'm used to living a certain way, and I couldn't afford it if I had to live on my salary. And Dad knows that, which is why he often reminds me of how he'd cut me off if I move out. So, really, it's my own fault for not wanting to give up what I've got."

Raoul knew what she meant. Still, there were always options. "Why not get a better job? You know, make more money?"

Anne shook her head. "I can't do that, either. Remember

how I told you I got the job through Dad, how the agency's owner is a friend of his?" Raoul nodded. "Well, I can't get another job without getting effectively thrown out and cut off. Dad thinks advertising is a good field for me, and pays me an allowance on top of my salary as long as I'm doing what he wants me to. What he thinks I should do." She looked at him, then away. Toying with her fork, she said quietly, "Pathetic, isn't it? You're so lucky, you know, to have all this." She gestured at the room. "To have everything be your own and no strings attached." She sighed.

"Are you done eating?" Raoul asked abruptly, pushing his chair back. "I'm not changing the subject, really. Let's go sit, if you are." Anne appeared confused at first, then nodded and stood. Raoul carried the wine bottle into the parlor, freshened their drinks, then stretched out in one of the large leather chairs, throwing his legs over one arm. Anne sat on the couch.

"I thought we'd be more comfortable in here," he said, then picked up the conversation where they'd left it. "It's not pathetic at all, Anne. I think everything comes with strings attached, especially in the kind of family situations I think we both have. All this," he copied her gesture of a few minutes before, "has its own strings. How do you think I happen to have a full-time housekeeper, on my salary? Don't get me wrong, it's great having Higgins here, but I couldn't ever afford her on what I make." Anne looked perplexed.

He continued. "It's my mother. She thinks I'd be unable to function without someone taking care of me, so she pays for Higgins. If I really wanted to, I suppose I could say no and just make her stop, or let Higgins go, but it's never seemed worth it. I just take it for what it's worth and try to live my own life as best I can. Eventually my mother will figure out I'm never going to be the way she wants me to. Maybe." He shrugged.

"Dad won't," Anne said glumly. "I mean, I suppose it's stupid that I try to fight him while at the same time keep doing everything he wants me to. He tries to control everything, he always has, but in other ways it's as if he just doesn't care about anything I do. I used to think it was because he wanted a son, and so he wants me to be the exact opposite of what I want to ... I don't know, sometimes I feel as if I'm two different people, one of them the little princess my father wants me to be, and the other trying desperately not to be that. I guess I do it to annoy him, in ways he can't say anything about. Or won't, anyway. All those stupid parties I go to, all the stupid people I go out with; I'm out every night, sometimes all night, but he never says anything as long as I'm the way he wants me to be in public. Or look it, at least. He won't say anything, so neither do I. It's such a stupid game. Do you know how many men I've brought home just to spite him? It's like I ... Oh, Raoul, I'm so sorry! You don't want to hear all this, I'm sure. I'm so stupid sometimes, I never *think* about what I'm saying or doing until it's too late ... I—"

Raoul waved her off. "It's okay, Anne. I understand."

She looked at him gratefully. "I mean, I've always felt like I'm some kind of display mannequin to him, not a real person at all. I need to act a certain way, look a certain way, and so on and so forth. I'm the daughter of a very important man, you know," she said acidly. "When I was little, I always wanted to be just like everyone else, but I never could. Everyone must have thought me a royal stuck-up bitch, for the things I couldn't do and the places I couldn't go. I think I hated my father for a long time, without ever actually saying or even thinking it when I was younger. I don't think I do anymore, though." Strangely, she laughed. "You know, that's the one good thing about all this—now he has to keep a low profile, trying not to attract 'negative publicity.' And do you know, lately I've actually had people sound like they feel *sorry* for me? And it's felt good! It's like being ... well, normal for once." She finished her wine. Raoul stood to pour another glass, but the bottle was empty.

"Hold on a minute, I'll be right back." He went off to

the kitchen, returning with a fresh bottle. He poured for Anne, then finished his glass and poured for himself.

"You must think me an awful bore, talking of nothing but myself," she said. "I'll shut up for a while."

Raoul shook his head and smiled at her. "No," he replied. "It's weird; I think I've always felt much the same way about my mother as you do about your father. I just started rebelling at an early age." He laughed, remembering. "I don't think I ever gave her a chance to think I might actually be able to act or even look normal, so she's never really expected me to. Your rebellion just took a different track, it seems. Nothing wrong with it, either way."

Anne shook her head. "You know, you really are something different. I mean, don't take this the wrong way, but you do come off pretty cold at first. Whenever you used to show up at parties and get-togethers it always seemed you only talked to Max . . . But that's not what I mean. You're just so different from all my other friends, and from the other professors I know. I think that's why I went out with you in the first place. You seemed kind of . . . well, dangerous. But there's so much more to you. I mean, you're so easy to talk to, and you understand all my neurotic ramblings, and . . ." She trailed off. "I guess what I'm trying to say is, thank you for listening, and I really enjoy being with you." She smiled, then looked down into her glass. "Is that sappy or what?"

Raoul wasn't quite sure how to respond. "No, it's not. Thank you. And believe me, I'm really not like this with most people. I don't make friends all that easily. I don't even like most of the people I have to deal with, and I certainly don't go out of my way to talk to them. I guess you're pretty easy to talk to yourself." He shrugged. "I usually don't even think about things like this, to tell the truth. I guess I'm not very introspective."

Anne smiled brightly at him, cheerful again. "Anyway," she said pointedly, "if we keep this up we'll both need insulin shots before the night's over. Enough about me, then. So how's your research going? I guess it looks like my father's in trouble, doesn't it? Or is this something you don't want to talk about?"

He didn't, but she seemed to want to. He decided he'd just leave out anything he didn't want to discuss. "It doesn't really matter to me," he replied. "Are you okay talking about it?"

She laughed. "I'm not going to go hysterical on you, if that's what you mean. It's something I've been thinking about. You know, for all my problems with him, I just can't picture my father doing something like that. You know, killing anyone. He's not the type, if you know what I mean. And from what he says, that's not even what the police are concentrating on at the moment. Those stupid notes! I can't see why anyone would want to blackmail him; I mean, I can see why they'd want money, but everyone knows that George Montgomery-Lewis' death was an accident. Especially Arthur Mowatt! And he and Dad had been friends forever. I just can't believe anyone could take the idea seriously. It just doesn't make sense." She took a deep breath, obviously trying to keep from becoming upset.

Raoul stood and walked to the fire. Taking up the poker, he stirred the ashes, then added another log. He wondered if he should let her know that it looked like the note received by the police and Bolton was a fake. It would reassure her, at least. He didn't think she was as unconcerned about it as she'd said when she raised the subject.

He stalled, saying, "I don't think it really makes sense to anyone at this point. There are just too many things that don't fit. Don't forget, it could all just be some kind of weird coincidence." Behind him, Anne made a noncommittal noise. He wished they hadn't started talking about this. He turned around to look at her. She sat staring into her glass, swirling her wine.

"Anne, you can't tell this to anyone, okay?" he began. "This is something even the police don't know yet, and I don't want to be the one to tell them, because, well . . . for a couple of reasons. But I'm pretty sure they'll figure it out before too long, in any case. So, you need to promise that it'll just be between us."

"Sure," Anne said quietly. "What is it, Raoul? Is it something about my father?"

He took a deep breath. "The note that was sent to the police and to Bolton doesn't appear to be a 'real' blackmail note. It wasn't done on the same typewriter, and it's pretty certain it was sent by someone other than the actual blackmailer. Right now, unless something else turns up, it looks like your father was telling the truth about never having seen that particular note, since there's no proof that he ever received it. And it's highly unlikely that Mowatt was involved in blackmailing him. So if that's what the police were using as a possible motive for your father, it's pretty useless.

"The big questions are going to be who wrote the first note and who sent it to Bolton and the police. Possibly the same person, but I'm not taking anything for granted anymore. So it looks like someone's trying to implicate your father. After all, the note was received, and most likely mailed, *after* Mowatt's death. If we knew who sent it, and why, we might know who the murderer is. Does that make you feel better about your father? Once the police figure this out, they'll probably turn their attention to finding out who sent it." He glanced at her. She was staring at him, her eyes wide, her face drained of color. "Anne! What's the matter?" he asked, crossing the room quickly to sit beside her. He took the glass of wine from her shaking hands.

She said something too quietly for him to hear. "What?" he asked. "Anne, what's wrong?" He put his hands on her shoulders, turning her toward him. "Tell me," he said quietly.

Instead of answering, she simply collapsed forward into his arms. He patted her back for a moment, then began to lightly stroke her hair. He noted how soft it was, even as he kept up a steady stream of hopefully calming words. Oddly enough, she didn't appear to be crying.

After a few moments, she mumbled something. "What?"

he asked gently, moving back a bit on the couch. But he kept his hands on her shoulders, holding her at arm's length. She shook her head, refusing to look up at him.

"Anne, I didn't hear what you said. Tell me again. Please."

"I didn't mean it," she whispered finally, still not meeting his eyes.

"I don't understand. What didn't you mean? What's the matter?"

She shook her head again, her hair falling forward to cover her eyes. "I didn't mean for this to happen. I didn't know it was different."

Raoul narrowed his eyes, thinking. He shook her lightly as he asked, "You didn't know what was different? Anne, are you talking about the note that Bolton got? Is that what was different?"

She nodded. "I didn't know what else to do with it," she said. "And Dad was being horrid again about me wanting my own place. I wanted to hurt him. I opened the letter by mistake, it was after Arthur died, but I don't remember exactly when. I didn't know what to do with it, so I mailed copies to Max and the police. I knew at least one of them would look into it. I wanted to get Dad in trouble, to get back at him. But I swear I never meant it to go this far." She brushed her hair out of her eyes and looked at him.

"*You* mailed the note?" Raoul asked. He didn't know what to think about this. She nodded. "And your father never saw it?" She shook her head, biting her lower lip and watching him attentively. "Damn," he muttered. "Are you going to tell the police about this?"

Her eyes widened. "Do I have to? I mean, is it that important? You said they'd probably figure it out anyway . . ."

"Anne, it's the only concrete proof that your father never saw the signed note, no matter who sent it. It's important. Very important." He stood up, walked across the room, sighed, then walked back and stood facing her, his back to the fire. "I can't believe this. Why is nothing in my life simple anymore? Why do you, of all people, have to be mixed up in all this crap?" He sighed again, explosively, and threw himself back into his chair. He sat staring at the fire. He hadn't wanted to think about this at all tonight, and now he couldn't think of anything else. He couldn't even relax anymore, it seemed. Damn Mowatt, he thought, damn him to every hell there is.

"I'm sorry, Raoul," Anne said quietly. Raoul glanced up at her but didn't respond. After a few moments she asked, "Should I go now? Do you want me to leave?" She stood. "I should go."

Raoul remained silent, not trusting himself to speak. Anne collected her coat from the rack near the door, then walked back to stand in front of him. "I'm sorry," she repeated. She waited for him to answer, to no avail. She threw him one last look before walking to the door.

"Anne."

She turned, her hand on the doorknob.

Raoul was standing next to the chair now, one hand clenching the back. "This isn't about you," he said. "I mean, it is, but there's more to it. I'm just not ready to deal with this now. Can you understand that? I'm frustrated with all of this, and I need to be alone for a while."

She nodded.

"I'll call you tomorrow, okay?" he said without moving. He was forcing his voice to sound calm, but it merely sounded tense.

"Okay. Good night, Raoul." She quickly turned and left. He spoke the spell to open the gate, then remained standing until the sound of her car disappeared. He closed the gate with another spell, then turned and looked down at the table. First himself, then Bolton, and now Anne were all in this, all having their lives screwed up because one stupid, stubborn old man had gotten himself killed somehow. He poured wine sloppily into his glass, took a large swallow, and flung the glass into the fireplace. The wine hissed for a moment among the flames. "Damn," he said. "Damn all of this." He felt a black fury growing inside him at his lack of control over the recent events of his life.

Raoul spent most of the next hour pacing, trying to calm down, but only becoming more upset. He wasn't sure just why he was so angry, and wasn't in the mood for self-analysis. He debated calling Bolton, but decided against it. This needed to be told in person. He thought about taking a walk, but decided against that as well; in this mood, it wouldn't help. He was just working himself up, thinking about everything at once. He needed to get out, get away from all of it.

Without stopping to think, he walked to the phone and called for a cab. He told them to get there as soon as possible, destination London. There was a club that he sometimes went to, a dingy hellhole that made the Seller look civilized and where it was too loud to think at all. He'd go there until it closed, then wait for visiting hours at the hospital. He stalked upstairs, swigging wine from the bottle as he went.

Chapter 10

"Good Gods, Rags! What happened to you?" Bolton asked as Raoul entered the room. "You look like hell! What'd you do, stay out all night or something?" He looked closely at Raoul; his hair was even more riotously tousled than usual, and his cloak was torn in several places, splotched with what looked suspiciously like blood. Large hollows under his eyes looked almost purple. "You look like you've been fighting, too."

Raoul nodded blearily. "Anything left in that?" he asked, gesturing with his head at the teapot. He stripped off his cloak, wrinkling his nose as he surveyed the damage to it. "Damn! Well, blood comes out, and I'll bet the cleaners can patch it." He sank into a chair, grimacing. He'd gotten into a fight, but it was just what he needed to work out his growing frustration with all that was happening. Something about hard fighting always calmed him down.

He sat up and forward with a jolt as Bolton reached out with his lightly bandaged left hand and poured a cup of tea. "Hey!" Raoul cried. "What do you think you're doing? Put that down! Let me do that!" He reached for the pot.

Bolton finished pouring, then carefully set the pot down. He was smiling broadly. "Not to worry, my friend. The healing's taken really well on the left hand. All new skin, soft and pink as a baby's tushie. Still kind of sensitive, but at least I can use the hand again. Now, if only I were left-handed! So drink your tea, and tell me why you've shown up at—" He glanced at the clock on the opposite wall.

"—seven-thirty in the morning, looking rather the worse for wear."

Raoul sipped his tea. "That's not important," he said. "But something else is. Anne came over last night."

"You dog!" Bolton broke in, laughing. "Looks like she was a bit rough on you . . ."

Raoul glared at him. "Don't be an ass. I spent the night at the Gaul."

Bolton registered the name with shock. "The Raging Gaul? What the hell were you doing there?" He was familiar with the club, which made the papers several times a year, usually for drug arrests or "accidental" deaths. Bolton had gone there once, looking into a rumor about an up and coming young barrister's seedy pursuits. He'd left in a hurry. He never understood why Raoul periodically went there, usually just to get into fights. "What happened?"

Raoul shrugged. "I got in a fight, that's all. I was in a pretty bad mood. Anyway, I need to talk to you about Anne—"

Bolton interrupted. "You know, Rags, sometimes I don't understand you. What in the seven hells were you doing getting into a fight at the Gaul again? People get killed there, don't you know?"

"I can take care of myself. Anyway, about—"

Bolton opened his mouth to interrupt again.

"Max," Raoul said quietly but firmly, holding Bolton's gaze, "shut up. This is important."

Bolton's mouth snapped shut. Raoul never used his given name, except when something very serious was afoot. He waited.

"Last night," Raoul said, "Anne told me that she's the one who sent the note to you and the police. She said it came in the mail after Mowatt died; she opened it by accident. She mailed it because she wanted to get her father into trouble. She hasn't told the police. So Whiting never actually saw that note until the police showed it to him. Plus," he added, "I spoke to Jean yesterday. She admits she's Jeanine Montgomery-Lewis. She's our blackmailer.

But she says she didn't write the note that Anne found, and I believe her. Also, Whiting knows that Jeanine is blackmailing him, but he doesn't realize that Jean is really Jeanine. That was pretty much my day yesterday." He stopped, waiting for Bolton's reaction.

Varying expressions had flitted over Bolton's face as Raoul spoke, but now he settled into a look of concerned confusion. He started to speak, then stopped. After a moment's pause he held up his hands and said quietly, "Wait. Give me all that again, would you? Just start from when you left here yesterday, and go from there. I don't think I quite followed all of it."

Raoul complied, describing the past day's events in full detail. Bolton listened attentively, occasionally stopping him with a question. Finally, Raoul reached the point in the story where he stormed out of Thornhold. "So I stayed out all night, then got here at about six," he said, "but they wouldn't let me up until a little while ago. What do you think?"

Bolton smiled, shaking his head. "I think I understand why you had one of your moods and picked a fight at the Gaul," he said gently. "Though it is an overreaction. And I think I can throw another wrench into the works."

Raoul quickly raised his head to look at Bolton, narrowing his eyes as Bolton held up a hand for him to wait.

"Brenda's been a busy girl," he began. "You know, I think she'd make a great detective. Hand me that folder, would you? Actually, no, don't give it to me, just look through it. The first page should be a summary of her notes." He waited while Raoul found the folder, opened it, and began to read. It didn't take long before Raoul's head came up with a jerk.

"Jeanine had a child?" he asked. "When? How did you find this out? What happened to it?"

"Like I said, Brenda's a great investigator. She managed to find some old health information on Jean, or rather, Jeanine. Brenda was researching Jeanine's skin disease, which apparently kicked in a few months *before*

Montgomery-Lewis died. Anyway, one of the questions Jeanine answered for health records was whether or not she'd ever had a child. The answer was no. Then, a little over a year later, another form stated that the answer to that particular question was yes. Doesn't take much to figure out what happened in the interim, does it? Hang on, I'll ring for more tea. This is thirsty work, eh?" He pressed a call button near the bed. "Hand me those notes, if you're not going to read, will you? Gently, please."

Bolton gingerly took the proffered file and laid it on his lap. He continued, glancing down occasionally to check the notes: "So with that information in hand, Brenda started tracing just where Jeanine went after her husband died. She got lucky; she located the woman who was the Montgomery-Lewis' maid at the time, who recalled that she was let go when the house was sold in September of 'sixty-eight. Turns out our friend Jeanine was planning on taking a 'rest cure' for her skin condition at a sanatorium near Bristol. Their records show she was not only treated for that, but was also relieved of a nasty swelling in the abdomen." He smiled grimly. "On March thirtieth, 1969, to be exact. Male child, six pounds and change. Now, get this part—no, wait, here's the tea. Hello, Liza, dear." Bolton smiled, closing the folder as the young candy striper entered, carrying a laden tea tray.

"I brought you some of those scones, too, Mr. Bolton," she said, smiling at him. She gasped, nearly dropping the tray, as she saw Raoul.

"Don't worry, dear, he's harmless. Liza, this is Raoul Smythe. Raoul, meet Liza, the only light in my dull and lonely days."

"Hello," she said nervously, looking at Raoul as she would a possibly vicious dog who might snap. "Pleased to meet you."

Raoul nodded at her, quirking one side of his mouth in a lopsided smile that more closely resembled a sneer. He didn't speak.

She quickly set the tray down and returned to the door. "I'll, uh, stop by to see you later," she stammered, then left quickly, closing the door behind her. Bolton scowled at Raoul. "Great. Scare off the only attractive thing around here. Thanks a lot, Rags. Where was I?"

"She had the baby in March."

"Right." He opened the folder again and looked at it a moment before continuing. "Anyway, Brenda's still checking what happened to the baby; Jeanine left the sanatorium six weeks later without it. There were no death certificates issued for any newborns there during that period, so it's likely that it was given up for adoption. Jeanine legally changed her name immediately after she left the sanatorium, by the way. And that's all I've gotten so far."

"March when?" Raoul asked.

Bolton followed his train of thought. "Thirtieth," he said. "Why?"

"Assuming the child went the full term, that means she was—" Raoul counted the months backward on his fingers. "—pregnant in July. The month *before* her husband died. So why give up the baby?" he mused. "She seems to love kids . . . So if he was born in 'sixty-nine, he'd be what now?" He paused, counting. "Twenty-five, right? A little younger than us." Bolton nodded absentmindedly. "What if it wasn't Montgomery-Lewis'?" he wondered aloud.

"What, the baby? Whose, then? Not Mowatt's; Jean said he'd never even said anything to her about how he felt back then, much less actually done anything about it."

Bolton held up a hand, thinking. "What about Whiting?" he asked. "And how's *that* for a blackmail motive? Didn't your old professor say something about the two of them?"

Raoul scowled, trying to remember. "Hang on, I'll check my notes." He rummaged through his bag until he found the file he wanted. Picking out one of the pages, he skimmed through, muttering quietly to himself as Bolton looked on. "Here it is: Marlowe always thought Whiting 'somewhat resented' Jeanine. Hey, wait . . . this is interesting. Marlowe says here that as soon as Montgomery-Lewis' affairs were settled, Jeanine left the country. But we know she told her maid she was off to a sanatorium, which is where she actually went. Two different stories. Why?"

Bolton shrugged. "Covering her tracks, maybe, which means she knew what she was going to do. Go back to Whiting, though. Anything else about him and Jeanine?"

"Not that I see, and I don't really remember hearing anything besides what I just found. However, it's interesting that Whiting became dedicated to his studies after all this; Montgomery-Lewis' death was apparently the catalyst."

"Or Jeanine's leaving, if the affair theory is right. Can you talk to her again? *Will* she talk to you again?"

"Maybe. I think the fact that I haven't run out and told the police what she told me will help. That is, unless they've now figured it out as well."

"I just wish you hadn't told Anne, though." Bolton said carefully.

Raoul bristled. "What's that supposed to mean?"

"Well, think about it. I know you like her, and believe me, I'm *glad* you like her, I think it's good for you. Hell, she's a friend of mine, too. But—and try not to get pissed off here—I think she may have more to do with this than we've thought, especially in light of what she told you." He leaned back, watching to see how Raoul would react. He realized that if his own perceptions were correct, Anne was probably the first woman Raoul had actually dated of his own volition, and probably a more sensitive subject than Raoul realized.

Raoul's reaction proved him correct. He glared at Bolton and uncrossed his legs. "My relationship with Anne—" he began stiffly.

Uh-oh, Bolton thought.

"—is strictly between Anne and me. I don't see what your point is, anyway. If you think about it, it's perfectly logical that she'd send the letter out, once she opened it by mistake. She's got a pretty bad relationship with her father. We talked about it; she was trying to get back at him.

Makes perfect sense. She just didn't expect anyone to take it seriously."

"No, you think about it," Bolton broke in harshly. He realized he was treading on thin ice, but he needed to make Raoul see the possibilities. "Sure it makes perfect sense for her to open the letter by mistake, realize what it was and fire it off to *either* the police or the press. That's the heat of the moment. What doesn't make sense is for her to go out, make two copies, and send one to each place. And, by the way, what happened to the original? Why not send that, since she says she didn't give it back to her father? Maybe because the note she opened didn't say what the note she sent did, have you thought about that? What if it was just another vague, unsigned note mentioning Montgomery-Lewis, like the other two?

"Do you realize we don't know how many notes Jeanine sent, only how many were actually found in Whiting's house? Anne could have typed it up, making it seem like it implicated her father in a previous murder as well as Mowatt's death, signed Mowatt's name, and then mailed it off. We know it was typed on Parker's typewriter, which anyone, especially Anne, had easy access to. So after you told her that the note wasn't written by the same person as the others, she gave you a song and dance about finding it in the mail 'by accident.' Hell, we don't even know that she didn't see a previous note and decide to frame her father for murder. What do you think about that, then?" Bolton stopped, breathing heavily. He eyed Raoul, who'd taken all this in silence.

Raoul's face had gone even paler than usual. His eyes were narrowed. "I think," he said slowly, "that that's the most ridiculous thing I've heard in a long time. You're just playing bedside detective. It doesn't fit with who she is; maybe if you knew her better you'd understand—"

Bolton broke in, speaking quietly. "I've known her longer than you have, you forget. Look, I underst—"

"Is that what this is all about?" Raoul asked, sounding forcedly rational. "Are you jealous? What, did you ask her out and she said no or something? Is that it? Man, I wouldn't have thought you—"

"What the hell is the matter with you, Raoul?" Bolton snapped angrily. "Look, I don't know what you two have talked about, and frankly, I don't care, but I don't know who the hell this Polly-pure princess you seem to be talking about is. Anne Whiting has some serious problems, believe me. Hell, she told you herself. If you'd just listen—"

"I can't believe this! You're fucking jealous!" Raoul stood up and crossed to the foot of the bed, needing to move. "What is it you have against her? Seriously, did she turn you down or something? Is Anne the one person Bolton the stud couldn't get into bed? What?"

Bolton was stunned. "Is that what you think of me? Well then, fuck you! And for your information, your sweet little friend doesn't turn many people down. Believe me, I know. She's great in bed, trust me. Maybe someday you'll even find out for yourself!" He shouted the last sentence at Raoul's back as Raoul stormed out the door.

"Shit!" Bolton cried, watching the door swing quietly shut. He slammed his hands down on the covers, wincing as they hit. "What the hell was that?" he muttered. Now that Raoul had left, he didn't feel angry, just drained and tired. He leaned back, sighing, and rang for the nurse to see to his hands. Hopefully Raoul would cool down after a bit and they could talk this out. He couldn't believe what he'd said about Anne; it was the last thing in the world he'd wanted to mention, and especially not the way he had. Bolton closed his eyes and waited for the nurse.

Raoul slammed himself into the back of a taxi. "Oxford," he said shortly. He could feel himself shaking, he was so angry. So Bolton had slept with Anne. Nice of him to say so. Especially after practically accusing her of starting the whole blackmail mess with the police. Especially after sleeping with Anne. And nice of her to have told me, as well, Raoul thought. He sat and seethed, unable to think clearly.

"Nice day, eh?" the driver asked.

"Just drive, would you?" Raoul snapped. The driver muttered something under his breath but didn't respond aloud. After glancing once at Raoul in the mirror, he fastened his eyes back on the road.

Raoul closed his eyes and began a meditation exercise. He didn't think it would work, but he couldn't just sit and fume for an hour. He breathed deeply, willing his anger to subside. At first snippets of the conversation replayed themselves in his mind, but eventually his breathing evened out as he fell into trance.

"Excuse me, I need the address."

The cabbie's voice startled Raoul. He leaned quickly forward as if to rise out of the seat.

"Where to, I asked. Are you awake back there?"

"Yes," Raoul said. "Give me a moment." The cabbie snorted but stayed silent.

Raoul considered his next move. Meditating had helped; he felt calm again, but knew that the anger was still there, waiting for an excuse to explode. Going to Thornhold wouldn't do any good. Neither would going to the office. He needed more information. Nodding, he looked into his bag, grimacing at the disorder of the files he'd crammed back in when leaving Bolton's room. He gave Jean's address to the driver.

When Raoul got there, he leaned on the buzzer, not letting his finger ease off until he heard footsteps approach. He waited a moment, sure that Jean was looking at him through the small peephole in the door. "C'mon, Jean, it's Raoul Smythe. I need to talk to you."

"Why?" Jean's voice was muffled. "I don't want to talk to you."

Too bad, Raoul thought and paused, carefully remembering the lock arrangements on her door before opening them with a spell. Jean gasped as he pushed the door open. "Invite me in," he said harshly, looking directly into her shocked face.

"Come—Come in," she stammered, looking from him to the locks and back.

He stalked into the house, leaving her to shut the door behind him. Looking at the empty and half-filled boxes lying around the room, he asked, without turning around, "Leaving? Don't you know there's a murder investigation going on?"

He could hear her moving toward him. "I—I have a medical release," she said. "What are you doing here? What do you want?" She sounded frightened.

Raoul didn't care. "Medical release?" he repeated. "Going off to another sanatorium? What's the matter," he asked, turning to face her, "pregnant again?"

She stumbled backward, grabbing a chair to keep from falling. "Oh, God," she said dully, then fell silent.

Raoul waited silently for her to speak. He figured the more nervous she was, the more she'd babble. After a few moments of facing him, she proved him right.

"I don't know how you know," she began, "but you have to believe that I just couldn't have borne having him around. I couldn't, not after what had happened. George's death . . ." She paused, collecting herself. "George's death was the end of my life. You can't understand, I know you can't, but please try. He was my life. He was everything to me. I know people thought it was funny, he was so much older, but it wasn't like that. We really loved each other. I know it sounds strange, but I couldn't have borne it, having a child without him. It would have broken my heart every time I looked at him. Can you understand that?" She stopped, looking at him.

"Sure I could," Raoul answered. He knew he was taking his anger out on her, being more cruel than he needed to, but he couldn't seem to help himself. "If it were true."

"What do you mean? It is true! What do you want me to say?"

He played a hunch, hoping she'd react. "I want you to tell me why, if you loved your husband so much, you had Reginald Whiting's child."

Her face crumpled. It was the only way to describe the

way her features seemed to fall into themselves. Her eyes filled with tears.

Score one for Bolton, Raoul thought. The asshole. "Is that why Whiting killed your husband?" he asked. "Because of your affair? Is that it? Or did you kill him, to protect your lover? There are a lot of drugs whose effects mimic heart attacks. Maybe we could have an exhumation. That might clear some things up."

"No!" Jean cried. "No! It was an accident! No one killed anyone! Oh my God, why are you doing this to me?" She fell into the chair she'd been holding. "Why?"

Raoul stepped toward her. She looked up, an expression of terror on her face. Suddenly, he felt guilty; he didn't need to be this cruel to get what he wanted. Moving aside to perch on the arm of another chair, he took a deep breath and forced his voice to sound gentle. "Look, Jean, talk to me. I haven't gone to the police with the other information. I just need to know this. Believe me. Just tell me what really happened, okay? How did your husband really die?"

"He saw us," Jean said quietly after a moment, sounding shaken. "And he had a heart attack. That was all. We came around as fast as we could, but by that time he was . . ."

"It's okay. Your husband saw you and Whiting together? Where were you?"

"We were in the woods, near the shore. We didn't think anyone would see us, but then we heard George shout." She looked up at Raoul, meeting his eyes. "He saw us, and he had a heart attack, trying to get to where we were. I was breaking it off, you have to believe me. I never meant for it to happen in the first place, it just seemed to . . . well, I couldn't help myself. We only had a few times . . . together; it had only started two or three months before we went to Scotland. But I didn't want it to go on. I loved my husband. I never really knew how much until . . . I wasn't lying about that. I never meant for anything to happen to him."

"Did you know you were pregnant?" Raoul asked. "Is that why you broke it off?"

"I didn't know then. I didn't know until . . . after. I couldn't bear the thought that it might not be George's, and I was willing to take the risk that it might be. I never saw him, the baby, I mean. I couldn't have stood it. I thought I'd have more children, that I'd make up for it somehow. I was wrong." She wiped at her eyes.

"So why blackmail Whiting, after all these years?" Raoul asked.

She looked up at him. "I needed the money," she replied simply. "But I can't tell you why." She chuckled bitterly. "Of course, you'll probably find that out, too, and come back again, but I don't care. Isn't it enough that I say I needed money? Why do you need more? It didn't have anything to do with Arthur. Nothing at all. It was between Reginald and me. Arthur didn't know. I've had to keep things, secrets, from everyone I've ever loved. And I never wanted that."

"One last question, and then I'll leave. How many notes did you mail to Whiting?"

"Mail? I never mailed any. I left them in envelopes in his office mailbox. There were three of them, over a period of two months or so. The last was just before Arthur died, just a few days before. Reginald only paid the first two, but that was understandable in light of what happened. Why do you need to know, anyway? Does this have something to do with that note the police received? Do they think whoever wrote it had something to do with Arthur's death? This had nothing to do with him, I told you that." She paused, her eyes filling again with tears. "Oh God," she said, her voice shaking, "I couldn't bear it if this had something to do with his death. It can't have. It can't. Not Arthur, too." She fell silent, shaking her head and rocking slightly back and forth in her chair.

"Look, I'm sorry," he began hesitantly. "Can I do any—"

"Leave," she said, not looking up. "Just leave. And lock the door behind you. Just leave."

He did as she asked. He stood on the stoop a moment after reclosing the locks, wondering what to do next. He knew he needed to think about this, but was afraid of what he'd discover. Bolton had been right about too many things so far. He started walking back toward town, thinking he'd go to the Hollow Man and collect his thoughts.

He didn't make it that far. He hadn't gone half a mile before ideas started crowding into his head, forcing themselves on him. Jean hadn't mailed any of the notes. She'd given Whiting three of them. What happened to the third? Had someone seen it, taken it, then rewritten it and mailed it *after* Mowatt's death to make it look like Whiting had a motive for murder? Who would do that? If Anne was telling the truth about finding it in the mail, then who sent it? If she wasn't . . .

Unwillingly, Raoul forced himself to wonder if her hatred of her father was strong enough to drive her to murder. Could she have killed Mowatt? Physically, he didn't think she was strong enough to overpower him, but how much strength did it take to hit someone from behind? Could she have done it magically? He didn't know. He felt as if he didn't know anything or anyone any longer. First he'd argued with his best friend, and now he was considering the possibility that the woman he thought he'd begun to care for could be a murderer. Oh, and he shouldn't forget that that friend and that woman had also slept together. Great, he thought to himself, just great. Nice life.

He stopped, looking around. He'd gone most of the way to the Hollow Man. He looked for a telephone kiosk, saw one just down the street. He entered and dialed Anne's work number. When the secretary answered, Raoul asked for Anne.

"Anne, it's Raoul," he said when she picked up, wasting no time on pleasantries. "I need to see you. Can you meet me at the Hollow Man in half an hour or so?"

"Uh, sure, Raoul," she replied, somewhat hesitantly. "Are you all right? You sound kind of upset . . ."

"I'm at a pay phone. I can't talk now. I'll see you later, okay? Thanks." He rang off, forcing himself not to think about Anne and Bolton together. Maybe someday he could bear to ask one of them about it, but not today. Probably not tomorrow, either, he thought ruefully as he started walking again. He shifted the strap of his bag to a more comfortable position, wrapped his ripped cloak more closely around him to ward off the wind, and tried to think about what he was going to say to Anne.

"She's already here," Edward said, walking up to Raoul as he entered the pub. "I gave her the back booth." He eyed Raoul curiously but didn't say anything.

"Thanks," Raoul said, and walked into the back room. Anne was sitting facing him in the booth. She watched as he approached, her expression somewhere between a smile and a look of concern. "Hi," she said as he took off his cloak and hung it next to the booth. "Is something the matter?"

"Hi." He slid in across from her. A pint of lager and a pint of Guinness were already on the table. "Thanks for ordering."

"I didn't," she responded. "The waitress just brought them over."

"Ah. Edward must like you." She looked bewildered, so he quickly explained who, and what, Edward was. An awkward silence fell when he'd finished. He felt confused now that his initial anger had dissipated.

Anne spoke first. "Why'd you ask me here?" she asked, toying with her fork. "It is about last night?"

Raoul shook his head. "I'm not even really sure myself," he replied. "It's been a really lousy day so far."

Anne looked confused. "What, like seeing me can't make it any worse? Is this about me, or about, well, what's happening with my father and the police? Raoul . . ." She paused, unsure of whether to continue or not, then went on in a rush, "Look, Raoul, I really enjoy being with you. You're different, and special, and I . . . I don't want to have to wonder whether you're with me because you want to be with me or because you're looking for information about my father or Arthur Mowatt's death. Things seemed to be going well for us for a while, but after last night . . . I just don't know what to think now." She looked at him, waiting.

Raoul didn't look up when she'd finished speaking. Quietly, he asked, "Did you sleep with Bolton?"

She dropped the fork. It dinged against her glass as it fell to the table. "Do you want me to leave?" she asked.

"You didn't answer the question."

"Well, what do you want me to say? You wouldn't have asked if you didn't know the answer. What do you want to know? That he and I ended up together one night after a party? That we were drunk, and that it never happened again? I don't know what he told you, or if you heard it from someone else, but that's the truth. I was going to tell you, but—"

"It's okay."

"What?" She looked up at him. He met her eyes.

"I said it's okay," he repeated. "I just needed to know. But it's really not that important." He sounded surprised. "I need to know that you're telling me the truth."

"About Bolton? I just said—"

"About everything."

She looked at him and nodded. "So this *is* about my father and Mowatt, isn't it? It's about that damned letter." She tipped her head back, looking at the ceiling. "You know, I wish I'd never mentioned it."

He felt so strangely about all of this. Part of him wanted to trust her, but another part needed reassurance that he could believe what she'd told him. He wasn't sure what he felt for her, but he recognized that it was something completely new for him. But he couldn't commit himself blindly, no matter what his hormonal response was.

The thought that he didn't really know her continued to flit through his mind. He hadn't had enough time with her yet. What they'd had together had been, on a certain level, superficial. He knew she didn't like her job, had problems with her father, had a quirky sense of humor, enjoyed his company, and had more than likely had quite a few meaningless affairs in the past. And that she hadn't told him about finding the note, or about whatever had happened between her and Bolton. And that she'd maybe lied to him when she did finally tell him about the note.

It would make sense to her to protect herself, Raoul thought, and I know that. She doesn't appear to ever think about the consequences of her words or actions; it's as if she doesn't think ahead at all, she just deals with the results as best she can. Maybe it's because she's always been protected, and now she's started doing things on her own and has to deal with the consequences. So even if she's not lying, I think she could be. I don't trust her. I think she's beautiful, but I don't trust her.

He tried to put some of what he was thinking into words. "Anne, look," he said. "I don't know what's going on here. I've always felt like I was ... well, in control of myself. These last few weeks, it seems like everything I thought I knew has been slipping away. My life, my work, my best friend. And now you've come along. This is new for me. All of it. And I don't know what to think or do about it. Do you understand what I'm saying?" Reaching across the table, he lightly touched the back of her hand.

"I think so," she replied. She turned her hand so that it was holding his. "What can I do?"

Gently, he pulled his hand back, running it through his hair, not wanting to say he wasn't sure there was anything she could do. He couldn't just ask her outright if she'd lied to him; his ability to believe had already been poisoned. He'd have to be circuitous, find out answers without asking directly. "Can you do magic?" he asked.

She looked baffled. "What?"

Raoul repeated the question, adding, "You know, do you have any magical ability?"

Anne shook her head. "No," she said, still looking confused at his apparent change of subject, "not that I know of."

"Can I give you a quick test? It's nothing complicated."

"Raoul, what does this have to do with what we were

talking about? I don't understand. And anyway, haven't we had this conversation before?"

He gave her a small smile as he reached into his bag. "Just humor me, okay, Anne? It'll make me feel better about all of this. Ah, here we go!" he exclaimed, producing a small leather pouch.

"What's that?" Anne asked, craning her neck.

Raoul opened the pouch, gently spilling a number of small crystals and stones onto the table. Picking through them, he chose one and held it up to the light for a moment, then handed it to Anne as he returned the others to the bag. "It's a black opal," he explained. "They're mostly used as a power focusing agent."

She examined the small polished stone. "It's beautiful," she remarked quietly, turning it in her hand. "Such a strange color. It's like smoke with a rainbow inside. Is it a true opal? I've never seen a black one before."

"It's just another color variation, but it's fairly rare. Most are snapped up by magicians; they're one of the most powerful stones, since they contain the colors and properties of all other stones. They're usually used as focusing agents because one of the stone's properties is to amplify magical power, or at least enhance it. Plus, you can charge it to either projective or receptive energy. Personally, I think it's relaxing just to look at them, not to mention using them for meditation. And, of course—" He grinned, and spoke in a reasonable imitation of Catherine's voice. "—the color matches my wardrobe." He held out his hand for the stone. Even the simplest magic could improve his mood.

Anne handed it back somewhat reluctantly. "So what are you going to do with it?"

"Not me—you. The stone will help you to focus. Don't be nervous," he added, noting her concerned look. "It's really easy. Watch."

He moved the pint glasses aside and laid his right hand, palm up, on the table. Placing the stone in the center of his upturned palm, he glanced quickly up at Anne, who was watching silently. "This is a simple spell to leave the stone where it is when I take my hand away. The physics behind it are intuitive, which is why it's used as a test. You just need to trust the spell. Now, watch and listen carefully. There are only eight words."

Raoul fixed his gaze on the stone, then raised his palm to eye height. Holding his hand still, he spoke, enunciating carefully. *"Penthuna ten rach zem sath mal thui tev."* Without taking his gaze from the stone, he lowered his hand. The opal remained suspended in midair. Raoul leaned back. "See," he said, gesturing vaguely at the stone. "Easy."

"That's really amazing," Anne said, almost to herself. "How long will it stay there? Can I touch it?"

"Touching it will break the spell, since it's not set very well. Also, if you break the spell by touching it, the stone needs to be recharged. In any case, the counterspell to return it to normal is simple, too." This time he only glanced at the stone as he spoke. *"Cul tev sal penthna am."* As he spoke the last word, he stretched his left hand out, catching the stone as it fell. "So, do you want to try it?" He handed her the opal.

She took it, more gingerly than before. "What did you mean by 'recharge'?" she asked. "What's a charge?"

He smiled. "Good question. Also a very complicated one, but I'll give you the short version. There are two basic types of magic: projective and receptive. It has to do with energy. Anything—stones, crystals, elements, cloth, people, whatever—can be attuned to a particular charge. It's not always necessary, but in complex spells it becomes very important. However, some things, because of their own magical properties, can only accept a certain charge. It's especially true of stones, crystals, and herbs. So what you use in a spell is just as important as how you use it. Does that make sense?"

Anne nodded, gently rubbing the stone between her palms.

"Good. Well, certain items are unique in that they're equally balanced between the two charges and can be attuned to either one. Opals are like that, and so is quartz. Do you remember when I looked at the stone before I spoke the spell? Well, that's when I charged it projectively. It's very simple, especially when the charge doesn't need to be strong and the stone charges easily to begin with. Anyway, you probably didn't want to know all of this, but it does lead into the next question. Which hand do you write with?"

"My right. Why?"

"Well, everyone has a projective and a receptive side. The projective is usually tied to whichever is the 'leading' side, the hand you write with. Are you ready?"

"I don't know."

"It'll be fine. Really. Now, what you have to do is concentrate on the stone, really concentrate, and repeat the words I'll say. You have to pronounce them exactly, so we'll practice without the stone first. Repeat each word after me, okay?" He spoke each word of the spell slowly and carefully, making Anne repeat them until they were exact.

"How in the world do you ever rememb—" Anne began.

"Shhh ... I'll explain later. Concentrate." He took her right hand and laid it palm up on the table, placing the stone in the center of her palm. "Concentrate on the stone," he whispered, raising her hand to eye level. "Visualize what you want to happen. Now say the spell."

Haltingly, but with the correct pronunciation, Anne spoke the words.

"Now lower your hand. *Only* your hand. Focus on the stone."

Slowly and carefully, she did as he said. The stone remained firmly in her palm. "Oh, blast!" she exclaimed, looking at her hand lying on the table as if it didn't belong to her. She raised her eyes to look at Raoul.

He shrugged. "Maybe we used the wrong hand. Try it again with your left?"

She repeated the spell, still with no effect. "You know, Raoul," she said, handing the stone back to him, "maybe I just don't have the ability to do magic."

"It looks that way, doesn't it?" He wiped the stone on his shirt before replacing it in his bag. Well, he thought, at least that's settled. Though he hadn't wanted to mention it, the spell he'd chosen was foolproof, if pronounced correctly. If she'd had magical ability but had wanted to hide the fact for some reason, it would have been impossible. Some spells needed full mental concentration, not to mention co-operation, to work. Others, like the spell he'd just shown her, worked whether or not the speaker wanted them to. So she definitely was magicless. Raoul picked up his Guinness.

"Then again, maybe I'm like my father," Anne mused.

Raoul looked up at her. "What?"

"Well, remember when you and I talked about magic?" Raoul looked at her blankly. "At the Seller, the first time we went," she explained. He nodded. "Well, I was inter-ested in what you said about people having varying amounts of magical talent, so I asked my father about it. I guess I was wishing I could do magic. Anyway, he said pretty much the same things you did, but he also told me that the ability isn't always there from birth. Sometimes it develops later. He said that he never knew he could do magic until he was in his thirties. He'd been tested when he was younger and couldn't do a thing, then one day he could. So, the same thing might happen to me, too. Is that right?"

Raoul's mind was racing. Of course; sometimes magical potential stayed latent and undetectable until something, usually but not always puberty, triggered it. He should have thought of that, since he'd seen it so recently with Mordechai. If Whiting could work magic, he could have erased the aura at Mowatt's house. Anne couldn't have, Raoul now knew. But if Whiting hadn't actually seen the note signed by Mowatt, there was still no reason to suspect him of murder.

Raoul realized that once again he wasn't thinking clearly. He'd come here halfway believing Anne had killed Mowatt, with some vague idea about getting her to reveal

whether or not she had magical ability. He'd also wanted to
know if it was true about her and Bolton, but now that he
knew, he recognized that it didn't matter. He hadn't even
known her then, and what would being pissed off prove?
That Bolton was a complete slut? He'd known that for
years.

He smiled, realizing he'd forgiven Bolton. They'd both
spoken in anger, that was clear. It would be difficult for a
while, he was sure, knowing that cruel thoughts were hidden under the veil of their friendship, but they'd get over it.
They'd had arguments before, though not as bad. Things
would work out.

He wasn't sure about Anne, though. It seemed that the
more he knew her, the more he liked being with her; but
the more he knew *about* her, the more uncomfortable he
became. He sat here now, enjoying her company but uncomfortable with the knowledge that he probably shouldn't
be. She'd come between him and Bolton, and he had to admit that she probably was more involved in the blackmail,
if not the murder, than he'd originally thought. And there
was something he couldn't define that made him want to
pull away, despite the physical attraction.

It might be best, he thought, to hold off doing anything
at all until all this was settled. That was safest, really. If
someone thought killing Bolton, or at least injuring him,
was worth the risk, then there was no telling what else
might happen—to Anne, for instance. On one hand, he dis-
trusted her, and on the other, he was worried that she could
get hurt. His protectiveness bothered him; after all, she
could probably take care of herself. He needed to remind
himself that he hated worrying about people nearly as much
as he hated people worrying about him.

He realized Anne was speaking. "What?" he asked,
shaking his head. "Sorry, I wasn't listening."

"Raoul," she said, concerned. "What's the matter? You
look kind of . . . well, rumpled, and seem out of sorts. One
minute it sounds like you're accusing me of I don't know
what, the next you're smiling and laughing and being . . . I

don't know. I mean, I still don't know why we're here. Was it just to see if I can do magic? Why is that so important? Or was it about Max? I don't understand what's happening." She seemed about to cry.

"Anne," Raoul began hesitantly, "I'll be honest with you. I don't understand a lot of what's happened lately. At first I was in this to prove that I wasn't involved with Mowatt's death. Then your father got implicated with this blackmail business, which effectively put me out of the running. Then Bolton was almost killed. And now you're involved, and we're . . . well, whatever we are."

He took a deep breath and continued. "Look, what's happening between you and me would be confusing enough *without* all the rest. I don't mean about you and Bolton, either. That's past, and frankly, I don't care. But you and me, well, I guess you could say all this is new for me. You've probably figured that out already. I don't know what I want."

Anne nodded, but didn't interrupt. Her expression was concerned and confused, as if she were trying to follow what he was saying but couldn't.

He rested his forehead on one hand and sighed, frustrated. He wasn't expressing himself very well, he thought. It's what came of trying to be gentle. He raised his head and met her eyes. Gesturing vaguely at her with the hand his head had been on, he continued, "What I'm saying is that . . . I need a break. I need to just sit back and think about all this. Alone. There's just too much going on right now, and I've lost what little control I have over my life. I need to concentrate on something, and right now it's got to be figuring out this murder. Someone tried to kill Bolton because of it, and I'm going to find out who it was. Period. Anything else, and that includes whatever happens with you and me, is going to have to wait until that's settled." He leaned back against the booth. "I'm sorry."

Anne closed her eyes tightly and took a deep breath. "I think I need to leave," she said shakily. She started to get up.

"Anne, wait," he said, reaching toward her, pulling back as she sat down again. "I didn't want to upset you like this." He felt like a complete heel. "This isn't completely about you, I want you to know that. It's because of a lot of things, too many to even go into. Everything is too complicated now, and I need things to be simple again." He knew he couldn't let things continue as they were, not while he also needed to look at her possible involvement with a clear eye. With that thought, he felt as if he were somehow slipping away, distancing himself from her.

"Why do you have to be involved in any of this, anyway? I mean, aren't the police taking care of it? And I can't believe you're letting my father come between us like this. I wish I'd never seen that letter, and I wish everyone would just leave us alone!"

Raoul wasn't sure if "us" referred to Anne and himself, or to Anne and her father. "Anne, I told you—"

"I know, I know, it's about Bolton. But you don't know for sure that it wasn't an accident, do you? And if there *is* danger involved, what about you? What about my father? What if something happens to him? I already told you how nervous he seemed, even before all this happened."

Raoul didn't remember her mentioning that. She plowed on, saying, "This all seems like an excuse to me. Have you thought that it might just be that you're nervous about us? Raoul, believe me, I don't want to pressure you into anything, I just want you to think about it. Please?" She started to cry.

Raoul didn't know what to do, what to say. "Anne," he began, "I . . ." He trailed off. *This* was one of the reasons he'd always avoided relationships.

"I'm sorry," she said, trying to calm herself, wiping her cheek with the back of a hand. "I'm sorry. I understand what you're saying, but it's hard for me, too. You've been there for me through all of this, and now . . . I don't know. It's all been so fast. I don't want to think about it anymore, okay?" Meeting his eyes across the tabletop, she slowly shook her head. "Maybe you should just go, okay? I can't think now."

He nodded and rose. Throwing his cloak across his arm and taking up his bag, he turned to leave, then turned back. She wasn't looking at him, so he decided not to say anything more. He thought about calling her later, just to make sure she was all right. As he passed through the front room on his way to the door, he caught Edward looking at him. Raoul averted his eyes and left without speaking. He walked toward Carfax Square, scanning the narrow streets for a cab to take him back to London.

He slept all the way to the hospital. Climbing blearily from the backseat, he felt drained, both physically and emotionally. Which was probably for the best at the moment, he thought ruefully as he prepared himself to open the door to Bolton's room.

Liza, Bolton's young candy striper, was changing the bed linen as he entered. She turned around as the door opened, the welcoming smile on her face changing to a look of surprise. "Oh!" she exclaimed, taking an involuntary step backward. Looking at her face, Raoul realized he probably looked even worse than he had that morning.

Raoul forced a smile. "Hello again. Liza, isn't it? Where's Bolton?"

She looked at him with wide eyes. "Mr. Bolton?" she repeated, "He's—He's in treatment now. Can I help you with something?"

Raoul shook his head and crossed to the guest chair. "No, thanks," he said, putting down his bag and cloak. "I'll wait." He settled himself into the chair. "Do you think he'll be long?"

She shook her head, still eyeing him nervously. "I'm not sure, really."

Raoul shrugged, "Oh, well, no matter. Go on with whatever you were doing, please. Don't let me stop you." Leaning back, he closed his eyes, planning to just sit quietly until she left.

Bolton woke him as he was wheeled back into his room.

"Rags!" he exclaimed. "What are you—" He stopped as Raoul bolted upright in the chair. "I . . ."

Looking warily at Raoul, the orderly rolled the chair farther into the room, then helped Bolton settle himself on the bed. Before leaving, he asked Bolton if he needed anything more, and reminded him that the nurse would be by with his medication within the hour. Bolton thanked him and asked that he close the door on the way out.

Bolton and Raoul sat in silence after the orderly left, neither wanting to speak first. Eventually, both began talking at the same moment, breaking the tension. Raoul held up a hand for Bolton to wait. "Me first, okay?" he said. Bolton nodded for him to proceed.

Raoul hesitated, unsure of just how to begin. "Look, Max, I'm sorry about what happened this morning. I was an idiot." That pretty much summed it up, he thought.

Bolton chuckled wryly. "You took the words out of my mouth," he said, then shook his head. "No, I'm the one who should apologize. I had no right to bring up . . . well, the past. Especially not the way I did. I'm sorry."

"It's okay," Raoul replied. "After I thought about it for a while, I realized it doesn't matter. Not," he added, raising an eyebrow, "that that means I want to know details. I don't. What happened happened." He shrugged. "And anyway, after this afternoon, I'm not sure I'll be seeing Anne anymore." Saying it aloud, he realized it was true, and that the idea didn't affect him all that much now that he was away from her physical presence. Again he wondered if the attraction had been just hormones.

"What?" Bolton sat straighter. "Why? What happened?"

"Let me start at the beginning. This whole day has been a bitch." He sat back, crossed his legs, and told Bolton what had happened since he'd stormed out earlier in the day. He didn't spare any details, including his conversations with both Jeanine and Anne.

"Damn," Bolton said when Raoul had finished. "I'm sorry, Rags." He shook his head. "You know, maybe if I'd never opened my big mouth this morning—"

"Bullshit," Raoul said, interrupting. "It was going to happen anyway. It's like I told her, I need to be back in control of my life, and there're things I need to figure out first. Who knows? Maybe when all this is over ... that is, if she's not involved. And maybe not; I don't know anymore. I hate to admit it, but the more I think about what you said this morning, the more I think it might be true. And then this afternoon, when she mentioned having said her father had been nervous even before the murder, it got me thinking again. I think she's lying about finding that note in the mail. I can't decide if she's trying to protect her father or implicate him. Hell, she probably doesn't even know. And then there's Jean's involvement, which gets ever more complicated. Frankly, I don't know what to think about any of this anymore. You know," he said, looking at Bolton and smiling, "if I'd known things were going to get this convoluted, I'd probably have killed Mowatt myself, just to make it easier."

Bolton laughed. "I think I'd have helped, at this point." After a short pause he said, "You know, Rags, I'm bothered about something Anne said to you."

"What?"

"Hear me out on this, okay? You said she asked why you were involved anyway, that the police were investigating the murder *and* the blackmail. What if she's right?"

"I don't follow you."

"What I mean is, through all of this the police have been doing their little investigation, and you and I have been doing our little investigation. Now we've come up with things they don't know, like Jeanine's identity and Anne's involvement. And now it seems that we're stuck. I'm not saying that we should give up our end of this, because I'd like to know if someone tried to kill me or not, and if I'm still in danger. Or if you are. But why not tell the police what we know? It's not like there's a race on to see who finds out first. Unless you want to keep Anne's involvement to yourself. I'd understand if you did."

Raoul thought for a moment. "Max," he began, "what

you're saying makes sense, but ..." He sighed. "I don't know how I feel about her. I've never felt like this. It's like when I'm with her nothing else really matters, but even then I can feel something's not right. Not wrong in any physical sense, just something *about* her. She seems so ... naive, that it's weird. But it doesn't matter. Until I think about it, that is. Am I making any sense at all?" Raoul shook his head. "I sound like a fool." He'd never spoken like this to anyone before, not even Bolton.

Bolton shook his head. "No, Rags," he said gently, "You don't. Listen to me for a minute, will you, and don't get offended ..."

Raoul nodded.

"You sound like someone who's experiencing their first crush," Bolton said. "Hear me out. There's nothing wrong with it, it's just taken you a while to get around to it. Look, I *know* that you've never gotten involved with anyone, never really opened yourself up to that kind of ... well, emotion. Maybe you've just never met the right person or some other platitude like that. Whatever. Anne's beautiful. She's funny, she's got a great personality, and she's also got a lot of problems." He held up a hand. "Don't say anything. She and her father are like you and your mother. So you're drawn to her in a lot of different ways. You sympathize. Not just because of the problems or the way she looks, but because of all that she is. You said she's naive in a lot of ways. Well, so are you, my friend, and don't look at me like that, you know it's true."

Raoul looked at him uncomfortably. "Do we really have to go into this?"

Bolton smiled. "Look, all of this is completely natural. Don't be so uptight about it, okay? What I'm trying to say is that I think you're confusing yourself. For the first time in your life you're letting your hair down with someone, so to speak. Think about it—this is the first time you've ever let yourself get past your own stereotypes. Think about Catherine—you've never really seen her as a person, only as a walking example of all the things you hate. But there's more to her than that, there's more to everyone. And Anne has opened that up for you. What you need to decide is whether you're confused because you care about Anne, or because you're letting yourself care about anyone. Caring means you can't control situations anymore, and you've never been too comfortable with things you can't control."

Raoul sat silently, looking at his hands. Bolton let him be.

"I don't know, Max," Raoul said finally. "I just don't know. You're probably right, but, damn it . . . why is this so hard?"

Bolton shrugged. "Welcome to the wonderful world of emotional involvement. You've always kept things bottled up inside. I know that, you know that. I mean, there are things you've never talked to me about, and I'm your best friend. And it's been fine until now, but sometimes you just need to let things out. And now you've been able to talk to Anne about a lot of those things, maybe for the first time in your life.

"But look at it this way," Bolton went on. "If we involve the police, the truth will probably come out, whatever it is. Maybe the real story isn't what we think it might be. Either way, you'll *know*, if you see what I mean. Right now you won't know what's right and what's not. Do you trust her, as things stand?"

"I don't know. I don't know anything anymore, it appears."

"Then what's to lose? Confusion? Emotional turmoil? Think about it."

Raoul did. "They'll take them into custody, probably," he mused. "I don't know if I want to see that."

"It's probably going to happen sooner or later, anyway," Bolton replied. "Someone else will eventually make the connection between Jean and Jeanine. And once people know that the third note wasn't paid, and that it's not even the note she wrote, they'll start looking at the Whitings even more closely. It'll come out, I'm sure. The only difference is when."

"And who, and how," Raoul added. "That's a pretty big difference. Both Anne and Jean will know where the information came from, you know."

"What about Collings?" Bolton asked, struck by a thought.

"What about him?"

"We could give *him* all the information, and he could say he'd thought it up himself. Or, wait, this is even better: he could say he'd received the information anonymously. That way, if it ever got back to us, we could say we didn't want to be involved, but didn't want to withhold information. That would cover us, no matter what Jean or Anne said."

"Yeah, but . . ."

They argued back and forth. Finally, Raoul agreed that they'd go to Rodger Collings with what they knew and let him pass it along to Barnstone or whomever. And that way, Bolton pointed out, Collings might feel more disposed to keep them informed about what happened. Raoul agreed. And handed Bolton the phone to make the call.

Chapter 11

"So now what?" Raoul asked as the door to Bolton's room closed behind Rodger Collings. He and Bolton had spent an hour and a half going exhaustively over everything they knew about the blackmail and Mowatt's murder with the police clerk, leaving out only Raoul's discovery of the aural erasure at Mowatt's house. Collings was now on his way to pass the information to Barnstone.

Bolton yawned. "Now I take those pills I was supposed to. Not that I need them at the moment; I'm dead tired."

Raoul grimaced. He'd forgotten that this had started with Bolton freshly out of a healing session. "How are you, by the way? You seemed to handle the phone easier than before, and you're going through tea at your old rate again. Are you better?"

Bolton finished swallowing the pills before he answered. "Yeah," he said, looking at his hands as he wiggled his fingers. Only the backs and palms were wrapped now, and thinly at that. "Just tired. It's taken well. The skin regeneration is almost finished. Apparently it's gone faster than anyone expected. Now we're just waiting for it to toughen a little more; the doctor said he'll probably turn me loose in a couple of days."

"Really? That's great!"

Bolton yawned again. "Sorry, Rags."

"I should leave now," Raoul said. "You need your beauty sleep."

Bolton lay back against the pillows, closing his eyes. "When're you coming back? Remember, Rodger said he'd call as soon as something happens ... Are you going back to Thornhold?"

"No, I think I'll stay in town until we hear something. I need to grab some fresh clothes and a shower, though, before they stop letting me in here. A little sleep wouldn't kill me, either. Why don't you call me when there's news?"

"Are you at a hotel?" Bolton's eyes opened to slits and his voice sounded distant. "How will I reach you?"

"I'll leave the number. Now go to sleep."

"Okay," Bolton mumbled, his eyes closing again.

Raoul rummaged through his bag for a clean sheet of paper and a pen, then wrote an address and phone number, to lay on Bolton's bedside table. Reconsidering, he picked it back up and scribbled a name above the number, then quietly rose and gathered up his cloak.

"Rags," Bolton said quietly as Raoul opened the door.

"Yeah?"

"You did the right thing, you know."

"Yeah, sure I did. Sleep." Raoul quietly left the room. What he wanted now was, first, to sleep, and then to think about what he and Bolton had just done. At the cab stand outside the hospital, the cabbie eyed his disheveled appearance and torn cloak warily, but Raoul stared him down. He gave the Bloomsbury address he'd written for Bolton, sighing at the thought of an evening with his mother, and hoping she'd made plans already.

Well, he thought, he had told her he'd try to drop by sometime. A small smile crossed his lips at the thought of her reaction when he appeared, then left his face as he realized she probably wouldn't react at all. It had been that way since she'd realized he wanted nothing to do with either her expectations for him or for the world she moved in. He supposed it would be nice to think she accepted him as he was, but knew it wasn't true. For years they'd lived separate lives. Still, she did keep a room for him, though he rarely stayed over. He sighed again, leaning back against the cab seat. Maybe Bolton was right about him sympathizing with Anne's relationship with her father. The thought was unwelcome.

The cab dropped him off in front of the house. The four-story town house had originally been built in 1731, but was rebuilt in 1814 after a fire completely gutted it. Harriet Gulledge liked to tell the unsubstantiated tale of how the fire had been started at a party by the young and notorious poet-mage Byron. Staring at the bronze lion's head knocker, waiting for the heavy wooden doors to swing open, it occurred to Raoul that the house still had its own notorious magician. Of course, he could have used his key or spelled the door open, but he'd never thought of this house as his, though his mother had owned it for almost fifteen years. All told, he had probably spent only a few months or so there, usually only a day or two at a time.

Finally the door swung slowly open. Laura, wearing her usual crisp brown suit, looked at him for a second in silence before her face lit with a smile. "Raoul!" she cried, "Oh, wait until Mrs. Stephens sees you! Come in, come in." She stepped aside for him to enter, chattering happily about how long he'd been away this time, what had changed since then, and repeating how surprised Mrs. Stephens, the cook, would be.

Raoul smiled silently through it all. Laura had been a lively girl of seventeen when his mother had bought this house and decided she needed someone to help Higgins and Mrs. Stephens. Although Raoul had been away much of the time, he'd gotten on well with Laura during his occasional holiday visits, probably because of the mere four-year difference in their ages. Since his mother sent Higgins off to work for him, however, Laura had had to assume the full responsibility of running the house. Still, the mantle of duty always slipped a bit when he appeared.

She stopped in mid-sentence, finally taking in his appearance. "Gracious! You look a fright! And me standing here yapping away . . . Well, your mother's getting ready to go out for dinner, so do you want to freshen up while I tell her you're here?" At Raoul's nod, she added slyly, "Should I assume you remember where your room is, or should I draw you a map?" Raoul didn't respond, except to raise an eyebrow, but then he unbraided her hair with a spell as he walked past. Her laughter followed him down the hall to the master staircase.

By the time he reached the garret, he felt as if the events of the last day or so had finally caught up to him. Closing the door of his room behind him, he dropped both his cloak and bag onto the floor and headed straight for the shower.

The phone rang as he stood in front of the open wardrobe, trying to decide what to wear. His mother kept the room stocked with clothes for him. She'd apparently realized that he never wore the colored pieces, since this time it was all black, though still not what he'd ever choose himself. He picked up the phone, knowing the single ring meant the call was from inside the house. "Yes?"

"Hello, darling. I hear you've stopped in for a visit. I've got a dinner engagement later tonight, but if you feel up to chatting, I'd love to see you before I go out."

"Sure. Shall I come down?"

"That would be lovely. I'll have Mrs. Stephens bring the tea things into the parlor." She rang off.

Mrs. Stephens was just leaving the parlor as Raoul walked in. He only had time to smile and say hello before his mother called for him to come in. He directed a shrug at the cook and entered the parlor.

"Welcome home, dear," his mother said, rising from the couch as he approached. "You look well. Didn't the jacket fit?"

He kissed her lightly on the cheek. "Hi. Thank you. I don't know. I didn't think I'd need one just to come downstairs. Should I go back up for it?" His voice came out more tense than he liked. He moved away, draping himself over one of the Louis XVI armchairs.

Harriet tilted her head at him and leaned gracefully back on the couch without answering.

"Sorry," he muttered, trying not to roll his eyes. "It's been a long day. Thanks for the clothes." He had to admit the pants to the Armani suit fit wonderfully. He'd thrown them on with a T-shirt, and had considered himself better dressed than usual, even with bare feet and no jacket. "You look lovely. Nice color." It was, of course, true. She was wearing a short-skirted black suit with only an antique silver cuff bracelet as ornament. Her short silvery-blond hair was loose around her face, not slicked back as it had been the last time he'd seen her. Raoul preferred it loose; it made her look even younger, not that she looked anywhere near her actual fifty-one years. If he didn't know her, he'd think she was in her late thirties. Harriet Gulledge always looked young, beautiful, well-dressed, well-mannered, and well cared for, no matter where she was or what she was doing. She was, in a word, impeccable. As usual, Raoul had trouble believing they were related. He smiled at the thought.

She smiled back at him. "Thank you, dear. Tea?" At his nod, she poured out two cups. "So what brings you to London? Were you at the hospital? How is dear Maxwell? Better, I hope?"

"Much. He says they'll release him soon." He sipped slowly at his tea, already running out of things to say.

"Well, give him my regards when you see him." She paused for a moment. "Will you be staying?"

Raoul looked at her speculatively. "Yes, if that's all right. I'm not sure for how long, to tell the truth. Probably a few days, if you don't mind. I don't want to impose."

"It's no imposition, Raoul, you know that. I was merely hoping we'd be able to have dinner sometime. I feel I've lost touch with you, especially with all that's happened recently. I've been . . . concerned." She seemed about to continue, but didn't.

Suddenly, Raoul felt a wave of anger wash over him. What the hell was he doing here, playing polite charades with this woman whom he really barely knew? She probably didn't give a damn about what happened to him, only how it reflected on her. "Yeah," he agreed, a cruel edge to his voice, "it must have been hell on the cocktail circuit.

Lucky for you we have different last names, so people may not have connected you with all the unpleasantness. Then again, you're pretty tight with the Whitings' set, aren't you? What a bitch that must be now. Has the tide of society turned against them yet, I wonder? You should be careful whose side you take, you know. People might talk."

Her only reaction was a tightening of the skin around her perfect red lips and a slight rise of her plucked eyebrows. She glanced at her watch and rose gracefully. "You must be tired, dear. Mrs. Stephens will fix you dinner if you're feeling peckish. Perhaps we could have lunch tomorrow, if you're feeling up to it. Do make yourself at home. No, don't get up, dear; I really must go. Good night." He watched her walk unhurriedly out of the room. He'd hurt her feelings, he knew, but at the moment he didn't care. He always felt out of place around her, as if he were intruding upon her life. It seemed he'd always felt that way, even when he'd been a child.

Raoul's earliest memories of his mother were of playing idly in her office at the gallery while she conducted yet another whopping sale. He supposed he must have been three or four at the time, maybe younger, since he didn't remember having a book with him. He hadn't yet discovered magic, that much he did remember. He'd been a fussy child, never satisfied with anything, never playing with other children, always preferring to be alone. Learning to read had opened up new worlds for him, and introduced him to magic. By the time he was five he knew he had ability, and by six he'd worked his first complicated spell, all on his own. Raoul smiled at the memory, reaching up to pull at a lock of hair. He could still picture the look on his mother's face when she'd seen what he'd done to himself.

At six, Raoul had been fascinated by the punkers he'd seen in the streets during his daily walks to the park with Higgins. Mrs. Higgins always appeared frightened of their spiky hair dyed in rainbow hues. Raoul remembered thinking that when he was grown up, he was going to look just like them; they seemed so vibrant, so different from his mother's sedately suited, well-behaved friends. Then one night he'd been struck by the idea that he could look like that *now* if he wanted to. He'd already done some simple transformation spells from a magic text he'd checked out of the library. It took two weeks of tinkering with the different spells until he succeeded.

Horrified, his mother had called in specialists from all over England, trying to change his hair back to its original light brown curls, all to no avail. And the specialists had so frightened Raoul that he'd been unable to even tell them what spell he'd used; he completely forgot it on the spot, and still could not recall it. And so when his mother had packed him off to public school, he'd been the only boy there with what appeared to be a fright wig of dyed black hair. It had stayed that way ever since. He smiled again, remembering. No wonder his mother had never known quite what to do with him, or he with her, for that matter.

Raoul sat silently, eventually hearing the front door close as his mother left the house. He was idly contemplating the cold tea in his cup when he heard a cough from the doorway. Mrs. Stephens stood just inside the parlor doors, nervously fingering a dish towel.

"Could I . . . Can I get anything for you?" she asked hesitantly.

Raoul replaced the teacup on the table and rose. "No," he said, crossing slowly to the door. "No thanks. I think I'm just going to sleep. I'm very tired." He felt a strange sense of *déjà vu*, as if this were a scene he'd played years before. He walked around her through the doorway, pausing to look back from the bottom of the stairs. "I'll just go to bed, I think. Good night, Mrs. Stephens."

"Good night, Raoul." She watched him climb the stairs, and called quietly after him, "Sleep well, dear." She wasn't sure if he'd heard or not; he didn't respond.

At the top of the stairs, Raoul realized he'd been counting each step. Fifty-four. He shook his head, trying to clear the feeling he had of being underwater. He couldn't recall the last time he'd had more than an hour of sleep. Carefully, he closed the door to his room, then drew the heavy drapes over the windows. He undressed mechanically and climbed into bed.

The phone's shrill ringing almost roused him, but he drifted back down into sleep when the sound stopped. He felt an undefined pleasure in his vague awareness of being almost awake, a feeling that intensified as he became aware of the warmth of the comforter around him. He smiled and nestled down farther into the covers, returning to sleep.

A while later, which was probably only minutes but felt like hours, a series of ever-louder knocks came at the door. Waking became a conscious decision that could no longer be put off. He opened his eyes sleepily and called, without moving, "Who's there?" His voice had a groggy sound, which further woke him. He struggled to sit, fighting his way out of the tangle of bedclothes.

"It's Laura, Raoul. There's someone on the phone for you . . . says it's important." The door muffled the pronoun.

Raoul blinked, still trying to wake himself. Probably Bolton, he thought. He finally gained a sitting position, then remembered Laura was probably waiting for an answer. He looked at the door, half expecting to see it open. It was still closed. "S'okay," he called out, "I'll pick it up." He half fell out of the bed and groped his way to the desk. He picked up the receiver. "H'lo?" he muttered, swallowing and blinking. The fog slowly began to clear from his brain. He'd slept too long.

"Professor Smythe? Raoul? Is that you?"

He couldn't place the female voice for a moment. "Anne?" he asked. "Who is this?"

"It's Miriam." She sounded irritated, Raoul thought vaguely. But then again, who didn't, when mistaken for someone else? "Are you awake?" The sound of another connection being hung up clicked in the background. "Professor?"

He leaned on the desk, almost but not quite sitting on the top. "Oh. Miriam. Sorry. No, I'm not awake. I mean, I'm awake, but not really. I just got up. Can you hang on for a second?" He put the phone down on the desktop, not waiting for an answer. He crossed into the bathroom and splashed his face with cold water. He walked quickly back to the phone, drying his face with a towel. Picking up the receiver again, he said, "Okay, I'm back. Sorry about that. I think I overslept. Hi, Miriam. You've been impossible to reach lately. What time is it, anyway?"

"Me?" she snorted. "*I've* been impossible to reach? At least I keep normal hours! It's the middle of the afternoon, and I've been programming my butt off for the last four days! That is, when I haven't been trying to track *you* down. I've got it, I think."

Raoul was instantly alert. "Got what? Did you find other spells with the same sound combination? Did you try the spells? What did they do?"

She laughed. "Wait, wait, wait! I've got my notes right here. Okay, so what I did was feed spells into the program. I used all of the spells I had in my computer, which was about twenty. I also added all the 'regular' spells from your office computer. I ignored your batch jobbies, by the way, since they're constructed slightly differently. We can do them separately later, if you'd like."

"Good thinking," Raoul muttered. "Go on."

"That brought the number of spells to well over a hundred. I also keyed in almost fifty more, mostly cantrips, that I got out of the *Oxford Book of Common Spells*. I took a couple from each section, to get as much variety in what the spells are supposed to do as possible. So I had almost two hundred spells of varying sizes and purposes. The first thing I did was run the entire master file through the phonetic program. I saved the resulting data in a different file, then recombined it with the original so I had a file containing two copies of each spell, one 'regular' and one phonetic—"

"Did you—" Raoul interrupted.

"Yes, Professor, I generated a unique identifier field in each spell record file before combining, so we'd be able to later identify and link each spell with its phonetic equivalent. Don't worry about it."

"Sorry."

"No problem. So after I had the master file, I ran a search program, looking for the same combination as in your aura-erasing spell."

"And . . . ?"

"And it turned up in four spells. Four *phonetic* spells. Then I realized I'd forgotten something, so I pretty much started from scratch again, only this time, when I ran the spells through the phonetic program I accepted *all* the phonetic variants, which gave me a lot more to work with. Don't worry, I modified the identifier field to take it into account. And then I ran it all through the search program again."

"And . . . ?" Raoul repeated.

"Twelve," she answered. "Still all phonetic. The original four and eight others."

"Yes, but were some of them duplicates of the same spells in varying phonetic versions?"

Raoul could almost hear her nodding over the phone. "Right. Two of the original four showed up twice, and one showed up three times. Simple phonetic variations that didn't affect what we're looking for. There were two other spells, one of which had three versions, the other only one. All in all, not counting the phonetic variants, six spells out of the two hundred or so had the combination we want. Three percent."

"What type of spells were they? Was there anything in common among them?"

"This is the fun part. I checked the original—not the phonetic—versions of each spell. All six are transformation spells. Different specifics, of course, but all involving physically transforming things on a level deeper than mere appearance. Creating and removing integral elements, mostly."

Raoul expelled his breath, which he'd been holding. "Well," he said. "Hmmm."

"So, is this what you thought the result might be?" Miriam asked.

Raoul spoke slowly, his mind busy with other things.

"Um, it's . . . yes, kind of." Then his voice cleared. "Look, I know I've been an unimaginable pain in the ass with all this, and believe me, you've done great work so far, but could you do something else for me?"

"Sure, I guess. I've been enjoying this. What do you need?"

"I'm probably going to be stuck here in London for at least another day or so. Could you somehow get out to my house and pull the files of archaic spell fragments off the computer there and do the same thing to them? I've got a disk with me here, but no computer, so it's easiest for you to get them at Thornhold. The fragments all contain the missing runes, the ones whose pronunciation has been lost. We do know, however, just what it was that all the spells are supposed to do. If you can run the fragments through the phonetic program, then replace the unknown runes with the new phonetic combination we've found, you can compare the spells with the six your program isolated. That may turn up enough similarities so that we'd know if we'd rediscovered the pronunciation of one of the missing runes. Does that make sense?"

"Perfectly. And it shouldn't take all that long. Oh, hey, do you want me to tell your housekeeper anything when I'm there? I got this number from Max Bolton, who said to tell you to call him and also to call your housekeeper. Apparently she's kind of upset that you haven't called."

"Blast. No, thanks, I'll call her myself. Let me give you directions to Thornhold. Damn! What day is it?"

"It's Thursday. Why, is something the matter?"

Raoul thought a moment. "Yes. You can't go there. I gave Higgins the rest of the week off, and the lock spells are too complicated to explain over the phone. Damn! This'll have to wait until I get back." He sighed. "So I guess I'll see you later, then. Thanks for all the great work so far—I think we're on to something."

"I'll say. Well, see you, Professor." She hung up.

Then Raoul rang Mrs. Stephens on the inside line. Funny how he still remembered the number, he thought.

"Good morning, Raoul, dear," she said brightly. "I hope you slept well? Shall I send a tray up?" she asked before he could say a word.

"Uh, you don't need to do that, Mrs. Stephens," he replied. "I'll be down in a few minutes."

"Don't you dare! I'll bring it up shortly. You just get yourself settled, and I'll leave it outside your door, like always."

"Thanks." Uncomfortable with the pampering, he rang off and headed for the shower before calling the hospital. If Bolton had wanted to speak to him because something had come up, he had to be ready to leave immediately.

Fresh from the shower, he dialed the hospital number as he ate.

"What?" he asked when Bolton picked up.

"Hi, Rags," Bolton said. "What what?"

"I just got off the phone with Miriam. She said you wanted me to call. Any news?"

"I'll tell you when you come by," Bolton replied tersely. "I've got quite the crowd of admirers here."

Raoul took that to mean he couldn't talk at the moment. "I'll be there within half an hour," he said. "See you."

He gathered up his bag, leaving his cloak behind and instead pulling on the brand new overcoat he'd found in the closet. He smiled wryly as he went downstairs, carrying his breakfast tray and idly reflecting that most of his "good" clothes at Thornhold came from his infrequent visits to his mother's house. He disliked the feeling that he was dependent on her for anything, but she refused to stop buying things for him.

He stopped by the kitchen on his way out, surprising both Laura and Mrs. Stephens as they sat at the small table having tea. He thanked Mrs. Stephens for the breakfast and asked them to let his mother know he'd gone out when she got back from work.

He imagined Bolton had news from Collings, and felt a strange reluctance to find out the truth. Knowing he was putting off the moment, he decided to walk to the hospital.

The weather was cool, but not cold, and the slowly falling twilight lent an almost magical cast to the buildings; in the fading light, everything appeared surrounded by a slight aura. He trudged along, hands stuffed into his pockets and head down.

"You're late," Bolton said accusingly when Raoul entered the room. "It's been over an hour."

Raoul shrugged. "I walked." He pulled up his usual chair, throwing his coat over the back. "What's the news?"

Bolton eyed the coat, smiling and shaking his head. "Your mother has the *best* taste. Pity it's not genetic."

"Bolton—" Raoul began, annoyance tingeing his voice.

"Sorry, Rags. I guess I'm stalling. Are you sure you want to hear this? Collings called a few hours ago with news about Jean." He paused, holding Raoul's gaze with his own as he added, "And Anne."

Raoul nodded. "That's what I figured this was about, anyway. Go on."

"Okay, then. Well, after we talked to Rodger yesterday, he went straight to Barnstone with the information, as we planned. He gave him the song and dance about having gotten the info anonymously, but he's pretty sure Barnstone suspects that we were responsible. Go figure.

"Barnstone was particularly interested in the information about Jean Morris being Jeanine Montgomery-Lewis, and assigned detectives to watch Jean, and Anne, full-time. Once he'd gotten confirmation of Jean's name change, she was called in for questioning on suspicion of blackmail. Interestingly, she'd recently bought a one-way ticket to Switzerland, saying she was going to some clinic there for her skin condition. Of course, planning to leave the country didn't endear her any more to Barnstone, once he knew who she really was. Is there any water left in that decanter? Pass me a glass, would you?"

Raoul waited silently, thinking of a particular clinic in Switzerland, while Bolton drank. His life had become a little too full of coincidences these days. Jeanine's child would be twenty-five or so, they'd figured . . .

Replacing the glass on the table, Bolton continued. "So Barnstone leaned on Jean, or rather Jeanine, about the blackmail. She eventually caved in and admitted to sending the notes, although Barnstone couldn't get her to say why. Your name was mentioned, by the way, and not favorably. In telling what she'd done, she also mentioned your visits to her house, and told Barnstone exactly what she'd told you, and when." He looked directly at Raoul again. "You were pretty close to being brought in on a charge of withholding evidence, Rodger said. A warrant was actually typed out."

Raoul couldn't stop himself from glancing over his shoulder at the closed door. "So what happened? Why didn't they come for me? C'mon, Bolton, talk . . ."

Bolton smiled thinly. "Calm down, will you? This is where it gets a little complicated . . ."

"Like it's all been so simple until now," Raoul muttered.

Bolton ignored him. "So Jean confesses to writing three, count them, three notes, and leaving them in Whiting's in-box in his office. She says she only received payments for the first two notes, the ones found in Whiting's house, and that the third note was never paid. This coincides with the banking information they'd already collected on Whiting, by the way. Jean also states that the third note is *not* the note received by the police and yours truly. So Barnstone has a signed confession to blackmail, as well as an excuse to haul your ass in for more questioning. Perfect, no? Well, the last step before formal charging is to call in Whiting himself to actually press blackmail charges. Which they do, getting the poor man out of bed late last night to do it. And guess what happens then?" Bolton paused dramatically.

Raoul nodded. In a completely screwy way it all made perfect sense. "Whiting refused to press charges, didn't he? No blackmail, no crime. No crime, no withholding of evidence. Nothing on Jean, nothing on me. That's what happened, isn't it?"

Bolton smiled. "Gee, you're good at this, aren't you? Right on the money, my friend. Whiting says the money paid was just a gift to an old friend, that the blackmail notes were just a joke between the two of them. *And* he emphatically states that he never received a third note at all, not the one Jeanine wrote, and not the one Barnstone and I got copies of. And he corroborates that neither of the previous two notes came in the mail."

"Why do I have the feeling this is where Anne comes in?" Raoul asked. "That doesn't agree with what she told me about finding the note in the mail."

"Right. Barnstone knew that as well, through Rodger, so he asks Whiting if Anne had said anything to him about the blackmail. Now listen to this part: Whiting hems and haws, not giving anything away, then breaks down. Rodger said Whiting looked like he'd been crying when he finally came out of the room."

"So what did he say?" Raoul asked impatiently.

"Apparently he started talking about how much Anne resented him, and what a bad relationship they had. He said he'd suspected her of sending the note out as soon as he heard about it. Mind you, this is *before* Barnstone tells him what she'd already confessed to someone that she found the note and mailed it to try and throw suspicion on her father. So Barnstone tells Whiting what she'd said, and the shit really hits the fan. Whiting starts talking about Anne being unstable, talking about all the things she's done out of resentment toward him. He especially tells Barnstone about all of her—" Bolton paused, glancing nervously at Raoul. "—all of her affairs and things like that. Making it absolutely clear that none of it is her fault, it's just that she thinks of herself as persecuted, though it's certainly not true, and he thinks she would be capable of just about anything if she thought it would hurt him. He does the loving father of a wayward child act, then hits Barnstone with two facts. First, that he lied about his own alibi for the night of the murder, namely that he argued with Anne all night before they both turned in. The argument part was true enough, but then our girl stormed out of the house in a fit of anger. He stayed up all night worrying about her, wondering what she could possibly be doing, out and about in such an unhinged mood . . ." Bolton paused to take another drink. "This, of course, throws Barnstone for a complete loop, since Anne's now got no alibi for the murder, and a fairly good motive for committing one."

"What was the other fact?" Raoul asked dully.

Bolton looked at him with concern. "Are you okay? I know this can't be easy for you. And believe me, it's not going to get any easier. Do you really want me to go on?"

Raoul sighed. "Just tell me," he said quietly. "What was the other thing?"

Bolton was silent for a moment, as if steeling himself for an ordeal. "There's no proof of any of this yet, I need to make that clear—"

"For Herne's sake, Bolton, just get on with it!" Raoul was starting to worry. Bolton usually didn't pull his punches. He leaned forward, tense.

Bolton decided to stop stalling and just blurt it out: "That business trip Anne took to Manchester—her father found a train stub a few days ago. She hadn't taken her car, you see. The stub was from the early morning train from Glasgow to London." He looked at Raoul, who was sitting perfectly immobile, leaning his head against the chair back, his eyes closed.

"Go on," Raoul whispered, thinking about how Anne never thought about the consequences of her actions, and how Glasgow was the closest major city to Killin.

"It was from the morning after the guest house in Killin burned down."

Both men were silent for a moment. Raoul said, without opening his eyes, "She called me from Manchester the night it happened. About ten o'clock."

Bolton sighed. "The police checked the phone records. No calls to your number from that hotel. She checked out at six that night. There was a toll call billed to her home number, though. To your house, at around ten."

"From . . .?"

"A pay phone in Glasgow. An hour and a half after she'd

rented a car there. The police found the agency that rented her the car. It was returned the next morning, an hour before the train left for London. She paid cash. The clerk identified her from a photograph earlier this afternoon."

"Anne . . ." Raoul breathed. Without moving his head, he opened his eyes and looked at Bolton. Bolton thought he'd never seen Raoul look as stricken as he did at that moment. Finally Raoul moved, shaking his head slowly from side to side, his eyes never leaving Bolton's. "The little fool . . . Oh, Max," he said, "I'm so sorry . . ."

Bolton chuckled harshly. "That makes two of us, my friend; I'm sorry, too, believe me. It looks bad for her, Rags, really bad. And I still can't believe it. Why would she want to kill me? Or even just burn down the guest house? Covering up clues? There were no clues! There was no murder!"

"Where is she?" Raoul asked quietly.

Bolton calmed himself. "Rodger said they brought her in for questioning early this morning. She'll probably be released on bail tomorrow, unless they hold her over for some kind of psychiatric testing. She's been charged with arson and attempted murder, and she's now the prime suspect in Mowatt's murder, as well. I'm sorry, Rags. I really am."

"Has she said anything? You said they've been questioning her since morning. Did she . . . confess?"

"According to Rodger, all she admits to is lying about finding the note in the mail. She now admits that she saw the third note in her father's office a few days before Mowatt was killed and took it. She held on to it for a while, but then after Mowatt died she retyped it on Parker's machine, changing it a little to make it look like it was from Mowatt, forging his signature, and mailing copies off to Barnstone and me. Purely to get her father in trouble, nothing more."

"What about the original?"

"She says she threw it away. She says she only did it to make her father's life miserable, she did it *after* the murder, and she didn't kill Mowatt. She sticks to the story that she was home when he was killed, and says she doesn't know why her father would lie about it."

"What about . . . the other thing?" Raoul couldn't bring himself to say what he meant.

Bolton understood. "She won't talk about it. At all. And that's pretty much it. Are you okay?"

"I don't know." There was an awkward silence as Raoul ran the facts over in his mind. Something was wrong, he was sure of it. But what? "Magic," he said aloud. "What about the aural erasure?" He didn't want to think about the attack on Bolton, so he concentrated on Mowatt.

"What?" Bolton asked.

Raoul briefly explained what Miriam had uncovered about the aural erasure showing up only in transformation spells. "And since the entire room was wiped, that means that something was done to the room itself, not just something in it. It's unlikely that Mowatt would do that kind of spell on his own, very unlikely. So we can be pretty sure that whoever killed Mowatt used magic to do something to the room, thereby erasing the aura. Anne doesn't have any magical ability. Yet, that is. She can't have killed Mowatt. It's got to be someone else. Doesn't it?"

"I don't know, Rags." Bolton continued, speaking as gently as possible. "That doesn't make her innocent, you know. There's still—"

"I know!" Raoul snapped. "Don't you think I know that? She tried to kill you. Period, end of sentence. She tried to kill you, and she's going to stand trial for it. Don't you think I know that?" he repeated. "But that doesn't mean she killed Mowatt. It makes a difference, don't you see?" An almost pleading note entered his voice on the last sentence.

"Rags—" Bolton began.

"I need to see Barnstone," Raoul said, rising. "I've got to tell him about the magic." He stood. "I'll be back in the morning." He bent to pick up his bag.

Bolton sighed. "Don't bother," he said.

His words brought Raoul up short. "What?" he asked. Had he offended Bolton again? Couldn't Bolton see that who killed Mowatt made a difference to him? That no matter what he felt, or didn't feel, for Anne, he just couldn't see her charged with a murder she didn't commit? "What do you mean?"

"I mean, don't bother coming up here in the morning. Come by my apartment. They're letting me go tonight."

At first Raoul didn't understand. He looked blankly at Bolton, who repeated himself, smiling.

"Oh," Raoul said finally, "that's great." He still sounded dazed. "Yeah, I'll stop by your apartment. Great. I've got to go." He left quickly, leaving Bolton staring at the door.

When Raoul had explained to Barnstone about the aural erasure in Mowatt's study, the detective said, "I don't get the connection. And what the hell were you doing in the house in the first place?" He regarded Raoul with annoyance. "Hmmm?"

Patiently, Raoul explained everything he'd done since the night of the party. It took quite a while, and included how he and Bolton had contacted Collings. He didn't want to get Rodger into trouble, but he needed to tell everything if he wanted Barnstone to understand what he was saying.

"And so I came here, to you," he finished, looking expectantly at the detective. "If the erasure of the magical aura really has something to do with the murder, then there could be clues still in the study, transformed into something else, and no one would know. Someone used magic to change something about the room itself, either just before or after Mowatt was killed. Someone with magical ability. Not Anne Whiting."

Barnstone shook his head, thinking that Raoul at least had a lot of balls to come in here as he had. "Look, it's interesting, I'll admit that, and you may be right. But even if you are right—" He held up a hand to stifle Raoul's interruption. "—even if you are right, there's no way to know what was transformed, correct?"

Raoul shook his head. "True, but—"

Barnstone's hand went up again. "So there can be no concrete proof. Not now, not ever. It doesn't affect the case.

I'm sorry, Professor, but that's the truth." He rose. "Look, the best thing you can do is stop thinking about it. It's out of your hands now. Leave it to the police and to the courts." He crossed the room to the door, opened it, then stood waiting for Raoul to rise.

Raoul did, slowly, forcing himself to move. He walked to the door and shook Barnstone's offered hand.

"Look, Professor, I understand you're upset. It's hard to know people," Barnstone said. "And it's even harder when you're involved with them." He patted Raoul on the shoulder. "You did all you could. That was a good bit of research on the magic." His voice became stern for a moment as he added, "Some of it was extremely illegal, and you're lucky your ass isn't in jail. But," his voice softened again, "you did some good work there. Now let it rest. Go on with your life."

Raoul took a step out the door, then turned. "Could I see her?" he asked quietly. "Just for a minute?"

Barnstone shook his head. "I'm sorry. It's against the rules."

"Fuck the rules!" Several heads in the outside office turned toward them.

Barnstone's hand came down on Raoul's shoulder again, more firmly this time. "Calm down, Professor . . ."

Raoul shook his hand off. "Look," he said, his voice low but intense, "you yourself just said I did good work on this. Frankly, if it wasn't for what Bolton and I discovered, you wouldn't have anything. I *gave* her to you. All I'm asking is a minute to talk to her. That's all."

Barnstone considered it for a moment, then nodded slowly. "Okay," he grumbled, "but it's just for a minute, and not in private. You can see her in the visiting room. I'll call now and they'll let you in. And then you're out of this. Understand?"

Raoul nodded. "Thanks," he said.

Barnstone grunted in response, walked back to his desk and wrote down an address. He handed it to Raoul, then turned his back on him. Avoiding curious eyes watching him, Raoul left quickly.

Outside, he hailed a cab. He read off the address and ignored the driver's look. The ride to the jail took only ten minutes or so.

"I'm sorry," Anne said. She's lowered her eyes as soon as she sat down across the small table from him. "I'm so sorry, Raoul." She kept her eyes fastened on her hands, bereft now of rings. Most of the nail polish had come off as well, as if she'd been worrying at it.

"Why?" he asked simply. "Why did you do it?" He found he could look at her. It hurt, seeing her there with no makeup, wearing a shapeless gray dress, and knowing all the time why she was there, but he could stand it.

"Which 'it' are we talking about?"

"Scotland."

"Oh." She paused, still not looking up. "That." She shook her head. "You wouldn't understand."

"Try me." He couldn't keep the anger out of his voice.

"I never meant to hurt anyone. Please believe that. Especially not Max. Why would I want to hurt your best friend?"

"I don't know. Tell me."

"I just wanted the building gone. I didn't know he was actually staying there. Why did he have to go there in the first place? I wouldn't have done anything, except he said he was going there for a vacation. Not there specifically, but he said the Highlands, and I knew, I just knew, that was where he was going. You'd told me you were looking into the murder, and it all came together. I had to stop him from finding out . . ."

"From finding out what?"

"What I knew. I'd gone there before. After I found the first note."

"The first note? What do you mean?"

"I lied about finding the last note in the mail. I'd actually known Dad was being blackmailed pretty much from the beginning. I found the first note lying in his box at the office. It wasn't sealed. I read it, but left it there. It got me thinking, though, about just how Montgomery-Lewis had died. I started looking for information."

"And . . . ?"

"And I did just about the same things Max did. I looked it up in old papers. And then I went to Killin myself to see if there was anything there. I went on a weekend, and didn't tell anyone where I was going. And that's why I couldn't let Max find out what I knew."

"Which was . . . ?"

She finally looked up at him, her eyes glistening with tears. "That there was nothing there."

Raoul was shocked, despite himself. "What?" The guard, standing to one side of the empty room, looked up sharply. Raoul lowered his voice. "What do you mean, 'nothing there'?"

Anne shrugged. "Exactly that. Montgomery-Lewis' death was an accident. I didn't want Max to find that out. I wanted everyone to think my father *had* killed him. Just like I wanted everyone to think he'd killed Arthur Mowatt."

"Why, Anne? Why?"

"So he'd leave me alone," she replied, looking down. "I just wanted him to let me live my own life and not treat me like 'the daughter of the man who runs Oxford.' That's all. I just want to be me."

"Anne . . ."

She looked up at him again. Her eyes were still wet, but bright. "Oh, Raoul," she said, "don't you see? None of this had anything to do with anything, and nothing to do with you. I love you. At least, I think I do, and I know I could if we'd had more time. And you care about me. I know that and you can't deny it. You care, not about what I am, but who I am. None of this would have ever happened if my father wasn't so hung up on image and power and would let me live a normal life." Her voice was gaining in speed and volume. "I mean, look at me, the way I am now. I'm not me, I'm not who I want to be. It's like Skank said that night at the Seller, I'm who my parents want me to be. And

I hate it. I know I'm shallow; I'm like a puppet for my father to yank around any way he wants. I can't even stand most of my so-called friends, because they're just the way I am and I don't want to be like that anymore. I just needed something that would make him leave me alone."

"Killing Arthur Mowatt?" Raoul asked quietly.

She shook her head. "No, oh no. I didn't. I couldn't have. I was home all that night after the party. I argued with Dad and then went up to my room. I was home. I don't know why he'd lie about it, but it's not true. I was home."

"Maybe he's still using you as an alibi?" Raoul wondered, almost to himself. He couldn't help it; he still didn't want to think she'd killed Mowatt. Wasn't it bad enough she'd almost killed Bolton? And anyway, she had no magical ability. But her father did.

"Dad kill Arthur? That can't be. I don't know why he's lying about me, he's probably just mad at what I did, but he couldn't have killed Arthur. He wouldn't have. They were friends. He knew the note was a fake. He had to. It was nothing like the others. Why is all this happening? I never meant for people to actually believe it." Tears had begun to drip slowly down her face.

Another bombshell, if she meant what he thought she meant. "The third note?" he asked. "The one you sent to Barnstone and Bolton? He saw it? You didn't destroy the original?"

She shook her head, running the back of one hand across her eyes.

"Answer me, damn it! Did you give your father the original of the note you sent to the police?"

She'd lowered her eyes again, and seemed somehow smaller than before. "Yes," she said, very quietly, "but he didn't kill Arthur."

"But you don't know that, right?"

"My father is not a murderer!" she cried. "He's not! He can't be!"

"That'll be just about enough, I think," the guard said, taking Anne's arm. She continued to cry, unable to speak.

"I think you should leave," the guard said to Raoul. He nodded.

He watched until the door closed behind the two of them, then walked slowly to the visitor's door. The cab was where he'd left it, the driver reading a paper and smoking. The meter was, of course, still running. Dully, Raoul gave his mother's address.

He still didn't want to believe it about Anne, but now he thought he knew who'd killed Mowatt. He'd call Barnstone later. He couldn't, didn't want to, think about anything at the moment. He closed his eyes, willing himself not to see Anne's crying face as she was led from the room. He pitied her, he realized. Nothing more than that.

Laura opened the door to the house once again. "Oh, Raoul, it's you!" she cried, flinging the door open and pulling him inside. "I'm so glad you're back. Mr. Bolton's been calling for the last hour. You're to call him immediately; he says it's urgent." She pointed him to the hall phone, taking his coat. "I'll hang this up."

He dialed the hospital number from memory. "What now?" he asked when Bolton picked up. "I can't deal with much more tonight, Bolton."

"Sorry, Rags. This is big. Phil just called me from the paper with a news flash. The lead story for tomorrow is about Whiting. I thought you should know."

"What about him?" Raoul asked, merely to be polite. He really didn't care anymore.

"He's out. There was an emergency meeting called this afternoon, once the news about Anne had leaked out. All the chairs, all the trustees. But kept very quiet. He's gone, effective immediately. Of course, the story in the paper will be that he's 'willingly stepping down,' to be with his family, taking an early retirement, that kind of thing, but it wasn't willing, from what Phil told me. He nearly blew the roof off. I thought you'd want to know."

"Thanks. I'll see you in the morning."

"Rags? Are you okay? Did you see Barnstone? What happened?"

"Yeah, I'm okay. Look, I can't talk. I'll tell you all about it tomorrow, okay? Right now, I just need to be alone for a while. I'll see you."

"Okay," Bolton said, the worry still in his voice. "Take it easy."

"Right. 'Bye." He hung up and stood for a moment with his hand still on the phone. "Laura?" he called.

"Yes?" She entered the room too quickly to have gone far. "Is everything all right?"

He forced a smile. "Yeah. I just need to get out for a bit. Where'd you put my coat?"

"In the hall closet. I'll get it." She turned and walked quickly down the hall, returning a moment later with his coat. "Are you sure everything is okay? Your mother is just upstairs if you want to—"

He reached for his coat. "Laura, I am nearly thirty years old. When I say everything is okay, you can believe me. And I'm a little beyond needing my mother, as well, even if something were wrong, which it's not. Things are fucking wonderful. Now give me my damn coat and leave me alone."

He tried not to see the hurt in her eyes as she held out the coat. "Good night, Raoul," she said stiffly, then walked away. He left the house and hailed the first cab he saw. He needed to go home, needed to think.

"Upper Slaughter, near Oxford," he said, giving the driver careful directions, describing the exact spot where he'd left the car the night Mowatt had been killed. "And don't talk to me until we get there," he added, then began to meditate.

Chapter 12

Thornhold's gate stood open when Raoul finally arrived. He walked slowly up the drive, gazing at the car parked by the front door. Dim light came from inside the house; Higgins must have left a light on for him. Someone, Raoul couldn't see who, stood in front of the door. Still, Raoul had a suspicion who it was. But when he had finally walked close enough to make out the man's face in the dim moonlight, a startled exclamation escaped him.

"Mordechai? What the hell are you doing here?" He glanced at the car again, sure he hadn't mistaken it. "And where's—"

"I need to talk to you, Raoul," Mordechai said, taking a step away from the door. "It's really important. I know I should have said something sooner, but—"

Scowling, Raoul motioned him away from the door. "Hang on a minute, would you? I'm freezing my ass off out here." He looked at Mordechai as he spoke the spell to open the door, idly noting that it worked faster than usual. "I don't know what this is about, but this is a very bad time. Why don't you just go home?"

"I can't. I need to tell you something."

Raoul stepped inside, holding the door for Mordechai. "Well, then, make it quick. I can't deal with too many more revelations today, if you know what I mean," he said, closing the door.

"Well, that's certainly unfortunate," Reginald Whiting said from the couch.

"You!" Raoul and Mordechai exclaimed at the same time.

Raoul looked from Whiting to Mordechai in confusion. "What the hell is going on here?" He glared at Whiting. "How did you get in here?" He took a step away from Mordechai, who looked baffled.

"I let myself in, of course." Whiting replied. "Very good spells on your locks, by the way. I almost didn't manage it. I must say, though, that I expected you to be alone. Who's your friend?"

"I know who *you* are," Mordechai responded tightly. Raoul and Whiting gazed at him in surprise.

"You do?" Raoul asked. "Why?" He wasn't sure what was going on or who knew what about whom.

"Frankly," Whiting broke in, "I'm not all that interested. You've complicated things, young man. I'm afraid I'll have to ask you to sit down and be quiet. Now." Rising from the couch, he began gesturing and speaking rapidly in Etruscan.

"Stop it!" Raoul shouted, starting across the room as he recognized the spell. He turned as he heard Mordechai fall to the floor behind him. "What do you think you're doing?" he asked Whiting angrily as he knelt to check Mordechai's condition. The young man's eyes gazed up at him in terror, but Mordechai didn't move. Raoul checked his pulse; it was racing, but steady. "Easy," he told him, leaning the limp body against the wall in a sitting position. "I'll get you out of this in a second."

"I don't think that's such a wise idea," Whiting said blandly. "I need to discuss a few matters with you, and frankly, your young friend makes it more difficult. Care for a glass of wine, by the way? I helped myself while you were out. A rather fine vintage, I must say. You have excellent taste."

"My housekeeper does," Raoul replied curtly, rising. "Hang on, Mordechai. I need my book." Glancing around, he saw he'd dropped his bag near the door.

"Leave it," Whiting said strongly. "We need to talk."

Raoul glanced from Whiting to Mordechai. The spell

was only immobilizing him, not harming him. He directed a shrug at Mordechai, hoping he understood, then turned to face Whiting across the couch.

"I wasn't sure you'd be coming home." Whiting's voice was normal, even conversational. "But here you are."

Raoul nodded. "Here I am. What do you want?"

"Quite the place you have here, Raoul," Whiting said, looking around. "I'd heard it was interesting, but this is just wonderful. It looks very much yours, if you know what I mean." Whiting poured himself another glass of wine.

"Get to the point."

"I suppose you know why I'm here," Whiting began.

"I'm not sure I do," Raoul said, stepping forward to perch on the wide arm of a chair. "I know the university let you go this afternoon."

Whiting nodded, unsurprised. "I thought you might have already heard. You seem to hear a lot of things."

Raoul shrugged noncommittally.

"I was fired, to tell the truth," Whiting continued. "There's going to be quite a scandal when all of this gets out about . . . what's happened. The university is just covering itself in advance. It's the smart thing to do." He sounded perfectly reasonable, not bitter at all. He paused to take a sip of wine. "But that's not the only reason I'm here."

"No?" Raoul asked, raising an eyebrow.

The cynical smile flashed again, then was gone. "No," Whiting replied. "There's actually a bit more. You see, all this nonsense, first with Mowatt, and then with Jeanine, and now with Anne, has somehow involved you. I'm not quite sure how it started or where you came in, but you've really proven to be the keystone to much of it. I'm sure you feel the same way about it."

Raoul shrugged.

"And I wanted to set the record straight, at least between us . . ." Whiting paused, as if waiting for a reply. When none came, he continued, still in the same conversational tone, "Anne's innocent, you know."

"Of what?"

Whiting appeared puzzled. "Why, of Arthur's death, of course. What did you think I meant?"

"Oh, I don't know. Maybe arson and attempted murder? Who knows? There're so *many* possibilities." Raoul couldn't keep the bitterness from his voice.

"Oh, that. Pooh." Whiting waved one hand nonchalantly. "Those things don't matter. Your friend turned out fine, and they can rebuild the building. No loss there. No, I meant about Arthur. She had nothing to do with his death."

"That's not entirely true, I think," Raoul responded, managing to keep his voice even this time.

It was Whiting's turn to raise an eyebrow. "What do you mean by that?" he asked.

"Exactly what I said. She had quite a bit to do with his death, I think. It's the only possibility that makes sense." He glanced up. Whiting, his eyes narrowing, regarded him with uncertain suspicion.

Raoul continued, "Well, I know that Anne knew you were being blackmailed, almost from the first. I also know that she didn't know who was sending the notes, although you did, though she knew it had to be someone who was present at the time of George Montgomery-Lewis' death. That narrowed it down quite a bit. She took a trip to Scotland and came up with nothing. So if it wasn't one of the Scottish people, it was either Jeanine Montgomery-Lewis or Mowatt. No one had heard from Jeanine in years, so Anne assumed it was Mowatt, though the notes were unsigned. She decided that the situation was perfect for throwing your world into an uproar."

Whiting poured himself another glass of wine.

Raoul continued. "So she kept an eye on your office in-box, where she'd seen the first note, hoping to intercept another one. She missed the second note, but found the third. Since she thought Mowatt was blackmailing you anyway, she retyped the note so that it was more specific, and forged his signature on it. She destroyed the original note, then replaced her version where she'd found it. After, of course, making a copy, just in case something happened.

All this, by the way, took place a few days *before* Mowatt was killed." He glanced over at his guest.

Whiting was nodding. "Makes perfect sense," he said. "Please continue."

Raoul plowed on. "The rest I'm not sure about, but I have a few theories. Since you've lied about never having seen the faked note, and you knew the first two notes were from Jeanine and not Mowatt, I should think you have some theories as well. Why don't you take the story from here?"

Whiting laughed. "You are a cool one, Raoul! Very well, let me give you *my* theory about what happened. Just a theory, you understand?" Raoul saw with surprise that the man actually winked at him.

Raoul nodded. "Of course."

"Well, you've been right on the money up until now. So my little darling knew about it all along, eh? I hadn't known that. I must say I'm proud of her, even though she did end up drawing the wrong conclusion. Still, it was bright work, and all on her own initiative. It's about time she started using her head. But enough about my dear daughter. You're right, I knew the first two notes were from Jeanine Montgomery-Lewis. You probably also know that I was unaware at the time that Jean Morris was actually Jeanine. I only found that out yesterday, when called in by the police to press charges. Imagine my surprise, if you can. She'd changed so much." He shook his head. "In any case, I hadn't minded her notes; she hadn't really asked for that much, all things considered, and it was easier to pay than to have all that old nonsense dragged up. Especially since no one, or so I thought, knew about the affair. And, do you know, in a strange way it felt quite good to know I was helping her, and that she still remembered what we'd had." He drank off his wine. "Looks like I need a refill. Would you care for a glass?"

Raoul shook his head. "No, thanks. I'm not in a drinking mood."

"Good for you, Raoul. I, on the other hand, am." He helped himself to another glass. "I'd like to drink until I can't think anymore. Until all this seems like a bad dream. Do you know," he asked, "that I spent a good part of this evening, while I was waiting for you, actually thinking about killing myself? Ending it all, you know? Ah, I've lost my topic again, haven't I? Where was I?"

"You didn't mind paying off Jeanine," Raoul replied evenly.

"Ah, yes. So imagine my surprise when I received a note—and yes, I did receive it—apparently from my old friend Arthur, threatening to expose the same business if I didn't pay up. Quite shocking, and somewhat intriguing. Because it hinted at murder, you see, whereas Jeanine's notes had hinted only at the affair. And Arthur *knew* that George's death had been an accident. He was there, you see. So I was quite annoyed with the idea of him threatening me with the revelation of something that was patently a lie. Do you understand that?"

"Yes, I think so," Raoul said. "So you confronted him with it, right?"

"Exactly. But first I spent a little time thinking about *why* he'd done it. And then it came to me. Do you know why he sent the note?"

Raoul was puzzled. "But he didn't send it. Anne wrote it."

Whiting's casual air slipped for a moment. "But I didn't know that then!" he snapped, then recovered himself. "At that time I believed he had. And so I came up with my own theory of causation. Arthur, you see, had been quite jealous of me for quite some time. For years after we first met, I'd followed his lead in everything I could; he was older, more experienced, and he always knew exactly what he wanted. His goal had always been to become chancellor of the university. A high goal for a schoolboy, unattainable, some would say, but he had the potential. So very intelligent, and gifted with such a strong ability to perform magic. And so dedicated. George doted on him, you know. Of course, Arthur and I both worshiped the ground George walked on, but I believe Arthur was always his favorite. It was the magic, you see. George didn't have any magical ability of his own, but I believe he secretly coveted it. And Arthur had so very much of it. And I had none."

"But—" Raoul began.

"Don't interrupt. So I followed Arthur's lead, except that I studied history where he studied magic. The only difference. And then George died. At first I was completely undone by the fact of his death. I'd felt guilty enough having the affair with Jeanine, as did she. We were ending it, believe me. But in addition we ended George's life. He saw us, you see."

"I know. Jean told me."

Whiting shot Raoul a glare, but didn't reply. Instead he continued as if Raoul hadn't spoken. "He saw us, and it broke his heart. It may have looked like a heart attack, but I know it was a broken heart. I'd failed him, in the most irrevocable way possible. And so I threw myself into my studies to atone. At first, anyway. Later, when I'd graduated, I threw myself into my work as well. By then, you see, I'd achieved a modicum of success, and I liked that feeling. And I began to become more successful than Arthur. And he knew it. We were still friends, of course, we never stopped being friends, but there was a change. Jealousy. He was initially hired as a tutor, I as an assistant professor. He reached the position of senior professor; I skipped that level and became chairman of my department. And so on and so on. And his jealousy grew. My success galled him." He paused for another deep drink and refill.

"So you see," Whiting continued, "why he would have wanted to blackmail me." He looked at Raoul, who shook his head. "Very well, I'll explain. I'd finally reached a point in my career where I can *change* things, make them better. Take yourself, for example. Oh, yes, this is all a part of it, believe me. You represent exactly what I wanted to do to the university community, because it's what you want to do with your magic. Change things, stop them from being done the same way year after year only because they've always been done that way. We're much alike, you and I. We love progress. Don't shake your head at me, I *know* what I'm talking about. And that's why Arthur hated you so. If not for my support, you'd have never been hired in the first place. He'd have kicked you out as an undergraduate if I hadn't stopped him. Because I knew, you see. Even then, I knew you might be the one to make a difference. You disagree?"

"Oh, yes," Raoul said, "I do." Silently, he continued the thought. I disagree completely and wholeheartedly. And if for nothing else, then for one simple reason: I'd never kill someone, at least not for something as insubstantial as "position." So this is where Anne gets it from. Aloud, he said, "But go on. So you went out to confront Mowatt with his blackmail attempt. After the party. And after you argued with Anne."

"Yes. As you say." He looked at Raoul piercingly, as if trying to fathom his thoughts. "And I accused him of blackmail to his face, the note in my hand. He, of course, professed innocence. And I, of course, didn't believe him. We argued. He accused me of trying to dislodge him from his position at the university, which of course made me suspect him all the more. But I very clearly explained, as I just did to you, that I wasn't trying to dislodge him or even cause him disrespect, but that the university needed to move forward, needed fresh blood. You were mentioned, actually."

Whiting paused, pouring the last of the wine into his glass. "Arthur became angry. He said that although he wasn't blackmailing me, he wished he'd thought it up himself. Perhaps now that I'd suggested it, he'd even go public with information about the affair, which he'd known about back then, and which would at least lend suspicion to the murder theory. An investigation was sure to follow." Whiting's voice grew more animated, his gestures larger. "He said he'd see me in jail and or dishonored, even at the expense of his own career, just to see me stopped. All because I favored change. The argument escalated even further, growing more and more ridiculous. He'd see me tarred and feathered, he'd convince my wife to leave me.

Finally ..." He stopped, standing, his arms open wide. Slowly, he lowered them. He drained the glass and replaced it carefully on the table.

"Yes?" Raoul asked. He'd leaned forward on the chair arm without realizing it. He waited.

Whiting's voice, when he finally answered, was quiet and slow, all animation gone. "Finally I just couldn't stand any more. Something seemed to snap inside me, as if some barrier had been broken. We were both standing in front of the fireplace. He turned away, unable to face me. I was livid, not thinking clearly. I picked up a candlestick from the mantelpiece and hit him with it. I can't say why I even did it. I certainly never meant to kill him, but kill him I had. As soon as he hit the floor I knew I'd killed him, even though it took a few minutes for him to actually die. His eyes—" Whiting broke off, staring at the floor as if he could still see Mowatt's body before him.

Raoul used the pause to glance over at Mordechai. His eyes looked intent, not terrified. Raoul wondered what he thought about all of this, and why he'd come by.

Whiting shook his head, recovering. "I stood for a long time, staring down at him. He'd been my best friend for so many years, you see. Finally, I realized I just couldn't stand there, I needed to do something. I thought about calling the police, I really did, but what good would it have done? Then both of us would be gone, the university would suffer, and I'd be unable to do anything about it. It wouldn't have solved anything. No, I decided that as long as Arthur was dead, some good might as well come of it. I'm sure he would have done the same had our positions been reversed. So I destroyed the note, burned it in the fireplace. I couldn't stand to take it with me, not after what had happened, but I couldn't very well leave it lying there, could I? Then I spelled the room back to exactly the way it had been when I entered. Used one of Arthur's own spells from his book to rearrange the fingerprints. No fingerprints, no clues to my identity. What? Why are you looking at me like that? He made me do it. He would have ruined everything."

Raoul shook his head slowly, not wanting to believe what he'd just heard. "No, it's not that. The spell. The second spell, transforming the room. That's what did it." Strangely, the stupidity of it all bothered him more than hearing about the murder.

Whiting sounded annoyed. "Did what? What are you talking about?"

"Aural erasure. The second spell you spoke erased all traces of magic in the entire room. I discovered it later. That's what I've been working on. It's one of the lost runes, I think. Just a chance combination of sounds, and someone checking the aura immediately after, while it was still blank." He snorted quietly. "Pure coincidence. It all goes back to you, and you had no idea what you'd done." All his work, hoping the magic would be a clue, all for nothing, he thought. A tragedy of errors, all of it.

"Shall I continue?" Whiting asked sarcastically. "Or do you prefer to keep on about your research?" Raoul gestured for him to go on. "I felt very badly, of course, but there was nothing I could do. I couldn't very well turn myself in, you know. I'm worth more—that is, I *was* worth more—to the university as its head than in some jail. So I left. I'd hoped it would just look like an unfortunate accident, a burglary gone wrong or something like that, but then my idiot daughter had to get herself involved. I see now what must have happened. When the murder was discovered, or rather, when she found out about it, she must have made more copies of the note she'd written, then mailed them off. I'd played perfectly into her hands, her spoiled little hands."

Whiting's voice changed. He sounded as if he were speaking to himself, as if he'd forgotten Raoul's presence. Raoul watched him with tired interest. Since Whiting's offhand revelation about the aural erasure, this all felt like an anticlimax. He forced himself to pay attention to what Whiting was saying.

"And she did it purely out of concern for her own interests, in retaliation for what? Some imagined slights; she's spoiled, that's what she is. How can she say I'm a poor father after all I've done for her and given her? She's the one who fouled everything up; it's *her* fault things got out of hand, got to this point. Now what do I have? Nothing, that's what I have. No position, no family, no university. Nothing. And *you*—" He raised his eyes to look at Raoul. "—*you* didn't help, pushing your nose into things, ruining everything with your silly investigation and then your stupid romance. In a way, you know," he sounded almost rational again, until he continued, "it's your fault, too. I've never expected great things from Anne; I've always known what she is and isn't capable of. But *you* . . . you have talent, have a power that might be unmatched, and the brains to develop and use it. But no. You had to go sneaking around trying to solve this, even when I'd already gotten you safely out of the picture. Oh, sure, I knew the police would look closely at you after I suspended you, but what could they have found? Nothing, that's what. And then, when it had all passed," he spoke as if in a dream, "then I would have had to make it up to you, don't you see? And it wouldn't have looked like favoritism, people wouldn't have wondered at it. And then, what couldn't we have done? The university could have been so enriched by your work, you could have had whatever you wanted, and I—" Whiting stopped, breathing heavily.

Like the calm before the storm, Raoul thought, his eyes going involuntarily to the mantelpiece. Lots of heavy candlesticks there. He turned his gaze back to Whiting, who'd gone red in the face, hyperventilating. His eyes were unfocused and staring into some imagined future. Slowly, Raoul stood up and took a careful step away from Whiting and the fireplace. What followed happened so quickly that he was only able to put it together in hindsight.

"You bastard!" Whiting shouted, springing at him. *"You ungrateful bastard! This is your fault!"*

A small part of Raoul's mind remained calm, watching almost idly, and thinking about how much sense it all made as Whiting lunged forward and grabbed the poker from its stand. He's either going to kill me or try and goad me into killing him, he thought. Silly man. Even as he thought this, Raoul had sprung back into a fighting crouch. Taking another step backward, he started to speak a spell to temporarily immobilize Whiting, the same spell, in fact, that Whiting had used earlier on Mordechai. He didn't want to fight him. He'd had enough of fighting lately.

Whiting recognized the spell and rushed at him, the poker held back as if it were a cricket bat and Raoul a particularly tasty pitch. He swung furiously at Raoul's head, forcing him back another step and interrupting the spell. This was the problem with using magic in fights, Raoul thought; it took too long. The observer part of him wondered why he'd never worked on a batch spell for just such a situation. Continuing his backward movement, he began the spell again.

Moving toward Raoul, Whiting laughed. "Magic's not doing you too much good now, eh?" He swung again, and again Raoul sprang back, only to find his way blocked by an end table. He stumbled, barely keeping his feet as the poker connected with his ribs. Agony laced through his right side as he bent double, the breath forced out of him. He clutched the table, willing himself not to fall.

Whiting closed in, still laughing as he grabbed Raoul by the hair. Raoul, straining to breathe, twisted out of Whiting's grip, abandoning the idea of using magic. He'd have to fight, after all. He moved quickly out of Whiting's reach, wincing at the sharp pain in his right side as he straightened. Ignoring it, he noted that Whiting was taller and heavier than he was. Still, he was younger and faster; if he didn't lose his head, this shouldn't be a problem. As Whiting closed in again, Raoul lashed out with his right leg, connecting with Whiting's left knee. With a cry of pain, Whiting fell heavily, landing on his right knee but retaining his hold on the poker.

Without thinking, Raoul reached forward to take the poker from Whiting's hand as he drew it back to strike at Raoul from the floor. As soon as Raoul had a good hold on the thin brass rod, Whiting grabbed Raoul's arm, using Raoul's own backward movement to pull himself to his feet. Taking advantage of Raoul's surprise, Whiting rammed the poker straight into his chest with all his weight behind it, shoving Raoul against a wall. Only a fast reflex movement of Raoul's hands saved him from being skewered. Instead he was pinned against the wall, the poker held horizontally across his throat, inhibiting his already labored breathing. This wasn't going so well, his mental observer noted. Raoul gasped as he shifted his grip on the poker, using the wall's leverage to push Whiting away.

It was Whiting's turn to stumble backward, losing his footing as his injured knee gave out beneath him and he fell heavily against the back of the couch. Unwilling to fall for the same trick twice, Raoul made no attempt to grab the poker this time. Instead, he stood still for a moment, breathing heavily as he rubbed his bruised throat with a hand. Whiting glanced up at him craftily from where he knelt, then swung the poker with all his might at Raoul's legs, sweeping him off his feet. Raoul crashed to the floor on one knee, one hand flailing out to grab the edge of an end table in support. The impact sent another wave of pain through his right side, doubling him over even as he tried to rise.

Whiting used the poker as a lever to raise himself off the floor. In two limping steps he stood above Raoul, and brought the poker down once across his back before heaving it aside. "How's that feel?" he asked through clenched teeth as, supporting himself with one hand on the end table, he lifted Raoul by the hair, twisting him as he drew his head upward. Raoul was too dazed with the pain in his side to answer. Even his mental observer had fallen silent. He was, he knew, in deep trouble. "Screw you," he whispered, struggling weakly. His legs felt like rubber, barely holding him up as Whiting drew himself up to his full height, pulling Raoul with him. His side felt as if it were aflame.

"This is your fault!" Whiting cried, *Your fault!*" He punctuated the last two words by slamming Raoul's head down onto the table two times in rapid succession. As he

raised Raoul's head again for another stroke, the observer
deep in Raoul's mind blandly noted the spray of blood on
both the table and the wall. Interesting pattern. The aware
part of Raoul threw his weight backward at the top of the
next stroke, however, throwing Whiting off balance and
making him release the hold he had on his hair. Raoul fell
backward, hitting his head against the wall on his way
down.

He lay on the floor for a moment, dazed and breathless,
as Whiting bent down and picked up the poker. Whiting
lumbered toward him, the poker held high for a killing
stroke at Raoul's head. Before it could connect, however, a
hand grabbed Whiting's shoulder, jerking him backward.
The poker fell out of his hand as Whiting tried to keep his
balance.

"Stop it!" Mordechai cried, vainly attempting to hold the
struggling Whiting by one arm. "Stop it! You didn't kill
him!"

Whiting looked at him in shock, not understanding how
Mordechai had released himself from the spell, not knowing, as Raoul did, that Mordechai's developing magical
abilities could work spontaneously.

Whiting used his greater weight to hurl Mordechai into
the fireplace. Ashes exploded from the impact. Wiping
frantically at the blood falling in his eyes, Raoul forced
himself to stand as Whiting clawed at the wood near the
fire. Whiting had already struck Mordechai twice in the
face with a log when Raoul fell against his back.

"Stop it, Reginald! He's your son, damn it! Stop!" Raoul
cried as he and Whiting toppled over onto the floor.
Mordechai lay, unmoving.

Raoul's statement stopped Whiting for only a moment.
"You lie!" he screamed, rolling over and reaching for
Raoul's throat. His hands closing around Raoul's neck,
Whiting drew himself to a kneeling position as he began to
choke Raoul.

Raoul writhed vainly, unable to draw breath. The agony
in his side was slowly being replaced by a red haze falling

over his sight as he felt himself begin to lose consciousness. Panic-stricken, he grabbed madly at his leg and did the only thing left to him.

As Whiting leaned over Raoul, his face apoplectic with rage, Raoul drove the knife he'd pulled from his boot deep into the larger man's side. Whiting's hands loosened, his eyes wide in an expression that would have been comical except for Raoul's blood splattered across his face. "Ah," he said quietly. Raoul rolled away as the older man crumpled slowly forward. Whiting crawled a pace toward the wall before stopping, turning to lean against the wall as he removed the knife and let it fall. Raoul, meanwhile, groped toward the armchair he'd originally been sitting in, using it to draw himself up. Forcing himself to breathe, despite the pain it caused, he swiped at the blood dripping down his face, blinking furiously to keep his eyes on the man on the floor.

Whiting, propped nearly in a sitting position against the wall, listed to the left and clutched his side. He breathed heavily. Raoul could hear a high whistling sound with each breath Whiting took. Whiting looked down at his hand, covered in blood. He reached his other hand out to Raoul. "I'm sorry," he breathed, "I seem to have . . . my *son*?" His eyes widened suddenly and his hand slowly dropped to his lap as he gasped for breath. He slumped sideways, his eyes rolling upward in their sockets.

Raoul didn't bother checking to see if he was still alive. He didn't care. Leaning drunkenly on the furniture, he slowly made his way across the room, one hand clutching his ribs, the other still wipely futilely at the blood on his face. Never taking his eyes off Whiting, who lay unmoving, Raoul put his back against the wall and sidled painfully over to the phone. He dialed carefully, glancing at Whiting after each number.

Finally, someone picked up the line.

"I need the police," Raoul said slowly, forcing the air out to make each word, "and an ambulance." He gave the address, then slid slowly to the floor as his legs gave out beneath him and the room disappeared.

Epilogue

Bolton and Raoul fell silent, watching as Raoul's mother gracefully alighted from the black Jaguar parked outside the café.

Bolton glanced across the table at Raoul. "Look, Rags," he began, "you can't blame this on me. I didn't call her."

Raoul smiled. "I know. I did." He chuckled at the look of shock on Bolton's face.

A moment later Raoul's mother appeared in the doorway. They rose as she crossed the room to kiss first Raoul, then Bolton on the cheek before sitting. "Well, look at this: my *two* favorite men." She smiled. Turning to Raoul, she added, "You haven't changed your mind about leaving?"

Bolton tried not to notice Raoul's wince of pain as he lowered himself gingerly back into his chair.

"No," Raoul replied. "I just didn't want to leave without saying good-bye."

A waiter arrived, taking their drink orders.

"Well, I'm glad you invited me," Raoul's mother said. "I haven't seen too much of you lately, what with . . . everything that's happened. You look much better than the last time I saw you."

Bolton laughed. "And he probably still looks better than Dr. Sandler does. I'll never forget the look on his face the day after he thought he'd finally gotten rid of us, when Rags shows up with two cracked ribs. I thought he'd have a heart attack."

Raoul snorted. "And the idiot had the nerve to give me *your* old room, to boot. Anyway, I'm much better now. It's

307

the wrapping that's annoying. Pinches like hell when I bend." The waiter arrived with their drinks.

"Salut," Raoul's mother said. "To health."

"I'll drink to that," Raoul and Bolton said at the same time. All three laughed.

"So this is it, huh? You're taking off?" Bolton asked.

Raoul nodded. He looked around the restaurant, not recognizing anyone. He sipped gingerly at his stout. "Yeah," he said finally. "The boat leaves at seven o'clock."

Bolton shook his head, smiling. "You know, I still can't believe they're letting you do this. Has the university hired anyone to replace you yet?"

"Not yet. Marlowe said he's got a couple of people in mind, though, so I'm not worried. And why shouldn't they give me a sabbatical, by the way?" He smiled, somewhat bitterly. "After all, I'm the 'new magical wunderkind,' to quote your cheesy news rag. I've discovered one of the lost runes. I'm a senior researcher. I was almost killed by the last chancellor. Frankly, I think I *deserve* a sabbatical. And the university powers that be agree with me."

Bolton laughed. "That's because they're now all personal friends of yours. Who's the new chancellor? Lloyd Llewellyn-Jones, your former colleague and one of the few who's believed in your work all along. Who's the college chair? Robert Marlowe, brought back by popular demand, at least for a while." He turned to Raoul's mother. "Hell, when Marlowe retires again they'll probably give his job to *Raoul*. Rough life."

Raoul chuckled involuntarily, then became serious again. "And anyway, everyone thinks it will be for the best if I'm not around for a while. It'll let the publicity die down a bit. And it's not likely they'll need me for a trial, what with Whiting still in intensive care."

"I heard they had to remove one of his lungs," Harriet interjected.

"They did," Raoul replied. "So it's best I'm away. Anyway, it's not as if they're really losing my research skills. Miriam is already busily working on the first draft of our paper. Which, I'm sure, will end up as a book, too." He shrugged, a twinge of pain in his ribs making him grimace slightly.

Bolton smiled, and studiously avoided asking Raoul if he was all right. "Ah, the joys of having a research assistant." He paused for a moment, debating whether or not to ask the next question. "What about Anne?"

"What about her? You both know it as well as I do. She's in therapy, trying to get well enough to stand trial for arson and attempted murder. They're still trying to figure out if she really had any idea what could happen as a result of her actions. They'll put the trial off as long as possible, I'm sure. It's over, Bolton. You know that. Old news."

"I know, I know. It's just so odd the way it all turned out. Do you know what they're going to do with Mordechai?"

"I still can't believe he was Reginald's son," Harriet said. "It seems so . . . unlikely."

Bolton smiled. "Apparently, neither of them believes it, either. Not that they'll have a chance to talk about it."

"Ah, but Mordechai will ask Jean about it, you can be sure," Raoul added. "They're releasing him from custody as soon as the magic removal is complete. Looks like he got his wish after all, the fool."

"Well, really, Raoul," Harriet began, "you can't blame him. He thought he'd killed Arthur Mowatt, or at least made Reginald kill him."

"You know," Bolton said, "I sneaked a peek at his confession. Really weird."

"How so, Maxwell? I haven't heard a thing about it," Harriet said, glancing at Raoul, who didn't look up from his Guinness. He'd avoided talking about it as much as possible.

"Well, it turns out that before he asked Raoul to help him get rid of his magical ability, he'd asked his mother to approach Mowatt about it. He didn't know that they knew each other in any way except working near each other. Apparently, when Jean went over to ask Mowatt about it, that was when he came out with the fact that he was in love with her. They argued, she left, and told Mordechai that Mowatt had said it was impossible. Mordechai then decided to ask Mowatt about it himself. Why he chose the night of the party to do it, I'll never know."

"He didn't know about the party," Raoul said. "Jean didn't tell him."

"Ah." Bolton nodded. "That makes more sense. So anyway," he continued, turning back to Harriet, "it turns out that Mordechai was waiting to talk to Mowatt when he arrived back at his house. He's the guy the cab driver saw. He went in, talked to Mowatt, who was apparently very rude and pretty much told him to get lost. Mordechai left, but went back for some reason when he saw a car pull into the drive. That was Whiting. Mordechai hung around, watching through a window in the study. He couldn't hear anything, he said, but thought they looked like they were arguing. He was still angry that Mowatt had told him off, and said that he remembers wishing something horrible would happen to Mowatt. Then something horrible *did* happen—Whiting killed him. Mordechai thought he'd somehow magically forced Whiting into it."

"The idiot," Raoul snorted. "I *told* him you can't make anyone do anything they wouldn't normally do . . ."

Bolton glanced at Raoul.

"Sorry." Raoul grinned. "Didn't mean to interrupt . . ."

"So, as I was saying, Mordechai thought he was responsible. That's why he was so frantic to get help. Which Raoul provided. But then before Mordechai left for the Swiss clinic, he had an attack of guilt and needed someone to tell him that he was doing the right thing, that he didn't need to turn himself in to the police. For some reason, he decided that Raoul was the person he needed to talk to. And you know the story from there."

Harriet was shaking her head in wonder. "It's all so complicated."

"It's kind of funny to think about it now," Raoul said, "but do you know that when Mordechai released himself from the spell and tried to stop Whiting, he shouted something like, 'You didn't kill him.' " He chuckled grimly. "At the time, I thought he meant *me*. Weird. What really pisses me off is thinking about what might have happened."

His mother and Bolton looked at him quizzically.

"You know," Raoul continued, "what might have happened if Jean had just gone to Whiting and told him she'd been pregnant all those years ago. If she'd asked straight out for the money to get rid of Mordechai's magical ability, instead of sneaking around with blackmail notes. If she'd told him he had a son. What might have happened then, do you think? What might *not* have happened?" His voice had grown tense.

Bolton reached a hand across the table to pat Raoul on the arm. "Hey," he said quietly, "nothing ever comes of that. Everyone's got twenty-twenty hindsight, remember. What happened happened. You can't change that. Not even though you're the new magical wunderkind." He shrugged, then changed the subject. "So where are you heading first? Do you have an itinerary yet?"

"Hell, no! When I said I planned to wander around the continent, that's what I meant. I'm not even taking a map! What do you take me for, a tourist?" Raoul smiled, bristling with false indignation. "I'm landing at Calais, isn't that enough of an itinerary? Seriously, the only place I'm sure I'll get to is Tuscany, for research, since they've got the best Etruscan collections. Everything else is up in the air." He shrugged. "What time is it, anyway?"

Bolton laughed again. "Still refusing to wear a watch, eh? Well, Mickey's big hand is . . . Okay, okay! Don't turn me into a frog, your wunderkindness! It's a little past four. Don't worry, I'll drive you to the boat, if you want. It's no trouble."

"No, I've got a ride." He glanced at his mother. "But thanks, Bolton." He smiled. "You know how I hate tearful good-byes . . . Anyway, I should go. Are you ready?"

Harriet nodded. They rose, Harriet kissing Bolton again.

"Please drop by whenever you'd like, Maxwell. It's been lovely seeing you again."

"My pleasure, as always." Bolton rose, watching as Raoul helped his mother with her coat. Initially, he'd been surprised that Raoul had spent his first few days out of the hospital convalescing at his mother's house rather than at Thornhold. Anne had frightened Raoul, he knew, because Raoul could picture himself doing the same things. Since leaving the hospital, Raoul had begun improving relations with his mother, spending time with her and talking as they never had before. In fact, Bolton thought, Raoul had been talking to him as never before, too. It was as if he'd made a conscious decision to stop closing himself off from people. Not that he'd suddenly turned into mister sweetness and light, to be sure. No, Bolton mused, Raoul was still his usual brilliant, irascible, unique self, only perhaps a little more mature, a little less protective of his own differences. Maybe because he didn't need to be defensive anymore, now that people were finally recognizing that, no matter what his appearance or methods, he was a magician of the highest caliber. Or maybe because Raoul himself had finally—

"What the hell are *you* smiling at?" Raoul asked.

"Oh, nothing," Bolton said. "Nothing at all, your wunderkindness."

"I wish you'd stop calling me that. Anyway, we've got to go. I'll be in touch." He stood up.

Though he'd miss Bolton and the rest of his friends, Raoul was anxious to get away. So much had happened, and he needed time to sort everything out. It was as if, having finally accepted the presence of others in his life, he needed to reaffirm magic's place in his personal universe. Even just thinking about doing on-site research into the earliest Etruscan magic thrilled him. In a strange way, it felt like going home. But he knew that he'd be back, knew that he needed his friends as much as he needed his work. They were all part of his life; he'd seen what could happen when one idea, one piece of one's life, took precedence, and had vowed that it wouldn't happen to him. And it wouldn't.

"See you later," he said, smiling down at his friend.

"Okay. Call me." Bolton watched Raoul and his mother walk away. As Raoul was about to pass out of the doorway, Bolton called out, "And *try* to stay out of trouble, okay, Rags?"

Smiling, Raoul raised his middle finger in silent salute to his friend, then turned and walked out into the growing twilight. I hate it when he calls me that, he thought, and smiled.

Acknowledgments

Very special thanks to: Deborah Morgan Hogan, Mark Del Franco, and Maria Vickers. I couldn't have done it without you.

Additional thanks:

Ashton, for the technical magic advice; Tim Abbot; the Bellusci clan; Marcy and John Blumers; Sean Boudreau; Veronica Chapman; Debra Dauphinais; Todd Fairchild; Viv LaBerge; Cyncy and Steve Mare; David and Cari Maslow; David and Karen Mertz; Julia and John Ryan; Sarah and John Ryan; Gwen (Slash!) Sanchirico; Dr. Robert Staszewski, for his help with dermatology questions; Alan Vickers; the Woodbury clan; and to everyone at Fajitas & Ritas (West Street, Boston).

A special note of thanks to Clif Gaskill and the assorted little brownies for a great party; and to Jennifer Kimball, for proving that dreams really do come true.

NOTE: Richard Dadd's *The Fairy Feller's Master-Stroke* hangs in London's Tate Gallery, Room 9. It's worth the trip.

DEL REY® ONLINE!

The Del Rey Internet Newsletter...

A monthly electronic publication, posted on the Internet, GEnie, CompuServe, BIX, various BBSs, and the Panix gopher (gopher.panix.com). It features hype-free descriptions of books that are new in the stores, a list of our upcoming books, special announcements, a signing/reading/convention-attendance schedule for Del Rey authors, "In Depth" essays in which professionals in the field (authors, artists, designers, sales people, etc.) talk about their jobs in science fiction, a question-and-answer section, behind-the-scenes looks at sf publishing, and more!

Internet information source!

A lot of Del Rey material is available to the Internet on our Web site and on a gopher server: all back issues and the current issue of the Del Rey Internet Newsletter, sample chapters of upcoming or current books (readable or downloadable for free), submission requirements, mail-order information, and much more. We will be adding more items of all sorts (mostly new DRINs and sample chapters) regularly. The Web site is http://www.randomhouse.com/delrey/ and the address of the gopher is gopher.panix.com

Why? We at Del Rey realize that the networks are the medium of the future. That's where you'll find us promoting our books, socializing with others in the sf field, and—most importantly—making contact and sharing information with sf readers.

Online editorial presence: Many of the Del Rey editors are online, on the Internet, GEnie, CompuServe, America Online, and Delphi. There is a Del Rey topic on GEnie and a Del Rey folder on America Online.

The official e-mail address for Del Rey Books is delrey@randomhouse.com (though it sometimes takes us a while to answer).